GREEN
GIRLS

Michael Kimball

GREEN GIRLS

WILLIAM MORROW
An Imprint of HarperCollins*Publishers*

GREEN GIRLS. Copyright © 2002 by Michael Kimball. All rights reserved. Printed in the United States of America. No part of this book may be used or reproduced in any manner whatsoever without written permission except in the case of brief quotations embodied in critical articles and reviews. For information address HarperCollins Publishers Inc., 10 East 53rd Street, New York, NY 10022.

HarperCollins books may be purchased for educational, business, or sales promotional use. For information please write: Special Markets Department, HarperCollins Publishers Inc., 10 East 53rd Street, New York, NY 10022.

FIRST EDITION

Designed by Bernard Klein

Printed on acid-free paper

Library of Congress Cataloging-in-Publication Data

Kimball, Michael.
    Green girls / by Michael Kimball.—1st ed.
      p.   cm.
    ISBN 0-06-008737-4 (hc.)
    1. Amnesia—Fiction. 2. Adultery—Fiction. 3. Violence—Fiction. 4. Fathers and sons—Fiction. I. Title.

PS3561.I4163 G74 2002
813'.54—dc21

                                                                    2002141567

    02 03 04 05 06 WBC/QW 10 9 8 7 6 5 4 3 2 1

For Sarah

And in memory of my nephew and
friend, T. J. Hawkins. Hi ho.

Piscataqua River Bridge

DONALD BULLENS

ACKNOWLEDGMENTS

Thank you to

Paul Callahan
Richard Callahan
Brian Chernack
Milt Davis
Chris Fahy
Kevin Farley
Jodi Frechette
Gene Glick
Nancy Graham
Rick Hautala
Herb Hoffman
Phil Jones
Chuck Landry
Chuck Lawton
Paul Mann
Bo Marks
Art Mayers
Gail Morse
Dan Peabody
Alan Philbrook
Nessa and Pete Reifsnyder
Brenda Reimels
Jon Richardson
Linda Richmond
. . . for reading many drafts and being honest with your opinions

Bert Allen, for showing me around the Piscataqua River Bridge
Michael Dow, for your carpentry expertise

John Mercurio, for your racing expertise

Bo Marks, John Pelletier, and Pamela Ames, for your legal expertise

Brett Hugo, expert bartender, for your bartending expertise

Todd Lyon, for hypnotizing me

Chris and Laurie Simpson, for introducing me to the Secret Garden

Howard Morhaim, my literary agent, for helping me get it right

Stephen King, forever, for your generosity

Jennifer Hershey, my editor, for your faith—and for helping me kill my darlings

Mauro DiPreta, for your kindness to orphaned authors

Bill Massey, my editor in the U.K., for your patience and wisdom and good editing

Glenna Kimball, for years and years of your love

Note: Although some character names were borrowed from friends, personalities, relationships, and events are totally fictional.

GREEN
GIRLS

PROLOGUE

A GREAT TIME TO FIGURE THINGS OUT. THE YOUNG MAN plummets from the top of the bridge, his mind scattered in the ocean wind, reaching for the sky, silent, weightless, balanced against the crescent moon.

Time slows down as the trussed steel of the bridge whispers past. The young man can not only smell the river that rises to meet him, he has time to consider how a particular mustiness tinges the odor.

It's metabolism, the reason time slows down. Hummingbirds, for example, have such a high metabolic rate, they perceive human movement in slow motion. To a fruit fly, we are statues; their day on earth lasts a lifetime.

In humans, fear increases metabolism . . . which is why the victim of a car wreck will describe the accident as though it happened in slow motion. Extreme fear causes extreme time stall. What is the limit? It's long been acknowledged that some people who fall to their deaths actually die of heart failure before they land. Perhaps they die of old age.

In the 4.03 seconds it takes to fall 250 feet, from the top of the Piscataqua River Bridge to the water, a man can do a lot of thinking. Not that Jacob William Winter is watching his life pass before him.

He is simply seeing how things came to be.

PART
ONE

1

"MY WIFE DIDN'T BAIL ME?"

"Apparently, someone beat her to it," said the lawyer, unlatching his briefcase. "Your wife did bring your car, though, and packed some things for you."

"Packed what?"

The lawyer pulled out a manila folder and set it on the table in front of him. "You were bailed by a woman named Alix Callahan."

Jacob didn't recognize the name at first.

"A friend?" asked the lawyer.

Jacob shrugged, mystified. "What did Laura pack for me?"

"Clothes, toilet articles, sleeping bag, your computer. You don't know anyone named Alix Callahan?"

"There was an Alix Callahan in college with me, fifteen years ago," Jacob said, but he was thinking more about the sleeping bag. "We weren't friends. Anything but. Why is she bailing me?"

"Maybe she's a fan," the lawyer told him in a sympathetic way. "I'm sorry, but I'm on a tight schedule today. Can you tell me what happened?" He snapped on his tape recorder.

Jacob said, "Whatever's in the police report."

"The report says you attacked the victim, then proceeded to demolish your house."

"I don't remember much," Jacob said. He could see his old Mazda outside the courthouse window—a cardboard box pressed up against the rear window. After two nights in the York County Jail, all he wanted was to go home and talk to Laura. "She brought my sleeping bag?"

The young attorney fidgeted with the pleat of his wrinkled trousers, waiting for Jacob to get it through his head: his wife didn't want him coming home.

He'd barely slept since he was locked up, pacing and pacing, needing to know. Now another part of his brain churned with this new information, about the woman who'd paid his bail.

"Mr. Winter, I'm sorry, I don't mean to rush you, but I have a two-thirty appointment," said the lawyer in a careful way. Men, in particular, tended to be careful around Jacob. Six-two and solidly proportioned, when he frowned—even when he smiled—it seemed a muscular function.

Frowning now, he lifted his eyes to the plaster ceiling as though it were a movie screen. Over the past thirty-six hours, Jacob had replayed the episode relentlessly: coming home from the Red Sox game with his son, Max, seeing Price Ashworth's green Z3 in the driveway.

He told the lawyer everything as it replayed: entering the house, he can smell the dinner before he sees it; in fact there's nothing on the kitchen table; the evidence is on the stove and counter: the empty lobster pot, the soup crock, the salad bowl, oily with remnants.

Even if Jacob wanted to abandon the film, he could not. The same scenes kept looping over and over in his mind.

"Looks like someone had a nice dinner," Max says, taking an ice cream bar out of the freezer.

Jacob thinks he can hear the Red Sox game playing. But the radio in the kitchen is turned off. And they have no television.

It's impossible to forget this much: It's the way he steps into the hallway . . . and stops there when he realizes the radio is playing in their bedroom. Then Laura comes out of the dining room. She stops when she sees him. It's the look of concentration on her face, the strange way she meets his eyes, or maybe the way she says to Max, "Hon, go down to the field and play, okay?"

"Play what?" Max's mouth is full of ice cream.

"Daddy and I have to talk about something."

"Okay, champ?" Jacob says, with a tightness he hopes Max won't detect.

Max complies, but only after giving his dad a quizzical scowl.

Jacob stands there listening to the boy's footsteps tumble down the porch steps, then he walks to the dining room without speaking, while his head churns with noise. Laura follows him, saying, "Jake, wait."

She's his wife of twelve years, Price Ashworth his former psychiatrist. Twice in the past two weeks he has come home from baseball practice to find Laura sitting on the couch talking to Price on the phone. She's explained that Price was thinking of moving his office and was seeking her counsel. Now Jacob stands in the dining room doorway, his head humming, his stomach clenched, while Price sits in his chair.

The table is set for dinner, actually its aftermath: two red lobster shells on the good Italian stoneware, oyster-minestrone soup, the half-eaten loaf of Italian bread on a cutting board, the half-drunk bottle of wine. Of this much, Jacob remembers every detail: The twin candles flickering. The stoneware coffeepot and mugs. Cream in the matching pitcher.

Price Ashworth speaks first, in his assured way. "The timing could have been better, to say the least." As if this were one of those episodes that might turn into a good story over time.

The movie flickers out of this war-torn corner of Jacob's mind, and he cannot stop it. Yes, he can even remember the label on the wine bottle. He stands there with his heart pounding behind his eyes. He can't think of a word to say.

"Jake," Laura says with a shiver in her voice, "we have to talk." She sits down in her place, beside Price. She's so beautiful, Jacob thinks, even in memory, the way her dark hair sweeps over the faithless flush of her cheek.

Price shows Jacob his hand. It might be the start of an apology, but Price Ashworth is not accustomed to apologizing beneath his station. Pompous when sober, wine exalts him. No, not apologizing, he's gesturing Jacob to sit down—at his own table, the table he built for their home. Table, chairs, hutch—Jacob built them all himself with hand tools—as he's built all the furniture in the house, cupboards and cabinets, bookcases, end tables, coffee table, bedside tables, kitchen table, kitchen chairs.

Jacob does sit, across the table from Laura. Three years younger than Price and lumbering by comparison, his chest is quaking; his lungs are filled. The ball game continues playing from the bedroom clock radio, a small, state-of-the-art piece of hardware he had bought for Laura with the advance on his third book.

Now Price looks at Laura and says, "Stay focused. Natural breathing." He's coaching her.

A crowd's cheer erupts from the bedroom radio. Laura takes a deep breath. Her owl-brown eyes are dilated black. When she exhales, her breath trembles. "Jake, our marriage," she begins again, but she needs another breath. She looks at Price helplessly. He offers his hand. She takes it.

Jacob stands up. His chair falls. He floats out of the room into the hallway, down to the bedroom. The ball game plays on. He walks to the bed, an exquisite hand-tooled piece of mahogany furniture that took him half a year to build—his engagement ring to Laura. Inset in the headboard is a backlit stained-glass panel that Price himself had created for the couple as a wedding gift, an artless depiction of two pines overlooking a moonlit ocean. The crescent moon is, in plain fact, a yellow hexagon.

"Jake, please. Can we go back in the dining room and sit down?" Laura has followed him in. Price stands beside her.

Jacob walks over to the radio. It's the radio that's getting to him. "I thought you knew it was a *makeup* doubleheader," he says to Laura in a tightly controlled voice. Then he explains to Price, "In a makeup doubleheader, people with rain check tickets only get to see the first game, the one that got rained out last month."

"Jake, please?" Laura says. Is she crying? Apologizing?

Jacob stares at the square of stained glass on the headboard. A powerful wave comes over him, and he snaps the radio's plug out of the electrical outlet. The room becomes suddenly, contemplatively quiet. His heart is dying.

Price says, "Jacob, is baseball really what you are wanting to discuss at this point in time?"

The movie flickers. The radio leaps.

"Jake!"

The lamp explodes.

Then something shudders up from Jacob's chest, a sickening dull horror at the sight of Laura bent over Price on the bed, holding his head in her hands. . . .

"KEEP going."

Jacob stared dizzily at the table. "I hit him."

"And?"

"I must have. With the radio. I don't know."

The lawyer studied his notepad as if he were afraid to challenge Jacob's reticence. "Dr. Ashworth went to the hospital with a severe concussion," he said. "He could have died. Your entire house looks like a tornado went through." He had photos in his hand. "Looks like some very nice furniture—which I understand you made yourself?"

Jacob wouldn't take the photos. His mind was engaged: Had he been too self-absorbed? Too caught up in his work?

"Personally speaking"—the lawyer turned off the tape recorder—"if I discovered my wife and friend—"

"Not a friend. Her employer."

"Another man," the lawyer corrected himself. "If I found them in my dining room having a candlelit dinner, I would've shown the guy the door and maybe given him a concussion doing so. You'd have a hard time finding a judge and jury who'd say I wasn't somewhat justified."

Jacob shook his head. Kittery was a small town. Did Max know what had happened? Had he already heard rumors about his mother and Price?

"Here's the problem," the attorney said, and he waited to continue until Jacob met his eyes.

"Dr. Ashworth never said anything about a dinner. He claims they were sitting at the table, having a cup of coffee, waiting for you to come home—when you marched in and attacked him in a psychotic rage."

Jacob's hands opened in disbelief. "Laura's not saying that."

"For the record, your wife has refused to make a statement. And Dr. Ashworth has declined to press charges—which ultimately doesn't matter. It's felony assault."

Jacob turned to the window and the sun blinded him.

"State of Maine versus Jacob Winter," the lawyer said. "With felonies, it's the state that charges you."

Jacob stood. "They were having a candlelit dinner, with good wine and oyster-minestrone soup. . . ."

The young man seemed to shrink in his chair. Seeing his discomfort, Jacob took a deep breath, then sat down again. He brought his fingers to his head. He felt as if he was suffocating.

"Jacob, are you presently under psychiatric care with Dr. Ashworth or another doctor?"

"No."

"I didn't mean to imply," the lawyer said. "You are aware that aggravated assault carries a potential ten-year prison sentence?" He gave Jacob a sympathetic look. "Can you tell me anything more? Did your son witness the alleged assault?"

Jacob turned his head to the window again, waiting for the tremor in his chest to subside. All his questions—What had he done to turn her away? How long had it been going on?—suddenly replaced by burning reality: Laura's betrayal. And the raw terror of being separated from Max.

"Did he perhaps see the dining room table, as you've described it to me? With the lobster and candles and wine, and the oyster soup?"

Jacob shook his head. "Oyster-minestrone soup. No. Max was outside."

The lawyer said, "What *is* oyster-minestrone soup?"

"Something she makes when she's in love," Jacob said. "May I go home now?"

The way the lawyer stared—as if Jacob hadn't heard a word he'd said. "I'm sorry," he said, pulling a document out of his folder. "Restraining orders. Under no circumstances are you to make contact with, or go anywhere near . . ."

"Laura?" Jacob said.

The lawyer looked closely at him.

"But how can I talk to her?"

"You can't."

"I've got to. I've got to talk to her."

The attorney was shaking his head. "And that goes double for Dr. Ashworth. I'm sorry, Jacob. That's the law now. You can't telephone her, you can't write to her, send her an e-mail. If you see her on the street, turn your head and go the other way. That's what it means. No contact."

"What about Max, my son?" Jacob said. "He needs me."

"In cases like this, visitation arrangements are usually worked out between the spouses' attorneys."

"I'm trying to make you understand," Jacob said. "Max is ten years old. He needs consistency in his life."

"I promise, we'll do the best we can." The lawyer pulled a cell phone out of his briefcase and set it on the table. Laura's cell phone. "Your wife wanted you to have this," he said, then produced a sealed envelope. "And five hundred dollars from your joint savings."

Jacob said, "Why?"

"Maybe she's feeling guilty," the lawyer said in a hopeful way. "And your paycheck."

"But I don't get paid till next Thursday."

"A Chief Adler called." The lawyer removed a paper clip from a piece of notepaper.

"I'm a part-time dispatcher at the Kittery Fire Station," Jacob explained, then suddenly realized why he was holding his paycheck.

"I'm sorry," the attorney said for the hundredth time. "You've been suspended, pending outcome of the case."

Jacob took another breath. He tried to picture himself in the dining room attacking Price Ashworth—over a cup of coffee? It was fiction.

"And a Donny Donnelly?"

"He's my coach," Jacob said, looking up with dread anticipation. "I manage my boy's baseball team."

The lawyer shook his head. "Again, I'm sorry. The league took a vote."

Jacob got back to his feet, unwilling to hear any more. In fact, he decided to hire his own lawyer, someone who could do more than apologize. He'd find some way of paying him, maybe trade for furniture.

"Call me when you get settled, and we'll arrange a time to talk," the lawyer said, then pulled Jacob's car key out of his pocket and slid it across the table. His house key and keys to the fire station had been removed.

Jacob picked it up numbly, along with the envelopes and Laura's cell phone. He could feel the blood pounding up into his head.

"It would be good to get another job as soon as possible—for custody's sake, to demonstrate to the court that you're a responsible parent."

"Thank you," Jacob said, turning for the door.

"One more thing. She wanted you to have this."

Jacob's heart gave a hopeful tug. He turned back.

"Not your wife," the lawyer said, handing him a business card, colored green. "Your old classmate. Alix Callahan."

As soon as Jacob was able, he broke the law. Pulling up in front of his house—Laura's car wasn't there—he didn't even have time to turn off his engine before the front door burst open and Max came running . . . limping, actually. He already had his baseball uniform on—SPEEDWAY TAVERN—and Jacob's heart swelled. He didn't know how he was going to manage this conversation.

"Mom went to the store for some things, you coming in?" Max said, stopping at Jacob's window. Laura had evidently told Max about the restraining order.

"Not right now," Jacob said. "What happened to your leg?"

"Nothing."

Jacob could see his ankle was bandaged and his glasses had been glued together at the bridge. He reached out and tugged the brim of Maxie's cap. "Let's take a ride."

"How was summer school today?" Jacob said, after they had driven a half mile.

"Same."

"Stick to your behavior plan?"

"I guess."

Normally Jacob would be there when Max got off the school bus, full of chatter about the day. "How many hours did you play computer games this afternoon?"

"I reached the seventh level," Max said nonchalantly. "Bet I'm the only one in this town. Probably the whole state of Maine."

"I wouldn't be surprised," Jacob said. "Did you fall off your skateboard?"

"Something like that."

"Broke your glasses too, I see."

"Yeah."

"Doing something crazy?"

Max shrugged, waiting for the real conversation to start.

Jacob pulled the car into Seapoint Beach and shut off the engine. The two of them sat and watched the waves for a minute. Finally Jacob began. "Max, you know how we always try to be honest with each other?"

"I got something for you," Max broke in. "When Mom was packing your things." He dug in his pocket and came out with a purple ribbon and brass-plated medallion. *Bravery, Gallantry, Honor.* Max turned it over and read aloud: " 'To Jacob William Winter, from the Firefighters Association, Town of Kittery, Maine.' "

"Want it?" Jacob said.

"It's your medal. Keep it, it's cool." He opened the glove compartment and tossed it inside.

"Maxie, I did something wrong." Jacob stopped, reconsidered. The boy didn't deserve this, he thought angrily. "What I'm trying to tell you is, I hurt somebody."

"You hit Dr. A with the radio, that's what Luke Fecto said." Luke Fecto, son of Phil Fecto, the detective who had arrested Jacob. Luke was also on the baseball team, one of the no-talent jackals who tried to distinguish themselves by ridiculing Max.

"I'm not exactly sure what happened," Jacob told him. "I did lose my temper. Dr. A was injured. And I got arrested."

"Luke said that's why the police won't let you come home—because you blew your mind."

Jacob shook his head. "Luke Fecto doesn't know his rear end from a hole in the ground. Did Mom talk to you about it?"

"She said that Dr. A fell off his bike, and you got arrested for speeding." Max rolled his eyes.

Jacob said, "Well, I guess Mom was trying to protect us both."

Max gave him a look. "I thought we weren't supposed to lie to each other."

Jacob sighed. "Maxie, you know how sometimes people have emergencies, like their house catches on fire?" He put his hand on his son's shoulder and could feel the heat rising off his young body. "Well, Mom and I have had an emergency in our marriage, and for a little while I'm going to be staying someplace else."

"Mom already told me that," Max said, staring down at his sneakers.

"I'm going to stay close by," Jacob told him. "You and I are going to spend lots of time together, just like we always have." Stay focused, Jacob told himself as he swallowed back the lump in his throat. "Maxie, Mom and I love you very much, and we're both making sure we do the right thing for you. Right now the right thing for you is to stay with Mom until we work things out."

"But what did she do that made you so mad?" Max said, looking up at him, his voice getting smaller. "I could hear you yelling and breaking everything."

And he thought things had already gotten as bad as they could get. "Maxie, this was my fault, not Mom's," he said. "I lost my temper. You know Mom loves you, and she'd do anything for you. Anything. You know that, right?"

He waited for his son to look at him, but Max was picking at his ankle bandage. It was true, what Jacob was saying. Laura had once gotten them all evicted from a year-round oceanfront cottage because the owners, officers in the local Boy Scout organization, had terminated Max's membership for climbing a forty-foot pine and hanging the troop flag at the top. Not that he shouldn't have been disciplined for the daredevil stunt—Laura punished Max herself: took away his computer privileges for a week—but they had all seemed so eager to get rid of him. So she marched next door and threw his uniform into their barbecue pit during their Labor Day picnic. Laura had loved that little house. But she protected Max like a mother bear.

"Come on," Jacob said, rubbing Max's head. "I'd better get you back so you don't miss your game."

Max gave him a look. "You mean *we*, don't you?"

Jacob started the car and pulled onto the road.

"Max, I have to take a break from coaching the team," he said, "just until we work things out. Mom and I will have to take turns going to your games. Tonight can be her turn."

Max watched the houses go past. Jacob felt the ache rising in his chest again. "You can pretend I'm there, okay?" he said. "You know what I always tell you."

"Lay off the high, hard stuff," Max said.

"That's right," Jacob told him. "Your heart wants a home run, but your head tells you you've got a much better chance of getting a single. Which are you gonna listen to?"

Max kept the back of his head to his dad. Jacob let him have some time, and quiet. Coming into their neighborhood, seeing Laura's car in the driveway, he pulled in front of the house, keeping his eyes on the windows, trying to get a glimpse of her. . . .

Then the side door opened and she was there, wearing jeans and a plain white shirt, looking achingly beautiful. But the way she stared—as if Max had taken a ride from a stranger. Then she went back in the house. And Jacob's heart sank into his lap.

"Are you guys getting divorced?"

Jacob gave Max a look of incredulity. "See, that's your imagination talking, Maxie. It's like I tell you with your baseball: don't let your emotions take over for your brain."

Max scrutinized him. "Mom was on the phone today, talking

soft so I wouldn't hear," he said. "Afterwards I hit redial, and a lawyer's office answered."

Speaking of high, hard ones.

Awaiting his response, Max turned to stare out his window, as though waiting for a doctor to stick him with a needle. The question was inevitable; also one that Jacob did not know the answer to. He stared out at his hollow house, his insides melting.

"Maxie, do me a favor," he said. "Let Mom and me worry about the adult stuff, okay? We'll figure things out. What you need to worry about is your swing."

"I know," Max said wearily, reaching for the door handle, while Jacob reached for his shoulder and felt it slide through his fingers.

"Maxie?"

Max looked back, his eyes watering, and Jacob remembered the stunned first days and weeks living without his own father. The ache rose in his throat. And he made himself a vow: He would not let himself fall apart. For Max's sake, he would be strong.

"I want you to remember," Jacob said, and he made the same promise to himself: "Your head, not your heart."

2

GREEN GIRLS, THE BUSINESS CARD READ. EXOTIC GROWERS.

The shadows stretched lazily across the road as Jacob drove through town, thinking about this woman Alix Callahan—in fact, she hadn't been out of his mind all afternoon—wondering again and again what she could possibly want with him. Having no plausible explanation, he speculated that perhaps her reaching out of the past to help him might have some connection to Laura's infidelity.

Of course, he really needed to see Laura herself—ask her the thousand questions he had—but he knew that making contact with her could land him back in jail. So he drove across the Piscataqua into New Hampshire.

According to the little map on the card, Green Girls was located on the Portsmouth bank of the river, in the shadow of the I-95 bridge—also called the high-level bridge. Because Jacob didn't like heights, he took the lower Memorial Bridge across, one of two older drawbridges farther downriver that connected Maine to New Hampshire.

As luck would have it, the gate arm swung down just as he reached the middle of the bridge. While the roadway rose up in front of him, he watched a two-masted sailboat float past, heading to the marina. He looked in that direction, where the green, arched bridge towered over the river—and a weightlessness went through him. He looked away.

To the best of his recollection, they'd been in only three classes together, he and Alix Callahan—Creative Writing, Modern Poetry, Shakespeare. Even in a school the size of UNH, she'd made a name for herself. Jacob first heard about her lesbianism in the locker room. Fueled by the lack of evidence to the contrary—namely, she'd never been seen with a guy—Jacob's baseball teammates concluded that it had to be true. Not that Jacob cared one way or another, except that Alix Callahan was about as disarming as a girl that age could possibly be: confident, cool, mysterious.

First time he ever heard the word *cunt* uttered by a woman—and it wasn't used derisively; rather as an object of affection—it came from Alix Callahan's lips, reading her poetry aloud in class. As soon as she'd said it, Jacob felt his face flush, and she caught him . . . and kept her eyes nailed to him while she read the rest of the poem, as though she were reciting just for him, or accusing him of something. And that was the last time she ever looked at him.

No matter. From that moment on, Jacob could barely look at her, either, without imagining this tall, aloof, brilliant girl making love to her roommate, a tattooed, fierce-eyed redhead named Emily Packwood, who sang in an all-girl power-punk band called Tongue in Groove, and who singlehandedly drove Jacob's teammates to distraction debating the fairness of such a foxy thing wearing those skimpy leather skirts—the fairness and, after all, the downright honesty. Although Jacob didn't take part in such conversations, the locker-room consensus was that Miss Packwood was simply riding the lesbian bandwagon and in time would come to her senses. For Alix Callahan, however—she had dated an equally fetching girl the year before—there was no such hope.

A car horn shook Jacob from his reverie. The gate arm was up, the roadway down, and traffic was moving again. He crossed into Portsmouth and worked his way through Market Square, rich with the fragrance of restaurants and crowded with tourists, then westward alongside the river. Just beyond the on-ramp to the high-level bridge, he made a right turn through a cozy neighborhood of small brick houses. As he watched the steelwork bridge rise up over the river, the road swung underneath the approach span and left the neighborhood behind, with tall pines growing in on both sides. Then, glinting out of a clearing on the riverside, the glass appeared, reflecting the setting sun.

GREEN GIRLS—EXOTIC GROWERS. The wooden sign hung above the front door. Looking less like a flower shop than an unruly two-story home, the building was attached at the back to an enormous greenhouse of the same height, stretching back for a hundred feet or more. Jacob wondered if it had been a solarium salvaged from some luxury hotel, or perhaps a defunct orangery—definitely not part of the original structure, nor anything he'd expect to see in Portsmouth, New Hampshire. In fact, he thought he could see a palm tree pressed against the glass.

He pulled his car into a tire-worn area of the lawn, beside a ten-year-old green Volvo wagon with GREEN GIRLS—EXOTIC GROWERS stenciled on the door. Not exactly a prospering business, he thought.

He walked up the fieldstone path and rang the bell, then waited a few minutes before the door opened and Alix Callahan stood in front of him. She was tall, as he remembered her, even in bare feet, and she gave him a pleasant look of recognition, not exactly a smile. Behind her, flowers and leafy plants hung from the ceiling, clung to walls, and exploded full-blown from pots on the slate floor.

"So it was you," Jacob said, his glance unintentionally drawn to a gnarled, plum-shaped scar on her right cheek.

"Come on up," she replied, and when he'd turned back after

closing the door, she was already climbing a circular iron stairway behind the checkout counter. He looked around the dusky showroom and noticed, on the opposite wall, glass doors leading out to the greenhouse, with signs reading NO ADMITTANCE. Squeezing behind the counter, Jacob ducked into the staircase and started climbing, wondering again: What in the world did this woman want with him?

AT the top of the stairs he emerged in a white room filled with more plants, floor to ceiling. A stereo system sat on a table, with a black leather love seat on the opposite wall facing it . . . which was how he and Laura listened to music, Jacob thought, sitting together on their couch with the lights turned off. In April they'd gone to a Bonnie Raitt concert in Portland and afterward took a walk on the Promenade, hand in hand. Three months ago. Had she already been involved with Price?

"In here," Alix called from the next room.

Jacob walked into a kitchen that was overwarm and humid, smelling of vegetation and bathed in green light. The far wall consisted entirely of sliding-glass doors that looked down on the enclosed jungle. Alix sat at an oak table with her back to the opening, her head framed by the fronds of a strapping young palm. Other trees clustered behind her, crawling with red and yellow flowers.

"Coconuts in Portsmouth?" Jacob said.

"It's a rain forest," she said, closing a book—in fact, his first book, *Berth*, a four-hundred-page ode to his bed on a train he had ridden from San Francisco to Boston following his mother's funeral. Alix's eyes met his with no particular significance. She did not invite him to sit—which was fine with Jacob. Something about perching at the edge of a twelve-foot drop . . .

"Want some?" A bottle of red wine sat by her elbow, and a half-filled tumbler.

"No, thanks," he said. "I just stopped by to thank you."

She slouched boyishly in her chair, studying him with a knowing glint that told him she was well aware of the power she held over him—this mystery. Clearly she hadn't lost her withering charm—

but there was also a weatheredness about her that he didn't remember. Her hair was chopped just below her jaw, the way it had been in college, but not as tidy. Hay-colored and parted unevenly over her left eye, it looked as though she had pushed a hairbrush through it once, maybe a week ago. And that scar.

"Actually, I'm a little curious," he said, "about why you'd help me."

"Because you needed help."

"Is it business?"

She frowned.

"Do you charge a fee?"

"For bailing you?" Alix said, then turned abruptly toward the garden.

"I mean, it's not like we're old friends," he said, then stopped, having spotted what had caught her attention. A girl was down in the garden. She was young, her shoulders bare and brown, and she held Jacob's eye fully for a second, then retreated back into the foliage.

"Let's just say I wanted to help a struggling writer," Alix said, pouring herself more wine. "Sure you don't want a glass?"

Jacob sighed. "I'm sorry, I don't mean to sound suspicious, but there must be some reason—"

"I know the D.A. who's going to prosecute you," Alix said. "Her name is Susan Evangeline. She's going to crucify you and take everything you own."

Jacob shrugged. "Everything I own fits in my car."

"Including your son?"

He stood rooted to her floor. A couple of inches above his head a skylight was open, presumably to let out the heat, but it did little good. A drop of sweat rolled down his brow.

"What exactly do you know about me?" he asked, studying Alix Callahan very carefully. Now the scar on her cheek looked as if a dog had bitten her. "Or my son?"

"I know a lawyer who can help you," Alix began—then her eyes darted.

It was the black-haired girl again, standing ten feet away in the doorway of what appeared to be a pantry. Even in the relative darkness of the small room, Jacob was struck by her beauty. Jet-black hair hung around her face, which was deeply tanned and oval-shaped. A brown dress hung lightly on her shoulders by ribbon straps, clung to her high breasts, and ended at the tops of her thighs. Her arms were velvety with moisture, her feet caked with mud to her ankles.

"July, this is Jacob Winter, an old friend of mine," Alix said to her. "He's a writer."

The girl seemed to glare at him for a second, then she spun away from them both and went to the refrigerator, opened it, and came up with half a lime. Steam enveloped her body when she turned to look at Jacob. "Are you a poet?" she said.

"No," he answered.

"Good." She kicked the refrigerator closed and, ignoring Alix, focused intently on Jacob while she stuck the lime between her lips and sucked on the fruit. Clearly the women were not getting along.

"Jacob wrote *Berth* after his mother's death," Alix broke in, with a gesture toward the book. "It's about a cross-country train trip back from her funeral."

"Then the berth," July said, "is a metaphor for the womb? And the train is the passage of time . . . or is it loss?"

"Honestly? I just wrote about a train," Jacob told her, wanting to get back to the reason Alix had paid his bail—though he was surprised by the girl's quick perception.

"Please. Spare us the false modesty," Alix said. "The entire book is metaphor."

Jacob sighed, not about to concede the point, not about to debate her, either.

"Look at the evidence," she said. "The author's mother kills herself, and he writes four hundred pages about a train trip in which we learn the history of rail travel in America and the origin of every object and fixture in his berth, along with a description of his mother's alcoholism and suicide in such clinical terms you'd think you were reading an engineering journal. It's such brilliant self-delusion: the author trying to convince the world he feels no pain." She gave Jacob a long look. "Which is precisely what makes the book so devastating."

Jacob could feel July's eyes lingering suspiciously on him. Obviously Alix did not want to discuss his legal problems in front of her, but he was tired and growing impatient with the conversation.

"I do have to admit," Alix went on, "even though there are never any people in his books, something about his writing is extremely sensual. The fire in Baltimore? The commotion in the next berth? I'm not sure if he treats violence sexually or sex violently." She gave July a pointed look. "Either way, I know you'd appreciate it."

Jacob glanced over at July, who gave him a sullen peek as she sucked on her lime. Was she flirting with him? Then he saw something else: her index finger was missing.

She said, "Have you always been afraid of heights?"

He gave her a look, as if to say, *What makes you think I'm afraid of heights?* But of course it was obvious, the way he stood back from the opened doors with his arms folded. He was practically cringing. Recognizing how he looked, he allowed a self-deprecating smirk, and July let go with a soft peal of helpless laughter.

"Okay, so I don't like heights," he admitted. "Look, it's been a long day," he said to Alix, hoping she'd walk him out to his car and finish their conversation about her lawyer friend.

But July interjected, "Some people believe it's dangerous to reveal your fears to anyone but your shaman."

Alix stood abruptly from the table, toppling her chair out the open door, and she held the table with one hand to keep from falling out herself. "I was just about to show Jacob the garden," she said, composing herself. "Do you mind?"

July shrugged her brown shoulders. "Why would I mind?"

ALIX led Jacob into the pantry, a six-foot room with facing doorways—kitchen and living room—and a second set of circular stairs on which they descended to the rear of the flower shop. Through an open glass door they stepped into a startling eruption of vegetation pushing out of the New Hampshire soil, a wild grappling of color, broadleaf, and blossom filling every inch of the humid, glassed-in sky.

"So, this lawyer you know," he said, eager to finish the conversation and get out of there.

"Shh." She entered the middle of three narrow paths, and Jacob followed. With every step the heat grew heavier, while leathery, fanlike leaves scraped his legs, and the big house disappeared behind the greenery. As he watched around his bare ankles for thorns, he spotted a tiny yellow frog crawling up the stalk of a leafy plant.

"They're more afraid of you than you are of them," Alix told him. Not that he had any particular fear of frogs—in fact, he'd never seen such a creature.

"How do you get a rain forest in New England?" he asked.

"I have a few people, birders mostly, who bring me seeds and cuttings," Alix explained. "Eight different heliconias, more than forty anthuriums, and various other species from South America."

"Is that where July came from?"

Alix glanced back at him with a glint. "Actually, I recruited July from the other side."

"Meaning what," he said, tiring of the game. "She's promiscuous? Bisexual?"

Ducking underneath a shawl of deep red blossoms, Alix stopped beside a small thatch-roofed hut climbing with vines. "When I met July, she was in the process of leaving her husband. I helped her."

"And this has something to do with my legal problems?"

Alix looked behind them and said softly, "Willard Zabriski is the attorney's name. He's the best lawyer on the seacoast. He can beat Susan Evangeline."

Jacob was about to say he doubted he could afford any lawyer, let alone the best.

"He's already agreed to defend you," Alix said, preempting him. To his skeptical frown, she added, "He knows your work, Jacob. He's a fan."

"Never knew I had so many fans."

She took a business card and pen from her pocket. "Do you have a phone? He wants to talk to you."

Reluctantly he took the card and wrote down the number of the cell phone Laura had given him. "Look, if you have something to tell me—"

Alix snatched the card and shot him a quick, furtive look, punctuated by the sudden rustle of leaves behind them. He turned and saw July emerging through the ferns, holding two drinks in her hands, with lime wedges floating.

"I could only carry two," she said, handing one to Jacob and taking the straw of the other into her lips. This close together, he could smell a keen acridity rising out of her sundress, and he was struck by the contradictions of her. She had such youthful vitality, such softness and symmetry in her face. Yet in her eyes, Jacob saw someone disarmingly knowledgeable.

"Why don't you take this," he said, handing his glass to Alix. "I need to go."

"Didn't you invite him to stay for dinner?" July said, sipping from her glass, staring darkly at him through the gap of her missing finger. If she wasn't flirting with him, she was doing a good impression of someone who was.

"He said he's tired," Alix replied flatly.

Recalling the way she had reacted when July mentioned something about a shaman, Jacob decided to probe a little deeper. "By the way," he said, "what exactly is a shaman? A priest? Medicine man?"

"Priest, physician, philosopher, psychiatrist," July explained. "My husband's a shaman."

"Really?"

The look that passed between the women fairly crackled with electricity.

"Where's your husband now?" he asked, remembering that Alix had said she'd helped July leave her husband. But now Alix was giving July a narrow, piercing look meant to shut her up.

Returning a delinquent look, July bent to pick a pale blossom from a plant, briefly exposing a plump breast as the top of her dress fell away. When she straightened, she said to Jacob, "In a cage."

"Prison?"

"Cute," said Alix. "If sex had a face."

As if taking the disparaging remark for a compliment, July leaned back against the hut and fixed the flower in her hair. Her eyes had the reckless glint of a child's. "I don't think I'm supposed to say any more."

Another charged glance passed between the women. Jacob didn't know exactly what he'd uncovered, or whether it had anything to do with his troubles with Laura or the law, but he knew he'd definitely touched a nerve.

"Well, anyway," he said, fishing his keys from his pocket, "it was nice talking to you both."

"Are you sure you can't stay? July's an incredible cook," Alix said, fixing him with an intense stare that may actually have been an invitation to leave. Either way, he'd had enough of trying to interpret her.

"Thanks, I can't." Glad to be finished with them both.

But something about the way July was watching him as he turned to leave—that knowing, mischievous glint—made him think they weren't finished with him.

3

THE SHAMAN'S NAME WAS SERENO. THE WAY HE STARED THROUGH the sunglasses, it was hard to tell if he was even awake.

"Is he coherent?" asked the warden from his perch on the Indian's bunk.

"I think," the prison guard said. "Hey."

Sereno sat barefoot on the concrete floor, dressed in white muslin trousers and a matching top opened to the waist. He wore wraparound sunglasses, as he always did, day and night. A pale, wedge-shaped scar showed just above his solar plexus; a second, similar scar winked out from between two ribs just beneath his left breast. Two more on his shoulder and neck. Gnarled indentations—apparently from bullets—were located above and below his rib cage and on his forearm. A longer scar ran diagonally from his collarbone across his neck and under his jawbone from a knife.

Warden Latham leaned forward in his blue suit, examining the prisoner with the compassion of a country doctor. "Mr. Sereno, you have been a model prisoner for the past four years, which means you have accumulated gain-time, and that means you get to leave Alligator Alley several months ahead of schedule." He turned to the prison guard, awaiting translation. "Officer Bishop?"

"I don't mean to be disagreeable," the guard said, "but just because the man works for me, that don't mean we chitchat—besides which he knows English as good as any of us, even if he doesn't speak. He's always reading those magazines." A stack of them—*Time, Newsweek, People*—sat on the small table.

"For the photos, I'm sure," said the warden, who was ten years Bishop's junior, though prematurely gray. He wore blue-rimmed glasses and blue alligator boots. "I asked for your help because of your rapport with Mr. Sereno."

"I get along with all my men," Bishop said. "Due to a minimum of bullshit."

After eighteen years on the job, Buford "Biff" Bishop was still OIC—Officer in Charge, lowest rank in the institution—of the Motor Pool, having four times been promoted and as many times demoted again, for insubordination. He was a proficient mechanic and a moderately handsome man of below-average height, with thinning hair, a thinner mustache, and a dimpled smile that might have been endearing if not for the scowl lines carved in his face—from trying to pay his bills on poverty-level wages, he was fond of saying.

"Biff, I'm not sure how much you know about this gentleman," the warden said.

"Probably what everyone knows. Guy finds his wife sexin' another man? In my book he's got a God-given right to waste 'em both." He turned to the Indian. "That's how it works back home, right, Sereno?"

Sereno continued staring through his shades.

"Well, that's the way it should be," Bishop said. "Only too bad you did it in the great state of Florida."

"Biff? The gentleman does not need to be tormented."

"Just trying to get a rise out of him. Part of my *rapport*."

Biff Bishop was his own man. He didn't alter his personality for anyone, boss or underling. He said what he meant and he meant what he said.

The warden stepped over to the table, propped his boot on the wooden chair. "I need you to tell Mr. Sereno, please, that I'd like to make him a one-time offer. He can accept or decline, as he pleases. But this will be his only chance."

"Okay," Bishop said with a sigh of futility. Then he turned to Sereno and said, "This is it. Listen up."

Warden Latham continued. "A week from today Mr. Sereno will be walking out of this institution a free man, scheduled to go home. To Colombia."

The Indian turned slightly and, for the first time, appeared to pay attention. The warden took a toothpick out of his pocket, stuck it between his teeth. "Now, just because the boys in Administration missed your INS hold when you were admitted," he said, "they sure-as-shootin' won't miss it when you're released. Y'all know what that means."

Bishop held up one finger to Sereno. "One week. Deportation. You go Colombia."

"And, of course, the possibility of retaliation from the drug underworld."

The warden nodded to Bishop, who leaned closer to Sereno. "You killed the wrong *hombre*. When you get off plane, you get"—he shaped his hand into a pistol aimed at the Indian's head—"whacked."

"Biff, I need you to speak to my prisoners more respectfully."

"Just trying to speak realistically, sir. Just acknowledging the unfortunate coincidence that the gentleman he murdered turned out to be a drug mule."

"Mr. Sereno was charged in that murder and was acquitted," the warden said. "The time he has served with us was for domestic assault, and he's served it admirably."

"Stabbed the guy forty times, from what I've heard—acquitted or not—then went home and bit off his wife's finger. God-given justice for both of 'em as far as I'm concerned. Sir."

Something about the warden rubbed Bishop the wrong way, and

it wasn't just his inadequacies at running the prison. More the refined southern drawl and down-home colloquialisms that flavored his speech, this from a northern-educated son of a Savannah lawyer. He liked to say "Y'all." Chew on toothpicks. Somewhere in life he got the notion that animals could be rehabilitated, given respect and the right opportunities. Meanwhile, since he'd taken over, Alligator Alley had gone to hell in a handbasket right under his nose. The man was a joke.

"Hey, Sereno," Bishop said, "I bet you were surprised to find out the little woman was packin' heat. Cripes, it looks like she put a dozen slugs in him, plus half the silverware drawer. And he still managed to bite off her finger. Now that's what I call domestic assault."

The Indian sat stoically while Warden Latham, wearing a pained expression, said, "Officer Bishop, this is what you may not know." He removed his boot from the chair and sat on Sereno's table, moving the stack of magazines to the edge. "When the drug runner's body was discovered, there was no money found, either in his wallet or anywhere else in the hotel room. However, according to the DEA, the victim probably had over two million dollars in his possession at the time of his death."

Bishop turned to look at Sereno, who continued staring through his sunglasses, emotionless.

"They figure the money must be hidden somewhere in the vicinity of Plantation Key," Latham continued, "where the crimes were committed."

"Two million?" Bishop said. His gaze intensified on the Indian. "Now that you mention it, I believe I heard something about that."

The warden nodded. "What Mr. Sereno needs to realize is that if he were to reveal the location of this money, the Justice Department would look very, very favorably on relocating him once he's released from this institution. New name, new identity, perhaps relocation to another country altogether, where his enemies will never find him. Can y'all make him understand?"

Bishop gave Sereno another look, and he stuck out his hand. "The *dinero*," he said. "They say you'll be protected. *Seguro*."

The Indian stared.

"Otherwise, they haul your ass back to Colombia. Remember? Boom-boom?"

The Indian stared.

"Hey. Stupid."

"Officer Bishop—"

"This is the way I translate," Bishop said, keeping his eye on the Indian. "You're not getting near that money, hotshot, so get it out of your mind. And you're sure-as-shit not breaking out of here. One week to go? Your trusty privileges are over. Doneski. *Terminado.* Y'all gonna be in lockdown from now until they shackle your legs and drag you onto that plane. No more brake jobs or oil changes out in the sun. No more library privileges."

"Officer Bishop, please don't threaten my prisoner," said the warden. He gave the Indian a look of reassurance. "No privileges will be revoked. Mr. Sereno has earned his trusty status through hard work and strength of character."

"A week to deportation, with two million on the outside?" Bishop gave an assured nod steeped in sarcasm. "Oh, I'm sure he's not a risk to flee."

Latham stood up from the table, walked over to Sereno, and placed his hand protectively on the Indian's shoulder. "As long as I'm in charge of this institution," he said, "Mr. Sereno is to be treated no differently than any other trusty due for release. He will continue working for you in your motor pool, and we won't be abrogating a single privilege he has earned."

"Oh. Well. A thousand apologies," Bishop said. "How about this? We put him in charge, give him my keys, let him take the vehicles out for a test-drive."

Latham said, "I'll add your offer to my report."

Bishop glared at the Indian. This time he knew Sereno was making eye contact.

4

TIRED AS HE WAS, JACOB WAS NO CLOSER TO SLEEPING THAN he'd been three hours earlier, when he checked into his one-room cottage on the highway and collapsed on the bed. His rebellious mind constantly wandered back to Laura, a picnic they'd had recently, their daily beach walks, and all the quiet nights and mornings they'd made love while Max lay sleeping—

He threw his pillow at the wall. *Why?* What had he done to make her hurt him so deeply? Why hadn't she warned him? Or if she had, why hadn't he understood?

Yes, Laura was emotionally complex, but what woman wasn't? She was also emotionally honest—or so he'd believed—and that had been the core of his love for her: He did not need to interpret her. He had never known, nor even glimpsed, a part of her personality that would pretend love once she'd lost it. So the question remained: When had she stopped loving him? Realizing that he could not keep asking himself, he finally got up, got dressed, and went out to ask the only person who could answer him.

THE house Jacob and Laura had rented was at the edge of Kittery's original suburban development, where men who worked at the shipyard had raised their families for the past half century. Sided in pink vinyl, the small ranch sat at the edge of a gravel pit a half mile from the strip malls that lined Route One. It was the fourth house or cottage they'd rented since the bank foreclosed on the new home they had bought in York Harbor nine years earlier, and it was filled with the furniture that Jacob had built with hand tools and wooden pegs and dovetail joints and months of evenings planing and sanding—the cherry dining room set, the cherry hutch, the maple cabinets, the pine bookshelves, the mahogany armoire and bureaus . . . and bed.

Now one of the chairs lay at the end of the driveway, waiting for the trash collector, with a leg broken and a stile separated from its rail. The leaf from the table leaned against the chair, split down the middle, along with a broken hutch door. Another flash of recollection: trying to sit in the dining room chair; trying to hold down his rage by holding on to the table. Then he was pacing again, up and down the hallway, from room to room, demolishing everything in his path, wielding a cherry-wood chair like an ax, smashing china hutch, stoneware, and glass . . . while Laura and Price huddled in the bedroom. God, how he must have frightened her.

Now when he walked into the kitchen—she had left the stove light on—he cleared his throat so she would know he wasn't an intruder. Maybe she'd call the police anyway. What did he expect, coming in like a thief, that she'd take him back? Did he even want to come back?

"Jake, you can't be here," she whispered, tying her bathrobe closed as she came in from the hall. The way she kept her distance, as if she were afraid of him . . .

"You know I'd never hurt you," he whispered, not wanting to wake up Max. "You *know* that."

It was a rampage. The last time it happened was before she knew him, out in California, at a reception following his mother's funeral. He'd gotten arrested and was hospitalized for two weeks of psychiatric observation. When he returned to Maine, by court order he started therapy, and that's where he met Laura, in Price Ashworth's waiting room. She was working as his receptionist. Turned out she was a baseball aficionado. The fact that she was a diehard Yankees fan only added fire to their flirting. The clincher, in Jacob's mind, was that Laura had transcribed all his psychological files—until they started dating, anyway—meaning she knew him intimately and still wanted him. In fact, she told him that she loved his imagination—which Dr. Ashworth had diagnosed as "overactive." For Jacob's part, he had loved everything about her.

She was intelligent and beautiful and spirited. She had her father's feistiness and her mother's drive and practicality, and she loved to cook, having mastered an eclectic cuisine that reflected her personality, a wholly agreeable marriage of Old World Italian and Down East Maine: haddock *alla fiorentina* with fiddleheads; potatoes *frittelle;* maple tiramisu; oyster-minestrone soup.

So here was Jacob, standing in the middle of her kitchen waiting for words to come, while she stood waiting for him to go. God, how he wanted to crawl into his bed beside her. Yet how the sight of her enraged him all over again.

"Just tell me this," he said finally.

She shook her head. "Jake, please."

"Do you love him?"

How could she? In the first place, Price was an incorrigible womanizer, but Laura didn't need to be told that. She'd witnessed the chaos of the man's love life for nearly fifteen years. In fact, she and Jacob used to laugh about his escapades. Now she only shook her head, refusing to listen, refusing to *explain.*

"Laura, if it's money—"

"It's not *money,*" she said. "It's me. It's you. It's Max."

"Max is doing fine."

"Max should have gone to Belnap years ago—the day we got his test scores." Belnap School for the Profoundly Gifted, in California—Price Ashworth's alma mater.

"The school costs thirty thousand dollars a year—" Jacob stopped, aware that he was no longer whispering. Besides, it was the same argument they'd been having for years. For some reason, maybe because it was familiar territory, they were having it again. "Max doesn't need to be sent three thousand miles away to school. He needs his family."

"His family is not enough."

"He needs me."

"Shh."

"He needs to see that if you work hard enough, you can make it in this world—not in some private school filled with geniuses. He needs to see it every day."

"Jake, he's seen you work all his life," she said. "All you do is work, day and night, a slave to your precious schedule, making sure everything you do is so perfect, so precise—and for what? Do you know what it's like watching you? Like watching a lion in a cage, pacing and pacing. Tell me how that helps Max."

He could see her eyes welling, and it tugged at the hollow of his chest.

"Every day of his life is hell," she said in a vulnerable, shaking voice. "Come in from the playground where's he's been ridiculed for being *smart*, then sit in a classroom where he's so bored out of his mind that he ends up in the principal's office because his parents refuse to let him take Ritalin. . . . Meanwhile, the rest of his world marches farther and farther away."

"The solution is not to numb his brain—or take the rest of the world away from him."

"Oh, stop. Did he tell you how he hurt his ankle?"

"He said he fell."

"He tied two kites to his arms and jumped off the school roof. Some older kids dared him."

A tear ran down her nose, and she wiped it away. But she did not avert her eyes.

"Jake, you'll never know how awful I feel for hurting you," she said. "I never meant for it to happen this way. But I can't be sorry for trying to make a better life for Max."

"By sleeping with Price?"

"You need to go."

"Just tell me why!" he whispered, then shut his eyes to stop the

rising rage. He opened his eyes and tried again. "At least," he said, "when it started."

When she shook her head, he could detect the fragrance of her shampoo, and he added that to the things he would miss about her. But how could he ever live with her again, after such betrayal?

"You need to go," she told him.

He could barely say the words. "You're going to divorce me."

She kept staring with those sad eyes, not denying it, though how he wished to God she would. The white refrigerator seemed to shimmer. And now he realized that he would never again see her come in from jogging—she ran three miles every morning before Jacob arose, rain, snow, or blistering heat—then tiptoe up to their bedroom and strip off her sweats and awaken him with a kiss, or sometimes crawl back into bed on top of him. She did that only two weeks ago. It was a warm, humid morning, and she was so wet with perspiration that they laughed while they made love. Two weeks ago.

He staggered back a step, unable to take his eyes off her. She was the first girl he'd ever loved and the only one, a woman now, and he had no idea how he'd lost her.

"You won't take Max away from me," he vowed, anger leaping up through his skin again; then he turned away dizzily, pushed the screen door open, and walked down the porch steps. Crossing the lawn to his car, he could feel the roaring approach of a monstrous despair.

"Hey, Dad—"

The voice floated on the air like a ghost. It was Max, calling to him from inside the house.

Jacob turned. In the dark, he could see Max's glasses glinting behind the screen of his bedroom window.

Jacob took a tight breath. "Hey, champ, how ya doin'?" The words forced from his throat.

"I was right, wasn't I?" the boy answered.

Jacob came closer in the soft grass while he searched for something to say. But nothing came. Reaching the window, he cleared his throat, an abrupt and conspicuous sound in the quiet night.

"Go back to sleep, Maxie," he said, and he touched the warm screen where his son's forehead lay. "We'll figure something out."

He didn't turn away, he backed away, hoping that Max would roll back from the window, back under his blanket, back to sleep.

"Hey, Dad," the boy whispered, sounding furtive. *"Dad."*

"Maxie—"

"Did you know there was a girl in our driveway?"

JULY, in fact.

"What are you doing?" Jacob asked when he went to her.

She said, "I was afraid to stay home."

He walked her out to the road, not wanting Max to overhear, or Laura. "Afraid why?"

July shook her head. "I don't want to bother you."

Jacob looked around for her car, but the street was deserted. "How did you get here?"

"Hitched," she said. "An old man picked me up. The bars just closed."

He wondered how she'd found him—telephone book, probably.

"I'm sorry to bother you," she told him, and started walking off.

"Wait," he said. "I can drop you somewhere."

"Are you sure?"

He opened the door for her. She was dressed in only a T-shirt and shorts, and she slid inside and shut the door.

He hesitated a moment, then got in himself. He said, "Do you have anywhere to go?"

She shrugged. "The truck stop, I guess. She'll be better in the morning."

"Alix?"

July nodded. "After you left, she kept drinking and started accusing me—" She stopped, and stared out at the darkness.

Not wanting to pry, Jacob started his car and pulled away from the house. "Do you have any money?" he asked. "I could drop you at a motel."

She shook her head. "I ran out of the house."

He studied her, trying to think of a way to extricate himself from the trouble. "If you really believe Alix is a danger to you," he said, "why don't you call the police?"

"I can't, and she knows it."

"Why not?"

"Because I can't."

And neither could he. Involve the police in some sordid affair between a lesbian and her bisexual lover, and he'd surely lose custody of Max.

"She's insane, jealous," July told him. "Her imagination speaks to her all the time, like a gossiping old woman."

Hearing the colloquialism, once again Jacob wondered where Alix had found her. "Besides, it's not me I'm afraid for," she said.

"What are you talking about?"

She looked at him with frightened, liquid eyes.

"Me?"

Jacob's heart kicked from the conviction with which she held his stare. Then his cell phone shrieked.

Jacob grabbed for his pocket. July grabbed for his arm.

"Even if it's Alix," he said, "she's five miles away."

July said, "She has a cell phone too."

The phone trilled again. Another thought occurred to him, that it might be Laura, lying alone in their bed, unable to sleep. He clicked it on.

"I know what you're planning," the voice said. Alix indeed, loud and monotonic.

He stopped the car as he glanced over at July, who hunched small and frightened against the door. He could hear traffic in the telephone and for a moment feared she was driving up behind them. But he turned and saw that the road was dark.

"What did she tell you about me, that I'm insanely jealous and, what—"

"Alix, I haven't seen your friend—"

"—that I'm a threat to your life?" she raved on in that same hollow voice. "Or is it your son?"

"Listen to me." Jacob spoke as evenly as he could. "I don't know what you're talking about, but I want you to stay away from my family—"

"Or what, you'll kill me?"

"Look . . . Why don't you call someone who can help you?"

She gave an ironic laugh. "Do you want to know why I paid your bail?"

"I want you to leave me alone."

She said, "Meet me on the bridge."

"I'm not going to do that."

"Then you'll never know."

He looked nervously out at the night. "Alix, if you've got something to say—"

"I'll make both of you very happy," she said, and the line went dead.

JACOB sat there studying the phone, replaying what she had said while July watched him with wide, worried eyes.

"What did she say?"

"I'm not sure."

"Jacob, what did she say?"

He turned the car around.

Then he gave her the telephone. "Call nine-one-one," he said, racing toward the highway.

"I can't," she said again, and it occurred to him that she might be an illegal alien, so he didn't press the issue.

"Was she depressed when you left?" he asked, as he pounded the Mazda through its gears, squealing around the deserted rotary. "Did she ever talk about killing herself?"

"Why?"

"I don't know. I think she's on the bridge."

July studied him in the darkness, her eyes pinpoints of light. "Jacob, it might be a trap."

He cut the wheel sharply, veering onto the I-95 ramp, trying not to think about what he was doing: driving onto the high-level bridge for the first time in years. Seeing no other choice, he pressed back in his seat and clutched the wheel, concentrating on slowing his breathing. "Do you keep sleeping pills in the house?" he asked. "Barbiturates?"

"Tylenol PM, that's all," she answered. "Why?"

"Her voice. The things she was saying."

"I told you, she's drunk."

He tore off the ramp onto the highway, the skeletal structure rising up steadily before them—Jacob's heart started to pound—trees and rooftops descending, the lights of the town spreading out below, the moonlit sky wrapping around.

"What are you going to do?" July asked.

Higher and higher over the river they climbed. "I don't know," he said with as much calm as he could muster. "Talk to her."

"You *can't* talk to her."

He looked over as they were swallowed up in the steelwork, the bridge lights flickering off her face.

"There!" July slouched down in her seat again.

A car parked on the side of bridge, a small, boxy station wagon, its right directional blinking red, red, red . . . and a shadowy figure standing at the rail. Jacob hit the brake.

July whispered, *"Don't. Don't."*

He pulled over just beyond the Green Girls wagon. Indeed, it was Alix standing on the other side of the railing. She was facing him, cradling the rail in her arms. He leaned over July and fumbled with the window switch. "What are you doing?" he yelled into a whistling gust.

Alix looked over her shoulder, down to the darkness below.

Paralyzed with fear, somehow Jacob managed to open his door. July grabbed at his shirt, but he was already stepping onto the pavement, legs turning rubbery beneath him.

"Alix, please," he said, his voice a shiver.

"Jacob, be careful," July warned, her face in the window.

The blast of an air horn shook him, and he grabbed the hood of his car, the bridge bouncing like a diving board as the trailer truck blew past.

Now Alix stiffened, a guileless look of terror in her face and she said, "You told me you were alone." Though she spoke to Jacob, she kept her eyes on July.

"Just climb back over," Jacob told her. His whole body shook, but he could see Alix was shaking more. She looked down beneath her feet, then threw her face in the air, as if she couldn't believe this was happening to her.

"Listen to me—" He left the relative safety of his hood and grabbed onto the Volvo's roof. "There are people who can help you."

Her expression turned incredulous, as though she were about to laugh. Still she kept her eyes on July. "You're so stupid," she said, and moved her hand toward the pouch of her sweatshirt—

"Jacob!"

A sharp bang behind him threw him to the roadway, where he watched Alix's face drop between the railings. He reached out, but she was gone.

Kneeling at the curb, frozen, he looked back and saw July staring out the open window, terrified. He pulled himself to his feet in a daze. "What did you do?"

Tears streamed down her face.

Behind them another trailer truck was coming. July threw open the passenger door and slid behind the wheel. He got in, and she was already driving.

"What did you do?" he said, as she sped down the bridge, a sharp, incendiary smell blowing past his face. He could still hear the squeak of Alix's fingers sliding off the rail. Then a siren rose up in the distance. Gunpowder—that's what he was smelling. And there was the weapon—a small black revolver tucked behind the stick shift. He looked at July, horrified. "*What did you do?*"

"I was afraid she was going to kill you," she said, aiming his car for the exit ramp.

"Where are you going?"

"I don't know. Home?"

He laid his head in his hands. "I cannot be involved in this," he said. "I have a son."

"You can drop me off," she told him.

He couldn't think. "What about the gun?"

"I'll hide it."

He stared at her in disbelief. Reaching the bottom of the ramp, she drove through the red light without stopping. "Don't get pulled over," he said. "Jesus, what did you get me mixed up in?"

He looked through the darkness at her, astonished, as she turned onto her road, driving very slowly between the neat brick houses.

"Did you shoot her?" he asked.

"I told you she was crazy. Crazy and jealous. She had a gun."

"Did you shoot her?"

"I don't know!" July cried. "She was pulling something from her pocket! I was afraid she was going to kill you!"

"Kill me, why?"

"Because she's done it before!"

When July reached the point where the river and bridge swung into view, he could see the blue lights flashing up on the bridge; men, converging like fireflies, waved their flashlights down at the river. Another siren sliced the night, moving from west to east behind them.

"What do you mean, she's done it before?"

July wiped tears from her eyes. "I can't talk about it."

"She was jealous of *me?*"

He studied her as she downshifted, approaching Green Girls. Divers would be coming, he thought, his logic returning, to pick Alix's body out of the current. Would they also find a bullet? He closed his eyes, trying to replay what had happened, Alix's hand going to her sweatshirt pouch . . . for a pistol?

"Okay," he said. "You've been home all night. They're going to trace her license plate. Then they'll come tell you the news."

She stopped with a jerk in front of her house. Jacob turned off the key, checked the road behind them, relieved that no other houses were in sight. He got out and walked around to the driver's door, opened it for her.

"Listen now," he said. "It's absolutely critical that neither of us knows anything about this. You were home all night. You haven't seen me."

July remained in his car, holding the wheel, as though in shock.

"Don't turn any lights on," he whispered, stepping aside so she could get out. "Just go to bed. Do you sleep together?"

"What?"

"You and Alix—do you share a bed?" Realizing the tense was wrong.

July realized it too, nodding up at him glassy-eyed.

"Okay, you went to bed early and never heard her go out. You'll do fine. No . . ." He raised his fists to his head, thinking, thinking. . . . "Okay," he said. "Turn all the lights on. Have your bathrobe on, whatever it is you wear to bed."

"I don't wear anything." The way she looked at him, her emotions pitching just below the surface—how would she ever be able to talk to the police?

"Whatever you wear to answer the door, then," he said, feeling a chill when he saw the revolver in her hand. Very gently, he led her out of the car. "When they get here, tell them you woke up when you heard Alix leave the house, and you've been waiting up ever since. You were worried because she's been so depressed. That way you won't have to act shocked when they tell you."

She gave a slight, fearful nod.

"A note," he said. "She may have left a suicide note. You need to find it before they do. Is the gun registered?"

July leaned against him, and he felt her warm tears wet his neck. "I don't think I can do this."

"You've got to. I can't lose my son," he told her. "Is it registered?"

"I don't think so."

"We've got to be sure."

"I don't know," she said. "It belonged to Alix."

"Okay. Just hide it."

"Where?"

"I don't know. Someplace where . . ." Jacob drew back. "Wait a minute. If you had Alix's gun . . . whose gun did you think she had?"

July stared at him, eyes pooling.

"You said she had a gun."

"I don't know," she told him. "Maybe it was a knife. I don't know. . . ."

"Shh."

She gazed up at him, barely able to speak. "I was so afraid of her."

"We know she was going to kill herself," Jacob said, trying to comfort her. "Maybe she meant to take me with her."

He put his hands on her arms, gently turned her toward her house.

"They're going to be here soon," he said. "Just stick to your story."

She let out a soft gasp, then turned back to him, a fearful look in her eyes.

"You'll do fine," he told her.

But the way she kept staring at him, Jacob's heart pounded.

"What's the matter?"

She shook her head, deadly earnest.

"Her cell phone."

"What about it?" he said, but then he knew. His was the last number Alix had called.

5

SQUEAKY FRENETTI'S BAR LOOKED DEAD BY THE TIME JACOB got there—one-thirty in the morning, only one vehicle parked on the road, and the SPEEDWAY TAVERN sign turned off. Not wanting his car to be seen, Jacob drove up the driveway in back, where Squeaky, his father-in-law, parked his Impala. The lot was dark, as was the Captain Norman House, the building it had once served. Originally built in the 1700s by a sea captain, the white mansion had once been a magnificent display of glass, gables, and chimneys, with an octagonal widow's walk on top overlooking Kittery Harbor.

Over the centuries of changing families and fortunes, the property had served as home to shipyard presidents and factory owners, then became a sanitarium and later a retirement home, until it was shut down by the town's code enforcement office. During the same lifetime, the old carriage house that hugged the roadside had undergone similar changes, from blacksmith shop to bait and tackle shop, candy store, ice cream shop, and then clam shack.

When Squeaky Frenetti bought the property at a bank auction in the seventies, he dreamed of transforming the main building into a restaurant and inn, notwithstanding warnings from friends that he might as well throw his money to the tides. They might have been right. Structural repairs to the foundation and roof of the mansion had drained Squeaky's savings, and when the town refused to let him turn the carriage house into a working garage, he decided to keep his little house in town, with its three-bay garage, and turn the carriage house into a bar, while the Captain Norman House—which Squeaky renamed the Spite House—remained empty.

When Jacob walked through the back door of the tavern and down the steps, he found his father-in-law washing dishes in the small stone-walled kitchen.

Without turning to look at him, Squeaky croaked, "Here comes the mild-mannered man about town. How'd you like your vacation?" Sounds of a televised car race came from the bar.

Jacob didn't know what kind of reception to expect. Nor did he know how much Laura had told her father. "You know I'd never hurt Laura," he said quietly.

"So how come she kicked you out, you smart bastard? You went ape-shit with a radio, that's what I heard, caved in her boss's skull." He took his hands out of the soapy water and dried them on a towel, then turned and peered up at Jacob. "The guy's over the house talking business, right? About moving his office, right? And you come in and throw a fit."

"Really, that's between Laura and me," Jacob said, not about to sully Laura in the eyes of her father.

Squeaky smirked. "For a so-called intellectual, you ain't all that bright," he said. "Women like a little jealousy in a man, it makes 'em feel wanted. A *little*. This guy demolishes his own house. Numb-nuts, you'll be buying her flowers till you're both old and gray."

Squeaky Frenetti was a stocky man, five-nine in his black penny loafers, a holdover from the 1950s side of the 1960s, with his rolled-up short sleeves and blue jean cuffs. He was bald on top, but the white hair around his ears was greased and swept around the back of his neck in a stiff ducktail.

"Something happened tonight," Jacob said. "The police are probably going to be asking questions."

The older man's face brightened. "Yeah?"

"I didn't do anything wrong."

"You didn't do anything wrong?"

"That's right."

Squeaky appeared to mull over what Jacob was telling him, then he stuck his head in the doorway that led to the bar, and announced, "He didn't do anything wrong."

Jacob gave his father-in-law a curious look, then stepped through the door to see Detective Phil Fecto sitting on a barstool, watching the car race on TV. Smiling, the detective snuffed out his cigarette. "Hey, Jake, come on in, I'll buy you a beer." Fecto patted the stool beside him.

"Smart bastard, he seen you drive up," Squeaky told Jacob under his breath.

DESPITE the fact that the tavern was across the street from the harbor, no fishing nets hung from the walls or ceiling; no lobster buoys, no harpoons or long oars. The walls of the Speedway Tavern were covered with pictures of cars and autographed photos of drivers: Buddy Baker, Dale Earnhardt, Richard Petty, and the local celebrity, Jeff Dakota, a twenty-four-year-old kid from town who had recently made it onto the NASCAR circuit.

Behind the bar hung a crumbled red hood from a '72 Impala, the car that Squeaky still drove. Beside the hood, framed in gilded chrome, was a poster-sized enlargement of the same Impala passing a blurred Wonder Bread sign on a racetrack wall. QUAKER STATE was written on the side of the car. A brass plaque on the bottom of the frame read: 1975 WINSTON CUP. FIRST PLACE, TWO LAPS TO GO.

"The woman who telephoned you tonight, around ten twenty-five, Alix Callahan?" Fecto gave Jacob a look, Jacob gave Fecto a shrug. "We found her car parked on the high-level bridge. Keys were in it, and it started no problem, so we determined that she didn't stop because she was broken down. But she called you, right?"

"I don't know why she called me," Jacob admitted. "I hardly know the woman." He knew it would be pointless to deny Alix's phone call. But were he to admit that he was with her when she jumped, and then left the scene—with July?—he would surely lose his son. And if Alix had been shot? He'd be charged with murder.

Squeaky came into the bar and set a glass of ginger ale in front of Jacob, then turned off the television. "Would you boys mind turning off the lights and locking up when you leave?"

"No problem," Fecto replied, and the old man returned to the back room and was gone. Fecto turned back to Jacob. The detective had soft blue eyes, crinkled at the corners by years of work. "Jake, I don't mean to be disagreeable, but wasn't she the same Alix Callahan who paid your bail?"

"I don't know why she did that, either," Jacob told him. "When she called tonight, she sounded depressed, so I drove to her house."

"Which would've been ten-thirty, thereabouts?"

"Thereabouts," Jacob agreed, and took another drink. It's impossible to have a panic attack, Price Ashworth once suggested when Jacob was under hypnosis, as long as you're breathing properly. Trouble is, Price never explained how to breathe properly while you're having a panic attack. Jacob's heart pounded at his chest.

"Because about the same time," the detective went on, checking his notepad, "ten forty-two, to be exact, a motorist radioed dispatch and said he saw two cars parked on the bridge and two people standing outside their cars—a man and a woman. He said it looked like the woman was on the wrong side of the railing." Fecto kept his eye on Jacob. "But that wasn't you on the bridge with her."

"I told you, I hardly know her."

Fecto leaned on the bar, gave a troubled sigh. "Jake, I know you've been through a lot lately, and considering all you've done for the town and kids and such, I'd love to close the book on this and let you get on with your life." The way Fecto looked at him, with that furrowed scowl, Jacob knew the book was far from closed. "But she did call you; and you did drive over that bridge."

"I drove over. I never saw her."

"When she called you, did she tell you she was going to jump?"

"No," Jacob said. "She was vague, but it sounded like she might take her life."

The detective picked at his lip for a moment, apparently mulling over what Jacob had told him. Then he reached into his windbreaker pocket. "By the way." He pulled out a book, a worn copy of *Berth*. "I caught hell from my brother's wife the other night for not getting this signed. She thinks you're another Shakespeare or something." He set the book on the bar, and Jacob took a pen from him.

"Just your name," Fecto said. "She's a collector."

As Jacob signed the book, Fecto tapped a cigarette out of his pack. "You know the funny thing, they dusted that railing and lifted prints from two people—on both sides of the railing." He stuck the cigarette in his mouth. "They're checking the prints against yours that we got on file."

"They might be mine," Jacob said. "I stopped when I saw her car. I looked over the rail, but it was too dark to see anything."

"I missed that part, I guess, where you got out of your car," Fecto said. "My problem, not being specific enough."

Jacob handed the book back to the detective, who examined the autograph. "This oughta get me back in her good graces for at least a day or two." He slipped the book in his pocket. "No, but it's quite a coincidence, when you think about it," he continued, "on that entire bridge you'd end up in the exact spot where the girl jumped."

"Phil, her car was there."

"True. True. But then there's this other thing—" Fecto paused to light his cigarette. "That little dent in the railing."

"I don't know what you're asking me."

Fecto blew a column of smoke and said, "It's a fresh marking— the lab boys think maybe it came from a bullet." He examined

Jacob with a tilted head, like an Irish setter watching a rock. "No offense, but you don't seem like the gun type."

Jacob said, "Phil, do you think I shot this woman?"

"No, no. I know you better than that. I'm just asking the usual questions. You don't own a firearm of any sort, do you? Nothing came up registered under your name."

"No."

Fecto snuffed the cigarette out in the ashtray and said, "Mind if I take a look at your hand?"

"Which one?" Jacob turned his right hand over. With obvious discomfort, Fecto took hold of his wrist and brought his nose close, sniffing the fingers, palm, forearm. "You're a righty, I guess. Leastwise, you signed your autograph righty. You throw righty." He took a pair of rubber gloves out of his pocket and pulled them on. Then, setting a blue plastic box on the bar, he flipped the lid and took out a sealed packet, opened it, and produced a small moist cloth.

"Could I have that hand again?" he said, and swabbed it, while Jacob wondered if he should call that public defender—whose name escaped him—or maybe the lawyer Alix had told him about. Zabriski.

"It's diluted nitric acid," Fecto explained. "Detects the presence of nitrates on the skin—which come from gas and powder residue released when a firearm discharges. Again, strictly procedure. Lab'll analyze it. Should get the results sometime tomorrow."

A week ago, had anyone suggested that Jacob could have been involved in any of the events that had transpired over the past five days, he would never have believed it. "Are we about finished?"

The detective stuck the swab in the bag, sealed it again, then gave Jacob a studied look. "The driver of that trailer truck isn't going to put you on that bridge the same time Alix Callahan was standing there, right? No chance?"

If the police really knew the driver's identity, Jacob knew he'd be standing in a lineup right now. "No chance," he said. Still, he wondered if July would stick to the story they'd agreed on. "Have they found a body?"

"You mean, maybe she didn't jump?" Fecto fished inside his windbreaker for another cigarette. "Or if she did, maybe she swam to shore?"

"I guess," Jacob said, hating himself for the suggestion. But he just wanted the conversation to end so he could leave, go back to his crummy cottage, crawl into bed, and sleep for the next twenty hours.

Fecto snapped a flame from his lighter and shut his eyes as he inhaled a full dose of nicotine. "Back when they were doing repairs to the bridge," he said, easing smoke into his words, "the workers would dump their bags of cement that got hard. I saw it. Eighty pound bag of solid cement hits the water, you'd think it'd plunge, right?" Fecto shook his head with a pained expression. "It explodes."

Imagining Alix hitting the water, Jacob shut his eyes.

"A lot of people have jumped off that bridge since I've been on the job. Some left notes, others left their families with big fat mysteries. One guy even jumped on a bet. In thirty years, you know how many individuals lived to tell about it? Two. Because they managed to hit the water feet first, legs straight, hands by their sides. Like a human arrow."

"Maybe Alix did the same thing," Jacob said, trying to sound confident.

"Those winds?" The smoke laughed sadly out Fecto's nostrils. "Up top it blows one way, down below it blows another—off the ocean, down the river." His hand scattered the smoke. "A couple of years ago I helped recover the body of a jumper. When the guy hit the river, the impact tore his arm off at the shoulder and broke every major bone in his body . . . flattened him like a gingerbread cookie. I don't mean to be gruesome, but if your friend jumped?" The detective took a drag off his cigarette, inhaled in a meditative way, then snuffed the butt in the ashtray.

"Alix Callahan was not my friend," Jacob said. "I don't know why she bailed me out. I don't know why she called me tonight. I wish I did."

"And that's what I'll put in my report." Fecto stood and clapped

Jacob on the shoulder in a friendly way. "Sorry to trouble you about all this, Jake," he said, then headed for the front door. "But my sister-in-law's gonna be some pleased."

"If I think of anything, I'll let you know," Jacob told him.

"Appreciate it. Anything I can do for you in the meantime— place to stay till you get squared away, anything—don't be afraid to give a holler."

"I will. Thanks."

"And tell your father-in-law thanks for the coffee."

In the dark, Jacob held the hood of his car open with his back while he jiggled the battery cable. Then he went back to his window, reached inside, and turned the key. The motor moaned tiredly but didn't come close to starting. He opened the hood again, wondering why Squeaky had left him there with the detective. It wasn't like Squeaky to trust anyone to close up his tavern. As Jacob jiggled the battery cable again, a pair of headlights suddenly turned up the drive. Jacob squinted into the lights, hoping it wasn't another cop.

The old Impala stopped beside him. "Won't start?" the old man asked.

"It turns over but won't fire," Jacob answered.

"They don't usually do so hot without a coil wire," Squeaky said, holding up the rubber-coated wire.

Jacob scowled at his father-in-law. "What are you doing?"

"Looking for answers," Squeaky said. "Like how you give a guy a concussion and wreck your house—and don't know how."

Jacob shook his head.

"You clocked 'im with a radio—Fecto told me!" From years of shouting, the old man's vocal cords had been scraped to a raspy gargle.

"We had a disagreement," Jacob said flatly.

"Oh yeah? We're having a disagreement now. You gonna hit me with a radio? What kinda disagreement?"

"It's personal," Jacob told him.

"Personal, like the skirt tonight?" Squeaky got out of his car, stepped over to Jacob with his chin out.

"Who?"

"The skirt that called you tonight. The skirt that took the plunge."

Now Jacob understood Squeaky's anger. He thought it was Jacob who'd been cheating on Laura. He sighed, exasperated, and explained, "The woman was a lesbian."

Squeaky's face folded into a scowl as if he'd bit into something rotten.

"Squeaky, she was helping me," Jacob persisted. "She bailed me out of jail."

"Why?"

"I don't know."

"You don't know. And now this other broad comes in asking all about you."

"What are you talking about?"

"Some schoolmarm type with a hair acrost her ass—the district attorney, that's who. Lady Evangeline."

Jacob paused while his body absorbed more adrenaline. "What did she want?"

"You—on a cross." Squeaky handed him the coil wire. "Follow me to my house."

"Why?"

"Because you got evicted," the old man said. "The owners of E-Z Acres don't take kindly to cops bangin' on their door after midnight."

PEEPERS were singing loudly in the woods when Jacob pulled his Mazda in front of the three-bay garage beside Squeaky's car. He grabbed his backpack and laptop out of the back, but before he went in the house, he opened the glove compartment and found his medal of valor—*Bravery, Gallantry, Honor*—and flung it into the woods.

The minute he walked into the kitchen, the smell was familiar, a dull combination of gasoline, hand cleaner, thirty years of cigarette smoke, and cat food. He spotted photos of Max stuck to the refrigerator and went over for a better look. There were a dozen or so, most of which Jacob had taken. Laura always sent the doubles to her dad.

"You can sleep in here," Squeaky called from the end of the hall, where he opened the door to Laura's old bedroom.

Walking down the hall and entering the room, Jacob felt a welling in his chest. Everything had remained as Laura left it twenty years ago—her small bed, her vanity, her posters on the wall, everything in place—perhaps in hopes that she'd come back someday. There was even her fragrance, faintly sweet, or so Jacob imagined.

Jacob set his backpack and laptop on the bed and said, "What exactly did Evangeline want to know?"

"She asked if you were mentally ill. I said yes." Squeaky took the laptop off the bed, set it on Laura's little desk. "See, you even got a nice place to write."

Jacob shook his head, realizing his mistake in coming.

"You and your goddamn books. Meanwhile Dr. Ponytail's gettin' set to buy my business."

Jacob gave him a look. "Price Ashworth wants to buy the tavern?"

"That and the Spite House," he answered. "I thought that's what the beef was about: you jealous 'cause you missed out on it."

"Does Laura know?"

"Does Laura know?" Squeaky blew a laugh. "She's his frickin' agent. Where have you been? Oh, yeah, Mr. Sensitive offered me five hundred large for the place. Gonna turn it into some yuppie bed and breakfast, with the frickin' seashells and fishing nets and all the beautiful people."

Stunned, Jacob sank on the bed, trying to make sense of things. "Where's he getting that kind of money?"

"Hey, far as I'm concerned, more power to him," Squeaky said. "He's made something of himself. Instead of dreamin' up books that no one wants to read." The old man kept his eye on Jacob for another few seconds, then shook his head again. "You must be nuts," he said, leaving the room, "you want to put the little man through this shit."

Jacob imagined Price and Laura raising Max at the inn, and every organ in his body sank. At least things were beginning to make sense. Price wasn't in love with Laura. He was using her to get his hands on Squeaky's oceanfront property—just as Laura was using Price to get Max into a good school. But the same question kept coming up, unanswered: how was Alix Callahan connected?

6

"YOU TELL ME DON'T WORRY? HE'S MY GRANDSON!"

Jacob awoke when he heard the raspy voice seep through the wall. He was lying on Laura's bed with his feet hanging over the end. The sun was out. He got up and walked down the hallway to Squeaky's bedroom.

"Yo," the old man called when Jacob knocked. His voice was a yelp.

Jacob pushed the door open. "Was that Laura?"

Lying in bed with his T-shirt on, Squeaky kept his eyes closed. "Your lawyers are hard at work," he said. "The little man's gonna spend the weekend here."

His first reaction was elation. Then Jacob felt that hollowness in his chest, thinking that, with Max out of the way, Price and Laura would have the weekend to themselves.

"What did she say?"

"Oh, not much," Squeaky answered. "Except your lawyer's been calling her friends, askin' did she ever have sex affairs, does she have drug problems, drinkin' problems, is she a good mother to her son." Squeaky's hands jumped out of the blankets. "What the hell are you tryin' to pull?"

"I haven't said a word to my lawyer."

"Zalinkski, Zaleski, Wahooski—"

Jacob stepped into Squeaky's bedroom. "Zabriski?"

"Frickin' bloodsuckers," Squeaky said. "They bat around your lives like a game of Ping Pong till you're both ass-high in debt. When they finally bleed you dry, *then* they settle. You get screwed for life, she goes on welfare, the kid turns to a life of crime. Great frickin' country." Coughing deeply, Squeaky waved his hand at the door. "Get outta here and let me sleep."

"I don't understand," Jacob said. "Price Ashworth offered you a small fortune. You'd be set for life. Why don't you sell to him?"

Squeaky wrinkled his face. "Go ahead, I'll lay here and you keep firing stupid questions at me."

Jacob remained in the doorway, waiting, while Squeaky glared up at the ceiling, his big chest heaving.

"You think he's the only one who wants that place? A week don't go by without some idiot tryin' to give me money. Two days ago some shyster from Rhode Island who wants to turn it into a yacht club." Squeaky swiped the air with both hands, like a drunken conductor. "I gotta sleep, shut the door before you give me a heart attack."

Jacob stared into the room. "Do you know what's going on with Laura?"

"I don't know what's goin' on with anything!" the old man yelled. "With Laura, with you, Dr. Ponytail, lesbians jumpin' off bridges, and this whole miserable rotten world. But I'll tell you this. There's a little boy involved, and if you're not careful, he's gonna wind up as frigged-up as the rest of us."

INSIDE a gas station phone booth, Jacob looked in his pocket planner under Green Girls, found the phone number, and made the call.

"The police came last night and told me about Alix," July told him. "I cried—I couldn't stop—but they don't know I was on the bridge with you."

"I'll be there in a while," Jacob said, not wanting to discuss it on the phone. But he needed to see her, needed to know everything she'd told them.

"Jacob, I'm afraid," she said.

Against his will, he envisioned her brown shoulder, an image that presented itself richly hued and detailed. Even the smell of her came to him, that botanical sweetness complicated by the pungency of her natural scents wafting out of her dress—

"Jacob?"

He extinguished the image. "Try to stay calm," he told her, trying to hide his own anxiety. "I've got a couple of things to do, look for a job and an apartment. I'll be there as soon as I can." He hung up, and paged through the phone book with fingers shaking, looking for his lawyer.

7

WILLARD ZABRISKI'S LAW OFFICE SAT ON THE PORTSMOUTH
bank of the Piscataqua, a block west of Market Square, with three
arch-topped windows that looked out at a black and red freighter
docked under a billowy gray sky. The nautical brass clock on the
wall showed eleven when Zabriski's assistant, a woman who intro-
duced herself as Miss Finch, brought Jacob into the conference
room and seated him at a long table facing the river. A pitcher of
ice water sat in the center, beside three drinking glasses. The overhead light was on.

After a minute or so, an oak-paneled door opened and a slender, well-appointed man stepped in holding a folded newspaper.
The first look he gave Jacob was one of thinly disguised wariness,
perhaps wondering how to defend someone Jacob's size who was
accused of bashing a man's head with a radio. The lawyer's hair

was gray, and it swept to his eyebrows from left to right. He looked to be in his early sixties, and he said, "So," when he came over and shook Jacob's hand. "First of all, let me say that I'm a fan. I found your first book totally absorbing and thoroughly delightful."

"Thank you," Jacob said, and left it at that.

"Secondly . . ." The attorney dropped the newspaper in front of Jacob, then went to the head of the table and sat down. "What should I know about this?"

It was the morning's edition of the *Portsmouth Herald,* with a boxed, late-breaking story above the fold. "Car Abandoned on Bridge," the headline read. "Woman Missing, Feared Drowned." Below was a photo of Alix Callahan—probably from her driver's license.

As a light rain began painting the windows, Jacob told the lawyer the same story he'd told Fecto, omitting July's presence, omitting the revolver.

"And the reason Alix Callahan telephoned you?" Zabriski said, as he scribbled on his legal pad. His suit was ivory linen, his shoes calfskin.

"I don't know why exactly," Jacob said. "I don't know why she paid my bail, why she hired you to defend me, or where she got the money."

Zabriski kept writing. "But she did telephone you," he said flatly, "then presumably jumped to her death. And gave you no reason for her actions."

"That's right."

Zabriski seemed to consider this, then flipped a page in his legal pad. "Your assault case."

"Can I get anyone coffee?" Zabriski's assistant broke in. Miss Finch wore a conservative tweed skirt and jacket over a white blouse. With her wire-rim glasses and stony face, she could have been Jacob's age; she could have been fifty.

"Thank you," Jacob said, shaking his head. She poured a cup for the attorney and set it in front of him. She kept her distance from Jacob.

"I've read the police report concerning the alleged assault on

Dr. Ashworth and the damage to your house," Zabriski said, sifting through some photocopied documents. He glanced at Miss Finch, and she started a small tape recorder. "I'm aware of the disparity between your claims, yours and Dr. Ashworth's—whether he was at your house having an affair with your wife, or there on professional business." He looked across the table at Jacob. "It appears that you're both in agreement on the substantive point that while the alleged assault on Dr. Ashworth did take place, he was not *in* bed with your wife at the time. And you saw no evidence that they *had been* in your bed, is that correct?"

"That's right."

"At any time, did your wife's dinner guest make a motion that you might have regarded as threatening?"

"I don't think so," Jacob replied, rising up stiffly in the straight-backed chair. *Dinner guest.*

"Did he raise his arm?"

"Probably—to protect himself."

Zabriski glanced up with an almost playful look in his eye. "You must be a mind reader."

"What do you mean?"

"If he raised his arm, how do you discern intent?" His expression had turned instructional. "Now. Let's try again. When you confronted Dr. Ashworth in your bedroom, did he raise his arm to you?"

"Possibly," Jacob answered.

Zabriski examined Jacob more determinedly. "Did your son witness the altercation?"

"I'd like to leave Max out of this."

Zabriski stretched his legs under the table and looked out the window, seeming to watch a yellow kayak glide through the mist. The sky was lowering.

"Mr. Winter . . . May I call you Jacob? Jake?"

"Either."

"Jacob it is. Are you currently a patient of Dr. Ashworth's?"

Jacob shook his head. "Thirteen years ago I had a few sessions with him after my mother died. Laura's the receptionist and transcriptionist at the psychiatric clinic where he has his practice."

Zabriski looked up. Jacob tried not to read too much into the lawyer's scrutiny, that he met his wife in a psychiatrist's waiting room.

"Laura," Zabriski said, flipping a page in his legal pad. "How often does she drink?"

Jacob felt a rumble in his stomach. "I'd rather not go that route, either, if you don't mind."

The attorney leaned back and pressed his slender fingers together. "Jacob, in both your criminal trial as well as your divorce proceeding and custody hearing, I will be defending you from your wife, who, together with her divorce attorney, the district attorney, and Dr. Ashworth, will use every means at their disposal to destroy and demoralize you, to put you in prison and take every dollar you may have saved—and every dollar you might earn in the foreseeable future. And win sole custody of your son."

Jacob took a breath to object but could not find the words. Zabriski cut him off anyway.

"I'm not trying to frighten you, nor am I overstating. Now, let me ask you again. Does your wife drink or use drugs, pharmaceutical or otherwise?"

Jacob sighed. "Laura doesn't have a substance problem. She's a good person and a good mother."

"I'm sure she is," said the attorney, closing his legal pad. "D.A. Evangeline has already made us an offer: you plead guilty to one count of aggravated assault, you'll receive a five-year sentence, all but two suspended."

"Two years"—Jacob gripped the arms of his chair—"in prison?"

"That's correct," the attorney answered. "With good-time credit, you could reduce the sentence by four months."

Jacob stared off at the river.

"On the other hand," Zabriski continued, "we could go to court, plead guilty and ask for mercy. If we can persuade the court that this was not an unprovoked attack"—he raised his brow—"you could get as little as three months."

Jacob shook his head helplessly.

Zabriski looked over at Miss Finch, then back to Jacob. "Your alternative is to take the case to trial. With circumstances as you've described them, the jury may sympathize. But if they find you guilty, you could get ten years, all but six suspended."

Jacob stared at the attorney, reality slamming him from all sides. "They were having a candlelit dinner. Who wouldn't understand?"

Zabriski gave him a searching look. "Are you aware of Dr. Ashworth's claim?"

Jacob shrugged. "He said he was there on business."

"A Detective Phillip Fecto, the chief investigator," Zabriski said, rising to his feet and pacing to the window, "will testify for the prosecution that Dr. Ashworth had come to the defendant's home to persuade him to take his Haldol, a medication usually prescribed to inhibit the symptoms of psychosis."

Jacob sat up in his chair.

"The defendant walked into the dining room, where he discovered the doctor with an empty bowl of *oyster-minestrone soup*," Zabriski continued, as though he were presenting the prosecution's opening argument. "Mr. Winter, how much do you weigh?"

Jacob shook his head, seeing the picture the man was painting. "Nobody said anything about medication." Or had they?

"The defendant marched into the bedroom where he picked up a radio," Zabriski went on, "and viciously attacked the doctor, sending him to the emergency room with a severe concussion."

Jacob felt his intestines start to crawl. "It's the clock radio my wife keeps beside her bed. They were listening to the ball game so they'd know when I was coming home."

Zabriski shook his head. "Again, that's your assumption, Jacob. And it might very well be mine. But neither of them admitted to that. And they're not going to."

Jacob sat numbly.

"Now, about your medication."

Jacob closed his eyes. "The pills were prescribed twelve years ago, for an overactive imagination—not psychosis. I took them for a couple of months, then I stopped. I don't take the pills anymore because I don't need the pills anymore. They inhibit my writing."

"Nevertheless, it's part of your medical record." The lawyer studied him. "Jacob, besides the oyster-minestrone soup, did you ever have reason to suspect your wife was having an affair with Dr. Ashworth?"

"Did I imagine this? No."

"Not what I meant," Zabriski said. "But that's the portrait the prosecution will paint—of you."

The humming behind Jacob's ears was getting louder.

"Has she ever had any previous affairs?" Zabriski asked. "Flirtations?"

Jacob took a breath of the stifling air in the room. "Not that I know of." Their relationship, from the start, had been ideal: lovers, mates, best friends, parents. His chest grew heavy with a sinking sadness. Or was it brewing rage?

"Jacob, I need to ask you again, did your son see his mother and Dr. Ashworth in the dining room, or have any contact with them when he came in?"

Jacob shook his head adamantly. "I went into the kitchen, saw the pots and pans on the stove. Laura came in and asked Max to go play at the gravel pit because she wanted to talk to me."

Zabriski looked up at him, his pen paused on the legal pad. "Gravel pit?"

"We call it a field. It's grown over," Jacob said, and left it at that, not wanting to explain that Max didn't have any friends in the neighborhood, that the other kids considered him strange, called him names like "geek" and "bug-eyes," and that Max compensated by being the schoolyard daredevil, risking his neck for their amazement and amusement—which only served to alienate him more.

"Would Max have seen evidence of the kind of dinner she had prepared, the lobsters?"

Jacob shook his head.

"Is there a chance he heard an exchange of dialogue before he left the house? Or maybe he's seen Dr. Ashworth in your home on another occasion."

Jacob's head kept shaking.

"No, he didn't hear or see? Or no, you'd rather lose custody of your son than involve him in your defense?"

"It's this: a man was having a romantic dinner with my wife, and I lost my temper."

Zabriski gave him a wry glance. "Jacob, I assume you're aware that Dr. Ashworth lost his license to practice medicine in Maine, for engaging in improper relations with a former patient?"

Jacob nodded. "Eight years ago. That's why he moved the practice across the river, to New Hampshire."

"Did you also know that his license is currently under board review in this state, for yet another ill-considered dalliance?"

No, Jacob did not know, though he wasn't surprised.

The attorney explained, "If it were known that the good doctor was concurrently having relations with the wife of a former patient, it might well spell the end of his career."

And he wouldn't be able to afford to send Max away to school, Jacob realized—which must have been the reason Laura was willing to hide the truth about their relationship.

"You'll also be interested to know that he's paying off two former wives, to the tune of twelve hundred dollars a month; plus he's carrying a two-thousand-dollar mortgage on his house and rental on his office. He can't afford to lose his medical license."

"But he offered Laura's father a half-million dollars for his property."

Zabriski shrugged. "Perhaps he hypnotized a loan officer," he said, with uncharacteristic humor. "Enough about Dr. Ashworth. Now, let me tell you something about the district attorney who will be prosecuting you." Zabriski gave a hint of a smile. "Susan Evangeline has more determination than a mile of army ants. She lives to prosecute violent men."

"I'm not a violent man," Jacob said, and felt Miss Finch's sideward glance.

"She is the women's avenger, Jacob. And even though she has been instructed not to speak with you about this case unless I am present, I promise you that Susan Evangeline will learn things about your past that you've long since forgotten. For example . . ." Zabriski flipped through his notes again. "In California, an altercation at your mother's funeral, and subsequent arrest?"

Jacob gave a forbearing sigh. "My mother had just died. I was upset. I started treatment when I got back to Maine."

Suddenly the rain was slapping at the window in waves. While the attorney continued on, using words like *pattern of behavior* and *conflict resolution,* Jacob thought of his mother again, the way she had clung to him and wouldn't let go when he left for his last semester of college. It was the last time he saw her alive. Two months later he got a phone call at school telling him she'd had an accident, which turned out to be an overdose of barbiturates mixed with alcohol, which turned out to be suicide, of course, but no one ever mentioned that small fact until the funeral.

His memory was interrupted by the lawyer's words, ". . . shared parental rights and responsibilities. The question remains, which of you will get 'primary physical residence'?"

Although Jacob tried to appear attentive, Zabriski gave him a knowing look.

"At this point the question is rhetorical," he said, "but that's what will be at stake." Then, glancing at his watch, he stood and extended his hand, an abrupt but well-practiced move.

"Jacob, I know you've been through a lot, but it would be disingenuous of me to suggest that this won't be a long and painful fight, and a particularly difficult one if we choose to disarm ourselves. I'd like you to think long and hard about your decision to keep your son from testifying on your behalf."

Jacob didn't have to think. "I won't do that to Max," he said.

The attorney gave him a nod of respect, but his look was tinged with a note of futility. "One more thing," he said, looking out across the river, at the bridge. "In reference to the incident last night, let me say that if you do anything to embarrass this firm, or if you are ever less than completely forthcoming with me, I will have no choice but to resign as your attorney."

Jacob stood there, only half hearing the words. He was also staring out at the bridge now, with a sudden and powerful revelation: his next book.

"Just so we're clear," Zabriski said, stepping back as Jacob passed through the door.

"We're clear," Jacob replied. "Thank you."

Bridge.

8

RAIN SHOT OUT OF THE DOWNSPOUT AND WASHED IN A RIVER across the fieldstone walk. It tore at the sheet of paper tacked to the front door, bleeding the words CLOSED UNTIL FURTHER NOTICE until they were barely legible.

As soon as Jacob touched the handle, the door flew open, and July was pulling him in out of the rain.

"I didn't know where you were," she told him.

"Who came last night?" he replied, not wanting to talk about his legal problems.

She closed the door, saying, "A couple of men. Detectives. They looked everywhere."

"For what?"

She shrugged. "A suicide note, I guess."

"Did they find anything?"

"I don't think so. They said they might come back today."

"What about the gun?"

"I hid it."

Seeing she was barefoot, Jacob stepped out of his wet moccasins. The slate floor felt cold under his feet. "What did you tell them?"

"Just what you said: Alix went out late at night, and I waited up for her."

"They didn't ask if you were on the bridge?"

"They asked, I said no." She turned away from him to deadhead a blossom.

"But what if that truck driver spotted you in the car?"

She glanced back innocently. "I wasn't there."

He said, "Did they ask about me?"

"What about you?" she replied, then walked over to the circular stairs and started climbing.

Jacob came to the bottom of the staircase. "What did you tell them?"

"That Alix invited you to dinner last night. And that you were lovers in college."

"Alix and me? You're not serious."

Stopping on the stairs, July looked back at him without a trace of a smile, then turned and continued upward as if she expected him to follow. He had little choice.

"Alix and I never spoke until yesterday," he told her. "As far as I know, she never had a thing to do with anyone of the opposite sex."

He emerged inside the pantry, where July was waiting for him. In the tight, windowless space, the muffled rain hitting the roof was a comforting sound. But with July blocking the doorway to the kitchen, his comfort was short-lived. She looked up at him from under her hanging black hair and said, "What if you stayed here?"

"What do you mean?"

"You said you were looking for an apartment. I could do the cooking—I love to cook. You could write, you wouldn't have to get a job."

Momentarily disarmed by her offer, by the way she was peering up at him, he abruptly turned away and went into the living room. "It's not that I don't appreciate the offer," he said. "But the way things are, I don't think it would be too smart. Okay if I look around?"

"I wouldn't bother you," she persisted, following him.

"How about the bedroom?"

"I'd sleep in the garden hut," she said.

"I mean, did they look in there for a note?"

"I think so," she said. "I'm not sure." She went ahead of him into a short hallway and opened a door. Inside the small room Jacob saw a queen-size mattress on the floor, skimpy green underpants thrown beside it.

"Do you mind?" he asked.

She shook her head, so he went in. As in the rest of the house, lush flowering plants dominated the space. Jacob lifted a corner of the mattress, peeked underneath, then lowered it and pulled the blankets back. The sheets were discolored in two places where July and Alix had slept. A musky odor blew back at him when he dropped the blankets down.

"I've got some money saved," she told him. "All you'd have to do is write."

Jacob gave her a look as he shook a pillow out of its casing. He didn't want any more of the conversation, and it must have shown. She spun away from him and walked out of the room.

"What about the pockets of her clothes?" he asked.

She didn't answer.

Undistracted by the lace bra that hung from the knob, he opened the closet door and ran his hands through the pockets of every piece of clothing.

"You checked the bathroom?"

Again, no answer. He left the bedroom and opened the door at the end of the hall. The bathroom was narrow and long, with a skylight set in the slanted ceiling. Rainwater ran in sheets down the glass. The room was pleasantly appointed: an antique claw-footed bathtub, pedestal sink, old-fashioned toilet. Against the low end wall, a washer and dryer rumbled and shook the floor. Above the appliances a small frosted window was open an inch or two, looking down toward the road.

Jacob opened the medicine cabinet. He found—no surprises

here—a pair of toothbrushes in a juice glass, a bottle of Tylenol PM, a stick of deodorant, two hairbrushes, a pack of plastic disposable razors . . . nothing, at least on the surface, that would look like a farewell message. Then, above the noise of the appliances and beating rain, he heard a man's voice in the house. He went to the frosted window and peered out the two-inch opening, saw a blue Explorer parked in front of his car. Phil Fecto's.

"How are you today?"

Jacob spun around to see the detective standing at the open door. "Didn't mean to startle you," Fecto said.

"I don't think she left a note," Jacob told him, as if to explain his presence.

Fecto gave him a look, not exactly suspicious but not benign, either. He'd even dressed the part this morning, in a beige trench coat and a smart-fitting felt hat, both of them dripping rainwater. "Wet one," he said.

"Should make the farmers happy," Jacob replied, playing along.

"We sure need it." The detective looked down the hall in a furtive way, then closed the door and muttered to Jacob, "Know anything about her?" Meaning July, apparently. "No record. Nothing." At the sound of footsteps approaching, he changed the subject. "Anyway, did you know the Piscataqua is the second fastest river in the country? And the number one deepest."

July, sliding into the room behind him, gave Jacob a careful look. Her wet hair stuck to her face, probably from having stood outside with the detective trying to keep him from coming in.

Fecto reached inside his trench coat and pulled out a plastic bag. Inside was a stainless steel steak knife, with a half inch of murky water in the corner of the bag. "Divers found it about a hundred feet downriver," he explained. Then he turned to July. "Look familiar?"

A look of seriousness came over her face. "It's one of ours," she said.

Which meant she had been right the night before—it was what Alix had been reaching for on the bridge . . . and July had indeed saved his life. Her eyes lingered on him, too long.

"You recognize it?" Fecto said to him.

"Me? No."

"I'll show you," July said, and left the room.

Fecto eased the door closed after she went out. "Often, when someone appears out of thin air," he said quietly to Jacob, "no history, no record other than a Social Security card? There's a good chance they're under Witness Protection. Not always stellar citizens." He poked a hanging flower pot, starting it swinging.

"What do you mean, no history?" Jacob asked, then spotted something that shot a chill through him. Up on the skylight the barrel of a handgun peeked into the room, washed onto the glass by the torrent of rainwater flowing down—and he realized: that's where July had hidden the revolver last night. The police must have arrived as soon as he'd dropped her off, and it was the first place she'd thought to put it. He tore his glance away as the door opened, July returning, a matching steak knife in her hand. Now Jacob gave her his own careful look: *Get this guy out of here.*

"That looks right," Fecto said, taking it from her. "Do you mind if I take it for a few days?"

July shook her head. Her red bra showed through her wet dress.

"Do you think she cut her wrist before she jumped?" Jacob asked, positioning himself in the doorway to keep the detective facing away from the skylight.

"We won't know that just yet," Fecto said, then he took a photo out of his pocket. "Something else we found." He faced it toward Jacob, a picture of a small, misshapen slab placed beside a ruler, a quarter inch around. "The lab boys picked it up this morning, in the southbound lane—which is why it got away from us last night. Could be a ricochet."

Jacob studied the photo, casually trying to move them into the hallway. "A bullet?"

"When a slug collides with something hard, like a steel railing, the lead will flatten and break apart," Fecto explained, not moving. "Which means—see?—no lands or grooves left for Ballistics to analyze."

He showed the photo to July, who said, "I don't understand."

But she gave Jacob a more concentrated look, probably wondering what was rattling him. She still hadn't seen the revolver.

"Fortunately, they've got some pretty sophisticated equipment at the lab," Fecto explained. "Even with a slug this beat up, spectrographic analysis can tell what gun it came from—or if it matches any bullets from the same gun—or even bullets still in the box." Sticking the photo back in his pocket, Fecto said to July, "You don't own a firearm, do you?"

"I told you last night, no," she said. Then she saw it. Her eyes flashed back at Jacob.

"No access to firearms, either of you?"

She looked up at the skylight again, straight at it. Jacob felt the heat rise to his face, knew he was flushed, and he walked out of the bathroom, hoping they'd follow him. It worked. Fecto came out, July too, and she shut the door behind her.

"You can imagine what goes through an investigator's mind," the detective said. "Here you've got a partial slug, a bullet mark on a railing, a steak knife that belonged to a woman who might've jumped off a bridge, might've been shot. . ." He seemed to be leaving, sliding his notepad back in his pocket. But he looked troubled, or preoccupied about something. "You want to hear the strangest thing. . . ." He focused on July, as though he wasn't sure whether to tell her. "It might be upsetting."

She shrugged. "After last night? I'm numb."

"Well, probably there's nothing to it," Fecto said. "You know Deborah McBride?"

July scowled. Jacob said, "The state senator?"

"Yeah, she lives down at Kittery Point, big old place on the water."

"Not personally," Jacob said.

The detective looked at July again, who shook her head. "I don't follow politics."

"Well, like I said, it's probably nothing. But the guy who delivers her newspaper said he saw Alix Callahan in Senator McBride's driveway this morning."

"Alix?"

"The senator's got a long driveway that winds through the woods, like a quarter mile. The guy came around a corner, and there she was, like a deer in the headlights. According to him, she ran off when he saw her, and disappeared into the woods. He wouldn't have thought that much about it, but her picture was right there in the paper."

Jacob said, "Did anyone ask Senator McBride about it?"

"I just came from her office. She has no idea what the guy's talking about."

Fecto looked at July, who'd obviously been affected by the story, her face given to a kind of preoccupied grimace, and he said, "It's probably the last thing you want to hear."

"What about the guy?" Jacob said. "Is he reliable?"

Fecto shrugged. "He's got a steady job and no police record—course, that doesn't mean he's got all his marbles."

Jacob could feel July's eyes, like spotlights, on him; he wished she'd turn the other way.

"I like murder mysteries, personally, when it comes to books," Fecto said. "Action-adventure, suspense thrillers, that's my cup of tea. Those books of yours? Personally speaking, I mean, they might be true and all, but I didn't much care for them."

"Unfortunately, you're not alone," Jacob replied, forcing a smile that the detective did not share. "Has anyone else reported seeing her?"

"I mean, four hundred pages about someone's kitchen?" Fecto's brow folded perplexedly. "I might be missing something."

"That one wasn't a big seller," Jacob said. His head was spinning with misgivings. "But this newspaper deliveryman—he's sure of himself?"

"Who knows with witnesses? Sometimes you get a feeling they're just looking for attention." Fecto ran the wet brim of his hat through his fingers. "Anyway, if either of you turns anything up—suicide note, anything at all—be sure to give me a holler."

"Okay," Jacob said, letting them both pass him in the hall. He went back into the bathroom and closed the door, then stood listening to their footsteps going down the iron stairs, then the shop door closing. He peeked out the window and, to his relief, saw

Fecto get in the Explorer and start the engine. By now the revolver, having washed down to the middle of the skylight, was plainly visible to the road . . . if the detective decided to look up at the house. But as his vehicle started moving, he seemed more interested in July, her red underwear.

Keep going, Jacob prayed, as Fecto shifted through the gears and disappeared around the corner.

Jacob unlatched the skylight and pushed it up. Rainwater fell in around the sides. He raised up on his tiptoes and reached his hand around the frame, but still couldn't get at the gun.

"He's gone," said July, coming in.

Jacob bounced the frame up and down so the weapon slid with a gnawing squeal down the glass. He just wanted to take it and get the hell out of there.

"I didn't know it was going to rain," July said defensively—probably still miffed at the way he'd dismissed her offer.

She climbed up on the dryer and braced herself on Jacob's shoulder, stretching for the weapon and giving him a distracting view of her red-silk crotch in the process. When she'd retrieved it, she climbed down and slapped it in his hand.

"You hide it," she said, and walked out of the room.

He didn't know whether to thank her for saving him from Alix, apologize for having doubted her, or talk about this new information—a man supposedly seeing Alix in a state senator's driveway. He decided it was best to just leave. But walking down the hall, passing her bedroom, he looked in and saw her standing at the window, looking out at the rain. He stayed outside the door, listened to the rain tapping at the roof.

"It could look suspicious, my being here," he said.

"Then go."

Yes, he told himself: go. "July," he said, "that knife they found . . ."

She turned toward him and stood for a moment, motionless, her eyes dark and full, her wet hair clinging to her face and shoulders. "Jacob, do you think she's alive?"

"How could she be?" he said, trying his best to sound reassuring despite this tapping in his brain. "We saw her jump."

The way she gazed at him, barely dressed, with those eyes . . .

He refused the libidinous tug. "If we stick to our stories," he said stupidly, the cold revolver growing heavy in his hand, "we should be okay."

She turned away from him. "You'd better go," she told him, and he did, before he lost the will.

9

✔10:00 SEE LAWYER
✔12:00 LUNCH; BUY NEWSPAPER
✔ 1:00 LOOK FOR JOB, APARTMENT
    2:00 AGENT
    2:30 LIBRARY
    3:30 OUTLINE

J ACOB SAT IN HIS FATHER-IN-LAW'S KITCHEN WITH HIS POCKET Planner, scheduling the rest of his day. This is how he contains his unruly mind—with order, not medication. He does not let his imagination rule his brain. Alix Callahan jumped off the Piscataqua River Bridge. July shot at her. The odds of her surviving were minuscule. She was dead, without question.

In his books—although Jacob hasn't written a word in several months—he describes objects, explains functions. He does not invent stories, does not create characters. He explores reality, never interprets it.

Likewise in life, he does not engage in speculation nor indulge himself in fantasies of sex or success. When he made love to Laura, he was always present with her and her alone. The furniture he builds is classic in design, always practical. He employs the golden section—that is, a dimensional ratio of three to five—because such relationships are aesthetically pleasing. His furniture is rectangular, the wood painstakingly selected and finished to a natural luster. His tools are always sharp. He returns them to their places at the end of every work session and always sweeps his shop clean. The work is meditative, it grounds him. This is how he contains his mind. With work. With order.

When his agent answered the telephone, Jacob did not waste time with small talk.

"I'm writing a new book," he explained, "about a bridge."

He heard Maury light a cigarette. "Jacob, I have to be blunt. Critics love you. Literary journals love you. I love you. But your commercial appeal?" Maury Howard was a kind and capable man, but hard as he'd tried to sell Jacob's fourth book, the only offer they got was a hundred-dollar advance from a university press and five free copies. "Jake, *Berth* was a phenomenon—twelve years ago," Maury said. "And your second book set new records for returns."

"This bridge," Jacob told him, "it's a monstrosity. It's sky-high, and it connects two old New England towns—a New Hampshire shipping port with a Maine fishing village."

"Readers want stories about people, not bridges," Maury said. "I'm not saying you need a gargantuan plot and a cast of thousands. But you need *someone*. For crying out loud, in *Tree* there wasn't even a woodcutter, not even a woodpecker."

"There's a person in this one," Jacob said, improvising.

Maury didn't speak for a moment. "Does he do anything?"

"He gets a flat tire and can't decide whether to change it or jump."

"What, jump off the bridge?"

"That's right, he's depressed."

"Wait a minute. Are you talking fiction?"

Jacob paced the kitchen at the limit of the phone cord. "I want to know if you can sell it."

"Can I sell a great novel by a writer named Jacob Winter?" Maury paused, then breathed a thoughtful sigh. "Jacob, you're a meticulous and masterful talent. If I had a checklist—the thousand rules of wonderful writing—you could check every one. Technically, there's nobody better."

"But—?"

"You're a nonfiction writer. A novel, that's an entirely different world."

"Are you saying I'm incapable of writing a novel?"

"It's not that you're incapable. It's just"—Jacob listened to the agent draw deeply on his cigarette—"well, your writing has no heart."

"No heart?"

"How else can I put it?" the agent said. "People want to feel emotionally connected to what they're reading. It's not something you get off a checklist, not something you get from being intelligent, or doing years of research, or writing a brilliant outline."

"Okay," Jacob said, tired of the conversation.

"Jake, don't be mad."

"I'm not mad. Will you look at my manuscript when it's ready?"

"I'll look forward to it."

"Thank you."

"Jake—" Maury paused again. "Is everything okay?"

"Everything's fine," he said.

They hung up, and Jacob began writing—not his outline, but the novel itself. He lost himself. Words poured from his brain to his fingers. Paragraphs fell rich and fat onto the screen, about the Portsmouth waterfront, the freighters and tugs that docked there, the quaint rows of red-brick buildings that overlooked the river, and all the narrow, winding streets.

Even when he began feeling hunger pangs, he never lost his concentration. When the evening turned dusky, he turned on a lamp and continued writing. Although he'd already spun out forty-five pages, so far the man with the flat tire had not been mentioned. In fact, Jacob had yet to describe the bridge. The pages he wrote described the Piscataqua River, the towns of Kittery and Portsmouth, and only hinted at the enormity of the steel structure linking them.

Finally, when the twilight turned to dark, he put on his darkest clothes, took Alix Callahan's revolver from under Laura's child-hood mattress, and went out quietly into the night.

HE drove ten miles up the coast, to a place he knew in Cape Ned-dick, just off King's Cove, where a dirt road cut back into the woods along the shore of a shallow duck pond. He made his way to the dead end, surprised at the number of houses that had sprung up over the past ten years. The night was quiet. He hoped it would stay that way.

Where the road ended, a grassy old trolley bed intersected it and led through the woods, straight, level, and black. He took the revolver and a flashlight, and he walked fast.

The place was about three hundred feet in, a massive rock where he and Laura used to picnic when they'd first met. They called it Whale Rock because of its shape. At its head was a soft patch of grass. It was the spot where Max had been conceived, and now, as Jacob peeled back the turf with a garden spade he'd taken from Squeaky's garage, he felt as though he was desecrating the place.

Of course he was, carving into this hallowed earth while he thought about July. She had offered her house. No, she had offered much more, to take care of him so he could write his book—to be his keeper, maybe his lover. She'd already been his savior. Indeed, despite the depth of his concentration while he had worked on his book throughout the day, he'd never managed to completely get her out of his mind: her face, the coffee tones of her skin, the lithe muscles of her arms, her slouching dark stare. . . .

When he hit bedrock, he laid the revolver in and began pushing the soil back over it. As he was doing so, something cracked behind him. He spun around, leaning on the rock. Holding his breath, he tried to see through the darkness but could make out only indis-tinct columns of pine trees piled up against the black night. He flicked on his flashlight, shone it around, turning the near trees white and darkening everything else. It had sounded like a footstep about fifty feet back—or so he imagined. Logically, he knew it must have been a passing deer or fox, perhaps a porcupine. But in the wayward corner of his mind, he could only picture Alix Callahan stalking him in the dark. He shut off his flashlight. As quietly as he could, he laid the turf back on his secret spot and tamped it down with his moccasin.

Then he tiptoed back to his car and drove away, as fast as he dared.

10

H EART RACING, HENRY LAMB SWINGS OFF THE APPROACH RAMP. *The green steel web opens up and swallows his car along with all the other cars and trucks. High above the river, ocean winds beat against Henry's door. Veinal fluids tap at his temples. He has just spent his last twenty dollars on gasoline and a bottle of chardonnay for his wife, Dolores. He has something to tell her.*

Off to his right, a small airplane cuts a white hook in the sky—it looks like the letter J, white on red. Henry takes in the view to his left, the wide river yawning out to the ocean, the two drawbridges opened up, welcoming a salt bulker as it plows its way past the Portsmouth docks.

"That was Laura," came a voice from above. *"Hey, Stephen King—"*

Jacob looked up from his work to see Squeaky standing over him.

"Remember your wife?"

The window shade flashed with lightning, followed by quiet thunder in the distance.

"She just called. The little man's ball game got rained out. She's bringin' him now."

"Okay."

"You gonna let her see you like that? Brush your hair, shave or somethin'. You look like a bum."

Jacob said, "I can't see her anyway."

"You can't see her, how you gonna straighten things out?"

"I can't talk to her."

"Well, I sure the hell can't do it for you!" Squeaky cried, already hoarse.

"It's a court order," Jacob said.

"What, court order and you lay down and die?"

"Hey."

It was Max, standing in the doorway.

"There's the little man," Squeaky said, lowering into a boxer's crouch.

Max threw off his baseball cap and Squeaky gaped, dumbfounded. So did Jacob.

The top of the boy's head had been shaved bald, so that the only hair left was around his ears and the back of his head.

"What's with the trim?" Squeaky said. "Cripes, you look like a sixty-year-old nitwit."

"I look like you," Max said, and he danced forward, tossing left-hand jabs into the old man's padded hand.

"Maxie, who did that?" Jacob asked him.

"The barber," Max said, still throwing punches.

"I'm your barber," Jacob protested. "I cut your hair."

"You weren't around," Max said. "Price took me to his barber—his *stylist*. The guy asked me how I wanted it cut. I said, 'Like my granddad's.' Cool, huh?"

"Maybe for a circus midget," Squeaky said, moving toward Max, dodging and weaving. The boy feinted two quick lefts, then scored with a loud smack to Squeaky's arm.

Jacob stared at his son, thinking that perhaps this was Maxie's way of making him pay for the separation. "Price let the guy cut it like that?"

"He told him to do what I wanted. He said I should follow my heart."

"What did Mom say?"

"Not much."

Jacob sighed. "Maybe we should shave it all off. Bald's cool."

"I like it like this," Max told him. With his thick glasses, the boy could've been dressed for Halloween.

"Don't sweat it, the hair'll grow back," Squeaky said, straightening.

Max said, "Gramp, you ever been in a real fight?"

Squeaky chuckled. "Once or twice."

"Ever knock anyone out?"

"Naw."

The boy waited for more.

The old man gave a thoughtful frown. "This is what you need to remember: Everyone makes mistakes in life. You, with your dumb haircut. Me. This guy." He hitched his thumb at Jacob. "The deal is this. Some mistakes are big and some are small. And some are real doozies. Know how you can tell a doozy?"

Max shook his head.

"Well, don't worry, 'cause this ain't one," Squeaky said, fitting the cap back on Max's head. "A real doozy," he said, and he gave Jacob a pointed look, "that's the one you can't never take back."

11

IN THE DARK, THE INDIAN SAT ON HIS PRISON BUNK WITH *U.S. News & World Report* opened to the centerfold. With his thumbnail, he bent each leg of the steel staple that bound the pages. Pulling the staple free, he flattened it into a straight steel wire an inch long. Then he began the task of sharpening one end against the concrete wall. Once he'd achieved a fine steel point, he rolled it against the wall with his thumb, back and forth, until it was true as a blow dart. Then he took the Polaroid photo from his cigar box.

Working in the dark as deftly as a blind man, Sereno wet the dart in his lips, then pushed it into the side of the photo, careful not to pierce the front or back, until the weapon was buried inside the paper, unseen.

Then he returned to the stack of magazines on his table. This time he selected *Entertainment Weekly*.

12

T HE JULY FOURTH WEEKEND SAILED BY UNDER SUNNY BLUE SKIES while Jacob entertained Max and worked on his novel whenever he could find a minute . . . and did his best to keep his imagination at bay. At the movies Jacob wrote notes to himself in his Pocket Planner, even during the fireworks display in Portsmouth. After Max went to bed, Jacob stayed up until three in the morning reading library books about the history of Portsmouth and Kittery and the construction of the Piscataqua River Bridge. Even during the few hours he slept, Jacob woke up repeatedly and wrote notes to himself in the dark.

At seven in the morning they went fishing for schoolies in Spruce Creek. In the afternoon they went bodysurfing at York Beach, catching ride after ride into the sand and splashing back out again—Maxie with his cap pulled down to hide his friar's haircut, his glasses strapped to his head, giving his dad a triumphant thumbs-up when he caught a good wave. When they walked to the pizza place for dinner, Max swung his arms high, the way he used to, when he was happy. Indeed, for Jacob the days with Max were some of the happiest of his life. Then they were gone.

"You hate Price, don't you?"

Jacob looked up from his notes as Max got in the car, a towel underneath him to keep the seat dry while he wriggled out of his bathing suit.

"Waste of energy," Jacob replied, starting the car.

Max studied his father through salt-stained lenses as the car pulled out of the parking lot and onto the road. "Well, I hate him."

"He's not that bad," Jacob said.

Max tossed the bundled suit into the backseat and changed into his baseball uniform, saying nothing more while Jacob drove through York Harbor, then took the back road to Kittery.

"Mom says he's a Renaissance man."

"Price?"

" 'Cause he does that stained-glass crap and rock-climbing and all that. So what? He hates me."

"He doesn't hate you."

"He never talks to me."

"Do you talk to him?"

"I listen, he talks, more like it." Max took off his glasses, spat on each lens, and wiped them on his uniform. "If Mom's around, he acts like he's one of my teachers. When she's not around, if I go in the living room, he goes in the kitchen. If I go in the kitchen, he goes in the dining room. I don't care."

And that answered Jacob's questions about whether Price had been to the house. "Maybe he's uncomfortable around you," Jacob suggested, while his thoughts, like car wheels spinning in beach sand, burrowed back into that awful hole: how long had the affair been going on?

"He thinks he's so great," Max went on. "He's writing this poem about Benedict Arnold, it's like three hundred pages long. Mom's all, 'Oh, Price, you're such a genius.' "

"That's a long poem," Jacob said, while his mind traveled back over some odd comment from Laura, some oblique look, or the times he'd called her at work and she was out doing errands. . . .

"I think he's jealous of you," Max said.

"Jealous of me. Uh-huh."

"He's always bragging about, you know, he's so smart, and he's this master of tae kwon do, and showing off how fast he is. He drops an apple and before it hits the floor he can pick four other apples off the table, one at a time." Demonstrating, Max threw four lightning jabs at the windshield. "I guess it's fast. Big deal." He pulled the glove compartment open and reached inside. "Hey. Where's your medal?"

"I threw it away."

Max gave him a look. "How come?"

Jacob sighed. His heart felt like a rock.

"Dad, how come?"

When the ball field came in sight, Jacob pulled the car to the roadside and stopped. In the distance they could see Price's Z3 parked behind the backstop. Laura was sitting beside him in the convertible.

"The medal?" Jacob said. "The guys at the firehouse gave it to me."

"I know."

Jacob shifted into neutral, then confessed. "Maxie, you know I was never an actual fireman, right? I was the dispatcher, the person that answers the phone."

"I know."

"It gave me time to write."

Max scowled. "What about the medal?"

Jacob said, "I climbed a stepladder one day, to change a light-bulb. They knew I had a fear of heights. It was a joke."

The way Max looked at him—kind of a smirk, the way you might look at a bug in your hand just before you tossed it away. "What-ever," he said, and reached over the seat to grab his backpack. Opened the door, started getting out—

"Maxie, wait a minute."

Max stopped, but didn't look back.

"Adults grow up, you know—just like kids do." Jacob turned off the engine, to make things as quiet as he could. "We all change, Maxie. And we both need to accept the fact that Mom is changing about certain things. She still loves you—just like I do. That part never changes. But as far as the way she feels about me. And Price."

Max leaned out of the car, trying to bail out of the conversation. "I know what you're going to say."

"Let me say it anyway."

Max waited, as though on a leash.

"Just between you and me," Jacob told him, staring out at Price Ashworth's car. "Even the Renaissance had its share of assholes."

"That it?" Max said, clearly relieved, but humorless.

Jacob squeezed his shoulder. "I had a great time with you this weekend, champ."

"Yup." Max started walking to the field.

"Good luck tonight," Jacob called. "Remember: Head, not heart."

"Later," Max answered, without turning back.

13

UNTIL HE UNLOCKED THE DOOR, JACOB HAD NEVER COMMIT-
ted such a crime. Now, as he crept into the lobby, his mind swarming with images of alarm systems, guard dogs, and roving patrol
cars, he reminded himself that a psychiatrist's office probably
wasn't that heavily protected. What was there to steal but some
cheap furniture and artwork the doctors obviously didn't want in
their homes?

It was a one-story brick building on a quiet Portsmouth street in
the old part of town, just west of Strawberry Banke. Each of the
four offices had two outside walls, two windows. The reception
space, centered in the building, was windowless, so that once Jacob
had closed the inner entry door he was able to turn on the overhead fluorescents without fear of detection. Technically, he had
already committed one crime tonight, breaking into his own house

while Laura and Max were at the game and taking her spare set of keys. Everything was relative, he told himself: crime, love, commitment. He had to know when Laura became more than Price Ashworth's employee.

In her desk drawer he found four different-colored appointment books, one for each of the doctors. Simple deduction: if Price Ashworth had been seeing patients every day, then he couldn't have been somewhere else with Laura. He opened the book to a random week and found Price's patients booked solid, from nine to five. He swiped a few pages ahead, and again, booked solid. A few more pages. There again. And again. Then Jacob stopped—

Turned back.

One patient's name stared up at him. Wednesday afternoon, 4:00–5:00.

He checked the previous week. Same day. Same time. Same name . . .

Alix Callahan.

14

SENATOR DEBORAH MCBRIDE'S OCEANFRONT HOME SAT ISO-
lated among the rocks and weathered pines, separated from neigh-
bors by six acres of rugged, gale-weathered woods, a quarter mile
from the main road. The house itself was modest compared with
the value of the land, passed down among generations of the same
fishing family until property taxes made the house too expensive for
people who made their living on the water.

McBride lived alone. Her constituents, she liked to tell the
media, were all the family she had time for. This night she was taking no calls from either—constituents or media. Not even her staff
was getting through. She sat in an overstuffed chair with a TV
remote control in her hand, dressed in a white cotton nightie, staring at some silly sitcom—not that she was paying the slightest
attention. On her telephone answering machine, a man was leaving

a message: "Senator McBride, I'm sorry to bother you at home, but we were unable to contact you at your office today. We know you've been bombarded lately regarding the disappearance of Alix Callahan and the rumor that you may have had some contact with her. If the reports are true, you might consider sitting down and talking with us, to set the record straight. If the rumors are false, then your statement to that effect would help close the book before the gossip gets out of hand. We know how election years can be. So . . . please feel free to call anytime, day or night."

The machine beeped once, then turned off. McBride continued staring, unblinking, at her TV. Looking older than her years—in fact, having cultivated such a look—she was neither alluring nor homely. She'd carefully maintained the image of middle-class refinement necessary to women in Maine politics: down-to-earth, capable, unflappable. In public she did not drink hard liquor or smoke cigarettes. But here in the privacy of her living room, the thread of cigarette smoke rose past her face. Her ashtray was full on the table beside her, and the bourbon glass was empty except for a few ice cubes. If the phone message had disturbed her, it was not evident in her demeanor. Even when the smoke alarm began blaring, she remained perfectly composed, still holding the remote control in her hand—although the cigarette smoke was noticeably thicker.

In fact, the cigarette was smoldering in her lap, patiently burning a hole in the nightie. But she continued watching the TV, not even blinking when the back door closed, or when the cigarette dropped through the hole and the cotton ignited. . . .

15

Something shakes Henry's car, suddenly pulling him toward the rail. He jerks the wheel, stamps the brakes. A screech of tires behind him, horn blaring, another horn, his car slams into the railing, he is traveling backward now, spinning north, east, south, steel trusses fluttering past every window, the open sky.

Jacob sat in his father-in-law's house, Laura's old bedroom hovering around him as his story oozed out of his brain, tangling from time to time with strands of his own life.

He wondered: Maybe it was actually Price who had paid his bail, by funneling money through Alix Callahan. On the surface, it seemed implausible—unless one knew Price Ashworth. Why would anyone pay the legal fees of the man who'd brained him? To take the edge off his conscience for stealing the man's wife. Or, as Price would have put it, to balance out his karmic debt. But would Laura have consented to the payment? Feeling the gnawing in his gut, Jacob put the mystery out of his mind.

The car stops with a jolt. The passenger window shears in two and sails like a butterfly over the rail. A trailer truck screams past, air horn blaring. The roadway bounces slowly in its wake, up and down. Henry leans his forehead against the steering wheel. His lip is bleeding. He deduces that his right front tire is flat.

Maybe it was Laura who put Price up to paying his legal fees. Despite her disenchantment with Jacob, despite the fact of her infidelity, she wouldn't want to see him go to prison, if only for Max's sake.

The wind shakes the car so hard that Henry thinks it might float up off the roadway and blow over the railing. He opens his window to let the wind whip through. The oxygen calms him, but he is helpless to ignore the tons of interlocked steel surrounding him, groaning under its own weight.

Or perhaps the reason Price had paid for Jacob's lawyer was more diabolical: enlisting a powerful attorney in Jacob's defense to ensure that Laura would not win sole custody of Max. Of course. Why would Price want responsibility for the boy?

"Hey, Hemingway." Squeaky's voice intrudes out of the distance. "Do you mind? There's people tryin' to sleep here."

Jacob looked up from the small desk, all his errant thoughts dissolving from his mind.

"Sorry, I'll get out of here," he said, saving the file, then closing the lid on his laptop.

"No one said get out," Squeaky said. "Christ, you're in here clearin' your throat, tappin' your toes. It's almost three."

Jacob got to his feet. "It was inconsiderate of me. I apologize."

"What's it, a crime now to wanna sleep?"

Jacob slung his laptop over one shoulder, his backpack over the other, and walked down the hall, having no idea where he'd go— but he was not spending another night in that room.

"Not to mention, now ain't the time to crawl inside the windmills of your mind," Squeaky persisted, following him into the kitchen. "If you expect to get Laura back, you'd better wake up to reality, Mr. Man, get yourself a paying job. Hey."

Jacob opened the door and stepped outside before he got drawn into another battle.

"All right, you want somethin' part-time, you can work for me—till you find a better job."

Jacob turned back. "Tending bar?"

"No, swingin' a radio over your head. Yeah, tendin' bar. Saturday's gonna be busy, you could make yourself a bill or two in tips."

Taken by surprise—never would he have imagined Squeaky hiring him—Jacob gave it a moment's thought.

"Now come in and get some sleep. You look like shit."

"I need to work on this book," Jacob told him.

"Frig the book, face reality!" the old man cried. "You ain't no frickin' writer!"

Dogs started barking in the distance. Jacob shook his head, meaning to walk away, but . . . "Squeaky, she's divorcing me."

For the moment, the old man stood speechless, and Jacob took his leave.

AT four-thirty in the morning Rick's Restaurant in York Village was bright and lively with fishermen and wisecracking waitresses. But Jacob Winter, nursing his bottomless cup of coffee, couldn't remember ever harboring such bottomless confusion.

That Price Ashworth would have used Alix to pay Jacob's bail and legal fees was understandable. But why would Alix have agreed to be the conduit? Maybe she owed him for his services. No. As little as Jacob had known her, she seemed to have too much integrity to do anything surreptitious for the likes of Price Ashworth—not in trade.

What if Alix had revealed something to Price in therapy? Jacob let the notion grow. He knew their relationship had been more than just doctor-patient—or why in Jacob's conversations with her hadn't she mentioned at least that she knew the man he had clubbed with a radio? Maybe he'd been blackmailing her.

But blackmailing her why? What secrets had Price learned from Alix Callahan? And what about the rumors that she was alive? After all, her body still had not been found, even though Coast Guard divers had combed the harbor bottom for days.

Jacob yawned, though he was jittery from the coffee. It was sleep deprivation, he told himself, the reason these crazy ideas were ricocheting around his head: Alix stalking him, stalking July, being blackmailed by Price. Not for the first time tonight, he wondered if he should start taking the medication everyone seemed so eager for him to put into his bloodstream.

He took out his Pocket Planner, intending to schedule the coming day. That's when he overheard the conversation from the far side of the counter.

"She never got up from the chair," someone said. "Just sat there and burned."

Jacob looked over at the knot of men, his attention awakened.

"She fell asleep smoking," suggested one of them.

"And didn't wake up when she caught on fire?"

"Maybe she was drunk."

"*McBride*? Doubtful."

A dull shock went through Jacob, weakening his already tired limbs. "Excuse me," he said to the waitress. "What happened?"

"You haven't been listening?" she said to him. "Deborah McBride, the politician. Her house burned to the ground last night—with her in it."

Jacob stopped breathing.

"Smoke inhalation, right?" said one of the men. "The chair smoldered while she slept. Some of those older upholsteries release gas when they burn."

"That's not the way it looked to me," said another, younger man wearing high rubber boots. His face was unnaturally red. A firefighter, Jacob realized. "By the time we got it under control—" He shook his head, not wanting to continue, and his friend picked up his sentence.

"Looked to me like she still had a remote in her hand—pretty much black plastic melted over black bones now. Sitting on black springs."

Jacob stood up and reached in his pocket, pretending not to listen.

"Check?" said the waitress.

He nodded, needing to get out of there.

"Know what I think?" said an older man from one of the tables. "That gal from Portsmouth who jumped off the high-level bridge. That's who done it. Because McBride seen her climbing out of the water."

"What, you think the woman survived the fall, then swam out to Kittery Point?"

"No swimming necessary," the old man said. "Not with the tide going out. It's downstream all the way."

"Yeah, well," someone said respectfully. "Maybe."

"Tell you what," the old man came back. "Someone else seen her too—that paperboy fella. Let's see how long he lasts."

"Ever hear of self-immolation?" the waitress said to the men. "Spontaneous combustion?"

"Oh, yeah," one of them replied. "I read all about it in the supermarket checkout line."

"Laugh all you want," she told him, setting Jacob's check in front of him. "They got documented cases—thousands of 'em."

"That's right, and space aliens in the White House."

The little restaurant rang with laughter as Jacob walked out the door and climbed into his car. He drove over to Long Beach, where he parked on the road and reclined his seat, to soothe himself with the sound of the surf, hopefully to sleep. . . .

BUT sleep won't come to Jacob, no matter how hard he tries. It's his body more than his mind, as though a second body were trapped inside him, trying to push its way out. It happens when he's overtired, overstressed, overworked, the images: Price and Laura at his dining room table; Alix Callahan falling past the railing; a woman's charred bones reclined on black chair-springs. And July, always July, with her soft black stare.

He tries to dispel the images with thoughts of Max, memories of a recent Christmas morning when they'd sat opening gifts under the tree, Jacob, Laura, Max. He lays his head back on the seat and concentrates on the surf. The ocean breathes heavily; stars burn in the sky. He closes his eyes. He counts the seconds between waves. . . .

But he cannot dispel this girl. July. He can almost hear her voice in the whisper of water sweeping the beach, he can smell the pungency of her skin mingling with the salty air. Powerless to stop the sensations, he finally allows her ghost to move over him, cover him like a blanket, and soon falls into a fitful, sexual sleep.

A car engine wakes him with a start, racing away. But no car is in sight when Jacob sits up, no taillights in his mirror. The car was in his dreams.

Then it hits him: Maybe July knows the answer.

He pictures her, allows her fully into his mind. Yes, she must know. He starts his car.

And goes to her.

16

THE MOMENT THE DOOR OPENED, JACOB SAID: "I THINK PRICE Ashworth was blackmailing Alix." Not exactly what he meant to say, but there it was.

July narrowed her eyes. "Who?"

"He's a psychiatrist. Alix was his patient. Did you know that?"

"He couldn't have been very good," she said, straight-faced. The sleepiness of her gaze did not diminish her beauty.

"But you knew Alix was seeing him."

July called his bluff with a fervent black stare until he closed his eyes and leaned against the doorjamb, so exhausted he felt like collapsing. He'd already decided not to mention McBride's death, not wanting to frighten her. After all, simple logic dictated that Alix could not have survived the fall, especially considering she might have been shot.

"Jacob," said July, taking his hand, and she led him unresisting down the aisle of her sweet green shop and out to her cool garden. Dew-covered elephant leaves blessed him as they passed into shadows; sleeping fragrances lulled him. Then he was going through the door of her garden hut, four wooden walls and a thatched ceiling from which hung dried herbs and fresh flowers, filling the air with fragrance. On the floor was a thin mattress covered with a cotton quilt. She eased him onto the bed, speaking in the softest voice he'd ever heard. "Jacob, you need to sleep."

She touched his face, another blessing, and he closed his eyes.

PART
TWO

17

JACOB WINTER AWAKENS IN A DEEP GREEN LIGHT. HE RISES IN silence, pulls on his shorts, and walks out the door of July's garden hut, surrounded by huge, leathery leaves. All around him the forest drips with golden, syrupy dew as he heads toward the house. Then he realizes that he has gone the wrong way, actually deeper into the green, glassed-in world. He comes to an intersection of paths and turns right, but after a few steps the jungle presses in closer. He feels a low humming in his head that tells him something is wrong. This is the way it happens in his dreams. He turns around.

Alix Callahan is standing there.

Taken aback, he says, "You're alive."

Her chest jumps with a laugh. "Are you serious? I jumped off the bridge."

"You jumped . . . because Price Ashworth was blackmailing you. Right?"

"Blackmailing me?"

"And you killed Deborah McBride—because she saw you."

Alix laughs again. "Jacob, you think too much. I'm dead. Go back to sleep."

Back to sleep. Yes, Jacob realizes he's dreaming, so he turns away from her and rolls over in bed. It's dark again. He closes his eyes.

Then a door opens, and he hears the hush of footsteps coming closer. He thinks it's Alix again, returning to tell him the truth, so he awakens again. And stares.

But it's his mother standing over him. She's smiling softly and, God, the way she's looking at him.

"Honey, it's so good to see you," she says. "Do you want to dream together?"

Jacob gazes at her, afraid that if he makes a sound, if he even blinks, he will cause her to vanish. But he can't stop the tears from burning his eyes, and then he loses her.

"Wait!"

THE echo of his cry hung in the garden hut, hot and heavy with silence. He tried to gauge the time of day by the light coming through the windows, figured it must be close to noon. But what a longing he felt. Seeing his mother, even in a dream, had been wonderful.

He took his Pocket Planner out and scheduled his day: 1:00 CALL Z, ARRANGE TO SEE MAX. 1:30 LIBRARY RESEARCH. 5:00 FIND MOTEL.

Aware of strange ticking sounds coming from a narrow door adjacent to his bed, and thinking it might be July, he stepped off the mattress and knocked . . . "Hello?"

He opened the door—and was attacked by hordes of crickets, a dense cloud of them. Furiously brushing the insects off him, he kicked the door shut and staggered outside into the green heat—and there she was, July, laughing that musical laugh of hers. "Frog food," she said, picking a grasshopper out of his hair. "I meant to warn you."

"You raise grasshoppers to feed frogs?" Dreaming or awake—he could hardly tell anymore.

"Not me, Alix did. See?" She pointed to his right, but all he could see was a dense wall of burgeoning plant life. Then he saw the movement, the tiny yellow thing crawling into a cool green shadow. "Poison dart frog," she explained. "It's the most toxic animal in the world."

Jacob looked around his feet. With the low-cut moccasins he wore, he might as well have been barefoot. She moved toward the frog, and it leaped off the path into thicker foliage.

"In Colombia, the Choco Indians still treat their blow darts with the skin secretions. One frog produces enough poison to kill a hundred monkeys. Or ten humans, if the dose is strong enough."

At first he avoided looking at her. But he could tell she was waiting for his glance, so he complied, and she laughed at him again. "Jacob, you're so paranoid." Evidently she'd still not heard about McBride's death. "Come up," she told him, starting down the path toward the house. "I'll make you breakfast."

He followed, considering his mistake in coming here, that she might believe he was accepting her offer to move in. When they stepped into her shop, the place looked closed. July opened a wooden cabinet and took out a sprayer. "See?" She misted one of the hanging plants. "She used the frog poison to make insecticide. It doesn't cause cancer."

"The Indians use it for hunting?"

She gave him a beautiful look, or perhaps it was just a look and she didn't realize how beautiful she was. "Jacob, you're worse than the cops. What do you want to know? I'm not Choco, I'm Kogi. Half Kogi. To be *precise.*"

"From Colombia?"

"That's right. My father was an American missionary in Santa Marta." Her defiant posture suggested she was betraying a dirty family secret.

"I don't mean to pry," he told her.

She continued misting plants. "My mother was a Kogi Indian who had come down from the mountains to work as a cook for him and his wife," she went on. "After I was born, my father decided I should be raised American too. So my real mother was fired, and I was raised by my American father and his American wife, who never stopped hating him for bringing me into the world. Okay?"

"Are they still there?"

"I wouldn't know. I left when I was twelve."

At the bottom of the staircase he noticed a pile of cardboard boxes filled with books. Alix's books, he assumed. July was cleaning house. "Left, like ran away?"

She sighed. "I went up the mountains to be with my mother's people, and I married my thirteen-year-old cousin." The coquettish glimmer in her eye made him question if she was serious, and again he thought he should leave—or at least say something before she got the wrong idea. Then it was too late. "Jacob, come here, I want to kiss you good morning."

"Where's your cousin now?" he asked, wandering away from her as if he hadn't heard—or was suddenly interested in Alix's books.

"He disappeared," she answered. "Jacob."

He pulled a book out of the box. "What do you mean, disappeared?"

"If I knew, he wouldn't be disappeared. Most likely down to Santa Marta, to rob graves or sell drugs. Or become a whore."

And suddenly Jacob was very interested—in a book: an anthropology textbook. In fact, the box was filled with textbooks. Fact and speculation intermingling, Jacob nonchalantly flipped through the pages. "Didn't you say your husband was a tribal shaman, in prison somewhere?"

"My second husband," she explained, when he spotted the stamp on the inside cover, BRANDEIS UNIVERSITY, just above Alix's penned-in name—apparently where Alix had done her graduate work.

July put down the sprayer and came toward him, and he replaced the book, not wanting to divulge what he was thinking. But the way she studied him, with those searching black eyes, it was as if she could read his mind.

"Maybe you shouldn't make anything for me," he said. "I've got a busy schedule today."

He was startled by the sudden sharpness of her gaze. Aware that she probably felt rejected, he came clean. "July, I can't stay here with you."

The way her gaze turned derisive, suddenly he saw something very American about her indeed, that disdainful look informed by shopping malls and negligent parents, by MTV, suburban schools, and bad web sites. It was the look of a girl used to getting her way.

"I appreciate the offer," he told her, "but it just wouldn't look right." It was the best he could come up with, lame as it sounded. The truth was, he wasn't sure he could continue to resist her, and he left her house before he changed his mind.

18

JUST BEFORE FOUR O'CLOCK, THE HOTTEST PART OF AFTER-noon, the prison motor pool crew moved like slugs, eight trusties wearing their outdoor colors—blue short-sleeved jumpsuits with white side stripes—working on the officers' vehicles—oil change, lube job, wash and wax. A single officer accompanied the men, OIC Biff Bishop, in his tan uniform.

Heat waves rippled off the asphalt, making the parking lot appear vaporous, so that up in their air-conditioned towers, even with binoculars, the tower guards would not be able to see every detail below. What they saw, if they were paying attention this close to shift change, was the crew finishing up, crisscrossing paths, shut-ting hoods and doors and liftgates, and heading leisurely back into the building. With the second shift guards coming on duty and the first shift leaving, the heat rippling, the inmate activity, no one was likely to notice that only seven trusties made their way back inside. Nor would they have suspected that one of the prisoners might have crawled under the canvas tarp in the back of Biff Bishop's Jeep, especially when it was Bishop himself who had closed the lift-gate while he was yelling at his boys to get their asses in gear. After he watched the last of them go through the door, he climbed in behind the wheel, to head home.

It was an effortless and bloodless prison break which, when eventually discovered, would be easily explainable. Bishop would say that he'd lost track of time and hurried the men back inside without taking a proper count. Hey, if the warden himself didn't consider Sereno a risk to flee, who was a lowly OIC to argue?

With the second shift dormitory posts coming on duty, even if they saw that one of their seventy men was missing, they'd figure that, being a trusty, Sereno was working in the chow hall or doing latrine duty or off somewhere else in the facility—probably in the library checking out a new batch of magazines.

Even if by some quirk the escape was discovered, and someone deduced that the Indian had taken Bishop hostage, police would assume that a Colombian Indian, unfamiliar with the area, would head directly for Miami or Florida City, where he could blend in with the population. No one would expect the Jeep to leave the highway and take the first access road into the everglades. Then again, no one would suspect that Biff Bishop, who had poached every mosquito-infested corner of the swamp, would be in on the break.

19

It took Jacob an hour to drive to the university and another hour to learn the name of the professor who had supervised Alix Callahan. Then he had to persuade the dean's assistant to call the man at home. To Jacob's surprise, the professor agreed to come talk with him.

"Mr. Winter, how are you?" Professor Nielsen said when he walked into the office. "Still writing, I hope."

Flattered that the man knew of him, Jacob took his hand and lied. Yes, he was fine, thanks, and happily writing. Jonathan Nielsen stood slightly hunched, slender to the point of bony. His face was an unhealthy shade of pink and his hair white and wavy.

"So, Alix Callahan," he said sadly. "You were a friend?"

"Not exactly," Jacob replied, realizing the old man had heard of her death. "We were undergrads together. I understand she studied anthropology with you?"

"Ethnobotany." The old man gave him a lingering look—watery eyes peering over half glasses. His nose was red and enlarged, probably from wine, his cheeks marked with spider veins. At last he smiled gently and said, "Care to walk and talk?"

THEY took a worn path that cut off the corner of the campus. Jacob listened while Professor Nielsen talked. "Fantastic dedication. Fantastic mind. Fantastic scholar. I always thought she'd be the one who really made a mark." They joined the sidewalk, and the professor hesitated. "Rumor had it she got her heart broken—which is why she left the country."

Jacob said, "I don't know anything about it."

The old man furrowed his brow. "Nor do I." They resumed walking again. "She went to Colombia, ostensibly to work on her doctorate. But she never sent a thing back, never wrote. I contacted her parents in Vermont, but they hadn't heard from her, either; not that they seemed to care. Then, a couple of years ago, someone said she was running a flower shop up in seacoast New Hampshire."

"Portsmouth," Jacob said.

"From what I heard, I guess she was drinking pretty heavily. I telephoned a couple of times and left messages, but she never called back."

At an intersection they turned onto a side street.

"What about Colombia?" Jacob asked.

"Indeed," the professor said. "All I know is, she went to live with the Kogis."

"The Kogi Indians," Jacob said, his suspicion confirmed: it was where Alix had met July.

Nielsen smiled reverently. "You know about the Kogis?"

"Not much. They live in the mountains, don't they?"

The professor gave an approving nod. "To be precise, on the northern and western slopes of the Sierra Nevada de Santa Marta, one of the most diverse ecosystems in the world: rain forest, woodlands, mountains, valleys. Fascinating, fascinating people. They're seminomadic, meaning they plants crops in several different environmental zones, depending on the time of year. . . ." He gave an apologetic laugh. "Listen to me."

"Not at all," Jacob said. "They practice shamanism, don't they?"

"They do, indeed," exclaimed the professor, unable to stifle his delight in sharing his knowledge. "In fact, the Kogi shaman is so revered for his metaphysical knowledge that priests from other, far more affluent tribes will travel hundreds of miles to consult with him about spiritual matters."

"Including American missionaries?" Jacob asked, thinking of what July had told him about her father.

The professor gave a woeful smile. "I'm afraid Western culture is utterly unequipped to understand Kogi traditions. For example, when a Kogi girl first menstruates, she is considered a woman and encouraged to marry. As part of the marriage ritual, the village shaman deflowers the bride."

Jacob looked askance at the man. "The priest has sex with twelve- and thirteen-year-old girls?" Once again he was thinking of July, who had married her cousin when she was twelve. Not only that, but her second husband—who was in prison—was most likely the man who had first bedded her.

"Don't get hung up on sex," the professor said, seeming to read his thoughts. "To the Kogis, everything that exists, both physically and metaphysically, has to do with sex and procreation. The sun's journey divides the sky into masculine and feminine halves. Huts are built with masculine and feminine logs. The very earth around them—mountains, valleys, forest, lakes, and ocean—these are erotic things, erotic ideas, erotic visions. Which is why I said, any Christian missionary who thinks he has a prayer of converting these people obviously has no understanding of them. Even their vocabulary. Did you know that the Kogi word for sunrise, *munse,* is also their word for vagina?"

"Sounds like a strange place to go if you just had your heart broken," Jacob said, although he was really wondering how Alix ever expected to fit into a society where everything centered on male-female union. Or perhaps that's the reason Alix went, hoping to understand herself . . . or punish herself.

"Unfortunately, what makes it strange has nothing to do with the Kogis. Theirs is a very structured hierarchical and spiritual society, unchanged for centuries. Did you know that the Kogis were the only people in South America who survived the Spanish invasion of the sixteenth century—by moving high into the mountains? But nowadays they're being invaded from all sides."

The two men started walking across a campus lawn, where the grass was freshly mown and fragrant.

"On the lower slopes are the *colonos*," Nielsen explained, "poor Colombian farmers who are rapidly moving into Kogi territory, slashing and burning the land as they come. And what do they grow? Marijuana and coca, because those are the only crops that pay a subsistence living . . . but that brings the drug barons, who in turn attract soldiers and mercenaries and thieves. Then you have the revolutionaries and professional kidnappers who use the mountains as hideouts, and that brings the counterrevolutionaries and the army. And of course, we gringos have always found ways to exploit their natural resources."

They approached the parking lot where Jacob had left his car, and the professor said, "In the end, it's all the same." He gave Jacob a sad, wizened look. "Money." He repeated the word as though it were a curse. "*Money*. Always and forever. The almighty fucking dollar."

Fearing a lecture, Jacob looked at his watch. He was saved by his cell phone ringing. He answered and heard Laura's voice.

"You're not coming?"

"Coming where?"

"I'm at the ball field," Laura said. "Maxie's play-off game."

"What play-off game?"

"He called you this morning on your cell phone. He said a girl answered and said you were still asleep." Laura paused, just enough for the accusation to sink in: *girl.*

Jacob turned his back on the professor. "Laura, it's not what you think—"

"They won last night," Laura said. "Maxie got two hits. He wanted to tell you."

"I'm sorry, I must have missed the message," Jacob told her, wondering how much Laura knew about July . . . or Alix. "Tell Maxie I'm on my way," he said, but she'd already hung up.

He shut off the phone and turned back to Nielsen, who'd put his hands behind his back in a professorial way. "Well, then," he said, rocking a bit, poised for a collegial good-bye. "I do hope I've answered some of your questions."

"Yes, thank you," Jacob said, but all of a sudden a doubt was niggling at some torn corner of his mind. Despite all the professor had told him about Alix Callahan and the Kogi Indians, something in the old man's demeanor—the stiff smile, the hidden hands—told Jacob there was something else he was hiding. Then it came out.

"An awfully troubling coincidence, I should think," Nielsen said. "Your Senator McBride."

Jacob shook it off. "That's just the news machine, trying to make the most of nothing."

The professor gave him a look of thinly disguised scrutiny, not buying Jacob's disinterest; or perhaps suspecting the senator's death was the reason he'd come in the first place.

"Anyway, I appreciate your time," Jacob said, turning for his car, deciding to put it out of his mind.

"I'll be checking the bookstores for you," the old man called after him, evidently deciding the same.

20

H EY."

Biff Bishop watched his side-view mirror to see that they weren't being followed, then checked the rearview, as he did every few seconds, making sure that tarp didn't start rising up behind him. "You decide what you're gonna do with all that money?"

The prisoner had been gone for a half hour, and the police scanner still made no mention of the escape. Nevertheless, Bishop had steered his Jeep deeper into the cypress swamp, where anhingas sat on the low branches drying their wings, and alligators lay like half-submerged logs along the roadside, watching the vehicle slide past them as though it were potential nourishment. A few more miles of swamp roads and they'd come out on Card Sound Road, the two-lane blacktop down to the Keys.

"Yeah, I figure you for a gold-plated low-rider, you and your shades and some big solid-gold cross around your neck, down in Tijuana, hustlin' all the pretty senoritas. No?"

He swung the Jeep abruptly left, taking a narrow pass into a vast prairie of saw grass. A squadron of brown pelicans flew over.

"Me? Invest my share. GE, that's it. Dollar-cost averaging, like maybe a thousand a week. No high-techs, no sucker bets." He checked the mirror again. "You got enough air back there?"

It could've been a couple of spare tires under the tarp, it lay so still. He opened all the windows.

"You know what this job pays after eighteen years? Thirty-two grand." Bishop blew a bitter laugh. "Land of opportunity. Which means you make your own opportunity. Am I right?"

While he checked his rearview mirror again, he felt under his seat for the .38 he'd stashed. For Biff Bishop, opportunity would come just as soon as Sereno led him to the loot. A bullet or two in the Indian's heart, and he'd head back to Alligator Alley a hero, probably earn him a promotion and medal of valor—and a cool two million for his troubles. Lay low for a year, go to his thankless job every day, spend none of the money. Come next summer, he'd take an early retirement—or maybe give Latham the satisfaction of firing him. Then pack his bags, collect his cash, and go north, baby, get the hell out of this miserable Florida melting pot once and for all, maybe head up to Montana or someplace where nights are cool and people aren't a bunch of criminals jammed together like multicultural sardines.

He looked at that tarp again, checked to see they weren't being followed, then let up on the gas and pulled to the roadside. "I think it's time we consulted a map. Right? So you can tell me where we're headed."

He started to think the Indian was sleeping. Stopping the Jeep, he was about to get out and check when he noticed a green pickup truck slip around the corner. The truck's headlights flashed in his mirror, then it pulled up behind him.

"Stay down," Bishop said. "Probably just a game warden lookin' for poachers."

He thought about getting his gun but decided against it. "Keep cool," he said under his breath as he watched the truck's door open. The young man who stepped out had a tan uniform, like his own. Game warden. Bishop stuck his elbow out the window, let his own colors show.

"Hot one," the game warden said, walking up to the Jeep. "From the prison, are you?"

"Just enjoying Mother Nature," Bishop said. "Hope I wun't speedin' or nothin'."

The warden was trying to see in the back. "What do you got under the tarp here?"

"Me? Tools, spare tires, why?"

The warden tried the liftgate. "I need you to unlatch the back, please."

"Problem?"

"Probably not. We've had some poachers."

"Yeah, I'm stowin' alligator hides back there. Arab terrorists." Bishop gave a laugh.

"I need you to open the back, please."

Bishop chuckled again. "Like I got a hundred pounds of anthrax." Watching the warden slide around behind the Jeep again, Bishop furtively pushed in the clutch, thinking he'd take off, get around a couple of corners, and pop the back so Sereno could hop out and hide in the swamp. He'd come back for him later.

"Shut the vehicle off, please, sir," the warden said through the back window. Christ, now he had his service revolver drawn.

"Okay, look, I had a couple of brewskis after work, that's all, and I'd like to get on my way and not lose my license. No harm, no foul."

"I said to shut off the vehicle. Now."

Bishop turned the key. The Jeep went silent.

"Open the back, please."

Bishop pulled the handle, and the liftgate latch released.

"I need you to keep your hands where I can see them," the warden said, reaching into the back with his free hand, grabbing the tarp, and pulling it out. Sereno sat up as the tarpaulin slid off him.

"It's a hostage situation," Bishop blurted out. "Watch it, he's got a piece back there."

The Indian's shades were fogged, his stringy black hair obscured his face, and a hollow Bic pen was stuck between his lips like an unlit cigarette. The warden held his weapon on him as he stepped back.

"Want me to get on the radio?" Bishop said from the front seat.

"No, sir. I need you to get out and lay on the road, facedown."

"Friend, we're on the same team here."

The way the game warden swung his weapon toward him, for a second it looked to Bishop as if he was about to be shot. Then the warden slapped at his neck, flinching as if he'd been stung. Still holding his weapon on Bishop, he pulled something out of his skin—a needle, by the looks of it. As if thinking it some kind of strange swamp insect, he brought it closer to his face, then looked back at Sereno, who remained in the back of the Jeep with the hollow pen still in his mouth . . . and now the Indian was doing something with a photo that the warden couldn't understand, picking at the edge.

"You, put that picture—" The warden's voice stopped suddenly, and he grabbed at his throat, making a tortured, quivering sound.

The Indian concentrated on the photo as if he hadn't heard the order, calmly withdrawing a needle out of its border.

"What about a picture?" Bishop said.

The young man staggered in a half-circle, bending at the waist to keep from falling. When he came around to face his truck, he collapsed on the road.

Bishop didn't see exactly what had happened. All he knew was that one minute he had a gun aimed at him and was looking at the possibility of life on the wrong side of the bars; the next minute it appeared that he was free to go collect his two million.

Curious, he stepped out of his Jeep and looked down at the game warden sprawled on the road. The kid's legs moved for a moment, then only his shoes twitched. Then he lay perfectly still, gaping out at the green swamp haze.

"You see what happened?" Bishop said to Sereno, bending and prying the gun from the deputy's hand. "Excitement too much for him?"

Then he was stung too, directly inside his ear. He slapped at the thing and cursed in pain, having driven it farther in. Pulling it out, in the pique of understanding he wheeled toward Sereno . . . who was no longer there. In fact, the Indian was on the other side of the road stepping down into the swamp. Not running. Not even looking back.

Bishop yelled. At least he tried to yell—but he couldn't make a sound. He couldn't even lift his gun. Then he lost his legs, did a stutter-step, and watched the road jump up and claim him.

21

J ACOB REACHED THE BASEBALL FIELD IN THE GATHERING DUSK, fully expecting the game to be over, but the kids were playing under lights, six blazing floods distributed around the perimeter of the diamond.

Stepping out of his car, he saw by the scoreboard that it was the bottom of the tenth inning. Speedway Tavern, Max's team, was losing ten to nine, and they were at bat—with two outs and a runner on first. He spotted Max in the on-deck circle, and he gave the boy an apologetic shrug. Max looked away.

As Jacob walked down the right side of the field, looking for a spot where he could be by himself, he noticed Laura and Price sitting in Price's little green convertible. He kept his head down, embarrassed to make eye contact with the other parents, and found a place to stand against the fence. Then a voice came up behind him.

"Didn't think you were going to make it."

So much for being alone.

Detective Fecto was sporting a golf shirt and doubleknit trousers, uncommonly upscale. Jacob understood the reason when he saw the woman who accompanied him, although it was immediately apparent—maybe not to Fecto but certainly to Jacob—that she was out of Fecto's class.

"This is Mr. Winter, Kittery's famous author," Fecto said to the woman.

Looking up at Jacob as though intrigued, she took her place on his other side, close enough to make him self-conscious. She was obviously not Fecto's date, he thought, taking in the black rectangle of her eyeglasses, the short brown hair, the well-made jersey and khaki slacks, the whole of her demeanor presenting an aura of fit conservatism.

"*Berth,* he wrote," said Fecto, popping a cigarette out of his pack. "Remember that, a few years ago, about a bed on a train?"

Now the woman seemed to scrutinize Jacob. "I remember," she said. "I thought the premise was fascinating."

"But that's some news," Fecto said. "About Deborah McBride, that house fire?"

Jacob let them have the conversation to themselves, turning back to the game in time to see the opposing pitcher blow a three-two count and walk the batter, putting runners on first and second and bringing Max to the plate.

"This pitcher's good, maybe the best in the league," Fecto explained to the woman, "but you can tell he's tired."

The boy—who was easily six inches taller than Max, outweighed him by thirty pounds, and had already started shaving—was in his last year of Little League. Max, two years younger, looked like a child facing him.

Fecto took hold of the fence. "A walk ties the game and loads the bases for Luke. That's my son," he told the woman. "Luke—on deck there."

They hardly know each other, Jacob confirmed. "Looking for a hit, Maxie!" he yelled, putting his fists together and snapping his wrists. Then he touched his chest, his elbow, his head.

"See that?" Fecto said to the woman, touching his own head. "It's a signal. He just told his kid to take the pitch—not to swing. Smart. Let him walk, load the bases for Luke."

Fecto was right about one thing. Jacob had indeed signaled a take, but not so Fecto's son could come to the plate swinging. The pitcher was clearly exhausted and would keep walking batters—and Jacob knew the opposing coach had no other pitcher who could take his place.

The pitcher took his stretch. Checked the runners . . . and fired.

And Max swung from the ground. The force of his missing propelled his body out of the batter's box and tossed his glasses off his face. Boys from both teams let loose with lusty laughter.

"Maybe the new coach changed signals without telling you," Fecto said, trying to be nice.

Picking up his glasses and fitting them on his face, Max shot a look back at Jacob, who held a hand up to his eyebrows, showing him how high the ball had been.

The right fielder, scrawny and beak-nosed, yodeled, "Batter's a geek! Batter's a geek!"

Max glared off in the kid's direction. Jacob whistled, reclaimed his attention. "Base hit ties it, Maxie," he called, even though he touched his head again.

"Anyway, the fire marshal was there all day, combing through the ashes," Fecto went on. "Near as they can tell, Senator McBride fell asleep smoking."

Jake tried to keep his focus on the game. The pitcher went into his stretch.

"You know D.A. Evangeline. Right?"

The ball came in shoulder high, a hanging curve. As Jacob gripped the fence helplessly, Max swung and missed again, by half a foot. His helmet turned sideways on his head. A spontaneous jeer exploded from the opposition.

In fact, Jacob had never seen the woman who wanted to send him to prison, until now. But he remembered Zabriski's warning not to talk to her. And here she was, standing two inches from him.

"Geekballs! Geekballs!" the right fielder yelled at his son.

Straightening his helmet and glasses, Max looked over. Jacob clapped his hands. "Ignore 'em, Maxie," he called, at the same time wondering why his son was ignoring him—or how he himself could ignore Evangeline. He felt surrounded. He touched his head again, signaling Max not to swing.

The pitcher, standing taller on the mound, shook off a sign from the catcher, then went into his stretch.

Fecto said abruptly, "But you didn't know the senator personally, did you, Jake?"

The ball sailed in head high, fat and slow, exactly like the previous pitch. Max looked as if he was going to swing—his hips turned, his shoulders jerked—but at the last instant he laid off. Ball one.

Jacob sighed, his chest full. "Way to watch 'em!" he yelled.

"I'm asking because, you know, being a kind of celebrity yourself—"

"I didn't know her," Jacob said, then called to Max, "Make him come to you!"

Max dug in his back foot. The pitcher tossed down his resin bag, then looked to the catcher for a sign.

"Low and away," Fecto predicted, "he'll get him reaching."

The pitcher went into his stretch . . . and Max stepped out of the batter's box.

"Time!" The ump stepped around the catcher, arms raised.

"No, but what do you think would make someone do something so drastic?" the detective continued. "Jump off the bridge, I mean, if she did . . ." Suddenly distracted, Fecto gazed off toward home plate. "Whoa," he said. "What's that supposed to be?"

Stepping out of the batter's box, Max had leaned his bat against his legs and taken off his helmet, as if to examine it. For a moment the entire baseball field became silent, as everyone—players and parents alike—stared at his friar's tonsure. Then the murmur started in the stands, a pocket of laughter here and there, and cries of ridicule from the opposing team. Even the ump was shaking his head, as Max's teammates howled in the dugout. Jacob heard the coach yell at them to shut up while stifling his own laugh.

But Maxie never cracked a smile. He scratched the hair above his ear, the way an old man might, then replaced his helmet, picked up his bat, and stepped back in the box, never for a second taking his eyes off the pitcher.

"Jeez, do you and Laura condone that?" Fecto said. He was the kind of guy who could be genuinely distracted by a haircut. But so was the pitcher, and Max seemed to know it.

Jacob yelled: "Go get him, Maxie!"

With supreme confidence, Max took his stance, cocked his bat.

The pitcher glowered at him as he went into his stretch.

"Low and away," Fecto said softly.

And it was. Much too low, too far way. The ball hit the dirt and the catcher lunged—then threw off his mask and scrambled to the backstop. The runners raced ahead to second and third.

Jacob clapped and shouted, "Good eye, Maxie!"

"Good eye? It was a mile wide."

The pitcher, who had run to the plate, took the catcher's toss with a disgusted swipe of his glove, then said something to Max as he stalked back to the mound. Max responded by removing his helmet again, and he kept it off until the pitcher had a chance to turn around and have another look at his head.

"You think maybe Alix Callahan had something to hide from?" Fecto said. "Theory of mine."

The noise rose suddenly on the field, in the stands, and in both dugouts as Max took his place in the batter's box, giving the pitcher a kind of smile. The pitcher did not smile back.

"I asked that other one, July," Fecto added. "I guess they were partners, in the personal sense."

Even though the pitcher took a full windup, the runners barely crept off the bases, probably unnerved by the older boy's size, the shadow of his adolescent mustache, or the savage way he flung his body off the mound as he fired again. The catcher leaped in the air, snagged the ball way over Max's head, then feigned a pickoff throw, but the runners were already back.

"Three and two, two out, pressure's on," Fecto said. "First time you met July, from what I gather, was the night Alix bailed you out of jail. You went over there, didn't you? Just you and the two girls."

Jacob kept his focus on the game. By now the players from both teams had come off their benches to clutch at their dugout screens. Parents were standing in the bleachers. Even Price Ashworth had lowered his book.

"Geekballs!" cried the right fielder. "Geekballs!"

"Just you and Alix and July, right?"

Jacob said, "Phil, could we talk about this another time?"

"Don't see why not."

The pitcher walked a circle around the mound, bent for the resin bag, squeezed it a couple of times, dropped it back on the ground. At the plate, Max stepped out of the box and removed his helmet again.

Jacob heard Laura call: "Maxie, hit a home run!"

Max looked back at the roadster, where his mother was conferring with Price. Catching his eye, she yelled, "Over the fence, honey!"

Again the jeering started, boys on the opposing team mimicking her. "Home run, honey!"

"Max!" Jacob started clapping his hands, trying to get his son's attention. "Maxie!"

But his son wouldn't look his way.

"Hey, Squeaky!" he yelled.

Now Max glanced over, trying to contain a smile. He leaned over his bat as if it were a cane, then bent at the waist and started shaking his legs, his impression of an old man, squinting out at Jacob.

"What's he doing?" Evangeline asked.

Jacob touched his head.

The boy stopped clowning . . . and held his father's stare.

"You're telling the kid not to swing," Fecto said, "with three and two?"

Max kept squinting, in earnest now. The umpire came out and said something to him.

Jacob touched his head again.

Max looked away. Pulling his helmet back on, he stepped back in the box.

"He's not going to take the pitch," Fecto said. "I mean, cripes, even a normal kid . . ."

Jacob leaned on the cyclone fence, trying not to listen.

"You know what I mean—too much pressure," Fecto said.

The pitcher started his windup.

"Here it comes. Big fat curve," Fecto said.

The ball came in bending, too high but tantalizingly slow, just as the detective had predicted. Max reared back, as though to pulverize it. Jacob squeezed the fence. Max stopped. Jacob caught his breath. Then, suddenly, the boy's shoulders jerked, and the silver bat whipped around, shoulder high. As the ball arced down to the catcher's mitt, a vicious ping shot it skyward, launching out over the infield, high above the bright, upturned face of the beak-nosed right fielder, and way over the floodlights.

"That's foul," Fecto said. But he was wrong. The baseball, lost in the night sky, cleared the outfield fence, actually cleared the playground beyond, and eventually bounced high off the well-lit school parking lot. While Max's teammates went on howling and drumming the dugout walls and running to the plate, and the parents cheered, Maxie threw off his helmet and rounded first, showing his big shiny head to the pitcher.

"Like father, like son. He's got a mind of his own," Fecto said, nudging Jacob as if they were buddies.

Jacob ignored the needling as he watched his son stomp chalk dust off second base with both feet. "Way to tag 'em, Squeak!" he hollered in spite of himself, waiting for Max to look up so he could wave at least. But Max kept rounding the bases without looking back. Then he was swarmed by his teammates and new coach. Laura was there too, giving Max a hug. Even Price was high-fiving him. And Max walked off with both of them.

Jacob could do nothing but watch, holding on to the fence while his chest felt as if it was being crushed.

"I went through the same thing with my kid." Fecto's voice registered slowly, as Jacob watched his son squeeze into the roadster with Laura and Price. "You know, after the divorce."

Jacob turned, gave the detective a look. He figured the folksy badgering was simply Fecto's M.O. Rattle a suspect with friendliness, rattle him and rattle him until he wore him down, until the guy couldn't think straight, couldn't sleep, couldn't stop brooding about all the ways he had screwed up his life . . . until he wanted nothing in the world so much as to confess his sins, clear his conscience, and get some peace, even if it meant a clear conscience in a prison cell.

"What the heck, it'll be good for the boy's self-esteem," the detective said, his tone perfectly amiable. He even clapped Jacob on the back as Jacob walked away. Meant as a consoling gesture, and probably a sincere one, it did not come close to penetrating the wall of anguish Jacob felt. Consolation? He felt like buying a bottle of Jack Daniels, driving down to the beach, and drinking himself into oblivion.

"Mr. Winter, could we talk for a minute?" Evangeline tried to keep pace with Jacob's stride, but he wasn't about to stop. "Mr. Winter, I know Alix Callahan talked to you before she jumped off that bridge."

Jacob shook his head, refusing to even look at her, and said, "I'm not supposed to be talking to you."

"This has nothing to do with your assault case," Evangeline replied, keeping up. "All I want to know is what she said to you."

"I told the detective everything," he said as he reached his car and opened the door.

"Mr. Winter, please," she persisted, grabbing the door. "I'm not here as a prosecutor. I'm asking you for a personal favor."

He stared off at the darkened sky.

"Alix Callahan has a mother and father," she explained, her voice suddenly quieter, almost vulnerable.

He turned to her, peered through her no-nonsense glasses—and found no glimmer of vulnerability in her gray eyes. In fact, she looked like a woman who had no potential for anything *but* prosecution. But if he ever needed an ally, this was the time.

"I will not discuss your assault case with you," Evangeline assured him, "nor will I take part in any discussion that you might initiate regarding that case."

Jacob lowered his head. "What do you want to know?"

Even while he gave his tacit consent, a part of his mind skittered back over the field of lies he'd already sown, wondering what new deception he'd have to concoct—and whether he could muster the composure to continue.

"Ms. Callahan's parents would like to make sense of this," Evangeline explained. "They're desperate to know why she did what she did. Absent a body, all they can do is speculate. And now all the gossip surrounding Senator McBride. Did Alix say anything to you, give you any reason for jumping?" The words, spoken by someone else, might have had a ring of despair. But exasperation was as much emotion as Evangeline conveyed, as though she just wanted to get this unpleasantness behind her.

"I told the detective everything. Didn't he show you the report?"

"Yes, he did," Evangeline answered. "But I think there's something he didn't show you."

22

THERE WAS NO POINT IN ASKING WHERE EVANGELINE WAS TAK-ing him. Jacob knew precisely. As she veered onto I-95, taking the ramp twice as fast as she should have, the black Saab leaned hard to the left, and Jacob grabbed the shoulder strap.

"We lost the light," she complained, as if it were Jacob's fault. The vista widened suddenly, the steel-truss arch rising into view against the sky, the beacon at its top blinking like a single all-knowing eye. Treetops and roofs dropped away beside them, while across the river, window lights spread across the town like the evening's first stars. In all respects it was the onset of a pleasant summer evening. But as they ascended underneath the steel beams, and the sky opened up around them, Jacob felt himself swimming against waves of panic. Then he saw the blue light flashing on the bridge, and as they neared he realized it was Fecto's Explorer waiting. He pressed back in the seat, and Evangeline jerked the wheel, pulling around the Explorer and stopping hard in the breakdown lane.

"Detective Fecto is here in case you want to revise your statement," she explained as she turned off the engine and switched on her emergency flashers. Already Jacob could feel the slow swaying of the bridge under them.

"You claimed you saw Alix Callahan's vehicle parked here," she said. "You stopped your car, got out, and put your hand on the railing. You looked down to the river, but you couldn't see any sign of her because it was too dark."

Jacob closed his eyes, trying to drive the panic from his chest.

"Mr. Winter," Evangeline persisted, "did you or didn't you see her down in the river?"

"I did not see her," he said, looking at the side-view mirror: Fecto sitting on the hood of his vehicle, smoking a cigarette, looking out over the river as if he were enjoying the view.

"The Coast Guard called off the search this afternoon," Evangeline said, as a trailer truck roared past. The roadway went up and down. "Which means that unless a fishing boat finds her in their nets or she washes up on shore, most likely her body will never be found . . . if there is a body."

Jacob looked over at her.

"The truck driver who saw Alix Callahan told the police that a man was standing with her," Evangeline said. "A little over six feet, two hundred pounds or so."

Jacob shook his head. "Not me."

"If it *was* you, if you saw her jump and you don't want to admit it because you're embarrassed that you didn't stop her"—she gave him a pointed look—"or maybe you're afraid this might complicate your assault case or custody hearing . . . Mr. Winter, I understand your reluctance."

Jacob met those determined eyes again. For a moment he considered telling her this much: Yes, he had been here with Alix, he tried to talk her out of it, but she jumped before he could stop her. As for the bullet, the steak knife, July's presence . . . No, he could not risk telling even a half-truth. He could not trust this woman.

"Do you know any reason Alix Callahan might have wanted to disappear?"

"I keep telling you people, I didn't *know* her," Jacob said. "I don't know anything *about* her. I never talked to her until the day she bailed me out of jail."

Evangeline sat quietly for a moment; then abruptly reached past him to pull a flashlight out of her glove compartment. "I need you to get out of the car," she said, opening her door.

Jacob sighed. "There's nothing I can tell you out there that I haven't already told you."

"You need to see something," she said, slamming her door. The change in her voice told Jacob it was pointless to refuse. Then she was at his door, opening it. "Please," she told him, not a request.

"Beautiful night," Fecto called, snapping his cigarette over the railing.

Jacob swung his leg out the door and tested his moccasin on the pavement before he pushed himself out. A couple of cars flew past, flashing their bright lights. The hot gust in their wake gave Jacob the sensation of being blown over the rail, and he leaned back against Evangeline's car, trying not to let her see his fear.

"This is where your prints were found," she said, already at the railing.

Fecto leaned back against his windshield, clamping his fingers behind his head. "Looks like another beauty tomorrow."

Not that Jacob intended to discuss the weather, but Evangeline interceded before he had the chance. "In your statement, you said that when you looked down it was too dark to see anything in the river."

Standing in front of Fecto's Explorer, she held the rail with one hand, waiting for Jacob to join her, but his leaden legs refused to carry him away from her car.

"Do you see this?" She slapped a vertical post with her hand. It was a hollow steel column, maybe three feet wide and perforated—as were all the structural members—with large oval ventilation holes. "Maintenance workers climb inside these columns, up and down."

Jacob just stared. Was she suggesting that Alix did the same?

"By the way, that kitchen knife was found down there," Fecto said, gesturing with his head as he tried to light another cigarette in the wind. "Upriver a hundred feet or so—which is pretty weird, considering."

Suddenly curious, Jacob left the relative safety of the Volvo and ventured over to Evangeline, breathing deeply to counteract the vertigo. "Weird why?" he managed to say.

"I mean, considering the night Alix Callahan disappeared," Fecto said, sparks from his cigarette flying crazily past his face, "the tide was going the other way."

Jacob looked at the detective, whose eyes suddenly flared as a screech of tires sounded behind them. Jacob spun around to see headlights explode against the back of the Explorer, and he caught the grill in his hands, the impact throwing him into Susan Evangeline, the Explorer ramming the railing and rebounding around them, but only after launching Detective Fecto from its hood.

The way time stretched out, Jacob saw the detective leap into the air, executing what looked like a handspring off the bridge railing as he vaulted over it, even twisting back in a last-ditch reach for Jacob, who was occupied in the seeming act of shoving the Explorer away. In the detective's startled eyes, Jacob saw the split-second recognition that his last slim chance at survival had passed, and he slapped three ringing beats on the railing and fell from sight, his hoarse cry immediately lost beneath the steady blare of a car horn.

Jacob felt the railing knock against his back as he fell to the pavement beside the damaged vehicle, watching curiously as a white Dodge Caravan with a folded front quarter rolled diagonally across two unoccupied lanes, horn sounding, its driver hugging the steering wheel. Beside Jacob, Susan Evangeline got to her feet and scrambled over Fecto's hood, shouting back at Jacob, "Get on my phone and call 911!"

He pulled himself up, trembling, while Evangeline limped across the lanes to the Caravan, waving her arms at an oncoming trailer truck. Jacob heard the fierce hissing of air brakes as the truck swerved to avoid her. Then, thankfully, the Caravan's horn stopped . . . and a painful moan rose up on the wind.

Jacob turned to the railing.

"What are you doing?" Evangeline cried. "I told you to call for help!" She was working to free the Caravan's driver, who was saying in wavering tones, "I never saw 'em, they had their headlights off."

Hearing the moan again, Jacob stepped onto the curbstone, clutched the railing securely in his arms . . . and looked over.

Ten feet below the roadway, Phil Fecto was sprawled on a ledge, actually a steel maintenance platform that extended four feet out from the girder that supported the roadway. The detective appeared semiconscious, lying on his side facing in toward the bridge. His baseball cap lay between his head and elbow. His knee started to bend.

"Phil, don't move!" Jacob called down, then turned back to Evangeline, who was leading the injured driver across the roadway.

Recognizing his urgency, Evangeline helped the driver into her car. "Wait for me," she told him, then hurried over to Jacob and looked down.

"*Detective Fecto!*" she snapped.

At the sound of her voice, Fecto's head lolled. His arm straightened, knocking his cap off the platform. Watching it tumble through the air, Jacob clutched the railing. His legs turned to rubber.

"*Detective!*" Evangeline shouted, shining her light on Fecto's face.

Jacob warned, "I wouldn't—"

Fecto moaned angrily, sounding like a boy being summoned from a good sleep.

"*Detective Fecto, don't you move!*"

Fecto's eyes opened. He looked up into the flashlight dazedly, his leg dangling out over the beam, exploring the open air.

"I said, '*Don't move!*'"

He threw his arm up defiantly, then turned his head to look out at the sky. With a startled jerk, he kicked himself off the beam.

To the detective's credit, he showed admirable alertness in putting into practice the advice he'd given Jacob. Almost immediately upon his descent, his body snapped to attention and he plummeted feetfirst, like a javelin. Unfortunately, as he had also explained, the wind under the bridge could be notoriously uncooperative. While Jacob and Evangeline watched helplessly, the detective's stiffened legs began drifting upward in the wind. When he hit the water, his body sent out a terrible spray halfway across the river, and in the moment it took for the sound of the splash to reach the bridge, the detective disappeared from sight.

Jacob's legs gave out. As he felt the concrete slam into his knees, a wave of darkness took his consciousness.

HIS face between the railings, Jacob watched the lights of a boat squirming in the ripples—and something bobbing as it moved slowly downriver, a piece of wood, a plastic milk jug, or was it Fecto's head?

Somewhere on the dark edge of his mind, he heard Evangeline snapping off commands into her radio. Behind his back, cars crawled past. His own shadow moved back and forth along the green railing. The roadway went up and down, up and down. Sirens wailed in the distance. In a daze, Jacob pulled himself to his feet and started walking away.

"Mr. Winter, you need to stay here," he heard Evangeline say.

He kept walking, into the headlights.

"Mr. Winter!"

He walked faster. Emergency vehicles were coming toward him, blue and red lights flashing, the bridge underfoot swaying.

"I'm not finished with you," Evangeline said, pursuing him now. "I know you were with Alix Callahan when she jumped."

He turned to face her, ready with another denial . . . but he just stood there. Words wouldn't come.

"You were with her, Mr. Winter," Evangeline told him. "You were with her on this bridge. I *know* you saw her jump. Did you see her *fall?*"

He could only stare, mesmerized, as headlights flared across her face.

Evangeline repeated: "Did you see her *fall?*"

He shook his head numbly. "No." Although he heard the word

come out of his mouth, he had not meant to speak. It was as though someone else was in control of his voice.

Evangeline looked back at the spot where Fecto had gone over. She took a couple of breaths too, evidently to regain her composure, then said in a subdued tone, "I'll have someone drive you to your car."

"I'll walk," he said, and started off into the glare of headlights.

"Mr. Winter," Evangeline warned him, "it's against the law to walk on this bridge."

"Then you can charge me with that too," Jacob said, and he went on his way.

23

WHEN JACOB GOT TO GREEN GIRLS, JULY'S CAR WAS THERE, BUT the house and shop were dark. He rang the doorbell, eyes moving from one corner of the building to the other. While he listened at the door for her footsteps, he turned and looked back toward the road. The night lay still except for the metallic ticking of his car engine cooling. He turned back to the house, and just as he was about to ring the bell again, the door fell open.

July stood in the doorway, wearing a T-shirt and underpants, peering sleepily out from her black curtain of hair. "What's the matter?"

Without waiting for an invitation, he stepped inside, shutting the door behind him and locking it. "Remember the detective who was here yesterday—Phil Fecto?"

She folded her arms as if she were cold. "What time is it?"

"He fell off the bridge."

The sleep left her face. "Fell—like jumped?"

Jacob shook his head. "There was an accident," he began, then he backtracked. "The district attorney took me up there—Susan Evangeline."

July's eyes narrowed.

"She and Fecto were questioning me, then someone ditched a car into us." He gave her a meaningful look.

"Jacob, what are you telling me?"

"I'm saying I don't think it was an accident. Whoever ran that car into us had their lights off. I mean, this could all be in my head, but after Senator McBride's death . . . you heard about that?"

She nodded, her eyes losing focus.

"I don't think that was an accident, either. I think Deborah McBride might be dead simply because she'd seen Alix alive."

July pulled away from him as if he'd given her an electric shock. He followed her through the flower shop.

"July, I looked over the railing. There's a beam below the roadway that Alix could've landed on, like a ledge. And a series of ladders and catwalks and hollow columns—"

She started up the stairs.

"That night," he said, climbing up behind her, "how many shots did you fire?"

"I don't know, I wasn't there."

"July, more than one?"

Reaching the pantry, she turned and gave him a fierce look, then spun away. In a few seconds he heard a door slam. He knew it was stupid to try and reason with her until she'd had time to absorb what he was saying. But stupid seemed to be what he did best these days—why stop now? He went to the bedroom and knocked.

"July?"

He opened the door and peeked in. The room was dark, but he could see her lying on her mattress, turned away from him. She'd had sex with the village shaman when she was twelve, Jacob reminded himself. Later she married him. At some point she'd taken up with Alix Callahan. There was a vicious fight, and the shaman ended up going to prison. Now she was living here, possibly under witness protection.

"Look, I'm only trying to figure out what's going on," he said. "If her body turns up and they find she was shot, then I'm their number one suspect. I'm their *only* suspect."

"Jacob, you weren't there, either. Remember?"

He sighed. "I told Evangeline."

She paused. "Told her what?"

"That I was with Alix when she jumped."

As he waited for July to say something to fill the silence, his eyes became acclimated to the dark and he realized he was not looking at the back of her head. She'd been facing him all along.

"Evangeline doesn't know you were with me," he explained. "But she was asking questions about you. Nobody knows anything about you."

She stared wistfully out of the darkness, like a rabbit in a burrow, hiding from a fox. He persisted. "You met Alix when she went to Colombia, didn't you?"

July turned away from him, whipping the quilt over her shoulder. "I already told you, Jacob, why are you asking?"

"No, you told me about your parents. Alix said she helped you get away from your husband. What happened?"

With an exasperated sigh, July rolled onto her back. "My husband is in prison. When he gets out, he'll be sent back to Colombia, where he'll be executed."

"Why?"

"Because. It's Colombia. Okay? And Alix is dead. She's not hiding. She was crazy and jealous, and she wanted to hurt me by killing herself and taking you with her. Now stop talking about her."

"But if she's not dead," he began, then stopped himself. "You're right." He watched her eyes in the near darkness, wet and blinking up at the ceiling. "I'm sorry," he said. "I must be crazy too. I'm out of my mind. I'll get out of here."

"Jacob, I don't think you're crazy," she said, looking up at him again. "I think you miss your son."

He breathed a laugh. Not that he disagreed. In fact, her perception, once again, was dead-on.

She said, "Do you think I can't see how much you love him?"

His chest expanded. He held his breath for a moment, then released it in a sigh. He'd never imagined how much it could hurt, being separated from someone. "You know the kind of kid who'll do anything on a dare?" He slid down the wall and sat on the floor. "Maxie's got a hundred-eighty-one IQ—and learning disabilities. So he's classified 'twice special,' which basically means he doesn't fit." Jacob stopped. "Do you mind?"

"Uh uh." She'd raised herself on her elbow to listen.

"He has no social skills. And he thinks he's indestructible. The kids egg him on. Want someone to rig the fire alarm? Jump off a roof? Climb the flagpole? Talk to Maxie Winter."

"He sounds like a lot of trouble."

Jacob chuckled. "He's had his share of broken bones. He can't sit still in school, can't pay attention to his teachers for more than five seconds. His mind moves at light speed, constantly juggling twenty things at a time. He can't have any sugar, no caffeine. But put him in front of a computer?" Jacob's throat closed up, he couldn't speak.

"Jacob, come lie down." She lifted the blanket and invited him in.

He considered her offer, tempting as it was—not that he was craving her, but having someone to hold right now, and someone to hold him back—he'd never needed companionship as badly. Nevertheless, he pushed himself to his feet. "I'm sorry," he said. "I shouldn't have bothered you with all this."

"Wait, don't leave," she said.

There was something in her voice, a hushed urgency that he hadn't heard before. For a number of seconds they held each other's eyes, Jacob standing there in the dark, humid room, July lying below, looking up fearfully. "Please," she said.

When Jacob spoke, he heard the same sound in his own voice. "You think she's alive too," he said. "Don't you?"

July nodded. Rabbit in a burrow.

UNCOMFORTABLE as her floor was, it was such a relief to finally lie down—with his head against the side of her mattress and his foot propped against the door—that as soon as Jacob closed his eyes, he began drifting off.

July's soft voice roused him. "Thanks for staying," she said, passing her fingers through his hair. "I feel safe with you here."

"Mm," he said.

She left her hand on his chest, warm and soothing, just enough to put him to sleep.

A minute later, or perhaps an hour, he sat up with a start, trying to save Phil Fecto from falling off the bridge. In a still panic, he looked around the darkness, utterly disoriented. Then he remembered where he was. He could hear July breathing deeply behind him.

He lay down again. His shoulder ached from the hard floor. He could hear the distant whine of a trailer truck crossing over the bridge, and he pictured Phil Fecto again, the way he had grasped for the railing, that startled, terrified expression on his face. Then he pictured Alix Callahan as she dropped between the railings, and he saw something completely different: the look of studied determination.

He checked the door with his foot to make sure it was still closed. He listened to each little sound in the dark, inside the house and out.

This is the way his nights had been after New York was attacked, he remembered, lying awake in the dark while Laura and Maxie slept, replaying over and over the moment that a jetliner penetrated the first World Trade Center tower in a cascade of fire; reliving the way each building sank from sight, its image momentarily preserved in dust while paper fluttered like ghost pigeons, around and around. Night after night, mistaking the dull roar of his furnace igniting for Boston being detonated by a nuclear bomb; wondering if the plane passing overhead was dusting his town with anthrax; incessantly going over contingency plans—the tent and sleeping bags packed in the garage, the jugs of fresh water, the batteries charged, bags of rice and pasta—over and over, getting out of bed every hour or so, checking on Max, turning on the radio to make sure Chicago was not on fire, Los Angeles was still standing. . . .

Over time he learned to live with his fears, and gradually he was able to sleep through the nights. He even got used to the fact of people he did not know hating him and wanting him dead.

Now here it was again, the dread, the uncertainty, the hatred—but now he felt it so much more acutely. Now he knew the person who wanted him dead.

Or so he believed.

24

THE FLORIDA BOY WOULD SEARCH THE TRAILER FOR HIS WHITE uniform, the one that said HIALEAH SCHOOL OF KARATE on the front. He would blame his mother for losing it, and she would tell him she didn't remember taking it off the clothesline. Of course, she wouldn't think to call the Hialeah Police, not for a missing uniform.

Neither would the police be notified when, in the same neighborhood, a family cat failed to report for breakfast; or when a bird feeder that had been filled with sunflower seeds in the evening was found emptied in the morning.

As for the Florida State Police, they were still fighting off clouds of mosquitoes as they ran their dogs along the swamp roads where Biff Bishop and the game warden had been found paralyzed. The police had set up roadblocks on Card Sound Road and begun stopping all boats leaving the sound. They'd canvassed the residents of houseboat row as well as certain sections of Florida City where the fugitive might have been hiding. But outside of the footprints that led from Bishop's Jeep into the glades, they hadn't found a trace of the missing Indian. With good reason. They'd not ventured deep enough into the fuming heart of the swamp.

Who in his right mind would imagine a man surviving—in bare feet, at night—in places where even bloodhounds were afraid to go? The glades were filled with saw grass that would tear human flesh to jerky strips, never mind the alligators. The mosquitoes alone were enough to bleed a man dry, if they didn't drive him to drowning himself first for the pure relief of it.

Sereno did not stay in the swamp, however. By ten o'clock he was northbound, courtesy of a sugarcane truck that slowed to avoid a dead alligator in the road, then he hopped the sugar train out of Miami. It was well past midnight when two state patrolmen finally stopped to drag the reptile out of the road . . . and discovered it was missing its heart.

25

WHEN HE REALIZED IT WAS LIGHT, JACOB OPENED HIS EYES. The bedroom door was still closed, his foot still propped against it, but July was not on her mattress. Sometime in the early morning, while he was sleeping, she had covered him with a second blanket and brought his backpack in from his car.

If he was going to stay here—and he was beginning to think it best, at least until Alix was found—then they would need a clear understanding of their relationship. He got up and opened the door, thinking that July might have no expectations after all. She was younger, certainly a free spirit unaccustomed to the conditions of marriage. Perhaps the arrangement could be ideal: he'd stay there until things were resolved, do repairs, maybe build her some furniture; they'd watch out for one another and keep each other company—as housemates, not lovers.

But as he entered the living room, he found that maybe they would have to talk. She was sitting at a desk wearing one of his work shirts over her bare legs. Not only that, she was working at his laptop. She raised her face toward him. "You're writing about the bridge?"

"It's unpolished," he said, trying to ignore the way the shirt, opened to the fifth button, exposed one of her breasts.

"No, it's *alive*," she told him. "Don't change a word."

"Listen, about my staying here," he began.

Her gaze darkened.

"How about if I make you something—you know—in exchange for my room and board?"

She smiled playfully. "Make me what?"

"I make furniture."

"I don't want furniture." Her nipple stood out enough to tell him that she knew she was showing—and was aroused by it. "I want you to write your book."

"Carpentry relaxes me," he said, "I figure out what I'm going to write next while I'm working."

"Okay, make me a bed." She gave him a look—defiant, seductive.

"If that's what you want," he said. "I just need a place, like a corner of the shop. I'll hang some poly to contain the dust. What kind of bed?"

"Big. With a big green headboard," she said. "Shaped like the bridge."

Her eyes seemed to dilate, and Jacob felt a sudden interruption in his heart, a bright thread of warning to the back of his brain.

"Jacob, look at you," she teased, mimicking his scowl. "You're writing a book about the bridge. I want a bed shaped like the bridge."

He said, "I don't use paint or stain, only natural wood."

She said, "Isn't there wood that's green?"

"Well, the heartwood of poplar is green, but that's a secondary wood, used for the insides of drawers where it won't show."

"Oh, so serious."

"Besides, the bridge is arched at the top."

"So?"

"I don't bend wood, either," he explained. "The work I do is traditional—straight lines, square corners."

She gave him a skeptical smile. "Jacob, the rest of the world isn't straight and square."

"My furniture is."

With an exasperated sigh, she spun the chair around and got to her feet. "Don't make me anything," she said, then walked out of the room with a playful gait, like some jungle cat with her tail high.

"How about oak or maple?" he said.

She flipped back her hair. "I'll make your breakfast. You write your book."

Jacob took a couple of breaths, decompressing. He sat in the chair and turned to his computer. For a few seconds, he stared at his story—Henry Lamb sitting in his car high on the bridge—wondering if he should even start, or if he should gather his things and leave.

"I don't hear you typing," she called.

He laughed to himself. He'd never known anyone like her—so daring and impulsive, so beautiful and sexual . . . and so much his opposite. Yet she'd been attracted to him, and—for the first time he acknowledged this to himself—he was undeniably drawn to her. In fact, as he listened to her in the kitchen, singing to herself while she rummaged through the refrigerator, he felt the pull of attraction, down in his chest and stomach, anxiously, almost as a kind of fear. . . . Then his mind took over. Leaning over his computer, he placed two fingers on the keyboard and settled in.

HENRY Lamb does not think about jumping off the bridge. He may have considered jumping a month ago, when he first lost his job, or perhaps on those nights lying awake beside his sleeping wife—Dolores still doesn't know—yes, on those nights he may have entertained the idea. Now that he is on the bridge, however, he thinks only about getting his scissor jack out of the trunk, because the bridge is nearly a mile in length, and he is stuck at the center point, over the middle of the Piscataqua River, and he cannot drive off the bridge until he changes the tire.

The wind makes a hollow sound against his cheek. The airplane slices the red sky like an apple skin, inscribing the letter E. *Below him, Henry watches a fishing boat move up the river, heading for the marina, where his own boat is waiting. He has told Dolores about buying the boat, which is why they've been low on spending money. He's told her about the boat because she has always wanted a boat—but he's been unable to bring himself to tell her about the job. Now that he's out of money, though—his checking account is drained, his credit card shut off—he's going to have to tell her.*

For now, he looks out over the river at all the darkening greens along the bank, the groves of white pine and sugar maple and white oak. He's never stopped here before, never seen all this beauty.

A scissor jack is in his trunk, along with a spare tire. He takes his keys out of the ignition, opens his door and steps out onto the pavement.

He is parked under a green sign that reads:

STATE LINE

NEW HAMPSHIRE

Attached to the signpost is a set of steel rungs enclosed in a cage. When Henry looks up to see that the ladder leads to a crow's nest, and from there all the way to the top of the arch, he has to lower his eyes—and that's when he sees the girl. She is inside the hollow steel column, peering out at him, and the instant he meets her eyes, she starts climbing.

Startled at first—too startled to speak, or Henry would certainly ask her what she was doing there—he goes over and puts his hands on the steel. The paint is wet from the fog. The oval hole looks too small to allow his shoulders through. But he pokes one arm inside, then his head, then pulls himself all the way in.

"You like a bird's nest?"

Jacob looked up from his writing—a girl inside the bridge—and smiled, slightly chagrined. "Bird's nest?"

July had taken off his shirt and replaced it with a pale green halter, and tied a white apron over a conservative muslin skirt. She carried a pewter tray. "Fried egg on toast," she told him. "Alix used to call it a bird's nest. Is that too radical?"

Resting the tray on his chair arm, she began setting things on the desk: a mug of coffee, glass of orange juice, and a platter mounded

over with bacon and eggs and home-fried potatoes, sautéed pep-
pers, red and green, and mushrooms. "Is everything okay?"

He laughed. "It's fine, thank you, it's great. Listen . . ." She
stood there as a waitress might, awaiting an order. "Can you stop
that?"

"I'm sorry. Did you want something else?"

"Yeah," he told her. "I'll make you the bed."

26

THICK AS THE MOSQUITOES WERE IN THE NORTH FLORIDA
woods—they were louder than the sugar train going away—most
of them kept their distance from the Indian. Those that landed on
his skin immediately flew away. Even in Sereno's native forests,
mosquitoes never bothered him half as much as did the brightness
of the sun. With his shades protecting his eyes from the morning
light, he crept down to the riverbank, where the water ran slow
and shallow. Cupping his hand in the current, already he knew it
was the wrong place. The water was too warm. He took a taste.
No salt.

He climbed back up the bank, worked his way away from the
railroad bed, then crawled into a bed of sweet juniper. A balled-up
armadillo awoke, gazed at the Indian, then took a couple of hops

and waddled out of the patch. Sereno laughed, and found a place where the juniper was soft. He ate a handful of berries. As the train grew quieter, he made himself a pillow.

There would come another train in the night.

27

H ARDER."

Jacob pulled on the wood with every bit of his strength, his biceps burning with the strain, while July screwed the clamp lever with both hands.

"Jacob, pull!"

They sat in the flower shop, bending the wood around the form, a piece of three-quarter-inch plywood he had sawn in a simple arch. Reproducing the bridge was not a simple task. The top of the structure was comprised of two overarching chords connected by thirty-two trusses. What complicated the project also gave the arch its beauty: the two chords were differently shaped. While the bottom one was a simple parabola, the top chord described a bell curve, so that while the chords ran parallel along the top, they gradually separated as they descended, the top chord sweeping out to join the roadway, the bottom chord continuing down to join the piers—or in the case of July's bed, the posts.

Jacob pressed his feet against the door jamb and pulled the long strips of green poplar against the form while July set clamps every six inches. Because he had slathered wood glue between the layers, they were battling time, needing to set the clamps before the glue dried.

"Tight?"

"Yes," she answered in a gasp, letting go. Her halter was drenched with sweat, and her shoulder slid against his when she reached behind her for the water bottle. As much as they had perspired—it was easily a hundred degrees in the shop—they had consumed a gallon of water between them. She took a drink and handed the bottle to him.

He drank, then slid back. To make sure the unclamped boards ahead of them remained aligned, he grabbed his mallet and a short board and pounded it along the side of the chord.

"Do you have any idea what made Alix the way she was?" he asked.

"Craziness," July said, as she picked up another clamp and set it in place, sliding a piece of junk pine between the clamp jaw and the poplar to keep the metal from gouging the wood.

He braced his foot on the jamb. "Jealous crazy?"

"Crazy crazy. Always accusing me of things." She propped her heel on the frame, and her other leg fell out to the side, briefly exposing herself to him. He felt his heart kick, and he looked away, but her scent had already risen up between them.

"Did you ever give her a reason to be jealous?"

"Jacob, go!" she said, and he pulled back on the wood with all his might. She was already turning the screw. Thick yellow glue oozed out of the seams. "Are you going to pull?"

"I am."

"Or do you want to keep interrogating me?"

He tried not to laugh, straining against the wood. "Just tighten that thing. My arms are falling off."

"Jacob, pull!"

He pulled, she pushed, their bodies pressed together, perspiration mingling, eyes locked intently on one another, both of them laboring at the limits of their strength, and Jacob suddenly wanting nothing so much as to slide down to the floor and stare into those defiant brown eyes while he slowly sinks into her. . . .

The wood cracked.

"Back off," he said, examining the work. "It's only the caul, I'll get another one."

She loosened the clamp while he grabbed another piece of junk pine and slipped it into place.

"Accusing you of what?" Jacob persisted, as he realigned his grip and July started tightening the lever again.

"Crazy things, I told you. I lie to her, I do this, I do that. Jacob, harder."

He pulled with everything he had, until his arms trembled. Finally the wood stopped resisting.

"Good," he said, relieved that he could finally let go. He lay back on the floor, and July lay beside him. His entire body felt fatigued, his hands ached. He said, "She must have been depressed."

"She was the liar," July replied.

He gave her a look. "She cheated on you?"

"She was insane," July said again.

His cell phone rang. He started to get up—the phone was on the floor beside his tools—but July answered for him.

"I'm sorry, he's busy now," she said, after answering.

"Wait. Who is it?"

She covered the mouthpiece. "A woman," she mouthed.

He crawled over, thinking it was Laura, and took the phone, July eyeing him intently as he said hello.

"Mr. Winter," the voice snapped authoritatively.

"Yes?"

"This is Attorney Zabriski's office. We need to see you."

As soon as Jacob walked into the lawyer's office, he spotted the newspaper on the reception desk. Miss Finch looked up and said, "You were there last night, on the bridge with D.A. Evangeline when the detective fell to his death?" Her scowl was heavy with astonishment.

"We didn't talk about my assault case," he explained, naive as it sounded. "She was asking about Alix Callahan. She said it was personal, that she was a friend of the family."

"Mr. Winter"—the woman exhaled—"how do you expect us to defend you?" Her use of the word *us* did not escape him. At least, he thought, Evangeline hadn't told the press that he'd admitted to being with Alix on the bridge. No, apparently she was saving that morsel.

"May I go in?" he asked. The way Miss Finch folded her hands, he could tell she wasn't finished scolding him.

"Frankly, I don't think we can help you," she said. "You claim that Dr. Ashworth's version of the assault in your home is a fabrication, yet you won't allow Attorney Zabriski to speak with the one person who might be able to shed some light on the incident."

"I won't drag my son to court so he can testify against his mother," he said.

"Mr. Winter, at least let *us* talk to your son," she replied, her tone softened dramatically. "Whatever happened in your house that evening, one thing is certain. If you end up in prison, custody will no longer be an issue."

Jacob looked out to the river, thinking once again about the way Max had climbed into Price's car the night before. Nothing in his life had prepared him for the pain he felt thinking that he might lose Max—not the loss of his own father, not Laura's unfaithfulness, not even his mother's death.

"Can I be in the room when you talk to him?" he said, though he could hardly believe the words were coming from his mouth.

Willard Zabriski's door opened. Standing stiffly at the threshold, the attorney gave him a long, sober look. "Bear this in mind," he said. "I will not hesitate to drag your wife and the good Dr. Ashworth through an open cesspool if that's what it takes to defend you. Are you prepared for that?"

Jacob looked back to the wide river, despising himself for giving in. Zabriski stepped over to the office chair and hooked his thumbs over its back. "If it gives you any comfort, I raised three children myself. I will do this in such a way that he does not lose an iota of respect for his mother or father. If we do go before a judge, the only time Max will be present is when I talk to him."

For the first time, Jacob felt that maybe he could trust this man.

"As far as D.A. Evangeline is concerned," the attorney continued, "while she is definitely not a friend of Alix Callahan's family, she did not lie to you about one thing. That case has indeed taken a personal turn."

Jacob watched him walk around the front of the desk. He shoved the telephone back and sat on the corner.

"Eight years ago, when Ms. Callahan did her graduate work at Brandeis University, she commuted from Ogunquit, where she held a three-year lease on a small beach house. Do you know who her roommate was?" The attorney raised his eyebrows, and the cauldron of facts bubbled up in Jacob's mind.

"Susan Evangeline?"

The attorney smiled. "No, but that would be an interesting coincidence. Does the name Deborah McBride ring a bell?"

Even if Jacob wanted to seem unruffled by the news, his face betrayed him. He felt himself go pale.

"Of course, she wasn't a state senator when she lived with Alix," Zabriski continued. "She was still in law school."

"But they were more than just housemates," Miss Finch said, unable to disguise her prurient delight.

"You can thank Miss Finch for uncovering that tidbit," Zabriski said. "The press doesn't know—at least not yet."

"Does Evangeline know?"

"Oh, I think so. I think that's why she had you up on that bridge."

In Jacob's mind he formed a picture of Deborah McBride and was immediately struck by her plainness. She'd worn glasses; her hairstyle and makeup were prudent, middle-class. Not that she was unattractive, but what he remembered about Alix Callahan was that she preferred the company of girls who were young, hip, exquisite, and wild . . . hardly erudite. Perhaps in this woman, he thought, Alix had found her intellectual equal. A perfectly suited pair, one earning her doctorate, the other her law degree.

"You may not know this," Zabriski added, "but six years ago, just before Deborah McBride made her run for office, she got married."

"To a man," Miss Finch said with a glint in her eye, "for all of eight months."

"At her divorce settlement, she did not ask for a dime."

"She got what she wanted," said Miss Finch, reveling in the scandal. "She pretended to be straight, just long enough to get elected."

In Jacob's mind the cauldron bubbled over. Alix Callahan had not only found her high-achieving soul mate, she had fallen in love. And Deborah McBride had dumped her for the sake of her career. Alix responded by going to Colombia . . . and bringing back July.

"According to the fire investigators, an autopsy probably won't be possible," Zabriski said, interrupting his thoughts. "As there's been no evidence of foul play, for now they're treating her death as accidental—publicly at least."

"What about you," Jacob said, a shiver inside him. "Do you think Alix had something to do with it?" He shrugged in a way that would make him look doubtful himself.

"Let's say, for speculation's sake, that Alix Callahan survived the fall," said Zabriski.

"She might've gone to McBride for help."

"Maybe."

"Maybe to *rekindle* the romance," said Miss Finch, giving Zabriski a devilish glance.

"Ah, yes, the jilted, obsessive lover," Zabriski speculated, "frustrated in her attempts to revive a dead relationship. An interesting premise, Jacob, if you ever decide to start writing mysteries. But wouldn't her guilt seem rather obvious?"

It wasn't difficult for Jacob to see the attorney's sober-minded logic—and the logical part of his mind agreed. But in his body the chill wouldn't subside. "In a crime of passion," he said, "people don't always behave rationally, do they?"

Zabriski allowed a smile. "You're right. And if I'm wrong, then Alix Callahan got her revenge." He stood up from the desk. "Pre-

pare your son, Jacob. We'll expect him here on Monday morning."
He glanced back at Miss Finch. "Nine o'clock?"

She looked in her appointment book. "Nine," she confirmed.

"If the boy's memory corroborates yours, hopefully we can get this settled out of court."

Jacob got to his feet. "Then what?"

"Best case? No time, no probation. In your divorce settlement, shared support, shared custody."

"What are my chances?"

Zabriski went through his office door. "Zero," he said, "if I find out you've talked to Lady Evangeline again."

28

WHEN JACOB RETURNED TO GREEN GIRLS, JULY'S CAR WAS NOT there. He let himself into the flower shop, then called directory assistance for Massachusetts. He got lucky. Professor Nielsen was home.

"I have to ask you something," Jacob said after identifying himself, "about Alix Callahan."

"Yes?"

"Just . . . how well you knew her," Jacob asked. Hearing a car, he looked out to the street and saw July pulling into the driveway.

The professor said, "In an academic sense, quite well, in fact. Are you talking about her personal life?"

"That's right." Jacob lowered his voice as he watched July walk around to the back of the Volvo.

"I'm not sure I can be of much help."

She pulled a grocery bag out of the wagon, closed the liftgate.

Jacob retreated toward the garden door. "Do you have any idea if she might've been afraid of something?"

"Alix afraid?" Nielsen made a deliberative sound. "She always struck me as particularly fearless."

As July came up the fieldstone walk, Jacob walked around his temporary wood shop. "The Kogi Indians," he said. "Are they violent people?"

"Not in the least. Good God, why?"

Jacob heard the key in the lock, and he ducked out to the garden. "What about the tribal shaman?" he asked, walking quickly into the cover of green.

"Violent?" The old man hesitated again. Jacob peered between a fan of succulent leaves and saw July walking through the shop toward the stairs.

"I'm sorry, something's come up, I'll get back to you," Jacob said quietly. He hung up, then listened to her footsteps on the stairs. Nielsen knew more than he was telling, Jacob was sure. He shoved the cell phone back in his pocket, then walked back to the shop and up the stairs, where he found July in the kitchen, putting groceries in the refrigerator.

"I didn't know where you were," he said. "I was a little nervous." He went into the bedroom, where he found his white shirt in the bureau.

"I had to pick up some groceries," she answered. "How did it go with your lawyer?"

"Not bad," he called, pulling the shirt over his head. "By the way, I start work today at the tavern."

He heard a skillet fall into the sink. He stepped into a fresh pair of khakis, then went into the bathroom and brushed his teeth. "Don't wait up for me, I'm going to be late," he said, returning to the kitchen . . . but she wasn't there. He went to the open glass doors, where he looked down and saw her pushing a wheelbarrow into her rain forest.

"July?"

She kept walking away from him.

Buttoning his shirt, he went down the stairs. He wanted to find out what she knew about Alix's prior relationship with Deborah McBride, or Evangeline's investigation into the fire. As he started along the main path, watching around his moccasins for yellow frogs, he heard a quick rustle of leaves, and she came pushing the wheelbarrow through the greenery. She was wearing a sleeveless T-shirt and her arms shone with perspiration.

"I wasn't sure if you heard me."

She muscled past him with the load, a single plant, a shovel, and pitchfork.

"July, is something wrong?"

She went a few more steps, then stopped at a small clearing, where she'd left the garden hose. "You're going to the bar, and you don't want me to wait up," she answered. "Fine." She grabbed the pitchfork, stuck it in the ground, and turned over a hunk of dark, moist soil. "If I wanted to see someone, that's what I would do."

"I don't understand."

"Oh, you're going to work for her *father*?"

"You're talking about Laura?" he said, while July filled the hole with water. "Laura's not going to be there—she hates the place. I told you, I took the job because I need the money."

"And I told you, I have money," she said as she set the seedling in and shoveled dirt around it.

"I need my money," he said.

"You need *your* money?" She firmed the dirt around the plant with her hands and stood up, smiling. Her knees were muddy, as were her hands and feet. "Oh, Jacob, such an American," she said, her eyes pooling with ridicule. "He needs *his* money."

With a good-natured chuckle, he said, "I'm already late. The boss wants me in early so he can show me what to do."

"And I want you to stay." She lost her smile, wiped her muddy hands hard down the front of her T-shirt, her breasts taking the brunt of the punishment, her nipples standing in the wake. "You know, Jacob, I'm very attracted to you."

"All the more reason I'd better go," he said dryly.

She turned from him. "Fine, go to your job." Taking hold of the wheelbarrow, she started walking away. "Anyway, she's been here."

"Laura?"

"Not her."

"You don't mean . . . who? Alix?"

"I could smell her," July said, then she was swallowed by the greenery.

Jacob stiffened, tempted to pursue her. But he didn't. He left. Walked back through the shop and out the entrance door, making sure it was locked. He wondered if July had been like this with Alix—or if it was Alix who had made her this way. As he headed down the walk toward his car—he had left it in the street to give the impression of transience—he was struck with a sudden and most unwelcome thought: the mystery vehicle that had caused the accident on the bridge. . . .

He walked around the Green Girls Volvo and glanced back at it. Seeing no damage to the fender or bumper—not even a scratch—he chided himself for his wayward imagination. But he couldn't help feeling a lift of relief, however short-lived.

When he looked back to the house, there was July, standing behind the shop door, watching out the window.

JACOB got to the tavern a half hour before it opened, which meant he was a half hour late on his first day at work. Before he got out of the car, Squeaky came out the back door and yelled to him, "They want you at the hospital. Your phone's been off."

"What?"

"The little man."

Jacob's heart stopped.

"He's okay." Squeaky held up his hands. "He got into somethin', had to have his stomach pumped. He's okay."

MAX was asleep when Jacob walked into the hospital room. His baseball cap was on his head, an IV in his arm. The television was on, but his glasses were on the bedside table, along with his Gameboy—meaning Laura had been in. When Jacob turned the volume down, the brown eyes opened.

"Maxie, what happened?"

"Price saved my life," the boy said.

Jacob picked up the glasses and gently slid them on Maxie's face.

"That's what Mom says anyway. Then Price tells her I took drugs, which I didn't." His eyes were glassy and a little bloodshot, but his speech seemed normal. "So Mom grounds me for a week."

Feeling a surge of weakness, which was probably relief, Jacob sat on the bed. "What happened?"

"I got home from school. Did the usual."

Jacob said, "Computer games."

"Next thing I know, I wake up here. They pumped out my stomach, which is pretty cool. But my throat hurts."

Jacob touched his son's face and felt comforted by the warmth in his cheek. "Maxie, why do they think you took drugs?"

Another voice pitched in, "Because it was a drug overdose."

Jacob turned to see a nurse in the room with them, with oversized glasses and a satisfied sort of smile. "Was it Ritalin?" he asked, certain that Price had finally persuaded Laura to start medicating Max.

"We're not sure what it was, but the contents of his stomach went to the lab for analysis."

Jacob studied his son. He couldn't help thinking of his own mother, wondering if suicide was genetic.

"He's going to be fine," the nurse said, then added, "for now. The doctor wants to keep him overnight, just to make sure." By the look she gave Max, she seemed to derive some pleasure in saying it.

"Thanks for taking care of him," Jacob said. "Could we have a few minutes?"

"As I told his mother and her friend, he *is* supposed to be resting . . . but I'll give you a few minutes," she allowed. "Unfortunately, the time to talk about drugs is *before* they get the temptation."

As soon as she left the room, Jacob pulled a chair close to the bed. "Maxie, I know this is upsetting, what's going on between Mom and me. But you wouldn't try to hurt yourself, would you?"

Max wrinkled his face. "I'm not dumb, you know."

Jacob breathed a sigh. But now he suspected that some kids had given Max the pills to swallow—the same assholes who'd dared him to fly. Maybe they told him it was candy, and Max was embarrassed to admit he fell for it.

"Anyone give you anything at school, food or anything?"

Max shook his head.

"Price didn't give you any pills, did he?"

"They said if it wasn't for Price I might be dead. He found me on the floor and called an ambulance."

"Well good for Price," Jacob said—then remembered promising Zabriski he'd bring Max in on Monday. He reached for Max's cap and squeezed the visor, rounding it the way Max liked. "Hey, that was some home run you hit."

"I did what you told me," Max said.

"How's that? I was telling you to take the pitch."

"Head, not heart," Max said. "Remember?"

Jacob slapped the brim good-naturedly. "You used your head, all right."

Max laughed a little. "Also, Price hypnotized me."

"What?"

"Yeah, while I was hypnotized I told him I wanted to hit one out of the park. So he told me to visualize it—and I did. Cool, huh? I shellacked it."

"You sure did," Jacob said, but suddenly he was thinking about Alix Callahan again. What if Price had hypnotized her . . . and she'd revealed something while she was under?

"Oh, yeah," Max said. "Remember that girl who came looking for you—the one in our driveway the other night?"

July. "Uh-huh," Jacob said, hoping he wouldn't have to explain.

"She was at the game," Max said. "But after you got there I didn't see her anymore. Who is she?"

"Oh, nobody special," Jacob answered, but he was wondering why July hadn't told him she'd been there—and relieved she hadn't come over to be with him.

"What about the woman standing with you and Mr. Fecto?"

Jacob understood. Max probably wanted to know who was going to take Laura's place the way Price had taken his. "Just a friend of Mr. Fecto's."

"Oh. Well, she was standing next to you. That's why I asked."

"Maxie, I need to talk to you about something," he said, then stopped. How could he do it, ask his son to testify against his mother?

"I've got a couple of things to tell you too," Max said.

"Okay," Jacob said. "You first."

"Not sure you're gonna like this," Max said. "Just, Price got me into Belnap, that's all. I go the end of August."

The casual way Maxie said the words, it felt to Jacob as though a vacuum had sucked up his heart. Two things bothered him, although he wouldn't be able to articulate either until later. One, Max sounded as if he didn't mind leaving him. Two, he had called Price by name again, as if they'd become buddies.

"Now you," Max said.

"Huh?"

"What were you gonna say?"

Hey, champ, you remember that day we came back from the Red Sox game. . . .

Without Max's testimony, Jacob knew he didn't stand a chance of winning his assault case—which meant he'd probably end up losing custody of Max. But how could he ask Max to talk to his lawyer? The boy wasn't stupid. "I guess I already told you," he said. "That was a great home run." He rubbed Max's shoulder, struggling to think of anything else to say, while he watched his last chance fade.

Then Max said, "Actually, I had something else to tell you."

"Yeah?"

Max looked off to the side and said, "I think it might have been the grape soda."

Jacob scowled. "What do you mean?"

"Ah," Max said, as though disgusted with himself, "it was in the refrigerator. I snuck some."

Jacob said, "Why was there grape soda in the refrigerator?" They never kept sweets in the house—no soda, cookies, candy . . . unless Price had left it. But Price was the one who'd told them to keep sugar away from Max.

"I drank it," Max said. "Half of it, actually. It sucked big-time.

Then I filled the bottle with water and put some food coloring in, so Mom wouldn't know."

"Yeah, but sugar wouldn't . . ." Jacob's heart walloped. "Maxie, did you tell Mom about the soda?"

Max shrugged. "Price already got her thinking I took drugs. Why make it worse?"

His brain stammering, Jacob grabbed the phone on the bedside table and dialed. When Laura answered, he said, "Look in the refrigerator."

"Are you at the hospital?" she asked.

"Laura, is there a bottle of grape soda in the refrigerator?"

"Why would there be?" She paused for a second. "Wait a minute. Yes."

Because someone tried to poison him. Jacob did not say that aloud. "Don't dump it," he told her. "Wait there."

"YOU'RE right about Alix Callahan," he said, when Evangeline answered her phone.

"Excuse me?"

"This is Jacob Winter. She just tried to poison my son."

Evangeline didn't respond.

"Someone broke into his mother's house," Jacob said, "and put a bottle of grape soda in the refrigerator. It was spiked with something."

"Are you at the house now?" Evangeline asked.

"I'm at the hospital, in the lobby," he said. "Max is okay. But I don't want him to know what happened. I don't want him frightened."

"And you think Alix Callahan had something to do with this."

"I know she did," he said. "Just like I know she was the one who murdered Deborah McBride, and tried to take me out on the bridge."

"Have you called the police?" Evangeline asked.

"I'm calling you," he said, and hung up. Then he called July. He was relieved to hear her voice.

"She tried to poison Max," he said.

July didn't speak at first, and he realized that he must have frightened her. She said, "Is he okay?"

"He's fine. They got him to the hospital on time. Is your door locked?"

"What happened to Max?"

"I'll tell you about it later. Do you have any other guns in the house?" Even as he said it, he considered digging up the one he had buried.

"No, but I have a big knife," July said, half joking. "And I'm a light sleeper."

"Do you want me to come home?" *Home.* The word came out of his mouth unplanned. But there it was.

"Oh, Jacob," she said, sounding apologetic. "I don't mind if you work at the bar. I just wanted to be with you tonight." A seductive softness had crept into her voice.

"I know." He thought about her going to Max's baseball game and was touched that she'd shown an interest in Max—also grateful that she'd left when he arrived, probably having spotted Fecto and Evangeline cornering him. "Does your bedroom door lock?"

"I'm not afraid of Alix," she said. "I'll shove a chair under the doorknob if it makes you feel better. But how are you going to get in?"

"I'll sleep outside your door," he said.

For a moment, she remained silent. Then she said, "We'll see about that."

29

WHAT THE HELL DID HE GET INTO?" SQUEAKY SAID WHEN Jacob returned to the Speedway. There were already a dozen or so people in the place, mostly men standing at the end of the bar, drinking beer.

"He'll be fine," Jacob said.

Squeaky studied him, but Jacob didn't want to tell him anything more—the grape soda, his suspicions about Alix, or even the fact that Max would be going to school in California.

"Go take care of the setups," Squeaky said, tossing him an apron.

"Okay, I don't know what setups are."

"Knives, forks, and spoons rolled up in napkins. Jeff Dakota's racing in Loudon this weekend. I gave his car a little touch-up the other day. I'm the only one he trusts to do his engine work. This place'll be packed if he stops in."

Jacob tied his apron in back.

"Another thing," Squeaky said, "I found a full-time job for you." He set a bin of silverware on the bar in front of Jacob, and a stack of green cloth napkins. "There's a guy, one of my regulars, he's a cabinetmaker, and he needs help. I showed him the carpentry work you did in here. He'll pay twenty an hour, cash-money, under the table."

"I'll have to think about it," Jacob said.

"Think about what? He's waitin' to hear from you." He handed Jacob a bar tab with the phone number written on it. "Only thing you gotta remember, you're not building the Taj Mahal. Cabinets. Bang-zoom, you're done. Not six months to finish a table."

"I need to use your office for a minute, okay?"

Jacob didn't wait for permission but walked into the office, aware of Squeaky's eyes following him all the way. He shut the door when he was inside, took out his cell phone, and started dialing Professor Nielsen's number.

The door opened. "So the kid screwed up, what the hell do you expect, with all this bullshit?" Squeaky standing there, fishing for more information.

Jacob said, "Give me a minute, please."

"You yourself, I bet, when you were his age, with the wacky tobaccy. Don't tell me different."

"Squeaky, I need to make a call."

"While you're at it, call about that carpentry job."

"I told you, I need to think about it."

"Yeah, well, don't think too hard," Squeaky told him and left the room, pulling the door shut behind him. Jacob dialed the number, and while he listened to Professor Nielsen's phone ringing, he stared at the photo of the Impala on the wall. It was from the same race that was depicted on the poster behind the bar. In this one, a newspaper photo, the Impala was lying on its roof, its front end mangled. BRISTOL, the dateline read. It had been Squeaky's last race. The article, if there had been one, did not accompany the photo.

The ringing stopped, and a voice began: "Please leave your message with the correct date and time."

Checking the Pennzoil clock on Squeaky's desk, Jacob recited the tavern's phone number and time, then said, "I want to know what the hell happened to Alix Callahan in Colombia."

30

THE BLACK '65 STINGRAY SWUNG THROUGH THE PILLARS OF Deltaville Estates, a cul-de-sac of luxury homes with a spectacular view of the river and bridge and, out beyond, the wide Georgia coast. As it pulled into a wide driveway, the garage door rose up, and the car drove inside. When the door went down again, the driver did not see the shadow that followed behind the car. A neighbor might have gotten a glimpse, if she were watching at that precise time of night—but she would've only thought a dog had got in.

The man stepped out of his car, briefcase in hand, a twenty-dollar Cohiba stuck in his teeth, and he disarmed the alarm system. Opening the entry door, he went directly into the kitchen and took a Corona and a block of cheddar cheese out of the refrigerator. He puffed on his cigar as he grabbed a steak knife from the dishwasher.

As he sliced into the cheese, he felt a sharp sting on the back of his neck. Swiping at it, expecting to find an insect squashed in his fingers, what he pulled from his skin confused him—a crude finish nail, by the looks of it. When he turned around, he swallowed his cigar smoke.

On the other side of the butcher block island stood a very short man with long black hair and sunglasses, wearing a white uniform that said HIALEAH SCHOOL OF KARATE, and holding a hollow ballpoint pen to his mouth.

The man dropped the cheese and raised the knife, then moved to his right.

The Indian went the opposite way, keeping the island between them.

The man changed direction. So did Sereno.

They did this two more times, until the man suddenly gasped, then fell convulsing against the refrigerator. In a moment he was still.

Sereno came around the island and pulled him flat on the floor. Taking the knife out of his hand, he unbuttoned the man's shirt, then located his heart with his free hand, felt the faint beat. The man stared up helplessly as the Indian leaned over him, retrieved the cheddar from the floor, and sliced off a sizeable chunk.

In the mountains, he was used to going for days without food or sleep, but here, without coca leaf in his cheek, he could no longer deny his hollow stomach. Sitting in front of the open refrigerator, Sereno ate leftover pizza and barbecued chicken legs and all the cheese he could find. He sucked ketchup from a squeeze bottle, drank orange juice from the carton, and when the orange juice was gone, he went into the large attached greenhouse where he sniffed roses and orchids and cannabis plants. Then he took the bottle of beer into the bathroom, where he ran hot water into a deep Jacuzzi tub and had a long, satisfied soak.

31

As it turned out, Jeff Dakota did come into the Speed-way Tavern, along with his entourage of fans, his pit crew, and old friends from town. By nine-thirty, Jacob had poured a reservoir of beer, a pint at a time, and mixed countless whiskey-gingers and rum-Cokes. He recognized some of the local guys, by face if not by name. Many of them worked at local garages or auto parts stores, some were aging gearheads, like Squeaky. Everyone showed up whenever Jeff Dakota was in town, especially if he did well—and tonight he'd come in second.

At one point Squeaky took Jacob aside. "Look at this kid," he said, with a fire in his eye. "They're all kissin' his butt, and all he can think about is those last two laps."

The cell phone rang in Jacob's pocket.

Squeaky gave a disgusted look as Jacob answered. "Must be your agent callin' with a movie deal," he said.

"Hello, Jacob! You're doing some detective work, I see."

It wasn't hard to tell that Professor Nielsen had been drinking.

"Hold on," Jacob said, and he covered the phone and said to Squeaky, "I need to use your office."

"That about the carpentry job?"

"I'll just be a couple of minutes," Jacob told him, going into the office and shutting the door.

"To answer your question, what happened to Alix Callahan in Colombia," the professor said, "as I told you earlier, I have no idea. She dropped out of the doctoral program. Dropped out of sight. Of course, now I'm afraid we'll never know."

"I don't think she's dead," Jacob said quietly.

The professor said nothing.

"Someone tried to run me off the bridge last night," Jacob told him. "Today someone tried to poison my son."

"You don't think Alix—"

"What I think? I think you're keeping something from me." Jacob waited for a reply but heard only the quiet hum of silence on the line.

"Jake, earlier you asked about the Kogi shamans, whether they are violent."

"That's right."

"It's not a simple question," Nielsen said. "In a physical sense, I would have to say no, because I don't believe that violence, as we *civilized* people know it, even exists as a concept among the Kogis. In the metaphysical, however—and here again I'd refrain from using the word *violence*—but you must realize that the shaman's duty is to protect his people and their world from evil, in all its forms."

"Meaning Alix?"

He heard the professor exhale, a forbearing sound.

"I don't know what you're telling me," Jacob said.

"The condensed version." Nielsen paused again. "A Kogi shaman is chosen at birth by the reigning shaman of a particular village. He is taken away from his parents as an infant, then raised by the shaman and his wife for several years, sometimes eighteen years, in total darkness."

"In darkness. And how this relates to Alix Callahan?"

"He's kept in a cave or a hut with no windows," Nielsen explained. "They take him outside at night, but only when there is no moon."

"For eighteen years."

"Give or take. You see, he must learn to use his vision."

"You mean, inner vision."

"That's right," Nielsen replied. "Before he can assume the position of shaman, he must learn to leave his body and fly over the forest and mountains among the spirits—"

"Hey—" The office door opened. Turning to see Squeaky looking in, Jacob covered the phone. "Just take the job. We got fifty people out there."

Jacob gestured he'd be a minute, saying to Nielsen, "I need to go."

He heard the professor speaking but hung up anyway, then said to Squeaky, "I'm not taking the job."

The old man gave him a smile. "If ignorance is bliss, you must be happy as a pig in shit," he said. "What do you mean you're not takin' the job?"

Jacob stood up. "How come you quit racing?"

"Don't start with me."

"Laura said you were good," Jacob persisted. "You were leading the pack at Winston, with two laps to go. What happened, did somebody die?"

"Yeah, somebody died."

"Who died?"

Squeaky's brow folded into a mask of sarcasm. "Nobody died. I had a kid to support—like you. And no job—like you." The way Squeaky stared, his eyes seemed to shine. "Just what the hell do you have to tell the world that's so frickin' important you wanna throw away your family?"

"Writing is what I do," Jacob replied.

Squeaky smirked. "What you *do* is sling beer for a buncha drunks. That's what you *do*." Squeaky swiped his hand across the top of his head, as if there were hair there. "Let me put it another way: you get on the phone and take that carpentry job—or you ain't got this job."

"You're firing me?"

"That's right, smart guy."

Jacob went to the door, about to walk out. But before he did, he tried again. "She said you loved racing," he said. "I've read the articles. You were one of the best."

"Get it through your head: You . . . ain't . . . no . . . writer!"

Jacob met the old man's eyes, waiting him out.

Squeaky stepped inside the room and slammed the door shut with the side of his fist. The calendar fell.

"I lost my ring toe. Okay?"

"What?"

"You heard me." He snatched the calendar off the floor and tossed it on his desk.

"What's a ring toe?"

A dangerous look of sobriety darkening him, Squeaky sat on the desk. "You're a writer," he muttered, kicking off his penny loafer. "Ever seen a dictionary?" He stripped off his white sock and said, "Ring toe."

Jacob looked at the pink foot. It took a second to realize that Squeaky's fourth toe was gone at the knuckle.

"That?"

"Go fry your ass." Squeaky pulled his sock back on and buried the foot back in the loafer.

"That's the reason you quit . . . because you lost half a toe?"

"A toe off my body, smartass. I had a daughter to support."

Jacob shook his head. "This is how I support my son," he said. "By *not* quitting."

Squeaky looked up, his blue eyes blazing. "Well, then, be my guest," he said, opening the door with a grandiose sweep of his arm. "Here's the rest of your life."

Jacob shone right back at him. "Fine," he said. "Just don't tell me you quit racing over a toe."

Squeaky's smile brightened. The two of them matched glares for another second or two, until Squeaky backed away from the door and Jacob left, to find the woman who tried to murder his son.

32

GREAT TIMING," PRICE ASHWORTH COMPLAINED. ALTHOUGH he'd just sat down to dinner, he managed to grab the phone before the third ring, his gold pen in hand, prepared to take the message from his answering service. Then the pen stopped. He said, "Thank you," then hung up and said to Laura, "I'm sorry. I'll call from the other room."

SITTING in the therapist's outer office, Jacob waited less than three minutes before the telephone rang. When he picked up, Price said in a low-toned voice, "I suggest you get the hell out of there. I just called the police."

Jacob thought for a second or two. "I don't believe you did," he said. "But maybe I will. You know, Alix Callahan left a suicide note." It was a fabrication, but one he hoped would shake some information free.

After a period of silence, Price came back in a whisper: "Alix Callahan was delusional. Same as you."

Jacob felt a glow of satisfaction, knowing he had nicked a nerve. "I see here that she was a patient of yours for a couple of months, every Wednesday, her last session June twenty-two."

"And?" Price's confidence returning, as if he was fishing to see what Jacob had put together.

"She revealed something to you in therapy. You used it against her."

"Doesn't her suicide note explain it?" Price, back on the offensive.

"So far, I haven't mentioned any of this to the police," Jacob told him. "But someone tried to poison my son today, and I think you know who, and why."

"You *are* crazy," Price shot back. Then Jacob heard him cover the phone and say, presumably to Laura, "I'm talking to a patient. Go ahead. I'll be right there."

Jacob said, "Sounds like I called at a bad time."

"Stay calm, everything will be okay," Price replied, his telephone manner changed.

Jacob smiled. "I'll bet Laura didn't leave the room like you asked her to."

"I'll be there as soon as I can," Price said in that compassionate voice.

"No, I'll bet she's standing right there," Jacob said, "giving you that look of hers that makes you wonder if she can see right through you."

"Fifteen minutes," Price told him.

"It's only a matter of time," Jacob said.

FIFTEEN minutes later he was still sitting at Laura's reception desk when Price unlocked the front door.

"If you want to call the police, go right ahead," Jacob said, sliding the phone to the front of the desk.

Price opened his office door, and Jacob followed him in.

The room was decorated with diplomas and framed photos—Price Ashworth rappelling down a cliff face, Price Ashworth in his tae kwon do robe, Price Ashworth drumming at a men's pow-wow—probably to demonstrate to his confidence-shaken patients the range of his many talents.

"In the first place," Price began, "Maxie's drug episode—which you interpret as attempted murder—was nothing more than a confused boy vying for the attention of his parents. Jacob, believe me, it's a commonplace occurrence among adolescents in the shadow of divorce."

"I see by your session notes," Jacob said, "that Alix Callahan started coming to you because she had a drinking problem." He walked in and opened a manila folder on Price's desk, started flipping through the sheets of paper inside. " 'Excessive drinking,' " he read. " 'Problems with relationship.' 'Promiscuousness of partner.' Not a lot of detail. Just enough psychobabble to satisfy the insurance companies or a judge in case you ever get subpoenaed. The details you keep somewhere else, right? Along with the tapes that Laura transcribes."

Price turned to face Jacob, his face a study in stifled aggression. "Jake, I don't doubt that's what you think—"

"Tell me what you had on Alix Callahan," Jacob said, cutting him short. "You know why she disappeared."

"Jake, you have an extremely active imagination. Do you understand that about yourself? This business about someone poisoning Max, and now . . . I blackmailed Alix? Alix disappearing?" Price shook his head sympathetically. "I know you don't want to hear this, but until you start taking your medication again, your imagination is going to continue running your life. And ruining it. Along with the lives of the people you love."

Jacob turned toward the window, the star-spattered sky outlining all the old gabled roofs. The night seemed to brighten with his mounting anger. He turned back to Price, gave him a studied look. "I'm not leaving here without some answers."

The psychiatrist folded his arms in a professional way. He stared at Jacob for a few seconds, then motioned him to the couch. He pulled his leather chair around for himself and sat down, elbows on knees, as if ready to confide a secret.

"The only thing I know that might be pertinent," he said, leaning closer, "is that one day when Alix came in to see me—technically, this happened before her session began, which is the reason I can divulge it to you—well, on this particular day Alix was pretty charged up, and she told me that her partner, July, wanted her to find a man for a threesome. Which was an obvious invitation."

"You, with Alix and July?" Jacob studied him doubtfully, trying to imagine Alix ever proposing a heterosexual fling—or sharing July with anyone—particularly with the likes of Price Ashworth.

"In case you're unaware, Jake, sex with a patient is one of those little ethical details the profession frowns upon."

"I'm sure you wouldn't want to be unethical."

Price absorbed the dig, then fixed him with a narrow look. "One does not need a degree in psychiatry to understand that pleasure was not Alix's primary motivation."

Jacob said, "I don't follow."

"Genetic material, my friend." Price was writing something on a pad—a prescription for Haldol, Jacob assumed. "She saw in me a potential seed donor."

"I see. Then why did she contact me?"

"Well, you *are* kindred souls."

"You mean we're both writers, or both homicidally jealous?"

"Jealous? Alix never struck me as particularly jealous."

Jacob gave him a wary look. "We're talking about the same Alix Callahan?"

"Profoundly depressed, yes," Price said, "mixed in with a cocktail of alcohol and other demons. But jealous?" He shook his head. "I never saw any evidence of jealousy."

He offered Jacob the prescription as he rose smoothly from his chair. "Please, Jacob. Take your meds. And see if you can't get your life back on track. For everyone's sake."

Jacob gave him a look. Alix Callahan, not jealous?

"I have nothing more to tell you," Price said, going to the door to usher Jacob out. "I'm sorry."

Jacob nodded perplexedly, pretending to think it over. He was sure now: When hypnosis broke down Alix's inhibitions, she ended up telling Price Ashworth something she'd never intended him, or anyone, to know. And Price had used it against her.

He got up off the couch and followed Price out to the reception area.

"Did she ever mention Deborah McBride?"

"Oh, I've heard all the rumors."

Jacob kept his eyes on him. Alix had been in therapy with Price—but never mentioned the lover who dumped her?

"I'm not one who buys into conspiracy theories, Jake. What can I say?" He pushed open the entrance door with his back.

Jacob took the prescription from him. "Sorry to interrupt your dinner."

"Well." Price raised up on his tiptoes, then lowered back down. "If we're a step closer to resolving these issues, it was well worth a little eggplant parm."

Jacob went outside and took three or four steps down the sidewalk before he turned back. "I'd appreciate it if you wouldn't tell Laura about this," he said.

Price zipped his lip.

33

THE BLACK STINGRAY SLICES THE NIGHT LIKE A PHANTOM, SERENO keeping the car on the old dark roads, his headlights off. Driving past sleeping farms and settlements of asphalt-sided houses, stalwart trailers, gas pumps and school buses, maybe some poor farmer's son is lying awake coveting any other future but his own when he hears the low sound come out of the south and roar past like a hot gust of wind.

Gleaming out over the steering wheel, a fat cigar glowing in his mouth, Sereno flies like a hawk, wide-winged and delirious. A white-tailed buck looks up from a magnolia blossom, amazed at the black thing going by. Skunk stops on the roadside, twisting back for a look. But fox is too startled to do anything but crouch and squint, water-eyed. It's not the car, or the speed, or the fact that the black thing has roared into their world with no warning. They're used to surprises. It's the *eyes* of the man soaring past. His eyes, and that cold, adrenaline-socked fear that stops each one: they know he has seen them.

34

PRICE ASHWORTH'S DECOROUS, SOLAR-POWERED HOME WAS SITU-
ated near enough to Kittery Point that in winter, when the trees
were bare, from an upstairs window he could boast of an ocean
view, and he did. The house had three bedrooms and three Jacuzzi
baths inside, a hot tub on the deck, and a glass-enclosed great
room, where Price and Laura were presently seated at a cherry table
Jacob had built in exchange for Price's treating Max.

Laura hadn't said much during the reheated meal except that she
was having second thoughts about Max going away. Price, who had
convinced her that the boy had indeed swallowed something in a
cry for attention—probably an overdose of over-the-counter diet
pills—promised her that a taste of independence was exactly what
her son needed.

Now, while they finished their dessert, and meditative Tibetan flutes played in the background, the motion detector on the front porch came on, lighting the pines that bordered the property. Price didn't pay any mind. The neighbor's cat triggered the thing twenty times a night. In fifteen seconds the light went out again.

. . . And Jacob sliced through the basement window screen.

HE had worked out the possibilities on the drive over. Because Price would have accumulated several years' worth of the files that Laura transcribed from his tape-recorded sessions—and neither the complete files nor any of the tapes had been in his office—he must have kept them somewhere in his house. But not in his bedroom or living room or great room or any room where guests might see them. Probably not even in his home office. The basement seemed the logical place.

Jacob was right. Price's wine cellar, a windowless, atmosphere-controlled chamber, was located in an alcove off the carpeted family room. With a penlight in his teeth, Jacob found the light switch and turned it on. The wine, maybe two hundred bottles, was stacked along an entire wall. On an adjacent wall stood a mahogany desk and three file cabinets with a cheap wood-grain finish, furniture probably scavenged from Price's early offices.

It was almost too easy. While he listened to the murmur of Laura's voice above him, Jacob quietly pulled out the *C* drawer, and there they were: three months' worth of Alix Callahan folders—April, May, and June. He shuffled through them, found that each contained a few sheets of typed single-spaced notes and two sixty-minute cassettes, their labels dated, one session per side. He was most interested in June 22, the date of Alix's final appointment, and went through the papers until he found the documentation. "Discussed excessive drinking, problems with relationship," the transcription read—and that was it. Unlike session notes in other files here, the record from June 22 provided no more information than did Price's office notes—with one exception: the added, penciled-in word *Florida*.

"I didn't say *lie*." Price's voice suddenly rang clear, as a door opened above. "I'm merely suggesting that you represent an alternative reality."

Jacob hurried to the alcove doorway, flicked off the lights, and waited in the dark.

Footsteps came down the stairs. "Are you sure you want pinot noir?"

Stuffing the tape in his pocket, Jacob felt his way back behind the file cabinets. Outside the room, a light came on, seeping under the door.

"Pinot noir is hardly a *digestif.*" Price's voice, more present. "I'll pick out a nice bottle of port, if you'd rather." The door opened, the room lights came on. While Jacob held his breath, he heard a bottle slide out of the wooden rack and Price say, under his breath, "Pinot noir it is."

The light went off again. The door closed. Jacob felt his heart stir. Maybe the honeymoon was over after all.

35

ALL BUT IN FLIGHT, THE INDIAN FEELS THE COOL NIGHT lift his hair and wash the back of his neck. A lazy half-moon has risen in the east, bright enough to turn the ocean green. He sees brighter light in the north, yellow-gray, a buzzing kind of light, and he steers toward it.

In his vision he has seen the girl many times, always in the north, crouching in a garden beside moving water, salty, deep, and brown, a wide river of ocean water. He has seen the tall arched bridge made of green steel. And a lush garden crowned with crimson bougainvillea. Such a garden must be in a warm place. Yet the river he envisions is cold. He cannot understand the contradiction. But this is where he is headed, to the lights of the north.

As the settlement appears in the distance, signs and streetlights begin flying at him. He puts his sunglasses on. When he sees the big yellow *M,* he steers into the parking lot, almost clipping the exit sign. Driving around the back of the building, he parks behind the fenced-in dumpster. On the other side of the rail fence, a convenience store sits up on an asphalt plateau, with two gas pumps in front. Sereno can smell the fried food blowing out the exhaust fans, and he feels a hollow pang in his stomach. Still, it's not food he's stopped for, or gasoline.

It's the silver-blue Porsche he spotted from the road, a 1957 Speedster with its top down and a short-haired woman sitting in the passenger seat, examining a road map. The Speedster, this silver-blue shark, has New York license plates, but Sereno does not understand their significance. Nor does he care about the music coming from the car's speakers, which sounds to him like thunder being released in increments.

He is more focused on the woman, the way she is trying not to look at him as he walks toward her, yet how all her other senses perk at his approach. In fact, her jaw is clenched, and she has stopped breathing.

The instant his hand touches the driver's door, she abandons the map and scrambles out of the car, walking quickly around the building. Sereno takes his place in the driver's seat. He steps on the clutch and turns the key. The gas gauge needle jumps to nearly full. The engine catches and rumbles, sending a warm vibration through his chest. He pulls the stick into reverse and backs out of the parking place, then watches a different girl walking toward the car, carrying a paper bag. She is a McDonald's girl, with an *M* on her shirt and an *M* on the bag she's carrying and another *M* on her hat, which is cardboard. The way her head tilts when she sees him, the way she shows her teeth, she appears to be smiling. Sereno steps on the brake.

"I have your specialty order," she says. "Fish sandwich without cheese?"

He studies her melon breasts.

"Large fries and chocolate shake?"

Sereno stares through his shades, and she hands him the bag.

"Would you like extra ketchup?" she asks.

Sereno stares, and she reaches into her uniform pocket and

comes out with three small packets, which she drops into his hand. He studies her head. Her red hair is streaked blue, and her hat appears to have no top.

"More?" she asks, reaching into her pocket again. The packets spill out over Sereno's hand. "This is all I have," she tells him, just as the short-haired woman comes around the corner and stops, pointing, while a boy wearing a topless *M* hat and a man wearing a baseball cap both come toward him, but tentatively.

Sereno shifts into gear and drives away, keeping his headlights off. By the time he's shifted into second, the Speedster has blended with the night.

36

A FINE DRIZZLE COVERED JACOB'S WINDSHIELD. UNDER A chilly, moonless midnight, the beach was quiet except for the pounding surf. Not a good night for tourists or teens to be out cruising. Jacob's dashboard clock showed 12:25, and he wondered if July would be waiting up for him when he got home.

He slid the cassette into the tape player, and Price's voice came on: ". . . imagining the most peaceful, most relaxing, most wonder-ful place . . ." Jacob hit fast-forward, then tried again. ". . . You take another step closer. Your breathing is slower, more relaxed . . . easy, deep breathing. You're so comfortable. . . ." Fast-forward again. This time when Jacob hit play, he heard Alix's voice. ". . . Plantation Key."

Price: "Plantation Key is in Florida?"

"Yes. When I was in Colombia, I'd heard stories about her sexual escapades with a shaman called Sereno. He was legendary as a mystic and healer, not only among the Kogis but all over the Sierra Nevadas. Her name was Juliette. After Sereno took her for his wife, they were banished. I found out they'd settled in Florida. I wanted to see if he was real."

"The Indian shaman. You wanted to verify his mystical powers. . . ."

A pair of headlights came down the road, flaring inside Jacob's car. He slunk low in the seat.

". . . how you come to meet them?"

"I met July first. I never actually talked to Sereno." Alix's speech, Jacob noted, was ponderous, no doubt hypnosis-induced. "I don't think he spoke English. Or Spanish."

Price: "Are you attracted to July when you first meet her?"

Pause. "At the time, I didn't think I was capable of being attracted to anyone. I did know that she was quite young and beautiful."

"Describe where are you *now*," Price suggested. "The moment you first see her, you are . . ."

"Outside, beside her house. She was working in the garden, transplanting into clay pots. I told her who I was and that I wanted to spend a few days studying her plants. While we talked, Sereno came home."

"Describe it for me. He drives into the driveway. . . ."

"No. Their property backed up to a canal where he docked his boat. He was a fisherman. When he saw me, he walked into the house. The way July watched him, I could tell she was agitated about something."

"Does she tell you what's bothering her?"

Pause. Jacob realized that Price's subtle attempts at getting Alix to speak in the present tense were his way of coaxing her deeper into trance—but Alix was holding back.

"She told me to come back in the morning, after he left. Then she went in the house after him, and I returned to my motel."

"Do you perceive any sort of suggestive undertone in her invitation?"

"I don't know."

"But you do return."

"No. She came to my room early the next morning and told me that she was afraid for her life."

"She tells you she's afraid of her husband?"

Jacob nudged up the volume, tensing as he recalled his own experience, July appearing in the driveway outside his house.

"She said she hadn't slept all night because he was so jealous. She was afraid he was going to murder her. She asked if she could sleep in my room for a couple of hours."

"Is this when your attraction turns physical?" Price said.

"Is that important?"

"It would help retrace the evolution of your relationship," Price replied. "When July first asks to sleep in your room, can you see what she is wearing?"

"She took off her top," Alix said.

"Yes, go on," Price told her. "Do you take that as a sexual proposition?"

Alix, breathing, not answering.

"Do you get into bed together?"

On the road, another car went by. The mist, Jacob noticed, had turned to a light rain on the windshield.

"Take your time," Price coached. "She takes off her top. Is that all?"

"She had on a pair of white bikinis," Alix answered.

"Are you aroused at this point?"

Again, the car became quiet except for the fingertips tapping at the roof.

"And you, Alix," Price continued, "can you see what you are wearing?"

Alix said slowly, distinctly, "I'd put my robe on when I answered the door. I kept it on. Is this turning you on, *Doctor*?"

Jacob chuckled. Even hypnotized, she hadn't lost her spark.

"Shall we stop?" Price said.

"No."

"Now. You get into bed together. . . ."

Pause. "July got in first. When I got in beside her, she held on to me."

"Does it occur to you that she might have sexual feelings toward you?"

Jacob turned up the volume.

"I wanted to kiss her," Alix replied, staying in the past tense, maintaining control.

"Do you kiss her?"

"I put my arm around her."

"And . . ."

"Her back was very warm. Her hair was cool. I remember that."

"You can feel this now."

"She curls up, like a little girl," Alix said, slipping into the present. "I can hear her breathing. Then she's brushing her lips against my neck."

"You're aroused. That's good."

Alix's breathing was suddenly drowned out by the rainfall's louder pattering. "We started kissing." Back into past tense, retaining control, yet speaking more slowly. "We made love most of the morning."

"Breathing. That's good." Price, coaching her. "Nice deep breaths. So relaxed. So safe here."

"I'd never imagined sex could be so intense. Then she asked me to give her a bath. I did. And we made love again in the afternoon."

"I see."

"And for the rest of the week . . ."

"Yes."

Pause.

Price again: "Go ahead. Continue, please."

"For the rest of the week she came to my motel room every morning after Sereno went out fishing. We made love, we slept in each other's arms, we worked in her garden. . . ."

"You are falling in love with her."

Silence.

"Alix, you're safe here. So safe in this room."

"Friday morning."

"Friday morning," Price said. "Four days later. Friday morning."

Alix took a contemplative breath. "On Friday morning July told me that she'd had an affair with a man."

"At the same time she is having the affair with you?"

"No, before. His name was Kiefer. He lived in Key Largo, and he had connections with a couple of fishermen who were running cocaine from Colombia. July let Kiefer use her dock when Sereno was out fishing. They would have sex in the house."

"How does this make you feel, July telling you she'd been with a man?"

Alix stopped again. Jacob heard the squeak of a chair.

"So relaxed," Price said. "Very good. Now . . . July is telling you about this man Kiefer, the man she's had the affair with. Are you with her now, while she is telling you about Kiefer?"

"Yes."

"Very good. And you can hear her, can't you? You hear the words she uses."

"He's dead."

Silence.

"She told me he was dead. The police found him stabbed to death, and July told me she was afraid Sereno had murdered him because he'd found out about them. And now . . ."

"Alix, your shoulders," Price reminded her. "Relax, that's right."

". . . And now she was afraid Sereno was going to kill her."

Rain pounding the car roof, ocean waves battering the beach. A car came toward Jacob, headlights flashing bright to dim.

"You're so relaxed," Price said softly. "So safe here. July is telling you that Sereno is going to kill her, but you are safe now. July says Sereno is going to kill her. . . ."

"I told July she should call the police, but she was afraid they'd connect her to the drugs and deport her—"

"Steady, slow. She tells you she cannot call the police. And you're afraid of Sereno."

"Afraid for her. That night I hid in the garden—"

"Alix, I want you to breathe. That's good. Now you're hiding in July's garden. What are you seeing? Hearing?"

"A gunshot."

"Steady—"

"Two gunshots. July screaming. I go up to help her."

"Are you running or walking?"

"Running."

"Where?"

"Upstairs, to the bedroom. They're—"

"Slow. Slow. Tell me what you see."

"On the floor, covered in blood, neither of them moving. . . . They look dead. . . ."

Price: "Stay with it."

"Her mouth is open."

"July's mouth, open—"

"Wide, like she should be screaming . . ."

"Alix, breathe."

"Sereno's got her finger in his mouth, and . . ."

"You're safe here."

"I'm stabbing him. . . ."

"With a knife."

"In the back, in the side, and he's not moving, not even trying to stop me, but he won't let go of her finger. . . . I can hear her bones—"

"So safe and comfortable."

"I pull him off her, he rolls over—"

"You pull Sereno off."

"His mouth is all blood, and he's staring up at me and not moving, not breathing anymore . . . and that's when I see inside. . . ."

"His mouth?"

"I just want to get her finger—"

"Breathe, Alix."

"I'm trying to get it!"

"Shhh. You're safe."

"He's dead. He looks dead. He *should* be dead. I'm just trying to get her finger. Then he jumps—"

"Okay—"

"He won't let go!"

"Alix?"

"I can hear his teeth going into my cheek."

"Let's stop here."

"July keeps hitting him with the gun. He won't die!"

"Shh," Price whispered. "Let's—"

"We run out of the room and down the stairs. I hear a siren—"

"Alix, I really think we need—"

"No! There's a man—"

"A policeman."

"I don't know. At the bottom of the stairs, with a pistol—aiming at me. But July has Sereno's gun, and she aims at him. And we all stop."

"Alix, you're safe now."

"July tells the man, 'He's dead.' "

"*He* meaning Sereno."

"Yes."

"And you know this man?"

"No. A friend of Kiefer's, he must be, someone who's come to kill Sereno."

"Alix, tell me what you see."

"We stand there. I keep waiting for him to kill me. But he doesn't. The siren gets louder, we know the police are coming, so he backs down the stairs and hurries out of the house. And July gives me her gun."

"A handgun."

"Yes. And I leave too."

"Where do you go?"

Long pause.

"Alix, where do you go?"

"I ran back to my motel," Alix said, retreating to the past tense, back in control. "I packed up my things and drove all night, with toilet paper on my face to stop the blood. When I got to South Carolina I found a hospital and told them a dog attacked me while I was jogging."

Jacob could hear her breathing.

Price said, "You've been through a terrible experience. But you're safe now. Sereno is dead, and you are safe."

"He didn't die," she said with an air of desperation. "He went to prison."

"And you had to testify at his trial. That can be very traumatic—"

"I didn't testify. Nobody knows anything about me."

"Then Sereno doesn't know your name, or where you live. If he was convicted of murder, he'll probably spend the rest of his life—"

"He was acquitted of murder. He's in prison for aggravated assault on his wife. When he's released, he'll be deported back to Colombia. I'm not afraid of him."

"That's right, because he is there, and you are here," Price said, "and you've done some very important work today. Now. I'm going to count backward, from five to one—"

"I am trying to tell you something!"

"You're agitated, Alix."

"Of course I'm agitated. I just told you I tried to kill someone."

"You have nothing to be ashamed of."

"You're not listening."

"Alix, you were protecting yourself. You were protecting some-one you loved—"

"Listen to me! I'm telling you—"

Her voice cut off. Jacob turned up the volume, but he heard nothing but tape hiss. He fast-forwarded for a second or two, then tried again. Nothing but the rain whacking at his roof, the ocean waves crashing in.

Then he realized why the tape had been left in Price's files. Whatever Alix had continued to say—Jacob shuddered to think it could be more incriminating than what he'd just heard—Price had erased it. Either that, or it was transferred to digital and encrypted, stored on a hard drive or floppy disk. Whatever the case, Jacob knew he was never going to find it.

Another car came down the street behind him, headlights brightening the interior of his car, then flashing past, tires slapping at the wet pavement. He glanced in his rearview mirror . . . then looked harder. Suddenly alert, he turned and peered over the seat, at the car parked behind him. About fifty feet back, dark, seemingly unoccupied . . . the Green Girls wagon? Through the rain-streaked back window, he couldn't tell. What troubled him most: the car hadn't been there when he'd arrived. Neither had he seen it pull up—at least he hadn't seen its headlights.

He turned to start his car—and jumped.

July was at the passenger window. Standing in the rain.

"Jesus," he said, leaning across and opening the door. "What are you doing there?"

"Aren't you coming home?" She sounded sad, or frightened. Thinking about what he'd just heard, he suddenly felt ashamed for ever doubting her.

"Come in out of the wet," he said, and she crawled in. She was shivering.

He shut the door and said, "How long have you been out there?"

Her arm was cold.

"July, what's the matter?"

She kept silent. Had she heard what he'd been listening to?

"Tell me."

She was shivering so hard. "There were noises at home."

He gathered her in his arms. "It's okay," he whispered. She kissed his neck, and it made him shiver too. "You're soaked," he said, and he turned on the engine, pushed the heater to full. Then he gently pulled off her wet sweatshirt—and found her wearing nothing underneath. So he took off his flannel shirt and dried her face with it, dried her hair, dried her shoulders and arms, and then with the rain pounding at the roof he was kissing her, and she was kissing him. He found the seat lever and pushed back, and they fit themselves under the steering wheel. He tried talking to himself, reasoning that if he can bring at least his faithfulness to court, the custody judge will have to take that into consideration. Perhaps even Laura will realize. Yet even as he began this inner counsel, he could feel her warmth under his hands, her breast ripe and swollen, and once again this other creature started pushing inside his chest, heavy-browed and mindless, and he unfastened the button of her shorts. She sucked in her stomach to let him pull her zipper down, then watched him intently as he pushed his hand down the front of her underpants, his fingers sliding through her fine soft nest. When his fingers found her, it was like pressing on some overripe, sun-swollen fruit. At the instant of his touch, she seemed to burst, at once sucking his fingers in and spilling out over them.

Clutching at his wrist, she pressed back against the door, gazing up at him through half-closed eyes. In some distant part of Jacob's brain, he pictured Laura . . . but seeing July's rapturous, inward-directed scowl, the image dissolved.

Then she was opening his own trousers, this younger girl, and the moment she touched him a shock of ecstasy raced through his brain. He reached for her, but she pushed him back down.

"I want to watch you," she whispered.

He thought of Laura again.

Oh, but the sight of July rising over him. Suddenly nothing in the world existed but this girl, her black hair hanging over his face, her eyes gazing down.

She lowered herself. At the instant of contact, she caught her breath. He felt the kiss of young resistance, then she sucked him inside with a soft, shuddering moan.

And there was nothing left for Jacob, nothing at all but the rain drumming down, and his poor ravaged mind spilling over.

37

THE NIGHT STIRS UP COLOR IN THE EAST AS THE SPEEDSTER pushes through the marsh, Sereno looking out at the last fading stars hanging up above the mango-toned horizon. He turns onto a dirt road that leads him into cypress woods. Mosquitoes thicken as the trees press in, and the road all but disappears in the undergrowth. He burrows the Porsche into a rough-cut clearing, perhaps the place where the workers who built the road had finally surrendered to the insects and quit. Night-blackened foliage shows the dawn's first green. When he gets out of the car, mosquitoes sing loudly around his head, but they don't land. He hears ocean waves breaking in the distance. He smells salt in the air. Morning birds have started, so he looks for a soft place to sleep.

PART
THREE

38

Y OU'RE SO STUPID."

Alix Callahan again, her hands around his neck, strangling him—
"No!"

Jacob snapped to consciousness.

"Shhhh."

July breathed heavily in his ear. She was on top of him, in the hot garden hut, her body in feverish motion.

Jacob's heart came to life. The sun sliced through the windows. July gasped . . . She stiffened, fingernails biting into the backs of his arms, while he gripped her hard buttocks to keep her from crushing him. She quivered in orgasm. Then she collapsed.

He listened to her breath in his ear, her entire body slick with perspiration. "I love watching you sleep." She moaned.

"I'm awake now."

"Mmm, I can see," she said, then laughed in her soft, musical way.

He pulled the blanket over himself. She captured his hand and kissed his fingers. "Don't you wish we could stay here forever?"

He watched goosebumps rise on her breast as her nipple stood up stiff and tender, not sure if he had ever seen anything so beautiful. Her name is Juliette, he thought. She cheated on her husband, and he killed her lover, then tried to murder her. She shot him, she stabbed him, she beat him with a pistol. She ran away with the woman who saved her—a woman more dangerous than the man she'd left.

"Never leave?"

"Never," she breathed, then ran her hand under the blanket. He took hold of her wrist to stop her.

"I'd love to stay in bed with you," Jacob said, reaching for his boxers, "but I've got to get to work."

"Jacob," she said, sounded wounded. "I want to talk."

He slid his shorts on. "About what?"

"I don't know. How was your job last night?" She pulled her hair out of her face. "You never told me."

"I quit."

"How come?"

"Things didn't work out."

She laid her face on his thigh, her gaze softening, her fingers creeping under the leg of his shorts. What did he expect, that she'd view their sex as a casual thing? Of course not. It was the consecration of a new love.

"What time?" she asked innocently.

"Hm?"

"Did you quit?"

"I don't know. Late." Was she fishing for his whereabouts between the time he left Squeaky's tavern and she found him at the beach? "I went for a ride," he explained, "trying to sort things out." Should he apologize and leave before he got in any deeper? Did he still want to leave her?

"Jacob, come down here," she said, trying to pull him on top of her. "Went for a ride where?"

"Are you checking up on me?" he teased, not wanting to tell her about breaking into Price Ashworth's house, especially since Laura had been there—but not wanting to have sex with her anymore, either, at least not until he made up his mind.

"I thought that was so romantic last night, in the rain," she said, and she opened her legs around him. He turned away from her, bent for his trousers.

"Really, July, I've got to write."

She slapped his butt, a surprisingly hard shot.

"Hey—" He could see the arousal the slap had brought her. His buttock stung. He resisted the urge to retaliate, afraid she'd consider it foreplay.

"Mustn't keep the famous author," she said, humorless.

He stood there for a moment, hesitating before he turned his back on her again, while another part of his mind flickered, like distant heat lightning, with a glimmer of fear. Perhaps sleeping with July had been a bigger mistake than he'd thought. In fact, it might've been a doozy.

39

THE HUMMING GROWS QUIETER AS HENRY LAMB CLIMBS HIGH
*above the traffic, safe inside the hollow steel. Each hole he passes looks
out right, toward the ocean, or left, upriver toward the marina, where
his boat is being painted. The way he's described it to Dolores—the
mahogany cabin has a stove and refrigerator and a bed for two—he's
promised her that on its maiden voyage they'd sail up the coast to Bar
Harbor, then head down to Provincetown.*

*When he nears the top of the column, he looks out a hole—and
sees the girl again. The crow's nest in which she stands is enclosed by a
square cage. They are near the top of the entire bridge structure, just
beneath the highest point of the arch, high over the roadway. Henry can
see the sky all around them, the flat ocean off to the east. When he looks
down, he can see the tops of cars and trucks disturbing the fog, oblivious
to his presence, rushing away to a far-off world.*

But the girl. Draped in a simple white dress that's smudged with rust and soot and bridge-green, this creature is possessed of more beauty than he has ever imagined.

Peering out of the hole, he asks her: "What are you doing here?"

She does not answer.

Afraid of losing her again, Henry does not ask anything else. He climbs out of the pillar into the open, naked air, where she takes him in her arms, takes him into the crow's nest, takes him down.

"I just wrote a sex scene," Jacob said when his agent came to the phone.

"You mean the guy on the bridge?"

"That's right."

"Wait a minute." Maury paused. "Isn't he alone?"

"No, there's a girl."

"*Two* characters?" Maury exclaimed. "Jacob, you're teasing me. Who's the girl?"

Jacob got out of his chair. "She lives inside the bridge."

Maury paused. "Inside."

"The beams are hollow."

"Why is a girl living inside the bridge?"

Jacob paced away from the desk. "Does she need a reason?"

"A girl living inside the beams of a bridge? Of course she needs a reason. Unless this is a fairy tale . . ."

Jacob paced back again. "See, this is why I don't write plots."

"Now wait." Maury softened his voice. "I'm intrigued. Do they fall in love? Does she end up saving him, talking him out of jumping? I mean, who exactly is this girl?"

"I don't know. Maybe he saves her."

"Saves her. From what?"

"The bridge—I don't know, I haven't figured it out."

"Jacob."

"What?"

"I need to ask you again. Is everything okay?"

"Everything's fine."

"Because I've got to be honest with you," the agent said. "A guy with a flat tire, a woman living inside a bridge. Who the hell do you expect is going to publish this?"

40

SITTING ON THE EDGE OF HIS HOSPITAL BED, BIFF BISHOP patted down his cowlick with his good hand, while an attractive redheaded nurse pulled his shirt over his shoulder. His arms hung by his sides, achy. His fingers and toes tingled. His tongue felt fat in his mouth, and he could barely hear over the whistling in his left ear, like a teakettle inside his head. The nurse was telling him he needed to rest for another couple of days, as far as he could make out, while Warden Latham stood at the foot of the bed, probably agreeing with her. Mostly Bishop heard the whistling.

"You people need to speak up if you want me to hear you," Bishop said. Christ, he could barely hear himself.

The warden came closer, leaning over him with his arms folded. In fact, Latham rarely sat down—which he considered his management style. He had brought in a cellophane-wrapped basket of fruit—big spender—then stood there yammering about god knows what, him and his blue alligator cowboy boots.

Bishop turned the tiny dial on his hearing aid, and Latham's voice cut through the whistling like a bullhorn.

"Christ!"

"MEDICAL LEAVE, CLOSE TO HOME!" that's what Bishop heard. Then, "Agent Connolly something something something . . . talk to y'all."

"Talk, talk." Bishop slid off the bed and stepped stiffly into his black suede loafers. "Last I knew, I was the goddamn victim." He turned to the nurse and patted his cowlick again. "Pardon my language, I've been through considerable trauma." Then back to Latham: "Man gets shot with a jungle dart, wants to take a little R and R, the FBI don't like it they can kiss my paralyzed ass, sorry again, ma'am."

He walked stiffly to the closet and got his overnight bag. When he turned around, the warden was right there, saying something to the nurse and smiling. She gave him a pointed look, probably meaning she hoped he would talk the patient into staying in bed. Then she went out into the corridor and shut the door behind her.

Latham closed in on Bishop again and put his hand on his shoulder—also part of his style. Touchy-feely. "I don't have to tell you the commission's gonna be looking at all aspects of this, Biff."

Bishop jerked back. "Goddamn whistle." When he stopped poking at his hearing aid, the warden was still there, just as close. "They can look at me all they want. Meanwhile, that cannibal psycho is off hunting for his wife to make her a five-course meal."

"Not that anyone is suggesting you were anything but an unwilling hostage. But they do need to understand how such a thing could have happened."

"What did I say to you? 'Put him in lockdown.' Did you tell the commission *that*?"

"I've taken responsibility for my error in judgment," Latham said. "What's perplexing everyone is how he was able to climb into the back of your vehicle in broad daylight—"

"Maybe I don't have eyes in the back of my head," Bishop said.

"Anyway, how's that game warden, the other poor bastard Sereno jungle-darted?"

"Still unconscious," Latham answered.

"Anyone know what he zapped us with?"

"Still being analyzed."

"Probably never be the same again, either of us," Bishop said. "But I don't suppose there's a promotion in the works, or some kind of fund for officers wounded in the line of duty."

Latham gave him a look. "Biff, y'all wouldn't be thinking of going after Sereno on your own, would you?"

Bishop chuckled. "You askin' if I give one solitary thought to that goddamn prison when I'm not stuck inside the walls?" With a bitter grunt, he picked up his bag and hobbled to the door. "I'll be taking my vacation now," he said. "Y'all help yourself to the fruit."

41

IT WAS EARLY AFTERNOON BY THE TIME JACOB CHIPPED OUT THE last notch in the upper chord of July's bed. Arm-weary, he had cut sixty-four such notches with a mallet and chisel, all precisely measured and spaced. It was delicate work, when what he really felt like doing was pounding something.

After all, Maury was right. His novel was preposterous. Henry Lamb and the mystery girl making love on top of the bridge. Not only the novel, but this other story he had concocted—of Alix faking her death and lurking about, causing Fecto's death, poisoning Max, immolating her former lover. . . .

It was his own imagination run amok. Just as Price had told him, as Laura had told him, and yes, Squeaky too. Even Max seemed to know what Jacob refused to face. He could not trust his own mind.

"Jacob, you're so lazy."

July's voice, a teasing lilt, came from behind him. Then she squeezed past him on her way out to the garden. She had on a short yellow shift, which her high buttocks tossed back and forth as she sauntered away.

"Federal law says I'm entitled to a coffee break," he replied, and pretended to go back to work, hoping to avoid the conversation he knew they'd have to have before the day was done. He was leaving as soon as he finished her bed, before they became more deeply involved.

She turned a graceful half circle and continued walking backward. "I've got something a lot stronger than coffee," she told him, running her hand up her thigh. "Sweeter too."

As she spun around and headed deeper into the rain forest, he sat there in the wake of her musky fragrance, determined to resist her, while his rising libido kept recalling the delicate pressure of her lips against his, her body receiving his. Then he knew he could put off the conversation no longer.

Dropping his tools on the floor, he started after her, wiping poplar chips off his chest while he came through the garden, strengthening his resolve, trampling the underbrush, heedless of whatever alien frogs might have wandered into his path.

42

A THOUSAND MILES AWAY, IN SOUTH CAROLINA, SERENO SAT on a sandy dune, with the sea smoke moistening the high grass in its breath. He could hear ocean waves. He could not see them.

Popping the top on a can of Sprite he'd found in the Georgia man's refrigerator, he took a drink, then lay back and pulled the snapshot from his pocket. He stared long at the image, stared and stared, until he fell under its spell.

The photo was creased with wrinkles, its edges ridged with the darts concealed inside. It was a picture of July from the waist down, naked, sitting in a garden. The image was off center, so that only one knee showed. Beside the knee was an elephant ear leaf; behind that the trunk of a sapling palm.

Looking closely at the picture, one could make out, through tiny breaks in the leaves, the top of an arched bridge in the distance, beyond the greenhouse glass, with a dark river below. A section of concrete pier showed a water line that was higher than the level of the river, an indication that the water was tidal. But it was the bird flying over the bridge—the black wingtips and yellow head—that spoke to Sereno.

Limon-cabeza.

When he was a fisherman working off the Florida Keys, in the winter he would sometimes encounter the seabird, a Northern Gannett, far from land, diving from great heights and plunging like an arrow into the cold water. When it burst from the sea again, shedding sundrops off its yellow head, Sereno would whistle, and the bird would swoop a great circle for him.

Limon-cabeza, the other fishermen called it. Lemon-head.

Sometimes he would see a long line of them, the lemon-heads, flying to their summer homes in the north. Sereno considered it a sign of luck when he spotted the bird.

Now he moved to the edge of the dune and looked northward into the fog. With the surf murmuring off to his right, he let out a whistle. Even as far north as he had already journeyed, he knew that this water, this summer day, were too warm for such a bird. Still, he whistled.

Then he stared into the fog.

And he waited.

And eventually a line appeared out ahead, the silver ocean mating with the sky.

He stared.

And golden sand ran away from his feet like honey.

He stared.

And out of a sighing breeze that rose off the ocean, the great yellow-headed bird appeared, slicing the whiteness with its wings, sweeping off toward the north.

Sereno stared.

And the fog gathered at its wingtips and chased after the bird. *Limon-cabeza.*

Sereno closed his eyes and gazed deep into the vision.

And the wide-winged bird flew a thousand miles.

Sereno stared.

And out of the fog, there appeared a green steel bridge, its arched top graceful as a woman's hip, spanning a wide salt river.

He rose into the air himself, mating his spirit with that of the bird, riding the air currents above the bridge until he could see it all: cars and trucks below him, racing past like hard-eyed demons blowing their gas into the air; the long flat ocean to his right, like a woman's belly undulating against the sky. To his left, the wide blue river impregnating the land. And there, on the southern bank . . . there, he could see it now, the glassed-in garden on the green bank, feverish and bright.

He knew she was there.

He could see her but not see her; hear her voice but not hear her. Like the knowledge of music when there were no musicians; the knowledge of heat when there was no fire.

Yes, he knew she was there.

43

JACOB FOUND HER IN A GRASSY CORNER OF THE GREENHOUSE, waiting for him, lying on a blanket with her head propped in her hand, watching him hungrily as he came and sat down beside her. Immediately she reached for the button of his trousers.

"July, wait," he said, stopping her. "We need to talk."

"God." She collapsed on her back. "No wonder your wife wanted somebody else."

"I know what happened in Plantation Key, with you and Alix and your husband, Sereno. July, I know he tried to kill you."

"If he wanted to kill me, he could have willed it in a dream."

Jacob studied her, knowing she didn't really believe that. "I also know that you and Sereno were banished from the tribe after he married you."

She turned her back on him. "The detective has been hard at work."

He persisted. "Did Sereno have something to do with your first husband's disappearance?"

He watched her shoulders sink with an exhalation. Outside their glass oven, the arched bridge reached high into the summer sky, while down on the river an oil tanker the size of four city blocks moved silently past.

"July, I'm sorry, I know it's painful, and I don't mean to bring it up, but"— he reached for her, and she stiffened at his touch—"I'm just trying to understand."

"Understand what?"

"Why it sounds like you still have feelings for him."

She sighed after a moment and rolled onto her back again. Her eyes narrowed as she stared up at the green canopy. "I torment him."

"How?"

A lewd, mischievous smile came over her, and she turned to face him.

"By staying alive."

Her words coincided with the crash of breaking glass, and she rolled to her knees, peering off into the garden as shards came raining, like ice crystals, out of the foliage.

Jacob sprang to his feet. "Stay here," he mouthed, while he pried a small rock out of the ground. Not much of a weapon, but it would have to do. Then she was gone, pushing through the leaves toward the middle of the garden, where the crash had come from.

"July?"

He crept onto the path, hoping to head her off. Now he was alert to everything—the tap of a water droplet somewhere ahead of him, the flick of a leaf under a sprung grasshopper. His eyes darted. He heard a rustle of brush—

"Jacob!"

The cry came from his left. He ran through the vegetation, heedless of frogs, and found her staring upward, terrified. At the top of the glass wall, a seagull was caught in the shattered pane, hanging by a leg and wing, its thin blood running down the glass.

Jacob put his arms around her, while she stood trembling, her eyes darkened with dread.

"It's just a seagull," he said. "That's all it is. We can fix the glass."

She gazed at him as though it was the stupidest thing she'd ever heard.

"He's coming," she whispered.

"Your husband?"

She lowered her eyes.

"July, he's in prison in Florida," Jacob said. "You told me yourself. When he's released he'll be deported back to Colombia. He's never going to find you."

She gave him that incredulous look again, and Jacob realized it was the same look Alix had given him on the bridge, just before she jumped.

44

As soon as he drove away from Green Girls, Jacob phoned Florida directory assistance, asked for the Department of Justice, then listened to the recorded menu. He chose Criminal Division. When at last a human voice came on, he was making his way through Market Square, heading for the drawbridge to Maine.

"I'm calling to check on the status of an inmate in your prison system," he said.

"Male or female?" the woman asked.

"Male. A Colombian Indian named Sereno. He was arrested on Plantation Key maybe five or six years ago."

The woman's tone changed. "Sir, do you have information on this prisoner?"

"That's why I'm calling you," Jacob told her, "to find out when he's scheduled to be released."

"Sir, could I have your name, please?"

"Isn't this a matter of public record?" Jacob asked, not about to jeopardize July's identity by telling who—or where—he was.

"The gentleman in question is currently classified 'Escapee.' From Alligator Alley Correctional Institution."

Jacob's heart jumped, and he turned off his phone. The Mazda's old air conditioner was blowing full blast, but it made no difference. There was no air inside or outside the car. At the end of State Street, just below the bridge, he pulled over to the curb and called the Florida Department of Justice again, asked to speak with someone in the Witness Protection Program.

"You mean WITSEC, the Witness Security Program?" the operator asked.

"That's right."

He got the number and dialed. When a male voice answered, Jacob said, "I'm calling with information concerning one of the people in your program. She may be in danger."

"To whom am I speaking?" the official asked.

"There's an escaped convict who may be looking for her," Jacob said. "He is a Colombian Indian who goes by the name Sereno. He escaped from Alligator Alley Correctional Institution."

"Your name, please?" the man repeated.

"To the best of my knowledge, the woman he is looking for is part of your program."

After a moment of silence, the Justice Department official said, "Sir, I appreciate your concern, but our policy is to neither confirm nor deny—"

"Don't you people use her as a decoy," Jacob said.

"I understand your concern, sir. If she is part of our program, she is quite safe." Everything the man said sounded rehearsed, as though he were reading from a script. "However, if she has violated the rules and is no longer part of WITSEC, then we have no information on her."

"What rules?"

"Any number of conditions, the violation of which would have triggered immediate forfeiture of protection. For example, if she ever tried to make contact with family or friends—or the prisoner himself—from that point forward, she would be on her own."

"You're not listening to me. She would never have made contact with his man. He tried to murder her." Even as he protested, Jacob couldn't help thinking about what July had said, about tormenting Sereno.

"If she is in our program, she is protected," the man repeated with a tone of finality. "If she is not in the program, then she's a citizen of some community, no different from any other citizen. If there's a problem, she'll need to contact her local police department. Now, is there a telephone number there, in case we need to get in touch with you?"

Jacob cut him off and drove over the bridge.

45

WHEN JACOB WALKED INTO THE TAVERN, THERE WERE EIGHT or nine customers, mostly men, watching a car race on TV. Making his way through the tables he took a seat at the opposite end of the bar.

"You just lookin' for an air-conditioned place," Squeaky said as he came over, never taking his attention from the TV, "or did you decide to take up drinkin'?"

"I quit writing," Jacob told him.

"Jeez, have you notified CNN?"

Jacob sat on a stool. "Can I have a beer, please?"

"Draft or bottle?"

"I don't care."

Squeaky went and poured him a glass from the tap, still watching the TV. When he came back and set it in front of Jacob, the others let out a yell.

"I told him!" Squeaky called down to them. "Stay high on the fourth turn. I told him, and he did it. He just moved up from fourth to second, that hot shit."

Jacob took a sip of his beer, the first he'd had since he was twenty. His eyes watered. "I quit writing," he repeated. "Think your carpenter friend is still looking for help?"

Squeaky gave him a skeptical look. "You come in for that?"

"That," Jacob said, "and I need an untraceable cell phone."

Squeaky stared at the TV again, but from the expression on his face, Jacob could tell he wasn't really watching.

Jacob said, "Do you know anyone?"

"Yeah," Squeaky said, "I know a guy." A scowl had dug into his brow and was deepening there. He reached below the bar and set a bowl of peanuts in front of Jacob. "Your buddy upped the ante, you know." He lowered his voice. "Eight hundred large for the Spite House. That's nothin' to sneeze at." He studied Jacob some more, maybe waiting for him to say why he needed the phone. Then he blew a disgusted sigh. "Bring your beer."

They went into the office, and Squeaky closed the door behind them. "All right, smart guy, you wanna know why I quit racing?"

Jacob waited.

"My wife left me," Squeaky said, holding the doorknob. "Okay?" Although he did not meet Jacob's gaze, there was no sarcasm in his tone this time, no anger. He had said his piece and was asking if Jacob understood.

In fact, Laura had already told Jacob that much. Now Squeaky told him more.

"Day I cracked up the car at Winston"—he motioned to the framed photo beside him—"afterwards I went after the sonuvabitch that ran me into the wall. We all got into it, pit crew, everyone. Couple of broken noses, couple of teeth. I got a suspension and fine. Not to mention my leg got screwed up in the crash, some broken ribs. And that ring toe I lost."

He tossed Jacob a glance, daring him to make some smart-ass remark.

"Next day, when I got home from the hospital, she had my bags packed."

"She didn't like you racing?"

"Didn't like the smell of gas on my hands, my greasy clothes, my greasy friends, their wives, that car." He gestured again at the Impala in the photo, the automobile he still drove. "Ever seen a woman jealous of an inanimate object?"

"So you quit racing," Jacob said.

"Oh, yes, I quit." A bitter glee crept into Squeaky's voice. "I got myself a steady job selling spark plugs up and down the East Coast."

"And she didn't take you back."

"Did I say that?" Squeaky gave him a look. "Yeah, I moved back. It lasted a month. Then *she* took off, and she took Laura with her. Said she never liked salesmen. So I quit the salesman job and bought this frickin' place. And that's my sad tale." He turned the doorknob. "So. You want a nine-to-five job, be my guest, make the call. In fact, you might as well come in here tomorrow. I'll put you to work." Squeaky shut the door again, leaned back against it, then lowered his voice.

"Wanna know the bitch of it all?"

Jacob gave him a look.

"She ended up marrying another driver."

Jacob almost laughed, then shook his head to show that he meant no disrespect.

The older man waved it off. "Go write your book. I'll call you about that cell phone."

46

W HEN JACOB RETURNED TO GREEN GIRLS, JULY WAS GONE.
Assuming she was out buying glass to replace the broken pane, he
gathered his glue and clamps, got down on his knees, and began
assembling her headboard. The work centered him, quieted his racing mind. As the hours clocked by, and he waited for July to come
home, he managed to glue the thirty-two truss members into
place, reinforcing the two chords into a graceful arch; then he
clamped his work tight. Finished, exhausted—it was almost eight
o'clock—he pulled himself up the stairs and took a long hot
shower.

While he was drying himself, he heard the shop doorbell chime.
After a minute, when July didn't come up, he thought of Sereno.
He thought of Alix. Stepping into his trousers, he went to the
kitchen and grabbed a paring knife from the sink, then went down.

Palming the knife as he walked across the slate floor, he opened the door a crack.

Susan Evangeline stood there, holding a clear plastic bag in front of her. "I thought you might like to know," she said, "your son's lab results came in."

"I was just making dinner," he said, to explain the knife in his hand.

"I noticed that yours is the only car here," she said.

He set the knife on the checkout counter but lingered in the doorway, stealing another peek at her bag. She wasn't exactly hiding it from him. He could see something red inside, maybe a shirt. "Is that something to do with Alix?"

"I can't discuss it with you, not without your counsel present—unless you give me permission."

Jacob smiled, but he said nothing.

Unruffled, Evangeline said, "The substance found in both the soda bottle and the contents of your son's stomach was a combination of acetaminophen—an over-the-counter pain reliever—and diphenhydramine, commercially known as Benadryl."

"Benadryl?"

"Commonly used for allergies. Some doctors prescribe it as a sleep aid."

"Laura keeps Benadryl in the medicine cabinet, for hay fever," Jacob said. Now he wondered about Price's theory that Max swallowed the pills deliberately. Would he have bought the grape soda to dissolve them in?

"But the combination of the two," Evangeline said, interrupting his thoughts, "acetaminophen and Benadryl, in this particular ratio—that's Tylenol PM."

"Tylenol PM?"

"Your wife said she doesn't have Tylenol PM at home."

"We never had grape soda, either," Jacob said . . . when something began nibbling at his brain.

"In a child your son's age, an overdose can be serious, even fatal. Fortunately, Dr. Ashworth got him to the hospital before his body had a chance to absorb it all."

"Alix," he said, tightening with dread. Now he knew where he had seen the bottle. Here, upstairs, in the medicine cabinet. He turned and headed for the staircase.

"May I follow you?" Evangeline asked, coming in.

Why argue? He led her past the cordoned-off area where the green headboard lay assembled behind a translucent plastic wall, and as they began climbing she said, "Do you expect the mystery girl home shortly?"

"I have no idea."

"I found it rather interesting," Evangeline went on, "that 'July' used to be the name registered as beneficiary on Alix's life insurance. Did you know that Alix dropped the policy six months ago?"

Jacob heard the plastic bag swinging in her hand, but he didn't take the bait, didn't even glance back—though he could hardly dismiss her inference: that Alix may have been afraid of July.

Emerging in the pantry, he led Evangeline through the living room, past the bedroom, and into the bathroom, where he went directly to the medicine cabinet and pulled it open.

Gone.

A pair of toothbrushes in a juice glass—his had replaced Alix's—a pack of plastic disposable razors on a shelf, a can of shaving cream, his deodorant, July's hairbrush. But no Tylenol PM.

Goosebumps blossomed on his skin.

A door slammed in the next room. Evangeline flinched, took one hand off her bag.

Jacob stepped out into the short hallway, saw that the bedroom door was shut. He went and knocked.

"July?"

He knocked again. Listened. Then opened the door.

There she was, with her back to him, pulling a sleeveless white T-shirt over her head.

"The district attorney is here," he said, trying not to sound as if he was warning her. Then Evangeline appeared beside him in the doorway.

July turned to face them both, innocently snugging the tight T-shirt over her breasts.

"She came to tell me the results of Max's lab tests," Jacob said. "Wasn't there a bottle of Tylenol PM in the medicine cabinet?"

July's head snapped around to him.

"It was in the soda he drank," he said.

"Maybe now you believe me," she replied. The way she slouched against her dresser in her tattered jean shorts—arms folded, chin raised—she looked like some street tough.

If it was for Evangeline's benefit, the D.A. seemed more interested in the open closet. "Do you mind if I ask you some questions?" she said, walking over and running her hand along the clothes hanging there.

"Ask whatever you want," July told her.

"Mr. Winter, you may leave the room if you want, or you can stay, as long as you're aware that anything you might say to me, you do so voluntarily. Do you understand?"

He smiled again at her persistence as he nodded, and Evangeline turned back to July, who continued leaning brazenly against the dresser. " 'July' is the name on your driver's license and Social Security register," she said. "Is that the name your parents gave you?"

July turned to Jacob again. It was that expression of hers, bewilderment, hurt, or whatever, impossible to decipher. "Stop looking at me," she told him. He averted his eyes, wondering what had gotten into her. She said to Evangeline, "Someone tried to kill me once, and I had my name changed."

"Was it a state or federal agency that facilitated the identity change?"

July shrugged, sticking her hands in her back pockets so her dark nipples showed through the T-shirt.

"You were Alix Callahan's partner for approximately five years before the disappearance, is that correct?"

July paused, apparently at Evangeline's choice of words. *The disappearance.*

"And in your statement to the police," the D.A. pressed on, "you said that you were here, in the house, on the night in question."

July stared straight at her. "I was in bed, waiting for her to come home."

Evangeline held her stare. "Can you remember what she was wearing when she left the house?"

The bag. Something had washed up on the rocks, Jacob realized. A jersey? Jacket? Sweater? He tried to picture Alix that night.

"A sweatshirt," July said.

"Describe it."

Maintaining her defiance, she said: "Red, with a hood. Black corduroy pants. Black leather sneakers."

Evangeline turned to Jacob. "Is that the way you remember her dressed?"

He said nothing. The more he tried to picture Alix on the bridge, the more his memory escaped him. Then it hit him: a bullet hole—

"Do you recall any printing on the shirt, a logo or insignia?"

Evangeline had directed the question at him, but July answered: " 'Plant seeds.' "

To Jacob, the image came clear: But it wasn't just the hooded sweatshirt emblazoned with PLANT SEEDS. It was that look on Alix's face that kept coming back to him: the way she had peered down beneath her feet, then threw her face in the air, trying to summon the courage to jump, as if . . .

Maybe it wasn't courage. Maybe she had no other choice.

In front of his eyes, the bag opened and the red sweatshirt came out, green stained. With some surprise, Jacob noticed that it was dry. Why wouldn't it be? Evangeline didn't unfold it but held it up still bundled, just enough for them to see: PLANT SEEDS.

"It turned up in a fisherman's net, not even a mile out," she explained. "Do you recognize it now?"

While he searched the fabric for the telltale hole, she quickly stuffed the shirt back in the bag, studying him as she did so.

"Is that what she was wearing, Mr. Winter?"

"Why are you asking him?" July asked. "Is there a bullet hole?"

She might as well have injected seltzer straight into Jacob's brain. His body stiffened, goosebumps raced down his back.

"Why would there be a bullet hole, if he didn't shoot her?" Evangeline said, continuing to scrutinize Jacob, as though waiting for some giveaway word or gesture. "He told me that he and Alix were the only ones on the bridge, that he stood there and watched her jump—"

"I *saw* her jump," he objected, caught in her cat-and-mouse game. "I tried to stop her—"

"Jacob, don't say any more," July said, moving toward him, no longer the slouching punk but suddenly the concerned girlfriend. The change did not escape Evangeline.

"May I see the shirt?" Jacob asked.

"Of course not, it's evidence."

"Why would I shoot Alix Callahan?" he asked. "She bailed me out of jail."

"Jacob, shut up," July told him.

He looked at her in astonishment, then turned back to Evangeline, who surprised him even more when she walked out of the room. "Make sure you notify my office if you're planning on traveling out of the area," she told him. That was it—she was leaving.

"Alix called *me*," he said, pursuing her. "She waited for me on the bridge." He followed Evangeline down the stairs, bristling. "You've got the bullet. You've got her shirt. You know I was the last one to see her. Why aren't you arresting me?"

All the way through the shop Evangeline didn't respond. But reaching the door, she turned, and the look she gave him reflected a certain exhilaration, like the glint of a hangman watching the condemned mount the gallows. "Mr. Winter, you should pay attention to your friend," she said. "Shut up. There is no bullet hole."

She opened the door and walked across the lawn to her car.

July came and stood beside him. With her hands tucked into her back pockets—that cocky, delinquent pose again—she watched Evangeline drive away.

"Were you flirting with her?" Jacob asked.

"No more than you were," she said with breezy innocence.

"Me? For Christ's sake, the woman is trying to ruin my life. I wasn't flirting with her."

July smirked. "Jacob, I saw you. Talking and laughing—"

"She's trying to take my son away! Why would I be laughing?"

"Don't ask me. I wasn't part of your little joke."

"July—"

When the phone rang, he jumped as if he'd been shot. July

turned and snatched it off the counter. She listened for a second, glaring at him, and snapped, "He's not here."

"Who is it?" Jacob reached for the phone, and she flung it at him. Though he blocked it from hitting his face, his forearm took the brunt of the blow. "Fuck yourself," she hissed, stalking away as he gathered the receiver and brought it up to his ear.

"Now that's what I call a secretary." It was Squeaky.

"What's up?" Jacob said.

"That thing's here."

Jacob flexed his throbbing arm, ran his fingers through his hair. As hard as she'd thrown the phone, she could have cracked his skull.

"That thing you wanted?" Squeaky said.

Jacob remembered—the cell phone. "I'll be right there," he said. Turning to go through the door, he saw July climbing the stairs. As the iron treads rang beneath her heels, he was suddenly certain of one thing: he had to leave her.

For some reason, that prospect frightened him more than anything.

47

THE PHONE MAN'S NAME WAS CHUCK LYON. ACCORDING TO Squeaky, he worked for the phone company in some capacity; computer programmer, Jacob guessed, because he had a reputation as a self-taught hacker of some renown—meaning he sold passwords to porno sites. He was one of the regulars at the tavern, usually came when the place opened and didn't leave till last call. He accompanied Jacob and Squeaky into the office, and Squeaky shut the door behind them.

"You're getting a deal," the phone man said quietly. "On the street these go for twelve, fifteen hundred."

"But this here's a barroom special," Squeaky said, taking the phone from him, "which means his tab is probably twice that, including all the nights I drove him home. Years of that shit."

"I know, I know," Chuck said, returning his attention to Jacob. "Anyway, absolute state of the art. I get the technician's code into the subbasement and reprogram them to emulate phantom switching cells."

"I'm sure we all understand that," Squeaky said, handing the phone to Jacob.

"Which means, basically, I stick over three hundred cell locations and owner stats into ROM, and they keep switching, randomly, from one to the other, as soon as you turn it on."

"In other words, it can't be traced," Squeaky said. "Right?"

"Impossible," Lyon said.

JACOB drove back toward Portsmouth but didn't cross the bridge; instead, he left his car in the parking lot of a lobster restaurant that overlooked the river, then walked along the roadside toward the drawbridge, where he could talk without being overheard. Though the inland sky was holding on to twilight, downriver the moon was already up, and stars had begun assembling. Under a streetlight, he called Florida directory assistance and got the number of Alligator Alley Correctional Institution.

"Warden Latham's gone home for the day," the prison receptionist said. "You'll be able to reach him tomorrow morning."

"It's in reference to your prisoner who escaped," Jacob said.

"Give me your number, please. I'll see if I can reach him."

"I'm not giving you my number," Jacob said. "This may be urgent."

"Hold, please." The phone clicked off and music came on. Jacob walked onto the bridge. In a minute the phone clicked on again.

"This is Warden Latham," a voice said. "How can I help you?"

Jacob didn't answer at first. How indeed? "Your escapee, Sereno," he said. "Do you have any idea where he is?"

The warden hesitated before he answered. "The FBI is coordinating an all-points search. Do you have information for us?"

"I might," Jacob said. "Do you know where he might be headed?"

He stopped walking while he waited for an answer, stood there with the cars passing behind him, looking upriver at the high-level bridge and all the headlights moving. He wondered how many agents were trying to trace the call.

"First things first," Latham said finally. "Sir, you do understand this prisoner's most likely got a number of folks workin' the other side of the street, so-called, who'd love to get their hands on him before we do. What assurance do I have that you're not one of them?"

Jacob said, "Would they call the warden?"

"They might. Yes, indeed."

Jacob said, "I may know something about his wife."

The warden said, "Such as—?"

"I have no intention of revealing my whereabouts—or hers," Jacob assured him, "and I'm on a secure phone."

"Do you know what this man was in prison for?"

"Yes, I do."

"You may have an idea," the warden allowed, "but I doubt you know the half of it. Has anything happened to make you believe his wife's identity and whereabouts have been compromised?"

Jacob stared out at that high arched bridge, thinking of Alix again. "I could give you an answer if you tell me where you think he might be headed."

The warden hesitated. "I'll put it this way: if your friend is on the coast of Georgia, y'all might want to get her relocated."

"I see."

The warden must have detected relief in Jacob's voice because he said, "Friend, I don't know the nature of your relationship with the woman, but I do know this: you do not want to put yourself between her and this Colombian."

"I don't intend to."

Latham said, "You do know he was charged with stabbing a man to death over her."

"Yeah, a drug dealer named Kiefer," Jacob said, showing the warden that he'd done his homework. "In fact, wasn't Sereno acquitted of the murder?"

Latham paused again. "Acquittal doesn't always mean innocence," he said, not particularly impressed with Jacob's knowledge. "Admirable as our judicial system may be, it is far from perfect. Maybe the man wasn't given Miranda in his native language, maybe a piece of evidence was mishandled—I'm only just beginning to look at the details of the case. But I can tell you this: the victim was stabbed more than forty times. Even for a drug dealer, that's a nasty way to go. And then Sereno went after his own wife. She was armed, do you know that? She had a gun and she emptied the clip into him, even got his knife away from him and sliced him up with it. And he *still* managed to bite off her finger. Believe me, you do not want to meet up with this man."

"Should the local police know the situation?"

"Absolutely not," Latham said. "You tell the police, one of them tells a spouse or friend, word gets around. . . . As I told you, Sereno is not the only man who'd like to find this woman. You might be aware that there's a significant amount of Colombian drug money missing and a few dangerous men doing hard time because of Sereno and his wife. If the media gets wind of her location, her life's not worth the price of this phone call."

"What do you suggest I do?"

"Got a pencil or pen?"

Jacob took out his Pocket Planner. "Yes."

The warden rattled off a phone number. "That's my private line," he said. "I want you to stay in touch with me. Likewise, if I need to alert you, maybe you should give me your number."

Jacob hesitated.

"Don't think y'all can handle this yourself," Latham said. "This man is half monster."

"I'll call you," Jacob assured him.

"Count to five," Latham said. "Count to twenty. Now think about this: forty times."

Jacob disconnected, put the phone in his pocket, and he felt the night air flutter over his skin. Looking out at the high bridge, once again he imagined Alix jumping . . . but not to her death.

He was sure of it now. Jumping ten feet down to a narrow ledge that might catch her if she landed just right—or might spill her if she didn't. Risking everything to get away. Because she knew Sereno would be coming.

And that was exactly what Jacob planned to do: Get away. Drive back to Green Girls, tell July the relationship's not working out, gather up his things . . .

And leave her alone. To face Sereno.

He slapped the railing with both hands, then held on tightly, helplessly. Recalling Warden Latham's words—"*This man is half monster*"—he imagined the bloody scene in July's Florida home . . . and he knew he couldn't leave her alone.

He peered upriver at the massive bridge, the simple geometry of its arch, and he wondered how his small life had become so complicated. In fact, the reason he was still standing here with the night falling around him was that he simply didn't know what to do next, or where to go. He stared out at that bridge and imagined Alix crawling along the ledge, climbing down the rungs to the catwalk, disappearing inside the hollow beams, the tunnels, erasing herself from this life, abandoning all she'd ever accomplished . . . just to get away.

Yes, but she hadn't left July alone to face Sereno. She'd found Jacob.

WITH a chill, Jacob recalled Price's story about turning down Alix's offer of a threesome—and suddenly he understood Alix's true motivation: not to have a ménage à trois or harvest Price's genes, as the vain doctor had believed, but to fix up July with a man who deserved her—and who deserved Sereno. Unfortunately, with Price, Alix's plan had backfired.

Not so with Jacob.

He recalled the curious tension between Alix and July when he first went to Green Girls, and suddenly everything made sense . . . the reason Alix had bailed him out of jail in the first place—another deserving male, arrested for domestic assault. Oh, yes, the way Alix had praised his writing in front of July, even the words she chose: "I've never seen violence treated so sexually." Showing enough interest in Jacob to make July retaliate by flirting with him.

And what had she told him about July? "If sex had a face." "July's an incredible cook." Playing both of them at the same time. And they both did her bidding like puppets.

You're so stupid, Alix had told him. How right she had been.

But now he was getting smarter, and now he was walking back to his car, thinking about Price Ashworth again—and knowing exactly what to do.

48

I WOULD'VE KNOCKED, BUT I DIDN'T WANT TO WAKE MAX," JACOB said quietly, appearing in Price's dining room by way of the swinging kitchen door. Laura gave him a searing look. Price reached for her hand, but she moved it. In fact, they weren't getting along tonight, as evidenced by the dinner Laura had prepared: spaghetti from a box and sauce from a jar. Indeed, the honeymoon was over. And Jacob was going to make sure it stayed that way.

Jacob said, "Is he in bed?"

"Jake, you can't be here," Laura told him.

"How is he?"

"Fine, if appetite is any indication," Price broke in. "He must have cleaned out three concession stands at Fenway."

"Did I hear he's been accepted to Belnap?"

Laura sighed.

"As an alumnus, I have certain privileges," Price explained, "not to mention friends on the Board of Regents."

"Sounds like a good deal for everyone," Jacob said.

"A win-win situation," Price agreed. "For once Maxie will be in an environment that challenges his intellectual curiosity."

"Yeah, and why would you want a kid around the house all the time?"

"Jake, that's not what he meant."

"Baiting," Price cautioned her. She sighed again.

"You're not putting him on Ritalin," Jacob said to Price. He wasn't asking.

"No, we're not. Of course, we feel differently about the matter."

"*We* haven't finished discussing it," Laura said.

"I don't mean to start trouble," Jacob said.

"You're not starting trouble," Price was quick to say.

"Okay, Jake, you need to leave," Laura said.

"I'm sorry," Jacob told her. "I am." His sincerity bought him another minute. "The reason I came over was to see if we could get together sometime and talk things over."

"We're not *supposed* to be talking," Laura shot back. "You're not supposed to be here."

"Laura?" Price motioned to her wine glass, meaning she'd had enough to drink.

"Give it a rest, I'm not one of your patients," she told him.

Jacob showed them his hands, an apology, then pulled up a chair and sat down. "Okay," he said calmly, "we all want to save Max the pain of a drawn-out custody hearing, with lawyers parceling out every little piece of our lives. I'm proposing we have a meeting somewhere, in a quiet restaurant—"

"What are you doing?" Laura peered at him, dark-eyed.

"No lawyers," he said. "To act as mediators, you could bring Price, I'd bring July. We'll have a nice dinner, a bottle of wine or champagne . . . on second thought, champagne goes to July's head."

His eye glanced Price's for barely an instant, but with enough of a glint to convey something man-to-man, something sexual. In fact, Jacob had no way of knowing how champagne affected July. It didn't matter—as long as Price believed it was true.

"Jake, no," Laura said firmly.

Price raised a finger, appealing for her indulgence.

"I am not having dinner with his girlfriend," she told him.

Price nodded patiently. "I hear your concern, that such a meeting might be uncomfortable for you."

"It's not uncomfortable for me," she told him. "I just don't see the point."

"Ah, the point. Scorpios need a point," Price said with a smile. "Like it or not, we're an extended family now, the four of us."

"Five," Laura said.

"Five," Price corrected himself. "And what a wonderful opportunity for us all to come together in the spirit of cooperation and mutual respect. For Maxie's sake."

"And then what," Laura said, "when it all blows up in our faces?" She gave Jacob a long, resonant look. He couldn't tell if it was suspicion he was seeing, or regret. Whatever, it tugged at his heart. Still, he persisted.

"We probably won't agree on everything," he said to her. "But at least let's give it a try."

Laura lowered her eyes.

Jacob looked over at Price, who offered a conciliatory shrug. "It might be a step in the right direction," he agreed, tossing Jacob the man-to-man glance that sealed the deal.

Jacob knew he could count on the good doctor.

WHEN he got home, Green Girls was dark. July's car was there, so he knew she was home. What surprised him was finding the front door unlocked. He thought of Alix, of Sereno, and went in quietly, his heart making its loud presence known.

Feeling around the wall, he found the light switch, and the grow lights came on, bathing the shop in warm daylight. The place was empty and still, while outside in the garden the overhead sprinklers rained noisily.

He climbed the stairs and found the twin switches, lighting the pantry and darkening the shop below.

Stepping into the living room, he half expected to see someone sitting in the dark. But the room was empty. He turned on the floor lamp, then went directly to the bedroom and pushed open the door. The bed was disheveled, blankets strewn. He flicked on the light, then crossed to the closet and opened the door, bracing himself as he did so. But, of course, the closet was empty too.

"July?" His own voice startled him. He listened for a response, but heard only the artificial rain slapping at the artificial rain forest, and tiny frogs filling the night with their toxic mating calls. Convinced at last that the house was empty, he went to the kitchen, where he found her note.

I'm sleeping in the garden.

Which may have been an invitation to join her, or may have been a warning to leave her alone. Jacob took it as a warning. He went into the bedroom, pulled the mattress against the door, opened his laptop, and wrote until he fell asleep.

49

WHEN JACOB SMELLED COFFEE, HE AWOKE, SLID THE MAT-tress back from the door, and wandered out into the kitchen. Looking out to the garden, seeing July walking with her pitchfork, he remembered his dinner plans with Laura and Price. He called down, "Thanks for letting me sleep late."

July went deeper into the garden as if she hadn't heard him. See-ing a tail of yellowish smoke working up through the foliage, he went down to tell her his plan, wondering what she was burning. As he neared the fire, he began hearing a quiet crackling, and he smelled the wood smoke stronger, a sour smell, probably scraps of his poplar burning.

"July?"

He found her behind the hut, standing with her back to him,

holding a pitchfork over a flaming charcoal grill, as though toasting marshmallows.

"Hey," he said as he made his way over to her. "I didn't want to wake you last night, so I slept in the house."

She acted as though she hadn't heard him, eyes downcast, while the yellow smoke went snaking around her. She was wearing a pretty butterfly-print dress, and she'd tied back her hair.

"You went to see her again," she said.

"Laura? Actually, I went to see Price," he admitted, knowing she must've driven over there and seen his car.

July turned toward him, her face shining with perspiration, strands of hair sticking to her cheek. Then he saw what she had on her pitchfork . . . Not marshmallows. Stuck on each of the four tines was a tiny yellow frog, the steel inserted deep in its gaping mouth, where thick white foam bubbled out.

Jacob stepped back.

On the ground beside her was a glass jar filled with the foam, and suddenly Jacob was thinking about what she had said—that one frog could kill a hundred monkeys . . . or ten humans.

She scowled. "I told you, I make insecticide with it."

"No, you said Alix made insecticide," he replied quickly, as if catching her in a lie. But, of course, Alix was no longer around to gather the poison.

July's gaze lingered on him, her beauty stunned him, yet her expression was absolutely unreadable. Was it anger? Fear? Sadness? Bewilderment? Although he couldn't help but feel sympathy for her, he was unflinching in his determination to break free.

"July, the only reason I went over there is because I think I know how to beat the lawyers."

She turned back to the grill and lowered the pitchfork nearer to the flame, and he heard a high-pitched squeal as more froth oozed out the wide yellow mouths and gathered on the tines.

"I've made a good deal of furniture over the years," he explained. "That's all I want out of the settlement—besides custody of Max, that is—my furniture. Price, on the other hand, owns a big new house with ocean views, a hot tub, nice car. He's got all kinds of money, belongs to the yacht club, eats at the best restaurants. What I'm getting at is, he's also got his image to maintain: the attentive, sensual, sensitive lover. How would it look if he took all my furniture?"

He felt her arm stiffen.

"That's why I arranged for us to meet with both of them for dinner tonight," Jacob said. "Just the four of us."

He touched her again, but it was like touching stone. He took an uncertain breath and thought he should say something else, but instead he walked away. The plan was in play, past the point of no return. As the frogs kept steaming, he wondered if he should ever have started.

He went into the shop and removed the clamps from the headboard, then began sanding his bridge replica top to bottom, back and front, until the seams disappeared and the green wood took on a pleasant grainy sheen. The bed would be his thank-you to July for taking him in. It would be his ticket out.

Later, when he was painting polyurethane on the wood, he kept glimpsing July in the garden, uprooting plants with her pitchfork or hacking them down with a machete-sized blade. In fact, by the end of the day it looked like she'd torn out half the vegetation and left it on the ground to die. He wondered if she'd forgotten to replace the broken pane of glass and the plants had died of a night chill; maybe insects got in through the hole; maybe she was simply thinning out some weak plants as a normal part of gardening. Then again, perhaps his dinner plans had unhinged her.

Mystery girl. That's what Evangeline had called her.

For some reason, maybe because the polyurethane was affecting his mind, Jacob's thoughts turned to another mystery girl—the one in the book, the one he'd left at the top of the bridge making love to Henry Lamb. As he brushed the preservative painstakingly over the top of the green arch, he could almost picture them up there, the two of them in miniature, standing together way up in the wind. Henry Lamb, out of work, out of money, who'd started his day with a simple flat tire and ended up so high above the rest of the world. . . .

Jacob stopped painting.

He backed away from his carpentry, gazing intently at the arch. . . .

Then he went upstairs and picked up the phone. His agent's message machine answered.

"It's Jacob Winter," he said, keeping an eye on July, out in the garden. "The girl inside the bridge," he said. "I just realized who she is."

A great time to figure things out. The young man plummets from the top of the bridge, his mind scattered in the ocean wind, reaching for the sky, silent, weightless, balanced against the crescent moon.

Time slows down as the trussed steel of the bridge whispers past. The young man can not only smell the river that rises to meet him, he has time to consider how a particular mustiness tinges the odor.

It's metabolism, the reason time slows down. Hummingbirds, for example, have such a high metabolic rate, they perceive human movement in slow motion. To a fruit fly, we are statues; their day on earth lasts a lifetime.

In humans, fear increases metabolism . . . which is why the victim of a car wreck will describe the accident as though it happened in slow motion. Extreme fear causes extreme time stall. What is the limit? It's long been acknowledged that some people who fall to their deaths actually die of heart failure before they land. Perhaps they die of old age.

In the 4.03 seconds it takes to fall 250 feet, from the top of the Piscataqua River Bridge to the water, a man can do a lot of thinking.

"You're going to be late."

Jacob spun in his chair.

July tossed him a disdainful look. "What's the matter with you?"

"I didn't hear you come up," he explained, and she walked away from him. He realized that his eyes were blurred with tears.

From the kitchen, he heard a cupboard door slam. He pulled his handkerchief from his pocket and blew his nose. Funny, he couldn't remember ever getting choked up from writing. Seeing that it was almost seven, he shut off the computer, then went into the bathroom and showered. When he was through, July was still in the kitchen, pouring rum into the blender.

He said, "Are you sure you won't come to dinner?"

"So you can all laugh at me?" Her voice had a hollow ring.

"July, I told you what this dinner was about."

"Because you can't stand to be away from your wife," she said, and started the blender.

"Come on," he laughed, trying to keep the conversation light, despite the volume he needed to compete with the shrieking machine.

July turned around. Her eyes narrowed, as if she could see exactly what he was up to. Or perhaps she was going to say something. She didn't. To Jacob, it was the gesture of someone who had just made a decision. Or so he hoped.

50

EVEN THOUGH THE SKY WAS AFLAME WITH A BEAUTIFUL SUN-
set, the harbor restaurant managed to be pleasantly gloomy. Jacob
had called ahead and reserved a table at the window, and he asked
the waitress to bring a bottle of twenty-dollar champagne on ice.
Ten minutes after he sat down, they came in. Jacob stood and
pulled out the chair to his left for Laura, but she took the seat
opposite him. Price sat on his right.

"Are you alone?" Price asked. Laura was already perusing her
menu.

"July wasn't feeling well," Jacob answered, though he knew that
if his instincts were right—she couldn't bear the thought of him
being with Laura—she'd show up any minute. "Champagne?"

"Probably best not to drink if we're discussing business," Price
suggested.

"I'll have a glass," Laura said.

"None for me, thanks," Price said, casting her a glance she did not meet.

Jacob could tell they'd probably had words on the ride. As he filled Laura's glass, she took a steno pad out of her purse and set it on the table, opened and ready for business.

"Before we begin," Price suggested, "I thought perhaps we might discuss preliminaries."

"My father's watching Max," Laura said. "I don't want him out late." Her way of telling Price to shove his preliminaries.

"At the tavern?" Jacob said.

"He's got the boy sitting up at the bar, eating microwave pizza and watching a car race on TV," Price said, then placed his hand gently on Laura's. "What do you say we establish the ground rules?"

She pulled her hand away and lifted her glass, started to take a sip of champagne, then suddenly looked off toward the door, her eyes narrowed. "Oh, it must be prom night."

Jacob didn't have to turn to know that July was on her way to the table. But he did turn. And July did not disappoint. Lightly across the floor she came, wearing a very short, very light summer dress, with obviously nothing on underneath. The fabric fell off her shoulders, touched her nipples and abdomen, and brushed her thighs with each step. Every other man in the dining room watched her entrance, and most of the women too. Jacob wondered if they could see the glare she focused on him as she came.

Price pressed his long fingers on the table and rose to his full height, then pulled out July's chair. Jacob stood when she arrived, but she pretended not to notice, nestling in the chair without speaking.

Knowing it was his place to make introductions, Jacob nonetheless took his time pouring July's champagne, waiting to see how the cards would fall.

Price played first. "I guess we could all use a little relaxing," he said, sliding his empty glass toward Jacob. "I'm Price Ashworth," he said to July, "but you must know that. This, of course, is Laura."

"His assistant," Laura said with a smile.

"Not outside the office," Price said, then explained, as though confiding, "Professionally speaking, Laura is my transcriptionist and office manager."

Jacob topped off his and Laura's glasses, emptying the bottle, then hailed the waitress, who came directly. She looked like a college student, young and fresh-faced. He gave her an attentive smile and said, "Another one, please."

"Looks like a celebration," the waitress joked.

"Something like that," Jacob said, not taking his eyes or his smile off her. He could feel July bristle beside him.

"And perhaps an order of oysters on the half-shell," Price added, saying to July, "If you have a weakness for oysters—I crave them—they're positively delectable here."

"Oh, do they raise their own?" Laura asked, as the waitress went away.

Price gave her a quizzical look, then turned back to July. As she reached for a dinner roll, her dress fell away from her breast. "Let me," Price offered, passing her the basket while pretending not to look, but Jacob could tell he was already examining the mental snapshot he had taken.

"Now, do I understand you specialize in esoteric plants indigenous to the South American rain forest?" Price said. "That must be a gratifying pastime, staying in touch with your roots." He cleared his throat to punctuate his witticism. "So to speak."

"And such a cute sundress," Laura said to July. "I remember when I could wear things like that."

"Don't be silly, you can wear anything you like," Price said. "I only questioned your choice of denim this evening because I know the restaurant, and I was concerned that you might feel conspicuous."

Laura ignored him.

"I always thought you looked amazing in jeans and a plain white shirt," Jacob said to her.

The comment was as much for July's benefit, and she responded more or less as he'd hoped, angling a probing glance at Price, who said, "If I were to guess, I'd wager your particular heritage was from the mountains—perhaps the north coast of Colombia."

"Does that make you a genius?" she said, sinking her thumbs into her dinner roll and slowly tearing it apart.

Price allowed a subtle, confident smile, as he buttered his roll with a surgeon's precision. "Tell me, July, did your family live in a *selva?*"

"What's a *selva?*" Jacob asked.

"I'm sorry," Price said. "Rain forest."

"Why didn't you say 'rain forest'?" Laura asked.

"The word *selva* has cultural connotations," he explained.

"Something else you'll have to teach me."

"Laura, I meant to ask," Jacob said, "when does Max leave for Belnap?"

Price answered: "As you might expect with such a school, there's an orientation session for incoming students. For Max, school would effectively begin the third week in August."

"Will they let him come home for weekends," Jacob asked Price, "or would that be your decision?"

Laura let out a sigh.

The waitress returned with the champagne and a plate of oysters. Setting the oysters down, she covered the bottle with a towel and uncorked it, wincing when it popped. "Beautifully done," Jacob said, catching her smile.

Ready to pour, she offered first to July, who turned her head away. Jacob nodded, and the waitress topped off her glass, then moved to Laura, who covered hers. Jacob did the same. "I'll stick with water."

"A smidgeon for me," Price said.

She poured, then turned to Jacob again. "Are you folks ready to order?"

Jacob looked at July, who seemed to be glaring at the oysters.

"Is everything okay?" the waitress asked.

Jacob smiled. "Maybe you should give us another few minutes."

As soon as she went away, Price picked up the conversation. "I've actually sailed along the Colombian-Venezuelan coast," he said to July. "Spent a long weekend in Cartagena. Have you ever been there?"

July lifted an oyster to her mouth. "Mmm," she said, which may have meant yes, may have meant no, or she may have been simply enjoying the oyster—except, with July, nothing was simple. The way she pressed the opened shell to her lips, the way her gaze turned inward when she sucked up the meat, it looked like an obscene kiss. As if on cue, both Price and Laura lifted their glasses and drank.

July reached her hand under the table. "I need to use your napkin," she said, swiping her hand roughly across Price's thigh.

"Didn't you get one?" he asked.

"I don't want to get it dirty."

"Who said chivalry was dead?" the doctor piped up brightly.

Jacob knew that July's seduction of Price was nothing but revenge—for his smiling at the waitress, his arranging this meeting with Laura. He could also tell, by the way Price was downing his champagne, that it was working.

"So," Jacob said to Laura, "how are negotiations going on your father's property?"

She tossed her menu on the table. "Excuse me," she said, getting up and heading for the bathrooms.

Jacob watched her weave a path between the tables. "I think I upset her," he said, taking his napkin off his lap and placing it on his plate. "Would either of you object if I went and apologized?"

"Not at all," Price replied. "I think that might be appropriate."

"July, okay?"

She responded by sucking another oyster indulgently from its shell, keeping her eye on Price.

Jacob excused himself, stood, and walked to the lobby. Momentarily, Laura came out of the ladies' room.

"Laura, I'm sorry," he told her. "Can we please talk?"

Shaking her head, she walked briskly past. He followed, saying quietly, "I was wondering if your parents ever told you why they got divorced."

She stopped, turned to face him, folding her arms as if pleasantly unaffected. "Could you be any more obvious?" She moved a step closer, if only to make sure they weren't overheard. "Trying to dump your little girlfriend on Price—do you think we're that stupid?"

"No, you're very smart, I've never doubted that. I mean, look at the arrangement you've worked out. Price gets your dad's property, you get Max into private school. That's a very intelligent relationship."

She stared at him, her eyes so familiar, so deeply a part of him. Suddenly he felt that if he wanted to take her in his arms—and he did, terribly—she would have wanted that too. But the moment vanished when she spun away from him and headed back to the table.

"Because of the racing accident," Jacob said, keeping pace.

Laura kept walking. "That's not why she left him."

Jacob pursued her through the dining room. "He told me that after the accident, your mom wanted him to quit racing. So he quit and got himself a steady job."

"I was there," she said, stopping again. A man and woman beside them continued eating, pretending not to listen.

Jacob lowered his voice to a whisper: "But she left him for another driver."

"No, she left him for a winner," Laura said, then closed her eyes as though wishing she hadn't said it. Nevertheless, inside Jacob's chest, he felt the awful emptiness return, and he stepped back, to let her go. Then she touched him. "A man who had money," she explained. "Enough to get us out of Lowell."

"Laura, she left your dad for a guy who liked to chase married women."

"You think she didn't know that?" Laura raised her voice.

Beside them, the woman put down her fork and stared unabashedly. Across the room, July watched them too, while Price talked on.

"Jake, I was fourteen years old. I was in a bad crowd, drinking, doing drugs. My mother was able to get me away from all that."

"For money," he said.

"She did what she had to," Laura said distinctly, her eyes deep and pained. With that, she walked to their table, where Price was speaking in Spanish, and July was giving Jacob the keen examination of a cat ready to pounce.

Laura did not sit down. "I'm leaving," she said.

"Not hungry?" Price asked with a clandestine smile, wanting to keep things under control.

"Don't get up, I'll call a cab," Laura told him, already walking away.

Price rose to his feet and folded his napkin on the table. "Her electrolytes are low," he explained, pulling three twenties out of his pocket and dropping them on the table. "July, it's been a pleasure." He took her hand. "Jacob?" He took Jacob's hand. Then he left, his poise intact.

Jacob took his place beside July, who stared at the champagne bottle as if she were trying to shatter it with her eyes.

"I guess that could've gone better," he said.

Then she left too.

Jacob took a drink of water. In fact, he thought it went just perfectly . . . until the waitress came with the check and an envelope addressed to: "Man with white shirt and moccasins."

Jacob gave her a curious look.

"Some guy found it in the men's room," she said. "Maybe you've got a secret admirer."

"In the men's room?" He looked around the restaurant to see if anyone was paying attention. No takers. "Where's the guy who found it?"

"Gone."

He added a twenty to the cash Price had left. "I don't need change," he said, "thanks."

As he made his way out of the dining room, he stuck his thumb under the flap and ripped the envelope open. A restaurant receipt was inside, with writing on the back: "IT WON'T WORK. STOP TRYING."

51

THE MOON WAS FADING IN THE WEST WHEN JACOB GOT BACK TO Green Girls. July's car was not in the yard. He'd expected that much. He let himself in and made his way upstairs, turning on lights as he went. In the kitchen, he made a full pot of coffee, then went straight to his computer, his novel. In a matter of seconds he lost himself, his fingers massaging the keys.

Metabolism rises. Time slows down. Henry falls slowly, as in a dream.

So slowly, in fact, that the police cars on the roadway appear stationary. A white and orange ambulance pulls out to pass, frozen in time. Policemen themselves cling to the misty bridge like spiders . . . poised on top of the arch, in the crow's nest, on catwalks, on rungs.

But wait—

Under the NEW HAMPSHIRE *sign, Henry spots his own car, its trunk still closed, his tire . . . is not flat . . . was never flat.*

The roadway rises.

Henry looks for the girl, he looks up and all around, but the girl is not falling with him. He notices that the airplane is stationary, a cross hung in the red sky, caught in the process of finishing the V in the statement JESUS SAV . . . *which, obviously, is* JESUS SAVES. *But why is the pilot still skywriting hours after he'd begun? Why haven't the letters blown away?*

Not because time has slowed down. Henry realizes this with a jolt—and suddenly he understands: Because it hasn't been hours. Because sometimes things aren't real. The boat, for example, now that he really thinks about it, the boat may have been a story he'd made up and told Dolores so convincingly that he ended up believing it himself. It's happened before in his life, that he's been fooled by his own mind.

Henry can see people crowding the banks. The people are real. The boats on the river are real. The cars on the bridge, and the police: all real. Dolores is real.

But the girl on the bridge, who's lured him to the top and beckoned with open arms . . .

Henry looks down, sees the red sky reflected in the river, tiny insects flitting across the surface, the backs of two hungry stripers.

The stripers dart.

Yes, indeed, a great time to figure things out.

JACOB pushed away from the desk and lay back in the chair. Tears broke quietly and ran down his cheeks, wetting his ears. He didn't know if it was exhaustion, the reason for his emotions, or relief that he was finally finished. Or perhaps his own life was finally catching up to him, now that he was no longer distracted by his book, by July's bed.

Then he stopped wondering about it.

A noise stopped him. Jacob got up from the desk, fast enough that his chair fell backward. He walked through the pantry and turned on the kitchen light.

"July?"

His voice was dry. Outside, in the garden, the overhead sprinklers had come on, and a sweet, warm mist rolled in through the open glass doors. The noise he had heard was a wooden creak, the sound of an old wooden floor underfoot.

"Hello?"

He went back to the pantry; listened down the stairs but couldn't hear anything over the sound of the rain in the garden. He returned to the living room, then to the bedroom and bathroom, wondering if July had slipped in while he was finishing his book. But her bed was empty and her car wasn't in the driveway.

Which meant his plan had worked, maybe better than he'd hoped. She was spending the night with Price. To be sure, he took out his cell phone and dialed. After two rings, Laura answered, quietly.

"I wanted to tell you," he began. "The book I started last week"—although he didn't know why he was telling her this—"I just finished. One week."

"Jake, it's four in the morning," she told him, more with incredulity than annoyance. He could tell that she hadn't been sleeping either. Tempted as he was to let her know that July never came home, he was not finding this victory as pleasing as he'd anticipated.

"I'm sorry to bother you," he told her. "I don't know why I called."

"Jake, what I told you last night," she fairly blurted before he had a chance to hang up. "About my mother, the reason she left my dad."

"Uh-huh."

"I always thought she did the right—" Laura's voice caught on the word. She stopped, and Jacob heard her sigh.

He said, "Are you okay?"

"I forgot," she whispered. "I forgot how much I missed him."

Then she hung up the phone.

52

THE SILVER SPEEDSTER SOARS THROUGH THE NIGHT LIKE A BAT, Sereno making his way northward along narrow black roads, past houses, trailers, and barns. He can *feel* the river, can *feel* the bridge, even though they're still miles away. Eventually, as the Porsche follows a long bend in the road, he watches the horizon fall away and the river take its place, widening, snaking through marshland and dune down to the sea, while off to the west, the steel bridge arches up in the sky.

But Sereno is troubled, and all at once he stops the car. There, on the riverbank, is a flower shop with a large attached greenhouse. But he doesn't need to get out of the car, doesn't need to taste the water to know. She is not here.

The Speedster is low on gas. Ahead of him a small square building sits on the opposite side of the road, with an illuminated sign and three vehicles parked out front. When Sereno shuts off his engine he can hear a steady thud of music coming from the place. He takes the keys out of the car, turns the steering wheel hard to the right, and pushes the Speedster down the bank. The warm river swallows it with hardly a splash. The music rises up in the night.

LITTLE BOB'S BAR AND GRILL, the sign said, but Sereno could not read it. The building itself, made of concrete, squatted in a clearing carved out of the Virginia pines. Only three vehicles were parked there: two new SUVs and a forty-year-old Ford pickup, two-tone turquoise and cream, with fat whitewalls.

When Sereno opened the door to the truck, the dome light came on, blinding him. There were no keys in the ignition, so he tried the Speedster's keys. That's when the men appeared, one at each of the doors.

"*Mexican,*" one of them said, as though he was cursing, "rippin' off my damn truck."

Three more males came around the corner, and three females, all wearing baseball caps, and they surrounded the truck.

"Just like they steal our jobs," said one of them.

The truck's owner opened Sereno's door, dangling his jackknife key ring. "Here you go, Pedro, you want the keys?"

Sereno watched him through his shades, the hollow pen in his mouth.

"I don't think he understands English," said one of the females.

"Maybe we should teach him," the owner said. "He looks like he wants a lesson."

The passenger door opened. "Welcome to our country, *señor.*" The young man ducked inside and punched Sereno's ear, knocking the sunglasses off. "This word means 'ass-kick.'" He reached in to haul Sereno out of the truck—which is when something curious happened. He twisted away with a curse, grabbing at his throat.

One of the women laughed as if he was clowning—until he suddenly stumbled backward and sat hard on the ground. "What are you *doing?*" she said.

He answered with a pitiful groan, then curled up, shaking.

"Sonuvabitch anthraxed 'im!" yelled one of the others.

In the moment of distraction, the truck's owner also collapsed beside his vehicle and began convulsing, looking like he was trying to eat his tires. At the same time, the old truck roared to life, sprayed gravel in his face, and went fishtailing through the lot, no headlights, no taillights.

Then it was gone, joining the night.

53

WHEN JACOB AWOKE IN THE MORNING, THE ROOM WAS HOT and filled with sunlight. He looked at his watch, saw that it was almost noon. An empty kind of satisfaction came over him as he remembered two things in quick succession: he had finished his novel the night before; and July had stayed out all night, most likely with Price.

He suspected she hadn't come home because the bedroom door was closed as he'd left it; if she'd returned in the morning, she certainly would have awakened him to goad him with her infidelity— or simply for the pleasure of waking him.

Then he heard her voice through the walls. He picked up his head. Yes, it was July having a conversation—probably talking to Price on the phone. Hearing the ring of silverware, he realized . . . of course, she had brought Price back here to give Jacob the full treatment—which was better than he'd hoped. He could pretend indignation, pack up his things, and be free of her for good.

He got out of bed, put his pants and shirt on, and went out to the kitchen. His heart stopped.

"Hey, Dad!"

Max was sitting at the table, his back to the opened sliding doors. July was standing at the stove, giving Jacob a smile. She said, "We thought we'd surprise you."

Heart rapping at his chest, he went over to Max. "What are you doing here?"

"It was cool," Max told him. "She called Mom, then came and got me at summer school."

July said, "Actually, it was 'Miss Finch' who called—you know, the girl who's always calling you?" She gave him a covert glance that told Jacob she'd pulled a fast one—pretending to be calling Laura from his attorney's office so that Laura would instruct the school to release Max early, to Miss Finch's custody.

"Max, don't drink that," he said.

"Jacob?"

Though July wore an expression of innocent perplexity, he was suddenly thinking about the drugs in Max's grape soda, wondering now: was it Alix who had tried to poison him—or July?

"He's not supposed to have sugar," Jacob explained.

"It's unsweetened grape juice," July said, pouring a glass for him from the same pitcher. "Jacob, you're acting crazy. Sit down. I made a nice breakfast. Fruit salad, veggie omelettes, and home-made blueberry muffins. Everything healthy." As if there had been no trouble between them, no dinner with Laura, no night with Price.

"Max, remember your manners," he said. "Wait for the host."

July gazed blankly at him while she poured a glass for herself and drank it down. Then she went back to the stove, saying, "I wanted to do something nice for you."

Max gave his father a curious look, which Jacob furtively shook off. "Maxie, why don't you move over here," he said, pulling a chair out from the side of the table, but a thick manuscript—in fact, his manuscript, *Bridge*—was already sitting on the chair.

"Oh, I printed it out for you when I came home," July told him, picking up the manuscript and setting it in the middle of the table. "You were fast asleep—you must have worked so late."

Still holding the chair, he said, "Maxie, please. It makes me uncomfortable seeing you so close to the edge."

"Max isn't afraid," July said. "Are you, Max?"

"Really, like I'm gonna fall out of my chair," Max said, offended that Jacob had treated him like a baby.

"I'm sorry," said Jacob, sitting down. "I guess I'm a little nervous about your missing school."

"Your dad's a nervous Nellie," July said. With a potholder, she lifted the cast iron pan from the flames and carried it to the table behind Jacob. For a moment he waited for the skillet to crease his skull. But she reached past him and set it on his manuscript, then cut the omelette into three pie shapes, the sharp knife squealing against the pan. "Maxie, take your pick," she said.

Max pointed, and she served him with the blade. He lifted his fork.

"Max, wait for everyone," Jacob said. He wanted to move the frying pan off his manuscript, imagining the title page charring, oil soaking through, but he let it sit. July served him next, then took a piece for herself.

"That's your new book?" Max asked.

"Uh-huh."

"Cool. I didn't even know you were writing one." Max kept his eye on Jacob, his fork poised.

"Maxie has such good manners," remarked July, sitting opposite Jacob. "Muffin, hon?"

Jacob looked up, wondering if she was addressing him. But she'd slid the pastry dish toward Max. He took one. Jacob refused. July took one for herself. She cut it and it steamed, and she spread butter on both halves, taking her time doing so. She looked so poised, so triumphant, refusing to take a bite of her food . . . while Max sat watching Jacob.

"Dad?"

"Wait for the host, Max."

Did she feel justified in spending the night with Price because Jacob had spoken to Laura? Did she feel justified terrorizing him? What else would she feel justified doing?

"I thought you'd like to see your son," July said, staring at the butter as it melted. "If it's a problem, I'll take him back."

"That's okay, I'll take him," Jacob said, not wanting Max to see them having a spat.

She put her knife down, hard. Jacob imagined her pushing the table into Max, imagined watching his son disappear over the ledge. With the side of her fork, she cut a corner off her omelette and put it in her mouth, glaring at Jacob while she chewed and swallowed. He gave Max a nod, and they both started eating.

"You're going to like your dad's new book," she said to Max. "It's about a man stranded way up on the bridge." Max ate without responding. "And a mysterious, beautiful girl he falls in love with." She shot Jacob a teasing glance, too obvious for Max to miss.

Jacob stood up. "Max, I'm sorry. I've got to take you back to school."

Max screwed up his face.

"The girl turns out to be a siren," July said. "Max, do you know what a siren is?"

"That's enough," Jacob told her, his warning tone unmistakable. He took the fork out of Max's hand, then led him around the table. "Did you bring anything with you?"

Max scowled. "Just my backpack."

"In Greek mythology, a siren is a beautiful woman who lures men to their deaths," July explained calmly, while Jacob found the backpack on the floor. "Isn't that right, Jacob?"

"I'll come back for my things," he told her.

As he drove Max back to school, Jacob phoned Price's office, hoping to reach Laura, but he got the answering machine.

"Mom didn't go to work today," Max told him, so he tried calling her at home but once again reached a machine. He left a message that he was returning Max to school. Then he called Squeaky's house, but no one answered there, either, so he left the same message. When he dropped Max at school, he told the secretary that Max was never again to be released to anyone except his parents or grandfather. Then he was back in his car, phoning Alligator Alley Correctional Institution.

"If you're not going to give me your number, you need to check in more frequently," Warden Latham said when he took the call. "We've got some new developments."

"Has he been found?"

"No. But he surfaced."

"Where?"

"I think it's probably time you told me the whereabouts of this young lady he's hunting for."

"Tell me where he surfaced," Jacob said, "and I'll tell you if he's close."

"Virginia," said the warden. "Critically injured two young men and stole one of their vehicles."

Jacob said, "So he's moving north."

"That's right," said the warden. "I take it north is the right direction."

"That's right."

"You need to know something else," the warden said. "We've also got a prison guard missing."

"What does that mean?"

Latham paused. "I'm not proud to tell you this," he said, and he paused again. "The DEA knows that a significant amount of heroin and cocaine used to funnel through this prison—before I came aboard—and from here, on to the entire Florida correctional system . . . that is, until the day our friend Sereno murdered Mr. Kiefer, at which point the supply dried up. And somewhere in the neighborhood of two million dollars disappeared."

"Sounds like Mr. Kiefer was a powerful man," Jacob said, but his thoughts had returned to July, wondering how much she'd known about the business Kiefer was in, how she had acted with him, indeed, whether she'd been in business too.

"I'm talking about the entire Florida correctional system—from this facility," Latham said. "Now, even though Sereno's wife gave up a few names in exchange for immunity and witness protection—mostly Colombian drug runners and small-timers—the feds never learned the identity of Kiefer's prison contact. They did know it had to be someone here at Alligator Alley . . . cook, dental assistant, deliveryman—"

"Or one of the prison guards," Jacob said.

The warden hesitated again, then heaved a frustrated sigh. "His name is Bishop. Supposedly, he was Sereno's hostage. But we've been taking a closer look."

"Wait a minute." Jacob pulled his car onto the drawbridge, heading back to Green Girls to get his things. "You're saying this guard Bishop helped Sereno escape?"

"Possibly. Or possibly set it up."

Jacob's wheels hummed noisily over the grated surface. He was beginning to get an understanding of the web he'd wandered into.

"Why are you telling me this?"

"Two reasons," Latham said after a moment's hesitation. "One: You could help confirm my suspicions about this man Bishop. Maybe his name will ring a bell with Sereno's wife; perhaps she had an opportunity to meet him."

"I'm not sure I can get that kind of information," Jacob told him.

"The other reason?" said Latham. "I'm wondering how well you know this woman. For instance, the reason she was kicked out of Witness Security?"

"Tell me."

"Well," Latham said, "three years ago she tried to have Sereno killed."

Jacob's heart stopped. His car left the bridge, the tires growing quiet on the asphalt.

"You weren't aware of that incident."

"No."

"Neither was I," Latham continued, "until today, when I was going over some old records. It was another inmate, some small-potatoes enforcer, he went after Sereno with a shiv. Woulda finished him too, except for the heroic actions of one of the prison guards."

"Bishop."

"You got it. Singlehandedly waded through the other prisoners and disarmed the man—who later admitted to the feds he'd been hired by Sereno's wife."

Nervously checking his rearview mirror, Jacob turned down Bow Street, staying alongside the river.

"Couldn't blame her, really," Latham went on. "After what he did to her? They decided not to prosecute. But her little trick got her booted out of the program just the same."

"I don't understand," Jacob said. "Sereno kills Kiefer, then makes off with two million dollars of Bishop's money. Why would Bishop save Sereno's life?"

"Exactly."

Jacob answered his own question. "Because Sereno knew where the money was stashed."

"See where I'm going?" Latham said. "Only thing is, I don't think he does."

"What do you mean?"

"If you had two million dollars, would you be stealing cars and ditching them every time they ran out of gas? Would you be barefoot? Would you be wearing clothes you stole off a clothesline? Stealing food from McDonald's? The FBI believes the man is flat broke—and I believe they're right."

Jacob pulled out of Market Square, and the high bridge came into view.

"Which is why I asked you," Latham went on, "how much you know about this woman—his wife."

"You think she took the money?"

Indeed, the notion—which until now Jacob had avoided—could neatly resolve several small mysteries: It would explain how July and Alix were able to buy their riverfront house in the first place, then construct and maintain such an extravagant greenhouse— with so few customers to support the business. It would explain how Alix was able to come up with Jacob's bail money.

"If my hunch is right," Latham said, "y'all may be in more danger than previously thought."

Just before the I-95 on-ramp, Jacob pulled to the roadside to absorb all he was being told. "Does anyone know you're talking to me?"

"No. Does anyone know you're talking to me?"

"No."

"Good, let's keep it that way," Latham said. "But he's getting closer to you every minute—which means he's probably got her scent. Now you may want to gamble that we get him before he gets her. But that's not a bet I'd take. I think it's time you let us protect her."

Jacob said, "I'll call you later."

"This young woman," Latham said abruptly, to keep Jacob from hanging up. "I mean, how far do you want to stick your neck out for her?"

Jacob disconnected and dropped the phone on the car seat. Looking out at the massive bridge stretching out over the river, he thought of Alix Callahan again, wondering how she had stayed with July so long. Maybe the booze had made it possible, keeping herself in a constant stupor. And the sex. Or maybe she was simply afraid to leave.

Jacob peered up at the bridge, and again he imagined Alix jumping. Grabbing onto that ledge, maybe hanging by her fingers, swinging out to the catwalk . . . all to get away.

Maybe it wasn't Sereno she was getting away from.

WHEN he got to Green Girls, he was relieved to see that July was gone. Without hesitation, he went to the shop and started carrying the finished parts of the bed out to the garden hut, and that's when he got his first whiff of smoke. It didn't smell like burning wood, which she used to cook her frogs, but more a trashy smell. Putting it out of his mind—he wanted to get out of there before she returned—Jacob quickly put the bed together, sliding the rails into the head posts and foot posts so they would lock in place. Because July had no box spring, he had cut plywood to fit the rails, and set her mattress onto the plywood. Even though the finished bed took up half the floor space of the hut, it was a handsome piece of furniture, the headboard a good enough replication of the bridge to set Jacob on edge. He was glad he'd never see it—or her—again.

Right now, he was planning to gather his manuscript pages and computer, pack his clothes, drive to UPS, and ship the novel off to Maury Howard in New York, then go to work at the tavern. He'd stay in touch with Warden Latham. If Sereno stayed on course and reached New England, then Jacob would give him July.

Hurrying up the stairs, passing through the living room, the missing computer didn't register at first glance. But now, staring at the bare desk . . . Jacob dropped to his knees and looked under the desk, then went into the bedroom, searching through his backpack, and on to the kitchen, where he'd last seen his manuscript on the table. Smelling that smoke again, his heart hammered. She wouldn't . . .

Down the circular stairs he went, down and down, through the shop then stalking mindlessly out to her garden—

"July?"

Mindless of poison frogs, mindless of everything, he walked back toward the hut . . . then heard a snap underfoot. He stopped, lifted his moccasin, and saw a single keyboard key—the plastic letter *G*—pressed into the ground. And beside it, a *B* and *T.* Jacob fell to his knees and found the rest of his computer ground into the chewed-up earth, scattered among the torn branches and leaves. She had beaten the thing with her pitchfork, by the looks of it.

He wanted to scream but couldn't take a breath—

Then a spark of hope.

Marching back to the house, he went through the shop and out the front door, down the fieldstone walk to his car, where he threw open the door and pulled open the glove compartment. His backup disks.

Gone.

He turned back to the house, but he did not hurry. He walked in dazed disbelief, gray fieldstones passing slowly beneath his feet, though his mind was a red blur, and then he was in her garden again.

"You'd better not be here," he managed to say as he followed the path to the hut and around back.

With his first glimpse of the charcoal grill, he leaned against the back of the building and sank to the ground. Even though he'd prepared himself for the worst, here it was. A red gasoline can lay beside the grill near a rough circle of blackened soil. Flecks of ash lay scattered on the green leaves all around—his manuscript pages. Inside the grill, his computer diskettes lay curled and ruffled on the coals, black and smoldering.

54

FROM A POOLSIDE BAR, BIFF BISHOP MADE THE CALL. "WHAT'S THE good word?" he said when Latham answered.

"I've been waiting to hear from you," the warden said.

"Why's that?"

"Just wondered how you were progressing."

"Oh, progressing just fine, enjoying some well-deserved rest and recreation." Above the bar, a television showed a bass-fishing show. Beside him, a young girl stood on the pool apron trying to summon the courage to dive headfirst into the water. "How's things with you?"

"As a matter of fact, I've been wondering about a thing or two," Latham answered.

"Well, y'all *are* the wonderin' sort." The girl sprang out and slapped the surface hard, splashing chlorinated water up from her legs. A drop hit Bishop on the mouth and he dabbed it with his tongue. "Actually, I've been wondering myself: any word on that brown-skinned indigenous gentleman who worked so hard to earn your trust?"

Latham lowered his voice. "Biff, I got some people down here who would very much like to speak with you, you know, for whatever pertinent information you might be able to furnish."

Bishop chuckled. "More than I already furnished? Well . . ." The young diver was up on the apron again, examining her tan line against the red sting on her belly. "Like I said, I'm vacationing now. Tell 'em I'll be back in commission in a week or so, when I feel better."

"Biff . . ." Bishop could hear the hesitancy in the warden's voice. "Sereno will be in custody soon. We've had a positive ID."

"Yeah, Deltaville, Georgia. I saw something about that on TV. Pretty place, Deltaville. Overlooking the river, kind of an upscale neighborhood. Your kind of place."

Latham didn't speak for a few seconds.

Bishop said, "You mean a positive ID *after* Deltaville?"

"Biff, the Justice Department is offering a handsome reward for his capture. When he's found, some things may come to light."

Bishop took the remote off the bar and started searching for a news channel. "Hey, if y'all want, I'll cut my vacation short and recapture his ass for you. Who knows?—maybe I'll get that promotion after all. Hot dog. Make sergeant 'fore I'm sixty."

"Biff, they're quite persistent about you coming back here to help with the investigation."

"I see. They want my help down *there*."

Bishop stopped on a channel. And there he was, Sereno, his mug shot filling the screen.

"Well, speak of the devil," Bishop said.

CUT TO: Yellow police tape fluttering in a breeze, state troopers and detectives walking inside the crime scene. A roadhouse just behind, with the sign LITTLE BOB'S BAR AND GRILL.

"Biff, they do not want you in pursuit."

CUT TO: A Porsche being hauled out of the river; a road sign reading DEEPWATER.

"Where the hell is Deepwater?" said Bishop. Then he saw the tow truck's insignia, and he answered his own question. "Virginia, you say?"

WIDEN: The sign, the dripping Porsche, a florist's shop and greenhouse . . . and Bishop took notice. The house in Deltaville, Georgia—the last place Sereno had struck—also had a greenhouse attached.

"Let me see if I got this right," Bishop said to the warden. "Y'all don't want OIC Bishop in pursuit of the prisoner who stole his vehicle, took him hostage, and left him for dead."

"I believe you can take that as a direct order," said Latham.

CUT TO: The roadhouse; the police tape; and rising in the background, a tall, skeletal arched bridge above the treetops, a flashing beacon on top. . . .

While the warden continued talking, Bishop suddenly leaned forward, staring hard at the television . . . a single, clear thought dawning on him: The bridge looked exactly like the one he had seen in Deltaville. Same shape. Same construction. Same color.

"Well, then," Bishop said, "I guess you'd best cancel that promotion, then. 'Cause I earned this vacation, and I'm damn well gonna enjoy every last minute of it."

He hung up the phone, drained his drink, then pushed himself off his bar stool and said to the bartender, "Y'all got a decent library in this tourist town?"

55

WELL, DON'T YOU LOOK LIKE A BUCK NINETY-FIVE,"
Squeaky said, when he let Jacob in the back door.

Walking past him and on down the stairs, Jacob went behind the
bar and grabbed the box of napkins, the bin of silverware, then sat
on a bar stool and started putting together setups for the night.

"Whadda you, got a week to live?"

"I'll be fine."

"Don't wanna talk, no sweat off my brow," Squeaky said.

Jacob tried to dullen his mind in the quiet rhythm of his work,
but it did little good. He was aware that the old man was lingering
behind him. "Do you have something to tell me?" he asked.

Squeaky fluttered his lips. "To tell you, nope." Walking away, he
added, "Except it's your last day."

"You're firing me again? Fine."

"Nope, it's my last day too."

Jacob turned on his bar stool.

"He heard that, didn't he?"

"You're selling it . . . to Price Ashworth?"

"Kinda tough to do that, since I stuck a 'No gold diggers' stipulation in the deed," Squeaky said, "not to mention, him and Laura just parted company."

Jacob's heart leaped. He dismounted the stool and followed Squeaky into the back room. "Just tell me."

"Tell you what, she quit her job and they're moving in with me?"

He pushed past Jacob and returned to the front, dealing glass ashtrays down the length of the bar.

"Squeaky, don't screw around."

The old man smirked. "Laura and Dr. Asswipe had a little beef," he said, obviously delighted. "So she gave her notice, effective immediately. Doneski. Unemployed. Which means she can't pay rent, which means she and the little man are moving in with me. Meanwhile Dr. Asswipe thinks all he has to do is up the ante and I'll turn this place over to him. He called this morning, up to a million now."

"He offered you a million dollars?" Jacob examined the old man long enough to know he wasn't kidding—about any of this.

"You gonna stand there with your mouth open?" Squeaky said. "Get the setups done."

Jacob returned to his bar stool, head spinning. Over the next minute or so, silverware seemed to find its own way into the napkins. Suddenly life didn't seem half so bleak. So his novel was gone. Judging from past experience, the world wouldn't miss it.

"You want a few hours, come by tomorrow," Squeaky said, carrying two cases of beer from the back room. "I'm gonna need some help gettin' the Spite House ready for the new owners."

"What are you going to do with yourself?" Jacob said when the old man walked past him. "I mean, without the tavern."

"You didn't think I planned on slingin' beer the rest of my life," Squeaky answered, squeezing behind the bar. "You're lookin' at Jeff Dakota's new crew chief. I hit the road in two weeks. Pennsylvania Five Hundred coming up in Pocono. Then off to Indianapolis for the Brickyard Four Hundred."

Jacob couldn't help but admire the old man, who bent down to stock the beer cooler, acting as if the career change were nothing, loading in bottles six at a time. When he stood, he said to Jacob, "Listen to this."

Jacob listened.

"Just between you and me," Squeaky said. "Laura don't know this."

Jacob waited.

"Her mother came back. Ten years after the fact. She shit-canned the other guy. Laura was off at college. I'm here, everything sailin' along as usual, closin' up one night. Bang, she shows up." Squeaky chuckled, with a faraway look. "So we sit down together, that little table over there. I open up a bottle of my best wine. We're actually havin' ourselves a laugh or two. Then she pops the question."

Jacob said, "She asked if you'd take her back?"

Squeaky chuckled again, in a more resigned way. "Genius that I am, I said no." He pulled a rag out of his back pocket and wiped the bar as he walked away. "And that, my friend, was a doozy."

56

"TALK ABOUT DECADENCE." PRICE ASHWORTH MOANED WHEN he'd swallowed the first bite of his dessert, a chocolate torte layered with ganache and finished with butter creame frosting, "God must be a French pastry chef."

July sat across from him at Aquiline Gardens, Price's favorite breakup restaurant. He knew this wouldn't be easy. They had been together on and off—mostly in bed—for nearly twenty-four hours. With the moon rising over the river, and the water slapping at the wharf outside their window, Price raised his glass of port and gazed across the table at her.

"Not only are you stunningly gorgeous and incredibly passionate," he said, "but you are also the most uncannily perceptive woman I have ever known."

July returned a full glance, candlelight flickering in her eyes.

He gave her a tender look. "You seem distracted."

"I'm afraid."

"Of?"

"What he might do."

Price watched for a moment as she drained her glass. "You're talking about Jacob."

She lowered her voice. "I'm afraid to go home. You know how jealous he is."

"What is jealousy but fear with a romantic name?" He took a bite of his torte and his face melted in rapture. "We're such complex creatures, we humans. Do you know we're the only species that attempts to separate love from life's other negotiations?"

July stared at him, eyes slightly narrowed.

"Even in the most idealistic of relationships—take the two of us, for example: unencumbered, independent—love is nothing more than a series of negotiations. You give yourself to me, I give myself to you. Except"—Price produced a philosophic smile—"what is it we withhold?"

He held the smile as the waitress arrived with the check, then he continued with his discourse. "Interestingly, many studies point out that the inability in humans to enjoy a lasting relationship has to do with their difficulty in negotiating the materialistic stuff of love."

"Jacob has a gun," July replied.

"I see." Price looked around in hopes she hadn't been overheard.

"I think he shot Alix on the bridge."

Leaning forward, Price said in a hushed voice, "Speaking of confidential."

Her gaze darkened. "I'm afraid he's going to do you next. Jacob is very smart, you know. It would look like an accident—or suicide."

Though Price's confidence was waning, he rested his chin in his hands and replied in a patronizing way, "I'll keep an eye on him."

July's eyes dropped to her plate.

"Now as I was saying, about the negotiations of love—"

"Jacob could also have an accident."

Price's mouth opened, presumably to reply, then he had a second thought. "July, I need you to hear this in the right way. I'm not sure if you're aware that Alix used to see me."

She studied him.

"Professionally, of course. But outside of our sessions together, we had also entered into a business arrangement wherein she agreed to become the principal investor in a business venture of mine."

July's gaze darkened.

"How to put this so it doesn't sound mercenary . . . I have tape-recorded testimony from Alix—a confession, if you will—detailing the events concerning a Mr. Kiefer, and how you came to acquire a considerable sum of "—Price looked around the dining room again, then softened to a whisper—"*money.*"

Taking five twenties from his wallet, he looked around for the waitress. "Maybe we should . . . I was going to say, would you like to continue this while I walk you to your car?" He looked at his watch. "Frankly, there's not much more to say. I know you'd like certain information to remain confidential—your identity, of course, along with the aforementioned incidents." He wrinkled his brow as if to minimize his demands. "And I deserve consideration for the legal jeopardy that accrues to me for withholding knowledge of a felony, not to mention what could happen if certain, shall we say, adventurous parties were to learn that I knew your whereabouts."

July dropped her eyes to the table.

"Of course, you should consider this strictly as an investment, but I do think something along the lines of "—he showed her eight fingers—"*hundred thousand.* Which, incidentally, was the same figure that Alix had agreed to invest."

July removed the napkin from her lap and folded it carefully.

"Of course, as principal investor, you will begin earning dividends once the business becomes profitable."

She set the napkin on the table and started to get up, but Price put his hand lightly on hers.

"I probably don't have to mention that I've documented details of my offer in a sealed affidavit, to be opened by my attorney in the event of "—he shrugged—"an accident?"

He smiled again, as if July might share his humor. Indeed, the look she returned may have been one of amusement: a seductive sort of glimmer had crept into her eye.

Removing his hand from hers, he said, "I was a little worried about how you might take this."

He began to stand and pull out her chair, intending to walk her to her car, when she said, "I'll be fine."

Something about the way she said it, the emphasis on the word *I'll,* made him sit back down and watch her leave.

57

IN THE SPEEDWAY TAVERN, THE NIGHT BARELY CRAWLED. BY eleven o'clock, business hadn't shown any sign of picking up. A few couples and foursomes had drifted in for drinks during the course of the night, and they all wished Squeaky well, but no one stayed long. The four or five regulars sat at the near end of the bar and watched car race after car race on TV—as always—while Jacob rinsed beer glasses in the back room, wishing that Squeaky would just say his good-byes and send the stragglers home, so he could go find a place to sleep.

Tomorrow, first thing in the morning, he'd start looking for a job. Maybe he'd go to work for the cabinetmaker Squeaky had told him about. Maybe he'd find a house builder who needed help. The more he thought about it, the more he began to feel relief at not having another novel to toil over, agonizing over imaginary characters and trying to force them into some kind of story. Life was not a plot. Life was unstructured tedium. There was no balance, no redemption . . . and never a happy ending.

When he was nearly finished rinsing glasses, Squeaky stuck his head in the doorway and said, "You wanna feel better? Get a load of the poor bastard in the corner."

Jacob stepped to the door and looked toward the far end of the bar, where a thin young man sat with his back to them, holding a coffee cup in both hands as if warming them. The guy wore a baseball cap low on his face, which was turned up toward the television.

"Go see if he wants any more coffee," Squeaky muttered, "and get a load of the mug."

"What do you mean?"

"The face. Try not to gawk."

Jacob picked up the coffeepot and walked to the end of the bar. "Warm it up for you?"

"Don't make a scene," whispered the guy, not turning.

Jacob jumped back and an arc of coffee jumped from the pot.

Alix Callahan eyed him from the shadow of her brim. "We need to talk," she said quietly.

Jacob only stared. The sides and back of her head, which showed under her cap, had been shaved to a fine stubble, and she wore a green lumberjack shirt with the collar raised.

Knowing that Squeaky was watching their conversation, Jacob turned his back to him and spoke casually. "She's all yours," he said. "I never wanted her in the first place."

Alix tossed a couple of dollars on the bar. "I'll wait in your car."

"Good. I'll tell Evangeline where she can find you."

Alix pulled a yellow floppy disk out of her lumberjack pocket.

"What's that?"

She dropped the diskette back in her pocket as she swung off her stool. "I made you a back-up."

"My novel?"

"We need to talk," she said again.

Jacob leaned closer. "I've got all the trouble I need because of you," he whispered.

She shook her head at him, while they matched glares. "You

have no idea how much trouble you're in," she said, and walked out the door.

Nerves jittering, Jacob walked the length of the bar, trying to avoid Squeaky, who stood there nodding his head. "You must be a helluva writer, don't know the meaning of the word *gawk*."

Jacob took off his apron, heading for the back room. "I need a break, okay?"

"I mighta figured some weirdo comes in, you'd be involved. Cripes, it looks like a dog tried to take off his cheek."

Jacob tossed his apron in the corner. "Okay?"

Squeaky raised his hands. "By all means. You need any money from the cash drawer?"

"I'll be right back."

HE went through the storage room, up the stairs, and out the back door. The parking lot was dark, illuminated only by a light above the door and a single yellow bulb that hung on the porch of Squeaky's Spite House. Seeing Alix's silhouette sitting inside his car, Jacob approached cautiously.

"Hurry up," she told him, keeping her eyes on the road below.

Jacob watched her closely, ready to run if he saw anything in her hand.

"If I wanted to hurt you," she said, "I've had a thousand opportunities."

"If you wanted to hurt me?"

She said, "You can't go back to her tonight."

"I wasn't planning to," Jacob told her. "I palmed her off on your old friend Price Ashworth. You know how that goes."

Alix watched the road. "Unfortunately, July isn't totally imperceptive. Would you please get in?"

Steeling himself, Jacob walked around the car, opened his door, and slid in behind the wheel. He pulled the door closed, but not all the way, just enough to extinguish the interior light.

"See if I've got this right," he said. "You hear about Price Ashworth losing his medical license in Maine for having sex with a patient. And you figure that he and July would be perfect for one another. So you become his patient, intending to dump July on him. But it backfires. Under hypnosis, you end up saying too much."

She said, "Where's your son?"

The five-second stare. "Out of state," Jacob lied, not about to give her any information.

"Does July know where?"

He balked again, and she handed him the diskette. "When did you get this?"

"Before July came home."

"So that was you last night . . . and you who sent me the note in the restaurant." He peered across the darkness, trying to see her face. "'Local Author Arrested in Domestic Assault.' You must've thought you'd found her the perfect match."

She sighed. "I apologize."

He blew a bitter laugh. "You apologize," he said. "And now you've come back. Why, to set things right?"

She said, "Maybe I sobered up."

He shook his head at her, not accepting the answer. "Alix, I know what happened in Florida."

She shook her head. "Are you listening to me?" she replied, then suddenly peered down at the dark street, where a pair of brake lights glowed. "Jacob, get down."

"What?"

The reverse lights came on, and the boxy station wagon started backing up.

She lunged at him. *"Down."*

Slumped together across the seats, they heard the Volvo quietly climbing the driveway.

"What's she doing?" Jacob whispered.

"*Shh.* She can't help herself."

The car stopped beside them, headlights off, engine purring. Jacob could feel the pounding of Alix's heart through her back. Then the Volvo moved away, its engine noise diminishing. Jacob peeked up over the dash, saw the brake lights glow down at the street, then the dark wagon drove off.

Alix took hold of the door handle, seeming genuinely frightened. "I've got to go," she said. When she stepped out of the car, the way she surveyed the darkness reminded Jacob of a cat. "Don't let her find you," she told him, and began walking away.

"Alix, I know what happened in Florida," he said again.

She stopped short. "You don't know," she told him.

"Her real name is Juliette." Jacob spoke quietly, confidently. "In Florida her husband tried to murder her, but you came to her rescue. Sereno was sent to prison. July turned in a few drug contacts and went into witness protection. Then she hired someone to kill him, but it backfired, and she got kicked out of the program."

Alix shook her head. "You don't know a thing," she said, and walked off into the night.

Jacob knew she'd be back.

58

At one-thirty, when Squeaky closed the tavern for the last time, Jacob walked to his car with a liter of bottled water and a bag of pretzels—his bedroom, his breakfast—and the diskette containing his novel tucked in his shirt pocket. Not wanting to involve Squeaky in his problems, he planned on finding a logging road up by Mount Agamenticus and sleeping in his backseat until the sun rose. Then he'd decide what to do with the rest of his life. He was too tired to figure it out now.

Maybe he'd telephone Max and see if he wanted to go camping for a few days. Maybe if he got Laura on the phone, he'd see if she wanted to come too. Maybe they could all pack the car together, the tent and stove and sleeping bags, and take a long vacation. Maybe he'd call Evangeline and tell her everything, or he'd call

Latham back and tell him where he could find July. But, he realized, that would expose Alix to a vendetta from the drug world. And perhaps himself. And Laura and Max.

Right now, he needed sleep. In the morning he'd be able to put things in better perspective.

He got in his car and stuck his key in the ignition, and a voice whispered in his ear: "Don't jump."

"Jesus!"

In the backseat.

"I've got to tell you something," Alix said.

"I already know too much."

"Portsmouth," Alix told him. "Go to the salt pile."

"Look—"

"Jacob, drive."

HEADING over the Old Route One draw bridge, she stayed low in the backseat, though every now and then Jacob would see her in his mirror, peeking out the rear window. "We're not being followed, if that's what you're worried about."

"You wouldn't know if we were," she said, as he left the bridge and started wending his way through the sleepy, narrow streets of old Portsmouth. "July's father was an American missionary in Colombia," she began. "Reverend Arthur Whitestone. He and his wife lived in a walled-in compound. They had a maid, a gardener, and a cook—all young Kogi women with whom the Reverend had sex routinely. I heard the stories from other Kogis when I was there doing research. Eventually one of the women got pregnant: the cook."

"Right, July's mother. I know the story."

"If you knew the story, we wouldn't be here."

He worked his way over to Market Square, where a few late night stragglers were shadowing the sidewalks. Other than that, the town was deserted.

"After the cook gave birth," Alix went on, "it became obvious to the villagers that her baby was part white. Reverend Whitestone, being the only gringo she'd had any contact with, eventually confessed his sin to his American wife. Because Mrs. White-stone couldn't have children of her own, the Christian couple ended up adopting the baby and firing the cook—who was subsequently banished from Kogi society. The American couple named their little girl Juliette."

"July already told me," Jacob said. "Look, I'm very tired—"

"To Mrs. Whitestone's credit, she forgave her husband and raised the little girl as though she were her own," Alix continued, undeterred. "Showered her with affection, bought her American clothes and toys and dolls, brought in American nannies, and tutors to home-school her. They watched American TV and movies, listened to American music. But little Juliette preferred the company of the Kogi servants, and by the time the girl was ten, she was running away and painting her face and chewing coca with the Kogi boys."

"When she was twelve, she snuck off and married one of her cousins," Jacob said.

"That's right," Alix said. "And the Reverend and Mrs. Whitestone, who refused to recognize the marriage, decided that drastic steps were needed. They sent Juliette to a private school in Arkansas. Three months later she came back."

"Why?"

"She was expelled. I don't know why. Use your imagination. Slow down."

He did. A huge cargo ship—a salt bulker—was docked in the river beside the salt pile, a white, conical mountain that rose off the pier. Jacob pulled over, waited for a milk truck to pass him.

Alix looked around nervously. "Turn off your lights and drive around back."

He did as she'd instructed, pulling around the salt pile, where he spotted a new white Taurus.

"Yours?" he asked.

"I borrowed it."

He pulled close to the Taurus, hidden from the road. "Okay," he said, "July left private school and returned to her family in Colombia."

"Not her family. Her husband."

"Right, her thirteen-year-old cousin."

The way Alix's eyes pinned him in the rearview, Jacob felt a tingle crawl up his back.

"When July returned, she insisted on moving into the boy's hut. Kogi wives do not do that. They stay with the other women and their children. Men live separately. But July didn't like those arrangements. She wouldn't let the boy out of her sight. She would follow him to the *nuhue*—the men's lodge—where she'd flirt with all the other guys, trying to make him jealous. She insisted on going on hunts with him, she was always chewing coca—another taboo: girls and women are forbidden to indulge. Finally the boy brought her to the shaman and asked for a divorce."

"Brought her to Sereno?"

"That's right. And a few days later the boy disappeared."

Jacob looked around at the darkness of the docks. His insides had begun jittering.

"By the time he was found, there wasn't much left but bone and hair. The men who found him said it must have been a jaguar. But the boy's family suspected Sereno."

"Sounds like July must've made quite an impression on the shaman."

Alix said, "What do you know about him?"

"Sereno? Enough," Jacob said. "Raised in darkness, communicates with animal spirits, has sex with twelve-year-old girls. That's quite a religion."

"Yeah, nothing like a missionary screwing the converts."

Jacob shut up.

"Sereno was no ordinary shaman," Alix told him. "He was a legend among all the mountain tribes for his mystical and healing powers. When I was there, some people still prayed to him." Alix stopped talking and peered out the window, watching a car in the distance traversing the high bridge. "Anyway, after the boy's death, Sereno and July began spending a lot of time together—too much time for some tribespeople. Don't forget, July was the daughter of a white man many Kogis never trusted. Factions developed. Some people felt that July was an evil spirit sent to cast a spell on him. They came to believe that Sereno had transformed himself into the jaguar that had killed the boy. When he eventually took July for his bride, the *comisario*—he's the secular leader of the tribe—met with the *mayores,* the village elders, and they expelled them both."

"And they came north, to Florida," Jacob said.

"Because July was technically an American citizen, she was able to get Sereno a green card. July's father set them up in Plantation Key with a house and a three-lot parcel that was subdivided from a failed key lime grove. Sereno started fishing. July started raising native plants. That's when I found them." Alix was quiet for a second. "Do you understand now?"

"Understand?"

"The danger you're in."

Jacob shrugged. "Isn't it possible the kid was actually killed by a jaguar?"

"Jesus, do you think I jumped off that bridge because I wanted a thrill?"

He gave her a look. "You don't really believe Sereno turned himself into a jaguar."

She shook her head in disbelief, as though he hadn't heard a thing she'd said. "It wasn't Sereno who killed that boy."

He sat stunned, absorbing the implications. "You're not saying July . . ."

Alix opened the door and got out of the car. "I'm saying, anyone who ever tried to leave July is either dead—or about to be."

He shook his head, unwilling to accept what she was telling him—or unable. But things started making sense. The car without headlights that ran the white Caravan into Fecto's Explorer. Was it July—because she'd seen Evangeline with him at the baseball game? Or the night at the beach, when he hadn't seen her car pull up behind him . . .

"The first time you kissed her, she began to despise you," Alix said. "She's been following you ever since."

Jacob leaned over to his passenger window. "So she's got a jealousy problem. That doesn't mean she's a murderer."

"Oh, she's very jealous," Alix said, getting in the Taurus and starting the engine. "Unfortunately, it's not her problem."

59

A PAIR OF JASMINE CANDLES FLICKERED ON PRICE ASH-worth's night table. From his CD player came the sound of aeolian wind chimes ringing softly against the babbling of a brook. Price himself, unable to sleep, hung from his ceiling upside down, naked, his feet clamped inside his yoga boots, his long hair unbound, flowing freely to the floor. The only illumination in the bedroom came from deck lights shining through the stained-glass window he had created. It showed a butterfly feeding on ferns, an image Laura had said—when she told him to go fuck himself—looked like a kite tangled in a tree.

To Price, the butterfly was his *drishti* point, the object on which he focused his gaze to help center his mind. But he was far from centered, his thoughts stalking across a field of questions: Whether to phone Squeaky Frenetti in the morning and raise his offer on the property or wait till afternoon when the old man would have had his first beer. And July. Would she come through with the money—or fall apart, as Alix had? With July, you couldn't tell. Price had started negotiations high, prepared to be talked down, but the way she'd left the restaurant, saying, "I'll be fine"—may have meant she was willing to go the whole nut, or may have meant . . . what? *"I'll be fine."* July was not an easy read.

And what about Jacob? Price was pretty certain that July was only feeling the booze when she'd told him about Jacob's having a gun. And shooting Alix Callahan on the bridge? Didn't sound like Jacob. Although with his temperament, anything was possible.

Maybe, Price thought, he'd better write that letter he'd warned July about, and spell it all out. . . .

The wall clock interrupted his thoughts. The little wooden door sprang open and Krishna popped out—two oms. Price took a deep, calming breath and let it out slowly. That's when he noticed his butterfly move. At first he thought it was a vision, from the blood buildup in his head. He closed his eyes and gave his temples a light massage. When he opened his eyes again, the butterfly moved again, just a speck, enough so that he could tell the movement was real—actually a reflection from inside the room. Then he was stung.

"Jesus!"

He reached back with both hands, stretching under his arm, between his shoulder blades, then pulled the thing out of his back: a wooden-shafted dart, the kind used in dartboards. Then July was there, upside down, circling around him barefoot on his Persian rug, wearing a dress . . . and holding a revolver in her hand.

Price's mind leaped into gear. If you'd like to renegotiate terms, for heaven's sake, just say so. That's what he intended to say. But the moment he opened his mouth to speak, his heart kicked viciously and his chest seized up. Suddenly he couldn't draw a breath—couldn't inhale, couldn't exhale—as though someone had put a lock on his lungs. Christ, he couldn't even raise a hand to pull himself upright. The house started shaking violently, his antigravity supports rattling against the ceiling, the blood fizzling in his brain louder and louder, his vision exploding in light and color.

Then, as suddenly as the quaking had begun, everything went still. The dart dropped from his hand.

WAS this nirvana? Price hung there, staring. He did not even possess the awareness to comprehend that his mind had stopped. The totality of his consciousness was this: his bedroom, upside down. And silence.

Then he heard his own breath: a single short gasp.

Silence again.

He stared: His bed.

Another short gasp.

Silence.

Stare: His bed. His stained-glass butterfly.

Gasp.

Like a fish out of water.

Silence.

Stare. Bed. Butterfly.

Gasp.

Silence.

Stare. Butterfly. Bed. July . . .

Gasp.

60

WARDEN LATHAM ANSWERED ON THE FIRST RING, TIREDLY.

"Sorry to call so late," Jacob said.

"Are you okay?" Latham asked in a waking voice.

"I've had better nights," Jacob said. "Where is he now?"

"No one knows," Latham answered. "But Sereno may not be your biggest concern."

"What do you mean?"

"Are you alone?"

"Yes," Jacob said—or so he hoped. He was parked on the west side of the mountain, on a dead-end woods road, with his windows up and his door locked. Unable to sleep, every time the wind stirred he watched shadows steal through the trees.

"I've been doing some research into Sereno's trial," Latham

said. "After you hear this, you may think differently about that woman you're protecting."

Jacob said, "I'm listening."

Latham said, "Would you like to know the technicality that got Sereno acquitted of murdering that drug dealer, Kiefer?"

"Go ahead."

"Well," Latham said, "you do know that the jury found him guilty."

"You said he was acquitted."

"Because the judge wouldn't permit the jury's decision," Latham explained. "He called the entire trial a travesty and ended up throwing out Sereno's murder conviction and drug trafficking, and reducing the attempted murder on his wife to aggravated assault. Know why?"

Jacob sighed, not wanting to play a guessing game. "Tell me."

"On the attempt on his wife—whose name was Juliette Whitestone at the time—investigators found the blood of a third person at the scene."

Jacob already knew that Alix had been there, but he wanted to see how much Latham knew—and how much he'd reveal. "Whose blood?"

"That was never determined. Most likely, by the number of wounds on Sereno, it was someone who was helping Juliette."

"I see," said Jacob, unimpressed. "What about the murder charges?"

"You're not in the company of the young woman right now, are you?"

"I said I'm alone."

"Okay, the murder victim—Kiefer—when they autopsied his body they found his blood laced with something called *batrachotoxin*. I don't know exactly how to pronounce it, but it's no recreational drug. It comes from poison dart frogs in the Amazon rain forest."

Jacob's heart took a thud that he felt in his temples.

"By the looks of it, the man was paralyzed when he was stabbed," Latham continued, "and had to lie there and watch himself murdered."

Jacob saw something flutter past his window—a bat, he guessed. Once it passed, the night seemed darker than before. "And Sereno has this frog poison now?" he asked, trying to keep the shiver out of his voice.

"Don't miss the point," Latham said. "In Sereno's trial, prosecutors couldn't produce one witness who would testify to having any drug contact with him—which isn't, by itself, unusual in big drug cases. But the morning Kiefer was murdered, Sereno was five miles out to sea. His lawyer subpoenaed five independent witnesses—other fishermen—who swore to that."

Jacob pressed the phone to his ear while he kept his eye on the dark road below.

"Still there?"

Barely. Jacob's brain had all but seized up. "You're not suggesting it was Sereno's wife who killed Kiefer?"

"And made off with the money. A good lawyer—*any* lawyer—would've gotten the case kicked before it ever got to trial. But down in Monroe County, you got a Colombian Indian accused of various and sundry offenses, including he bit off his wife's finger? They couldn't wait to lock him up."

"And set *her* free," Jacob uttered.

"Worse," said Latham. "They lost her."

Jacob sat there, staring out at the night. The name Deborah McBride had come to him, the state senator who had chosen her political career over Alix Callahan and ended up burning to death while sitting in an overstuffed chair. It happened a couple of days after July learned that Alix had gone to visit McBride. Now Jacob knew why McBride had just sat there while the flames devoured her. And now he knew who had killed her. And why. His hand was shaking.

"You want to hear the kicker?" Latham said. "A few months after young Juliette tried to have her husband killed in prison, she started sending him Polaroids of herself. Naked. Nothing wrong with that, girlfriends and wives do it all the time. With this wife, though, we figured she was just trying to drive him crazy, using mailing services so the pictures came from all over the country.

Because she was no longer part of WITSEC, the prison officials let the photos go through."

Jacob remembered July telling him that she tormented Sereno. He guessed that was what she meant.

"Well, now we know the real reason she was sending him those pictures," Latham explained. "She'd soaked one or more of them with that same frog poison. Chemists found trace amounts on the other photos in his cell, probably from coming in contact with the impregnated one."

Jacob said, "You mean just handling the photo would be enough to kill him?"

"Kill him? Hell, she was trying to help him escape."

"Hold on," Jacob said, his head starting to pound. "If Sereno's wife was the one who murdered Kiefer, then she set up Sereno to take the rap—he already tried to kill her once—you're saying *she* was the one sending it to him, trying to break him free?"

"That's exactly what I'm saying. Yeah. The same woman you're risking your life to protect."

"Why?"

"Whys and wherefores, who the hell knows?" Latham said. "Maybe she's insane. But one thing's for sure. You need to tell me where we can find her. Now."

"I'll call you in the morning," Jacob said, and hung up.

61

THE MARYLAND FARMER WALKED THROUGH HIS KITCHEN AT FIVE in the morning, the eastern horizon glowing like chrome, more than enough light to start his chores. He'd done it this way for sixty years and would probably do it the same way till the day he dropped. He drank a glass of water to get his system going, then took his cap and jacket off the hook and opened the barn door. Stepped down to the spongy floor, felt his hip complain. Stomped his foot a couple of times to work out the creaks. Tina and Beauty rustled when he picked the shovel off the hook. Two cows milking, one beef critter on the hoof, three hogs getting fat. About all he could manage at his age. Truth was, he felt damn lucky to still get around, still do his chores. Lucky the old John Deere still ran for him. Lucky the pickup started every morning, which was nothing short of a miracle, considering how old she was and how hard he'd worked her over the years.

Yup. Some kind of luck, when you think about it. Here you got a billion people in China. A billion people in India. "And here we are, pretty as you please," he said, patting Beauty on the rump.

He went to the back and pulled up the latch, pushed the old door out. Swallows were flitting about through the sky, picking at their mosquito breakfast. Himself, he'd boil up some grits when he finished his chores. He propped the door open with a two-by-four and went to get the pickup—then stopped.

"Now there you go," he said.

Sitting under the old apple tree, where his old Dodge should have been, sat the most eye-popping two-toned Ford, turquoise and white, probably '64 or '65 vintage, with thick whitewall tires and a body that looked like it just rolled out of the showroom, shiny as could be. He went up to the window and saw the keys in the ignition, penknife dangling from a chain.

The farmer took a big breath of the morning air, took hold of the pickup's rail, and bowed his head. People starving in Africa, people uprooted all over the world, plague, famine, earthquakes, war. He prayed to God, saying, "Now why am I the lucky one?"

PART
FOUR

62

JACOB LEAPED AWAKE, DISORIENTED, HEART POUNDING. THE sun was in his face, hot and high over the trees. He was drenched in sweat, his car an oven. He peered dazedly out at the thick woods surrounding him. By the position of the sun, he figured it was late morning, but he felt as if he hadn't slept at all. Between the stuffiness in his car with his windows closed, and the mosquitoes when he opened them, he'd spent most of the predawn hours in a state of nightmarish delirium, thinking of everything Alix and Latham had told him—about Sereno, about July, the frog poison. Now all he thought about was protecting his family.

He started his car and backed out of the woods. As soon as he hit the hardtop, he tried phoning Laura, but no one answered. It was Saturday, he thought, she couldn't be picking Max up from school. Then he remembered Squeaky saying that Laura and Max were moving in with him, so he called Squeaky's house, but the phone rang and rang. Figuring they might be at the tavern, helping Squeaky prepare the place for the new owners, he drove there, keeping his eye on his mirror all the way.

"CLOSED UNTIL FURTHER NOTICE. COMING SOON: SEAVIEW INN." The banner hung over the tavern door. Sure enough, he saw Laura's car next to Squeaky's up in back, along with a large moving truck.

Jacob pulled up the drive to the parking lot, where a pair of men were carrying a bed up the stairs of the Spite House. But the bed—with a rectangular hole in the headboard . . .

"What are you doing here?" Laura practically stammered, emerging from the back of the truck.

She was wearing jeans and her gray T-shirt with the little hole in the shoulder, and carrying a chair—one of the square-back kitchen chairs he'd made. Jacob stared into the truck, seeing the bureau he'd built for Max, the armoire, and dozens of cardboard boxes. Yes, he realized, that was his old bed that the movers were carrying, Price's stained glass missing from the headboard.

"I thought you were moving in with your dad—into his house," Jacob began, then realization broke through the haze. "*You're* the one who bought the place?"

She was standing inches away from him, searching his face. And God, how he wanted to hold her. Just to touch her, to feel the warmth of her body. But there was something strange, almost fearful, in her look.

He said, "Or is it you and Price?"

She said, "You don't know?"

"Know what?"

Her eyes, Jacob realized, were drawn as though she hadn't slept, either.

"Laura, what?"

"He's dead."

Jacob pulled back, far enough to see that she was serious. "Price?"

"He was shot last night, in his house," Laura said. "The police are looking for you."

"Wait a minute, you don't think—"

"Someone who claimed to be our ex-neighbor told the police you used to take target practice in the gravel pit behind our house."

"Target practice?"

"An anonymous tip," Laura said. "Anyway, they went out there and found some bullets that match the bullet found on the bridge and"—she gave him a wounded, uncertain look—"the ones from last night."

"Laura, last night I was here, working . . ." Until Alix Callahan showed up. "What time was he shot?"

"A woman said she heard the shots around two."

Where was Jacob at two? Either with Alix, at the salt pile . . . or alone at the mountain. "Laura, you believe me, don't you?"

"Jake, there were six," she said.

Jacob scowled. Six what?

"He was shot six times at close range—his arms, his legs. . . ." Her eyes pooled over with the horror of it. "He was tortured."

Jacob shook his head. July had to have planted the bullets in the gravel pit. But how had she found the revolver? He had buried it, and only he knew where.

She said, "What are you going to do? You can't run."

"*Hey—*"

He looked back and saw Max coming out the front door. His heart froze.

"He doesn't know what happened," Laura told him. "Jake, I need to tell you—"

Something in her voice . . . Jacob met her eyes, dark with intent.

"I was never in love with him," she said softly, then she turned and walked away as Max came running over.

"Hey, champ," Jacob said, trying not to let his voice betray the turmoil in his heart.

"Cool, huh?" Max was wearing one of Jeff Dakota's T-shirts, autographed, and a leather tool belt with a claw hammer hanging down to his knee. "Owner financing, zero interest rate," he said nonchalantly. "All we have to do is replace about eighty windows and sand ten thousand feet of floors, then start painting."

"Very cool," Jacob said, giving Laura another look as she walked up the ramp into the back of the truck.

"It's called the Seaview Inn now," Max said. "Mom and I are gonna sleep up in the widow's walk tonight."

"Up there?" Jacob said, looking up at the glass turret, but with his head spinning, he could barely listen.

"Know what else?" Max said. "Mom quit her job. I actually think she dumped Dr. A, the way she's all hush-hush, but I saw that coming all along." His eyes twinkled up at his father.

Jacob put his hand on Max's baseball cap. "Where's your gramp?" he said. "I just stopped to tell everyone good luck."

Max turned toward the porch. Jacob did too. Squeaky was standing in the front door, looking out at them with a studied frown.

Laura stuck her head out of the truck. "Maxie, come help me carry the coffee table. Daddy needs to talk with Grandpa."

Jacob went up the steps, and Squeaky backed inside the musty foyer, making room for him. The room was big, dark, and brown-hued. From the high ceiling, twin unlit chandeliers hung on either side of a wide oak staircase. Squeaky shut the door.

"What's going on?" he said, his face seeming wrinkled and old.

"I don't know," Jacob said, looking out. Laura and Max had gone inside the moving truck. "Do you have a gun?"

"Not for you, I don't."

"Keep it with you," Jacob said. "For the next day or two, whatever you do, don't let Laura or Max out of your sight." He turned to leave.

"Hey—" Squeaky pounded the doorjamb. "You gonna tell me what the hell's goin' on?"

"Take care of them," Jacob said. Then he turned and walked down the steps, passing the moving truck without saying good-bye. As he drove down the driveway, he saw Laura and Max in his mirror. They were walking down the truck ramp, carrying a rectangular coffee table he had made, both of them watching him leave.

Thinking it could be the last they'd ever see him, Jacob didn't wave, afraid that waving might make it so.

THE drive took ten minutes. He left his car on the dirt road that bordered the duck pond, then ran past the new houses. Even though it was daylight, he didn't care who might be watching out their windows this time. He ducked under the chain and continued running down the old trolley bed into the woods.

Though he had buried the weapon in the dark, he knew exactly where it was—at the head of Whale Rock, in the grassy spot where he and Laura had first made love. When he got there, he found he didn't have to dig. Someone had beaten him to it.

Staring at the desecrated ground, Jacob began to believe what Alix had told him . . . Somehow July had followed him that night. But how? As he recalled, he'd been alone in the pitch black. No headlights had followed his car. The cool, dark hole stared up at him, making irrelevant his denial. However she had done it, she had the weapon now, with his fingerprints on it. And she'd eventually plant it for Evangeline to find.

As he ran back to his car, a more frightening thought occurred to him . . . that she would claim more victims first.

63

JULY'S VOLVO WAS PARKED AT GREEN GIRLS WHEN JACOB pulled up. Caution was no longer an issue. He walked directly to the front door and let himself in. The door had been left unlocked for him—an obvious trap.

Or else . . . What if Sereno had caught up with her? He let the chill wash through him before he called out.

"Okay, July. I'm here."

The place was wrapped in silence. Flowers and plants in the shop were withered and dry. The glass doors to the garden were closed. His adrenaline pumping too hard to be wary, he walked directly up the stairs.

"Let's get this over with!"

But she didn't answer. He went from room to room but didn't find her, so he concentrated on finding the revolver. In the bedroom, he tore through the closet and bureau, searched under the mattress and through the clothes on the floor. But no gun.

"You want to shoot me?" he shouted. "Here I am!"

He proceeded into the kitchen, searching through the cupboards and refrigerator. The gun could have been anywhere—if it was here at all.

On the ride over, he had thought once again about surrendering himself to Evangeline and telling her the truth about Alix and July and Sereno, the truth about everything. But he was afraid of whatever planted evidence might rise up against him once he was in custody. He was more afraid of what might happen to Max and Laura if he weren't around to protect them.

Maybe it was time to get on the highway, pick them up and start driving . . . but with the police looking for him, he knew he wouldn't get far.

He looked down to the rain forest. Everything so quiet. Too quiet. Like the suffocating stillness before a thunderstorm. He went down the stairs to the shop and opened the door to the greenhouse.

"July?"

His shout died in the foliage. He walked up the main path, thinking the garden hut would be a good place to stash a revolver—better still, the grasshopper room. But when he reached the hut, he was suddenly afraid to go in. Was she waiting inside, lying in the bed he'd made for her, with the revolver aimed at the door? No. She couldn't use the gun on him, he realized, or how would she explain the bullets that killed Price. She'd use a knife—and have a perfect alibi. Jacob Winter, the twice spurned lover, on a rampage of vengeance. She'd plant the gun in his hand.

He took hold of the latch, braced for an attack—

—and heard a noise from the house. Jacob pressed up against the hut and crept to the corner. Peering through the leaves, he could see the glass doors open upstairs, but nothing suspicious, no movement inside. So he left the relative safety of the hut and went back down the path until more of the house was visible. . . .

The shop door was closed.

Had he closed it himself? He couldn't remember. Why would he?

Hearing another sound—this a creak from the trees above him, Jacob looked up into the thick green canopy. A quick shadow moved above the leaves, then a harsh, jangling crack. The leaves rustled sharply, and something came whickering down, slicing through the foliage and crashing into the earth two feet away from him—a guillotine of safety glass, embedded in the ground. Severed leaves drifted down around him.

Again glass broke overhead. Jacob jumped against a palm as the flash of another heavy pane came slamming down. Through a clean break in the trees, he saw July standing on top of the greenhouse in her white sundress, straddling the frame. With her bare heel, she stomped on the glass, and another crystal blade tore through the canopy. Jacob twisted and dived over a spiny bush, and the sheet of glass crashed in the spot where he'd been standing. Scrambling out of the thorns, he ran for the house, while more glass shattered, cascading out of the trees behind him, brilliant, icy shrapnel. Covering his head, suddenly exposed to the open sky, Jacob slammed into the door, grabbed the handle, turned and pulled, but it wouldn't give.

Above him, he heard a pistol shot, and the pane came down in jagged pieces, shattering all over the ground behind him. He looked up, saw her balanced on the frame, aiming down. The shot fired, the glass exploded, and now Jacob was racing back under cover of greenery, followed by ringing gunshots, raining glass.

Trapped inside the garden, he sought shelter in the hut, running inside and closing the door, hoping for a few seconds to collect his thoughts. Maybe . . . he looked around . . . he'd pull the mattress off the bed and use it to crash through the greenhouse wall, then make a run for his car.

Outside, a muffled shot sounded, and the thatched roof jerked as a thick pane tore through, slicing viciously into the mattress. Jacob pressed back against the wall, when suddenly the small inner door flew open, swarming with crickets, and an arm reached out—

He spun for the outer door, but was hauled to the floor as more glass detonated overhead, thatch bulging down, and he realized who had saved him.

"I told you to stay away from her," Alix whispered harshly.

"The police are looking for me," he said. "Price Ashworth was murdered last night."

"Don't you understand? She can kill you now, and it's self-defense."

"So what are *you* doing here?"

"Move!" she yelled, pulling him out from under the hole in the roof where July, balanced in a gleam of daylight, aimed down with both hands. They sprang through the door just as the gunshot rang and glass fell.

"Here!" Alix pulled him against a sticky gumbo-limbo, where the overhead growth was thicker. Grasshoppers clung to her cap and clothing and crawled over the backpack slung on her arm.

He whispered in her ear: *"Tell me."*

"Shh." July's shadow crept across the treetops, searching for them.

"I want to know," Jacob demanded.

Alex mouthed the word: *"What!"*

"Why you came back!" he whispered. *"And don't say it's because you sobered up."*

Above them, the shadow stopped. They heard a soft tapping, almost like rain, then brass casings came falling out of the leaves.

"She's reloading," Alix said. Pointing to the barbecue grill behind the hut, she made a swinging motion—meaning, Jacob guessed, that they could break the glass and make a run for it.

But he shook his head, demanding an answer.

She spread her arms impatiently. *"I don't know,"* she breathed. *"Maybe for once in my life I wanted to make something right—instead of running away from it."*

Though she'd barely made a sound, Jacob watched in horror as July's shadow suddenly changed direction and came directly toward them. He grabbed Alix's arm and they broke for the grill, crashing through the brush into the clearing behind the hut, while the overhead shadow cut across their path. Without breaking stride, he grabbed the grill by a leg, and they ran through the middle of the thicket. With vines and branches grabbing at them, Jacob didn't see the wall until he slammed into it, glass shattering on his shoulder. He stepped back and swung the grill. A pane blew apart, simultaneously with a louder crash above them, then the violent swiping of leaves. Sunlight flickering, July came crashing down, snapping off branches and ending up draped across the crook of the tree, hair hanging, eyes open but dazed.

"Go!" Jacob yelled, pushing Alix toward the break in the wall. Instead, she went back toward July and dropped to her knees, coming up with the revolver.

Jacob froze.

Alix rose, stepping back again, the weapon raised, aimed at July's head.

"This isn't how you make it right," Jacob said, but he knew he couldn't stop her.

He saw July blink, a glimmer of light returning to her eyes. Her nose was bleeding. But she managed a groggy smile.

"You don't know," Alix told him in a shaking voice. She held the revolver with both hands.

July's arm moved. Her leg bent. Slowly she gathered her body up and crouched like a cat on the limb. Staring defiantly at Alix, she reached up and wrapped her hand around a branch, then began pulling herself back up into the canopy.

Alix followed her with the gun, her hands shivering. Jacob took hold of the barrel and gently lowered her aim, then took the weapon from her. As they watched the girl disappear above the greenery, a siren rose up in the air.

"Come on," he said, and they ducked through the broken pane and ran out to the road. The siren sounded louder. Knowing the police would be watching out for his car, Jacob thought about taking the Green Girls wagon. "Do you have keys?" he asked Alix.

"No. Give me that." She grabbed the gun, turned to the Volvo, and fired. The hubcap rang and flew off the wheel. She fired again. The car sank. "Hurry up."

Jacob got in his car and started it, and she jumped in, throwing her pack in the backseat. "Kittery," she said, slamming the door.

Jacob sped out of there. "What are we doing?"

"Getting away."

Another siren joined the first. "They're already looking for my car," he said.

"Then move," she told him.

Jacob looked over at her, the revolver in her hand, and he began negotiating the back streets to Market Square, then wound around the roads and alleys behind State Street until he reached the Memorial Bridge. He could still hear sirens, but they were farther away. Driving onto the bridge, he said, "Maybe I should turn myself in."

"You can't," she told him flatly.

He looked at the gun in her hand. "You're not planning to use that, are you?"

She turned and looked behind them. "Faster."

He pressed the accelerator, the floor of the car singing as they passed over the grating. When they reached the midpoint of the bridge, she opened her window, saying, "Get over to the right."

"What are you doing?"

She reached out the window and flung the revolver over the rail into the river. "Making sure we're not armed and dangerous." Pulling herself back inside, she said, "Now get us to the Trading Post."

He left the bridge and drove through a pair of intersections and around a rotary, then north up Route One, a wide boulevard of malls, outlet stores, and lobster restaurants. "Here," she said, and he pulled into the parking lot of the Kittery Trading Post, a sporting goods store. "Right there."

Spotting the same white Taurus he'd seen at the salt pile the night before, he stopped and she got out, grabbing her pack. "Pull around back," she told him. "I'll pick you up."

THEN they were driving south again, Alix at the wheel. Neither spoke a word until she turned onto I-95 south, heading for the high-level bridge. "By the way," she said, "nice bed."

In the distance the arch poked up above the trees, then they were climbing up the approach span, the sky opening around them. "It was July's idea," he told her.

"I'm touched."

As they sailed under the web of green steel, Jacob pressed back against his seat. Down on the Portsmouth pier he saw the rusty salt bulker flying Panamanian and American flags. Dump trucks drove on and off the deck, loading Maine gravel.

"What's your problem with heights?" Alix asked.

"Gravity," he answered, hoping to deflect the conversation.

"Ever fly?"

"Twice."

"Were you afraid then?"

He closed his eyes, dizzy with the sensation. "First time, no. Second time, petrified."

"What changed?"

"I don't know. Maybe I got smarter."

"Why were you flying?"

"First time? Disney World. Would you mind telling me where we're going?"

"Second time?"

He sighed. "My father died. My mother and I flew to California to find a place to live."

"So, now we know," Alix said, the skeletal steel racing past her face.

"Know what?"

"It's not a fear of heights. It's a fear of losing your family."

He didn't respond, but looked out his window. As the bridge retreated in the distance, he felt he could breathe again. He sat up in the seat, relaxed his shoulders. "What's in the backpack?"

"Something to make sure she can't get away."

"Frog poison?"

Alix didn't answer.

"You do know that's how Sereno escaped," he said. "She sent him Polaroids laced with the same stuff."

Alix watched the highway.

"It's probably how Deborah McBride was murdered." Jacob watched her, saw her eyes fill up. "Were the rumors true? Did you go see her?"

Alix wiped her eyes. "She was going to try to help me. I don't want to talk about it." She kept driving.

"I'm not sure we can handle this ourselves," Jacob told her, but he stopped short of suggesting they turn July in to the police. He knew that if July's identity were disclosed, Alix herself would be exposed to retribution from the drug underworld, possibly criminal prosecution for McBride's murder, and who knew what else. But at this point, exposure seemed inevitable. "Sereno's on his way," he told her. "He was in Virginia yesterday."

The determined way Alix stared out at the road, she didn't need to say a word. Jacob suddenly understood.

"You don't want July arrested," he said, "because you want Sereno to find her."

"He's coming, that's all I know," Alix answered. "July knows it too. That's why she's coming apart."

"And you're just going to let it happen."

Alix gave him a look. "I don't know what's on her mind—or his," she said. "Even if you thought you had some vague idea about what makes these people tick, you'd be wrong."

Jacob said, "So what are we doing?"

Alix gave him an obvious look. "Hiding."

64

THE SENSATION WAS INTENSE, LIKE A NAP INTERRUPTED BY A fall. Jacob lurched up, opening his eyes. Sleep left him in a flurry, reality swarming in its place. They were parked in the driveway of a suburban house, a gray cape with white shutters and two stately maples in the front yard. Alix turned off the engine and got out. Jacob saw the front door open; a man—Professor Nielsen—stood there smiling.

"Maybe we should move the car away from the house, so it doesn't attract attention," Jacob suggested as he stepped out.

"It belongs here," said Alix, who got out of the car and went into the house, stopping to give the professor a hug on her way by.

Jacob followed her, his knowledge expanding as he went. The professor had been in on her faked death from the start. He had hidden her, perhaps even helped dry her out. Now he shook

Jacob's hand as if this were nothing more than a social call. "I certainly hope you two can stay for dinner."

"I don't know," Jacob answered, then called in to Alix, "Honey, do we have any plans?"

"Yeah," she answered dryly. "Staying alive."

65

Even at nine at night, the traffic pours steadily over the Bourne Bridge onto Cape Cod. From the rocky bank of the canal, where the diminutive Indian stands in a heavy trance, the stream of taillights means nothing. In fact, he is not even conscious of the dark water rushing past him. With an East Coast road map opened in his hands, he has risen above it all, land and water, high above the arched bridge. In his mind, he is soaring northward, the traffic below him as insignificant as a line of ants. Cars traverse highways, neighborhoods lie quietly. The wind rushes all around. Sereno soars. He passes over Plymouth Harbor and Massachusetts Bay, the jagged, sparkling crown of Boston. He looks down on Salem Harbor, the peninsulas at Marblehead, Gloucester, and Cape Ann, where a single boat trails a soft wake in the water. He sees the river emptying at Newburyport, then glides over miles and miles of sandy beach and an ocean that's soft as velvet.

In the distance, he can already see the wide Piscataqua mating with the ocean. And then in his vision the bridge rises up over the river, with cars and trucks coming and going under its towering arch, utterly unaware of what is hovering above them—or down below: the glass house on the bank, filled with flowers and trees that Sereno hasn't seen in years, and may never see again.

A gunshot intrudes on his dream. He feels the fire bite the back of his thigh, and he drops to the rocks.

"JUST like fixing a car, this detective work. Always go for the simple solution."

Sereno lowered his head. He didn't need to turn around to know who had shot him. Bishop walked out of the darkness, stopping at the edge of the bank.

"Did you know that the last two places you've been spotted, there's been a bridge exactly like this? Not just any bridge, but what the library books call a 'cantilever through-trussed-arch bridge.' Well, check the facts: there just aren't that many of these bridges in the whole damn country, let alone ones that cross over tidal rivers on the East Coast, like the one you've been looking for."

He stepped down onto the rocks with his .38 aimed. "Know what else? There's been greenhouses too. And the fact that I found you here—no greenhouse—leads me to two conclusions. One: this ain't the right bridge. Two: there's only one more like it on the East Coast, and I know where it is. So you're gonna come with me, and we're gonna find her. Together. Only this time the split's gonna be eighty-twenty—the price of your betrayal."

Slowly, the Indian came around.

"If I see a ballpoint pen in your mouth, Mr. Man, I will drop you in this canal," Bishop promised him. He took another step closer, straightened his aim. "So don't try my patience."

A shout rang out behind him. "Police! Drop your weapon!"

"I'm on the job," Bishop yelled back. "This man is a fugitive from justice!" He ducked down into a crevice between two boulders, his revolver ready.

"You need to stand up and put your hands in the air!" the cop commanded.

"You dumb Yankee, clean out your ears," Bishop yelled, staying low. "I am an officer of the law! I've been tracking this renegade sonuvabitch over a thousand miles!" He peeked his .38 up over the rock. Instantly the flashlight caught him, and he ducked back down.

"Sir! I need you to throw your weapon out, now!"

"Yeah, well, I *need* a lot of things."

The flashlight beam wandered away from Bishop and went bouncing over the tops of the rocks, left to right. The place where the light stopped—on the rock, where Sereno had fallen—all that was left was a blood splotch glistening.

Bishop yelled, "Meanwhile, while you're playing Boy Scout, I'm about to lose my prisoner."

The beam went searching again, and Bishop peeked up. He saw where the cop was standing, at the top of the bank, behind a craggy scrub oak. He ducked down again. "You Massachusetts State Trooper, I suppose."

The cop didn't answer.

"Well, you oughta know you're interfering in federal law enforcement. I *will* be speaking to your superiors."

Suddenly the cop's light flashed across the trees, and a gunshot rang out. Bishop ducked down. But, hearing two or three heavy footsteps in the sand, he jumped back up, both hands on his weapon, and saw the shadowy figure stumbling toward him. He fired once, twice, and got lucky the third time. The man collapsed at the top of the bank.

Ducking down again, heart pounding, Bishop listened for some sound, a groan or something.

"That it?"

He heard only the lapping of water behind him.

"I get up, I'd better see Yankee hands in the air."

Suddenly a car engine came to life. The police car, Bishop realized. But he knew it wasn't the cop. It was Sereno escaping.

Cautiously he stuck his head up from the rocks. The cop's flashlight lay on the roadside, its beam shining on the body of its owner. Bishop aimed his .38.

"Here we go," he said, feeling foolish, like someone talking to himself. He was. The man was plainly dead, the moonlight frozen in his gaze, pistol on the ground beneath his fingers. A nickel-sized dark spot showed on his khaki shirt in the middle of his back. Just above the wound, Bishop spotted Sereno's mark: the silvery pin poking out of his neck.

He picked up the fallen weapon, then returned to his Jeep, to go to claim his fortune.

66

For dinner they had a tuna casserole and steamed broccoli. The professor baked a fresh raspberry pie for dessert and opened a bottle of red wine, but ended up drinking alone. Nobody had much to say. After dinner, while Nielsen and Alix had coffee, Jacob went into the living room and lay on the floor in front of the couch. He found a news channel on TV, hoping to see a report of Sereno's capture—hoping not to see his own face—but he promptly fell asleep.

When he opened his eyes again, he was staring dazedly at the silent TV, where a great white shark was patrolling a reef. His head was propped against the couch, and his neck ached. He could hear snoring from another part of the house. He wished he hadn't left his cell phone in his car—which was sitting in a Kittery parking lot—because he wanted desperately to call Laura, to hear her voice and make sure Max was safe. But even if he wanted to call from here, he knew the police would probably have taps on her line, and Squeaky's too.

"Mind if I sleep now?" Alix asked. She was lying on the couch behind him, reading a book.

"Was I snoring?"

"No, but one of us needs to stay awake."

He saw a hammer on the coffee table. The blinds were drawn and shut tight, and it looked as if every light in the house was lit.

"If the police find us here, then they find us," he said. "I'm not running anymore."

"It's not the police I'm afraid of," she said.

"You don't mean July—?"

"Don't you understand? We're talking about a level of perception that's beyond anything you can imagine."

"This is *July*," he said. "Sereno's the shaman."

"Jacob," she said.

He turned to look at her.

"Sereno trained her." She turned off the lamp. "Give me two hours."

WHILE Jacob sat against the couch, flipping through channels, looking for another news station, outside a car passed slowly on the road, its radio booming as it went by. Then the professor's snoring stopped. Now Jacob listened to every sound in the house. He remembered the night he buried the revolver, how he'd heard a snap in the woods. Now he knew. It was July. She'd followed him in the dark. With the highway traffic in the distance, he wondered if he'd even be able to hear footsteps on the lawn, or a window sliding open.

Above him, Alix stirred.

"Did I wake you?" he asked.

"I'm not much of a sleeper," she said.

"Want me to turn off the TV?"

"No, it's okay."

He switched channels again, stopped on a Boston news broadcast showing Red Sox highlights. He left the volume down. From the bedroom, Professor Nielsen's snoring resumed. In the distance, the highway sounded like the ocean.

"I really am sorry, you know," Alix said softly. "For dragging you into this."

Jacob said, "I guess you didn't have many options."

"Well, I owe you."

"Don't worry about it," he told her—though he was grateful she'd said it. "So what are you going to do with yourself, now that you're no longer dead?"

"Seriously?"

He turned his head to see her. She was quiet for a moment, then she propped her head on her elbow. "I think I'd like to take in wayward kids."

"Wayward kids."

"Yeah."

"Like, delinquents?"

"Delinquents? No. Kids," she explained. "Kids who've lost their direction. Disillusioned, alienated from their families: wayward kids. They'd live in my house and apprentice in my nursery till they got their feet on the ground. Till they were fit to live with people."

He looked at her again and saw a glimmer in her eyes. He laid his head back against her leg, and was glad she didn't move it.

He said, "How would you do that?"

"Teach them about planting things and making them grow."

"Exotic flowers?"

She chuckled. "Nah. Hearty New England things. Trees. Fruit trees, nut trees, sugar maples."

Suddenly her leg moved, and his head fell against the couch. "Jacob," she said.

Hearing the fear in her voice, he turned. "That's him," she breathed, staring at the television.

The Indian's face filled the screen, a blurred photograph, in fact a mug shot—brown face, long black hair, piercing eyes—a chill shot through Jacob as he grabbed the remote and pushed up the volume. Then another photo appeared, of a young uniformed policeman. Jacob heard the newscaster say, "As police and federal agents hunt for this brutal killer, and our elected leaders attempt to deal with the myriad problems of immigration, underfunded prisons, and violence in our society, tonight this quiet Cape Cod town finds itself at the center of a national tragedy. And asks why."

"Cape Cod," Jacob said—and suddenly he couldn't sit any longer.

He got to his feet, stepped into his moccasins, and went into the kitchen, where he grabbed the telephone and dialed the tavern.

Alix came in behind him. "Jacob, who are you calling?"

"My family." He listened to the phone ring.

"What if there's a tap on their line?"

"Then the cops can come get me." He let the phone ring three more times, then he hung up and snatched the professor's car keys off the counter.

"What are you doing?"

"Going to protect my family," he said, stepping out into the night. As soon as he got in the car, the passenger door flew open. Alix got in, her backpack slung over her shoulder, her sneakers in hand.

He started the engine. "I got myself into this," he told her.

She closed her door. "Just go."

"You don't owe me."

"Jacob, drive."

He backed down the driveway, then started off through the quiet town, past the Brandeis campus. As he merged onto the highway, he tried again.

"Look," he said, "I know what you've been through. You did what you had to."

"You don't know a thing," she said

"Sereno tried to murder July," he said. "You came to her rescue. That's called self-defense."

She stared out at the road racing under his headlights.

"Alix, I know you stabbed him. I heard the tape."

"I lied," she said.

He looked over at her. "Under hypnosis?"

"Just shut up about it!" she yelled. "Drive."

67

WHEN THE DEAD TROOPER WAS FOUND BESIDE THE CAPE
Cod Canal, an all-points bulletin went out for his vehicle, along
with a description of Sereno. Despite the fact that the Massachusetts State Police, local police units, and FBI were scouring the surrounding towns for him, it would be another two hours before
they located the cruiser he'd taken, sunk to its axles in a cranberry
bog three miles away from the crime scene—and another few minutes before the man who owned the cranberries would realize that,
yup, he was missing his old stake-body flatbed dump truck. Which
at present, loaded with empty crates, was cruising unsteadily across
the Merrimack River on I-95, entering New Hampshire.

68

For the better part of an hour, from Lexington to Salisbury, Massachusetts, neither Alix nor Jacob spoke a word. As the Taurus crossed the state line into New Hampshire, Alex finally said, "Sereno was not trying to murder July in Florida."

"Alix, I heard you on the tape. I heard you."

She said, "We were trying to murder *him*."

Jacob rolled his head toward her. She stared straight ahead. Another mile rolled under the wheels before she spoke again.

"We waited for Sereno to come home," she said. "When he walked into the bedroom, July shot him, and shot him again. But he kept coming, so I came out of the closet . . . with the knife."

Jacob waited for her to continue; she didn't. Returning his attention to the highway, he watched the night continue to swallow them both.

"July murdered Kiefer," he said. "Didn't she?"

Alix nodded. "I didn't know it at the time."

"So Sereno never killed anyone."

"Of course not. He's a *shaman*."

"Did July kill Kiefer for the money?"

"I doubt it. Probably because he wanted to break off the affair with her. But the money was there for the taking."

"And then she convinced you that Sereno had murdered him—and was coming after her next."

"That's the way she works."

"But why did she want Sereno dead?" He pulled up to the toll plaza at Hampton, dropped four quarters in the basket, then drove on. After a minute he answered his own question: "Because he was getting ready to leave her, too."

Alix sat back in her seat saying nothing, just staring out at the road rushing toward them.

"So now we know," Jacob said.

"Know what?"

"Who sent Sereno the poisoned Polaroid. It wasn't July, was it?"

Alix gave him a look but did not deny the insinuation.

He drove on.

69

THE CRANBERRY TRUCK STOPPED AT THE MIDPOINT OF THE high-level bridge, tight against the curb, and the flatbed rose up, dumping crates all over the roadway. A trailer truck sounded its horn as it blew past, shattering the crates to splinters. Then the Indian stepped down from the cab and began walking across the lanes, oblivious to another eighteen-wheeler rushing past.

The driver got on his radio. About the only reason a man would stop here—which is why there was a law against it—was if he wanted to jump. But this crazy Indian, the driver reported, kind of hunched over and hobbling, wasn't jumping, not by the looks of it, not yet anyway. He was straddling the curbstone, holding on to the railing. Looked like he was sniffing the air. Christ, it's two-thirty in the morning and the guy's wearing shades, he's operating a commercial rig without running lights or even headlights—Miles Standish Cranberry Farm stenciled on his door—dumping the load all over the highway. Whatever the hell's in them cranberries must be some potent.

In fact, the Indian was entranced, surfeited with a woman he hasn't seen or heard or touched since she was a girl, filled with every aspect of her. Weakened from blood loss, drunk on sensations, he held on to the railing and stared out over the river.

Even with the salt wind whistling through the columns, he could detect her scent in the wet wind from below. In fact, he could sense her all around him. He could smell the flowers she had planted, he could see the house in which she slept.

Ignoring the cars rushing past, ignoring the pain in his thigh, ignoring a weakness so strong that it felt like seven nights of sleeplessness riding on his back, he crawled over the railing and grabbed hold of the steel rungs, lowering himself down into the sweet black wind.

PART
FIVE

70

IT WAS THREE IN THE MORNING WHEN JACOB AND ALIX ARRIVED
at the tavern. The place was dark, as was the old inn up above, the
Spite House. Laura's car was parked in the lot, and so was
Squeaky's—which meant they were there. But . . .

"The porch light's usually on," Jacob said when they stepped out
of the car. He wished Alix had returned a more confident expression. The night was still, disturbed only by their footsteps on the
gravel lot and the breath of the tide spilling into the harbor below.

As quietly as he could, Jacob climbed the porch steps and tried
the door. He was relieved to find it locked. The boarded-up windows on the ground floor were intact, another fact that eased his
mind.

Suddenly the porch light came on—in Alix's hand. "It was

loose," she whispered—then unscrewed the bulb again, and everything went dark, much darker than before.

Jacob backed down the steps, staring up at the building.

"Where are they sleeping?" Alix asked softly, coming close.

Jacob whispered, "Max and Laura are up top, in the cupola. I don't know where her father is."

They backed up far enough to see the glassed-in cupola poised silently against the sky. Jacob shivered, imagining that July might have gotten inside—that she might be up there still.

Alix grabbed his shirt and pointed: a window above the front porch was open—only two or three inches—but open.

He took in as much of the building as he could, trying to see if anything was moving behind the windows on the second floor. All he could see were reflections of pine boughs twitching. Then a whisper:

"Jacob—"

It was Alix, crouched at the corner of the building. "Phone line," she said, holding the severed wire in her hand.

Jacob's heart surged. His mind flew in all directions.

"Do you have a key?" she asked, coming back to him.

"No." He picked up a couple of small rocks sturdy enough to reach the second floor. Targeting a window in the corner nearest him, he managed to hit the wooden shutter. A slat broke and hung down. His second shot was on the mark. Glass shattered, and Jacob stared up at the massive house, watching for a light to come on. Every second that passed frightened him more.

Then Alix grabbed him and pointed to the opposite corner of the house. Up in the window, a movement. Yes, someone's head. Then a flashlight came on, and the window opened.

"You lost your mind?"

"Squeaky, where's Max?"

"What time is it?"

"Where is he?" Jacob repeated.

"They're asleep," he answered, "upstairs, in the widow's walk. I'm camped out at the bottom of the stairs." He showed his pistol. "Everything's copacetic."

"There's a window open," Jacob said.

"What window?"

"Over the porch."

Squeaky pulled his head back inside. The flashlight rippled off the sheer curtains. Then Squeaky returned. "The lights don't work. We got power out?"

"Go up and check on them," Jacob called. "Squeaky, hurry!"

As the light dimmed on the window curtain, the window to its right picked up the glow. Jacob paced in the same direction. Then the house went dark. He stopped pacing. He felt Alix's hand on his back. For a moment, neither of them breathed. In the center window, the one that was open, the flashlight approached the curtain. The window went up.

"Somebody opened all the doors," Squeaky said, then turned away, silhouetted.

"Jesus."

Suddenly the windows blazed with light, the room light on. Squeaky returned to the window. "They unscrewed the frickin' bulbs."

"Squeaky, go up and check!"

As Jacob watched, a window on the third floor lit—the stairway light, he assumed. He could hear Squeaky's footsteps now, clocking upward. A door slammed. The light went out. Jacob broke for the porch. Alix grabbed his arm. "Wait—"

Suddenly the cupola came aglow. Jacob stepped back, his legs shaking. From up top they heard a murmur of voices. Then Laura's cry.

"Maxie?"

"God," Jacob breathed.

The turret lit up like a lighthouse. Squeaky threw open a window, pushed back the curtains. "He's not here!"

"He might be in one of the rooms," Alix suggested.

Laura came to the window and cried desperately. "Jacob?"

"Get to a phone," he yelled. "Call Evangeline!"

71

THE TAURUS SPED PAST THE DARK WOODS, THEN SLOWED WITHIN sight of Green Girls. July's Volvo was still parked in the street, its tires repaired.

"Light's on upstairs, she's expecting us," Alix said, her voice as soft as the rainfall inside the greenhouse.

Jacob stared hard at the place, trying to think of a strategy, but his adrenaline-soaked brain was useless. "Cover your face," he said, hitting the gas as he cut the wheel and the car plowed across the lawn.

"Jacob, stop—"

"Duck!" He pulled her down as he crashed through the glass. The impact was more violent than he expected. The greenhouse frame gave way, and glass hailed over the car as it stopped with a jolt against a palm.

Jacob picked himself off of Alix, ignoring the pain in his shoulder. "Okay?"

"So much for a sneak attack," she answered.

He got out of the car and started walking into the garden.

"Wait—" Alix grabbed her backpack and ran after him, caught hold of his shirt. "You're in the dark," she whispered. "She can see everything we do."

"She's got Maxie," he said, pulling away, but she grabbed him again with both hands.

"She wants you dead." Alix spoke into his face. "That's all she wants: You. Dead. And you're walking right into her arms."

Jacob looked around. The artificial rain fell all over them, washing down their faces. "Leave if you want," he said, and turned away from her.

But she kept hold, whispering, "Stay off the path. It won't be as easy to ambush us." And they wandered into the thicket, where the foliage was wet and impossibly dark, and it caught noisily at their arms and faces.

"Wait—"

Alix stopped him again, sounding petrified, as she gaped through the darkness beside them. Her grip tightened on his arm. He turned.

A pair of eyes shone back at them in animal iridescence, someone lying on the ground.

"Maxie?"

"No." Alix pulled him back.

Jacob stiffened.

"Not July, either," she breathed.

WITH the dark and the rainfall, they could see nothing but the shining eyes that tracked their approach. In fact, Jacob did not see the body until they were almost on top of it, glistening among the foliage about halfway between the garden hut and the greenhouse wall. They stopped there.

The dark-skinned man lay in the downpour, his hair draped over the wet leaves.

"He's hurt," Alix said, and started toward him. But when the Indian raised his hand, Jacob caught her arm. "It's okay," she said, and he saw that Sereno's gesture was directed toward the glass wall behind him. In fact, he seemed to be focused on something outside.

Alix went closer to the wall and looked out. Then she caught her breath. *"Jacob."*

He went to the glass and peered off at the bridge, the beacon at the top of its arch flaring at two-second intervals, illuminating . . . the glass fogged. He wiped it with his shirtsleeve; then felt Alix's hands on his shoulders as if poised to hold him there. The beacon came on, then went dark again. Something . . .

"What—?"

The beacon lit. His legs gave out. She kept him from falling. He pulled toward the Taurus.

"You can't," she said, clutching his arm. "Jacob, wait for the police."

He shook his head, his mind frozen. "If the cops go up there, she'll throw him off," he said, getting in the car and shutting the door. "You told me yourself: She wants *me*!"

"What do you expect to do?" Alix said.

He turned the key, revved the engine. "I don't know!"

"Can you kill her?"

He backed outside, ripping more glass from the greenhouse. She came out after him.

"Jacob, if you go up there, you'll have to kill her," she told him. "Or she'll kill you."

He kicked the accelerator and tore across the lawn.

THE Taurus screeched onto Woodbury, flying under the overpass, then swerving left onto the approach ramp. Jacob was doing seventy when he joined the highway, eighty-five when he hit the brakes, the car shrieking to a stop at the bridge threshold where the arch began its upward sweep. Ahead of him he could see highway flares blocking the right lane where a flatbed truck was broken down. Blue lights of a police car were flashing there too, preventing him from reaching the ladder rungs. Were they even aware of what was going on high above them?

He got out of the car and went to the railing before the fear hit him. As though shaken from a dream, his legs buckled again, and he knelt hard on the curbstone, looking out over the lights of the sleeping town, the dockside cranes stretching up into the dark sky. Grabbing the railing, he pulled himself to his feet again and forced himself to look at the job at hand.

On the other side of the railing, level with the roadway, was the surface of the upper chord—his only way up. It was a hollow steel rectangle, four feet deep but only eighteen inches wide as it arched up into the sky. This was the same chord that Max was standing on, he told himself, Max and July, high above him. He looked up as far as he could but, because of the curve, was unable to see its top. Probably the reason the police weren't able to see them, either.

He grabbed the top rail under his arm, prepared to swing his leg over. The bridge architects, to aid maintenance workers, had thoughtfully strung a cable handhold along the outside of the chord, about waist-high, attached to stanchions positioned every eight feet. But to discourage daredevils, the cable did not begin until the chord had already risen about twenty-five feet off the roadway. Which meant that, for the first one hundred feet of his climb, Jacob would have to balance on the chord, with nothing to hold on to but the wind.

A roaring wave of weakness threatened to pull the railing out of his arms. Jacob clutched it tightly as he tried to slow his breathing, tried to find some courage. Maxie was up there, he told himself. . . .

And suddenly he remembered what Alix had told him—that his fear of heights is actually a fear of losing his family. If she was right—reason cutting through his panic—then perhaps it follows that his determination to save his family might overpower his fears.

And that's exactly how he proceeds.

SETTING his mind to the single purpose—shutting out every other impulse—he throws his leg over the top railing. Saving his family. As he stretches his foot to the outside curb, his moccasin feels loose, so he kicks it off and it goes fluttering down and down with the wind. He kicks off the other moccasin too, before he swings his other leg over. Then, holding the railing, he steps barefoot onto the narrow chord—and immediately regrets losing his shoes. The steel is cold and wet with dew. It doesn't matter. The cold will keep him alert.

He looks ahead of him. Saving his family. The chord rises up like a water slide, and the cable handhold is far ahead of him, but Jacob thinks only of Max. Saving Max. There is no thought of danger, no weakening of the limbs, only strength and purpose. Steadying himself with his left hand on the railing, he starts climbing. Simple as that. A trailer truck blows past, blasting its air horn, as though to warn him. Jacob barely hears it.

As the chord beneath his feet rises, the roadside railing under his left hand falls away, and now he must let go. This is when he first notices the wind teasing and tugging at him, but he is spurred on by an image—he and Laura and Max together at the dinner table. Arms outstretched for balance, he does not even need to watch his feet. The strain in his calves tells him he's climbing.

Another eighteen-wheeler rushes past, then a UPS truck, both signaling with their headlights that they're aware of him. But they're well below him now, farther and farther distant. Jacob is aware of the open air on both sides now, and the black river way below. None of it frightens him. He is saving his family.

About ten feet ahead of him, the cable handhold begins. Anchor-bolted to the outside of the chord, it rises diagonally to the top of the first stanchion, four feet high. Seeing the cable reminds Jacob of his precarious position, and suddenly he stops, arms out-stretched, up in the dark, up in the crosswinds alone, telling himself over and over about his family.

But his legs won't listen. They start to wobble beneath him, and suddenly he makes a desperate lunge for the cable, but his bare foot slips off the steel, and his leg follows, pulling the rest of his body along. Then he's hanging by his hands.

It's remarkable. Is he dreaming? His eyes are closed. But the cold steel under his cheek tells him he's awake.

He opens his eyes and sees that his right hand has managed to grab the cable at its base. His left hand clutches the edge of the chord, but it's a useless grip. The wind dangles him like a marionette. *Max,* he thinks, and throwing his left arm over the top of the chord, he catches the opposite edge, then swings his leg up and over. Quivering muscles transformed to energy, he hoists himself astride the steel, holding the cable to keep from sliding back down.

Off to the east, he sees a deep red line appear on the flat blue horizon. Yet the moon is still in the sky, and dock lights twinkle like stars on the surface of the river. Remarkable, indeed. He can feel the hum of traffic through his face. And it's such a relief, just for the moment, to close his eyes.

In his imagination, he is seeing his marriage bed being carried by the movers, his fine mahogany bed with the rectangular opening where Price's stained glass had been, Price's brash attempt at art. Then Jacob envisions his radio, black and streamlined, as it floats silently over the bed at the end of its power cord, flying toward the stained glass . . . when Price's hand leaps up to intercept its flight, and the radio swings around his arm——

Lying there on the bridge, suddenly Jacob realizes with perfect clarity: He was not trying to smash Price Ashworth's head. He was trying to smash his stained glass.

Jacob opens his eyes. The cable clenched in his fist, he pulls him-self to his knees. *Breathe,* he tells himself, and sucks his chest full of ocean air.

Now climb.

72

Alix knelt beside the Indian in the wet garden, nurturing him with a cup of water. She had shut off the sprinkler system and covered him with a wool blanket, then propped his head on her backpack. Sereno drank greedily, though his breathing was shallow. She was not aware of footsteps behind her until the flashlight beam swept across the foliage beside them.

"Well, outstanding," the man said. The light stopped on Alix's face, blinding her. "But is this the same Mrs. Sereno I remember? I don't think so."

"He needs an ambulance," Alix said, believing him a cop.

"I'm sorry, you'll have to speak up."

"He needs help!"

"You didn't call already?"

"The phones aren't working."

"Yeah, not workin'," he said in a skeptical way, "like the minute you call, your cover's blown, the old boy gets shipped back to the jungle, et cetera, et cetera, which doesn't really concern me as much as getting back what's rightfully mine."

Suddenly she recognized the man. Five years ago, in Plantation Key, he had appeared at the bottom of Sereno's staircase and aimed a pistol at her. Now he was here, aiming at Sereno.

"Just so you know I'm serious," he said, and fired the gun. Sereno jerked. Alix fell back, screaming, *"Will you stop?!"*

"This man is a dangerous killer," Bishop explained, "not to mention thief."

"He doesn't have your money!" Alix cried, throwing a handful of dirt at him, and stuffing her backpack under Sereno's head again.

"I know he doesn't have it." Bishop shone the light on the Indian again, the blanket bloody at his thigh—and now his shoulder, where he'd just been shot. Then the prison guard leaned in closer, lighting Sereno's face. "Besides, they're just hobbling wounds. So far."

The Indian squinted defiantly at the light, while Alix felt his fingers moving against her palm, surreptitiously handing her something. She took it, concealed it, just as Bishop swung his flashlight at her.

"So now, where *is* our wild child tonight, the lovely Juliette?"

"She doesn't have your money, either," Alix told him, while she tried to divine the object hidden in her hand . . . cigarette lighter?

"Ma'am, I'm trying to show restraint, but I guarantee you, the next bullet ain't gonna be a hobbler." He turned his aim to Sereno's heart.

"I'll take you to it," Alix said.

Bishop grinned. "Well, outstanding."

"First call an ambulance for him."

"I fully intend to call an ambulance," he assured her, "but first I'd like to get my money."

She glared into the light. "The money's here."

"On the premises?" He shone his light in her face. "Well, then. Lead on."

"Call first," she said.

"Ma'am, who's got the gun?" Showing her the weapon, he gestured toward the house. "Now move it."

Alix stood up, surreptitiously slipping the lighter into the pocket of her pants. "It's not in the house, it's out here," she said, turning toward the garden, knowing full well that, money or not, he was not going to leave either of them alive. But what was she supposed to do with a cigarette lighter, set him on fire?

"I guess you know if you're stalling for time—"

"I'm taking you to the money," she said, pushing a branch aside.

"Don't snap that."

She held the branch back, and he caught it with his shoulder . . . and there was the hut, dark and misshapen. A piece of greenhouse glass crunched under Bishop's shoe.

"You saying my money's in there?" He shone the flashlight on the caved-in roof, then back at Alix, but she didn't shrink. "No one ever told you about offshore banks?"

She pulled the door open. Inside, a slab of the thatched roof hung down. She felt his pistol poke between her shoulder blades as she stepped inside.

"Got a light in this place?"

"No."

He shone his flashlight around the small room. "Now there's a bed you don't see every day," he remarked. His beam reflected off the arched headboard, the broken glass on the mattress, down to the thatch-littered floor, then swung up the wall and through the hole in the roof, illuminating a severed palm frond. "What the hell happened in here?"

"Thunderstorm."

Bishop chuckled. "You got some set of balls, lady. Take money that don't belong to you, then act all sullen when you gotta return it." He shone the flashlight on her face again.

"It's in there," she told him.

"Speak up."

"Move," she said and, pushing past him, swung the outside door closed, revealing the smaller green door on the side wall. What did Sereno expect her to do, lock him in the room and torch the hut?

He tapped the narrow door with his pistol. "In there?"

"That's right."

"Open it up."

"Open it yourself," she said, and his pistol smashed her face. She dropped to her knees, pain radiating through her skull with such intensity—her cheekbones, her sinuses, even her teeth—she had to hold on to the floor to keep from passing out.

Bishop tapped her arm with the flashlight. "I'm used to men," he said. "By way of apology. Now let's get this over with, so I can leave you two in peace."

Alix leaned forward, blood seeping from her nose— and she felt the glass under her hands.

"Come on, I didn't hit you that hard," he said, and gave the wooden lock a twist. The door popped free. The instant he pulled it open, the grasshoppers sprang out at him, and he fell back with a shout, swiping his flashlight and weapon at them but leaving his throat exposed to the swipe of glass in Alix's hands. She heard the rip of flesh, and the man stumbled backward, gun and flashlight reeling. Alix tore the door open and ran. Bishop, his cheek pressed to his shoulder, bounded after her and tackled her at the turn. Folding under his weight, Alix hit the ground so hard she might have lost consciousness. But here, with Bishop kneeling over her, swinging his pistol like a hammer, she did not allow it. Dazed though she was, she threw her head to the side, and caught hold of his wrist. He yanked it from her grasp. She reached with her other hand, but he got his finger on the trigger. With both hands she grabbed the gun barrel and lunged with all her might, pushing his arm up to the sky. The pistol fired twice, answered by the chime of breaking glass, then the fierce hissing of leaves—and Alix spun out of the way.

As the crystalline sheet slammed down between them with a bone-jarring crack, Bishop's arm swung down, point-blank at her chest. Alix froze, helpless.

Bishop winced purposefully once, twice . . .

But the shot never sounded.

In fact—Alix stared in amazement at the sight in front of her— the man's arm was no longer attached to his shoulder, a fact that Bishop himself was presently trying to comprehend: his very own arm on the ground with the pistol still clutched in his hand, his short white finger pointing stiffly through the trigger guard. Staring through the windowpane at the lost part of himself, the man looked like a baby who had opened his mouth to scream but couldn't catch his breath. Then the softest sound came out, a shuddering, "Ahhh."

Carefully Alix removed the weapon from the disembodied hand, as though she feared the brain could somehow will it to fire. Then she went and crouched beside Bishop, taking his other pistol from his shoulder holster. She was not gentle doing so. Summarily, she stood again and tossed both weapons off into the brush, looking back at Bishop, to ascertain that he was unable to pick himself up and go find them. Blood spilled out the slice in his throat and gulped from his severed shoulder like oil from a pipeline. He began to shiver. And that's when she realized what the lighter was for.

She turned away from him and stepped over to where Sereno lay under the blanket. Gently removing the backpack from under his head, she slung it over her shoulder and returned to Bishop. "Still want your money?" she said, her voice devoid of sympathy.

His gaping eyes followed her as she went back to the hut, where grasshoppers continued pouring out the door. Opening the backpack, she poured its contents into the hut, a seemingly endless flurry of hundred-dollar bills, some in banded stacks, some loose. She tossed the backpack in after it, then picked up a fistful of dry thatch from the floor and snapped a flame from the lighter Sereno had given her. Bishop's mouth opened in objection.

Turning back to the garden, she showed Sereno the burning thatch, then tossed the fire into the hut. Though the Indian was barely visible in the darkness, she could see the sparkle of his eyes.

The thatch made good fuel. Flames swept across the floor and up the walls. Jacob's bed became quickly involved. Windows cracked, and the front wall blossomed into light and heat. Escaping the fire, grasshoppers sprang over Bishop, who shivered silently in the firelight. His mouth seemed to be moving, as though he were quietly conversing with someone, but he wasn't making a sound. Above their heads, the trees began to squeal, and the garden lit up brightly. Then a woman's voice cried out.

"Freeze!"

Susan Evangeline, wielding a flashlight and small service revolver, pushed through the brush. Seeing Bishop in the firelight, sprawled across the pool of glass and blood, seeing his estranged arm, she looked warily toward him.

"What happened here?" she said.

After a moment's hesitation, Alix replied, "How much time do you have?"

"The police are on the way, you can talk to them," Evangeline said, checking Bishop for a pulse. Head turned toward the fire, the man lay flat and glaze-eyed, motionless. He was dead, by all indications.

"Help me move him back," Evangeline said, shielding her face from the heat.

"I'm not touching him," Alix told her.

"Who is he?"

"I have no idea," Alix said. "Evidently, someone hunting for July."

Evangeline studied her, agitation giving way to concern. "Are you okay?"

"I'm fine,"Alix told her, though her hand glistened with her own blood, and her mouth and cheek were streaked.

Evangeline holstered her weapon and pulled a handkerchief from her pocket.

"I'm okay," Alix said again, when Evangeline offered it. "He's the one who needs help."

"He's dead," Evangeline told her, stuffing the handkerchief in Alix's wounded hand. "Wrap this around it."

"Not him," Alix said, and she turned to where Sereno lay. But he was gone, as was his blanket.

Evangeline directed her flashlight to the place where Alix was looking. "Who are you talking about?"

"No one," Alix said absently. Suddenly a car pulled off the road onto the lawn, heading straight for the greenhouse.

The car came to a sudden stop with its headlights shining through the broken wall, and two people left the car and ducked through the break, a woman and older man hurrying toward the flaming hut, the woman crying, *"Maxie!"*

"Max isn't here," Evangeline said, heading them off, to keep them away from Bishop's body.

"Where the hell is he?" Squeaky demanded. "Where's the boy's father?"

"Jacob?" Laura cried. Then, glimpsing the body in the firelight, she tried to push past, but Evangeline stopped her. "That's not your husband, Mrs. Winter. Now you need to calm down. The police are aware of the situation—"

"What situation?" Squeaky shouted hoarsely. "Someone better tell me where my grandson is!"

Outside, his car roared to life. The old man's head snapped around to see the headlights retreating to the road. Then, with a squeal of burning rubber, his Impala was gone.

73

HIGH ABOVE THE REST OF THE WORLD, JACOB WINTER CLIMBS, right hand clutching the cable. Although he is almost to the top, and his ascent has begun to level off, he still cannot see the beacon. He cannot see his son. All he can see is the chord under his feet as it rises ahead of him. He has formulated no plan, no strategy, but he seems to have gathered strength as the world has slipped away—the traffic, the river, the awakening town. Far below he sees the red lights of the salt bulker. The ship is also flying a red flag, which means it's fueling—Jacob wonders why he knows this, and why he bothers to think of it now. Perhaps it's because the ship is preparing to leave, and that means the crew members might be heading home to loved ones. Up here there is only the sky to embrace him, wide open and torn apart, becoming blood-colored in the east.

"Dad!"

Jacob stops, terrified. Suddenly he can see two heads atop the structure—now bright from the airplane beacon, now black against the sky.

"*Dad!*"

Jacob wants the cry to be a seagull's, because he's never heard such terror in his son's voice. And so it happens that a seagull swoops up from below him, balances on the breeze, then dives away.

"*Dad, don't come up here!*"

July stands behind Max with her arm wrapped around his chest. Beside them the airplane beacon flares again, and Jacob can make out the metallic glint of something in her hand.

"July, let him go. Please!" Jacob's poor voice, sliced with fear, barely comes out of his mouth.

Then he sees a small movement ahead of him. At first he thinks it's a loose bolt rolling on the chord . . . until it takes a timid hop. Yellow and glistening, a tiny frog. And another one, about two feet away, crawling up from the underside of the cable he's holding. Then he sees them everywhere, like dandelions, inching along the chord, clinging to his handhold.

"She told me you were up here!" Max cries out. "She said you were depressed and you were going to kill yourself! That's why I came!"

"Maxie, hang on!" Jacob yells.

Max stares down at him, terrified. His lenses reflect the beacon when it shines.

"Good morning, Jacob," July calls.

Jacob watches the frog nearest him clinging to the cable. Wide-eyed, the tiny creature crawls purposefully toward his hand, leaving a glistening trail on the steel. Knowing he must let go of the cable to let the frog pass, Jacob lowers himself to the chord, gripping the edges in both hands. He feels himself pushed by a gust of wind, but he crawls ahead, shivering uncontrollably. When he tries to stand again, he is not able. The muscles will not return to his legs.

She yells across the wind. "We thought you deserted him."

Jacob gets up to one knee and lunges toward the cable, catches it in both hands, then pulls himself back up on his poor legs.

She swings around to him. "Stop coming!"

Now he can see what's in her hand: a dart. He doesn't need an explanation to know—the tip is laced with frog poison.

"July, you're out of danger," Jacob says as calmly as he can, within thirty feet of them now. "Your husband Sereno is in custody."

"Oh, Jacob, all this way just to lie?"

"I'm trying to tell you, there's no reason for doing this," he answers, stepping ahead. "You're safe now."

Suddenly July grabs Max by the arm, swings him so violently against the cable that his foot slips off the chord. "You think I won't?"

"*Max!*"

The boy catches the cable under both arms, finds the chord with his foot. "*Dad?*"

"Jacob, stop where you are," she warns, holding the steel tip at Max's ribs, "or the boy will fly."

Jacob clutches the cable, no longer concerned about the frog slick. "Please," he says to her. "What do you want from me?"

"What makes you think I want anything? God." She sneers in that teenage way of hers. "It's your son who wants something. That's what I think. I think Maxie wants to see you jump."

Max shakes his head. "Uh-uh."

"Okay, then," she says to Max. "You jump—and your dad won't have to."

"Max, no!"

July nods her head up and down, like a little girl. "One of you has to."

"Please," Jacob says.

"Look at the big baby," she says. "I bet Max is a brave boy, not a coward like you."

"Max, I mean it."

He sees Max lean out over the cable, looking down at the river.

"*Maxie, no!*" Far below them, sirens sound like music, distant and disconnected. "Max, look over here," Jacob says to his son. "Promise me."

July laughs. "Oh, like you promise? You're such a fucking liar."

"Just tell me what you want," Jacob pleads.

"I already told you," she says lightly. With each flare of the beacon, he can see the oily glisten of her eyes. "I want you to jump."

"Jump," he repeats. *"Why?"*

She wraps her arm tighter around Max, her dart angled up by his ear. "I'm going to count to five," she says. "And if you don't jump, then your boy is going to. *One.*"

"Stop it!" he shouts. Then softens his voice. "Just tell me."

She prods the back of Max's hand with the dart. A tear falls out from under his glasses, blows across his cheek. "Let go, baby," she teases, but he squeezes the cable tighter. So she touches the tip to his side and he bends his back.

"July!" Jacob moves toward her.

"Come closer. I'll stick him. *Two.*"

"What do you want me to say?"

"It doesn't matter what a liar says," she replies. *"Three."*

"Okay, I'll jump!"

"Four."

"Will you wait!" he shouts. "I told you, I'll jump!"

"Dad, no!"

"Don't worry, Max, I know how to do it," he says. "Feetfirst, body straight as an arrow, I'll be fine." Jacob nods at his son with all the bravura he can muster, but he's actually instructing him. "Something I never told you—I used to do cliff diving."

July wrinkles her nose, but he can tell that his confidence has begun to undermine hers.

"Do it," she says, studying him with intense satisfaction, the way she had when they made love. Suddenly a helicopter rises up above the Portsmouth horizon. July tightens her grip on Max.

"No problem," Jacob says, as he pushes and pulls on the cable like a diver testing the springboard, but his legs have weakened beneath him. "Does it count extra if I add a back-flip?" He tries smiling at her.

July's eyes move to the side, aware of a man crouched on the opposite, southbound side of the bridge—while Jacob furtively inches forward.

"Maxie, hold on to that cable," he says, creeping closer. "No matter what happens, don't let go."

July snaps back to him, glaring suspiciously.

"They're sharpshooters," Jacob tells her. The helicopter hovers about a hundred feet out from them, turning slowly to the side, revealing another man kneeling inside the open door, aiming a rifle. "If anything happens to Max, you know they're going to shoot you."

"Stupid, they're aiming at you," July says, hiding the dart in her hand. "I'm protecting Max from you because you've lost your mind. Everybody knows. As soon as you jump, I'll let him go."

"Okay," Jacob whispers. He can only whisper. Staring straight out across the red sky, he lets go of the cable.

"*Dad?*"

"I can do this, Max."

"Jacob. Now." The words ooze from her lips.

He looks back at his son, only six feet away from him, and tries not to let on how hard he's shaking.

"July, would you take off his hat?"

"*Stop it!*" She squeezes Max's shoulder. The pain makes him wince.

"Just let me have one last look at him—without the hat. July, please. One look. Then I'll go."

"There," she says, and whips off Maxie's cap, revealing his friar's head.

In the instant of her distraction, Jacob makes his move—lunges at her—but his foot slips off the steel, and he has to catch the cable to keep from falling.

July turns back toward him, betrayed. Seeing his desperate grip on the cable, she almost laughs—then looks as if she's going to be sick. "I hate this," she says, and turns her dart to Max.

A booming horn stops her, the departing blast from the salt bulker below, the ship's farewell answered by the startled squealing of seagulls as the birds scatter from the understructure of the bridge, hundreds of seabirds exploding upward as though bursting out of the river itself, rising up in a furious flutter of wings, higher and higher, and suddenly they're attacking the arch, picking tiny frogs off the cable and chord, screeching and bickering over their bounty, while July waves her dart in the air, screeching back at them. . . .

Then she stops.

Jacob sees it too.

Coming straight at them through the barrage, its wings spread four feet wide. July lets go of Max as the yellow-headed bird swoops up at them, wings beating hard, July slashing fearfully with her dart.

At the same instant, Jacob leaves his feet—*I'm doing it,* he thinks, *actually doing it*—and tackles her.

The moment expands. . . .

Jacob watches the yellow diskette fall from his shirt pocket and go fluttering away. He swings out over the river, hanging on to July's waist. She stands at the edge of the chord, having caught the cable under her arms, her strong back bent, straining against the pull of his weight.

His knees bang up against the side of the chord. If he can swing a leg up . . .

But her own knees knock at his ribs, and he slips lower.

"Dad!" Max drops to the chord, trying to reach his father.

Jacob gasps, "*Max, no—*"

July rears back with one knee . . . and drives hard into his chest.

The impact loosens his grip. He slides down, catches her waistband with his thumb. Her button snaps, shorts opening. He wraps his other arm around her hip, hanging there helplessly, with the river waiting silently below.

He hears machine-gun fire—no, it's the helicopter coming closer. Wind from its rotors beats at his back. He can almost feel the bead of the sharpshooter's sights. Cheek pressed against July's bare stomach, her warmth is an odd comfort to him . . . until he hears her chiming laughter above.

He looks up. She's hanging on to the cable, straining, but beaming down at him. She simply wiggles her hips, and he slips farther down.

"*Dad!*"

"*Maxie, get away!*"

"Dad, the dart!"

And he realizes: The dart squeezed in her fist. Having to hold their combined weight with the strength of her arms, she cannot move her hand to poke at his head or the back of his neck. Neither can Jacob get at the dart, with his arms wrapped around her. But he tries just the same, raising his chin as if to begin climbing up her body.

Glaring down, July's black eyes flare with purpose. Just as suddenly, Jacob realizes what she's about to do. Her fingers open.

The dart, pressed into her palm, releases itself slowly, rolls out of her hand and falls, turning point-down in its descent toward his face. Jacob throws his head back. Sharp feathers scrape his cheek. He waits for the sting in his neck. Feeling only a dull poke, he looks down and sees: the dart has pierced the fabric of his shirt from the inside where his collar protrudes.

He turns his head, forces his chin into his chest. July suddenly starts trying to shake him free, loosening his grip. He gets the feathered end in his teeth. She kicks at his chest. He hooks his thumbs in her pockets. But she merely sucks in her stomach, and her zipper begins letting go, tooth by tooth.

Clutching at her thighs, he lets the tip of the dart touch the smooth, stretched skin below her navel. She hardens her muscles. He pecks at her, and she gives a fierce, throaty objection. Her knees strike his shoulders in tandem, once, twice—

Then he lunges. The tip pierces her skin.

She lets out an enraged shriek, and he forces the shank in farther. Her knees struggle against him.

Then he sees a man grab onto Max, saying, "You can't help, son, they'll pull you off!"

July's knees stop. A drop of blood forms around the steel shaft. She gives two more feeble kicks. Jacob looks up, sees the helpless rage in her eyes. Then her heel slips off the chord. Jacob swings to the side. . . .

They fall.

YES, metabolism rises and time slows down, but not as much as Jacob had imagined. He is reeling his arms furiously as he falls, trying to maintain his upright alignment, while beside him July falls placidly, her arms uplifted by the wind.

The green steel whispers past. Traffic on the roadway appears stationary. Indeed, the cars are not moving, because roadblocks barricade both ends of the bridge. The roadway rises up to meet him, blue lights flashing on police cars, the red sunrise flashing off windshields—and suddenly Jacob is seeing the stained glass of his marriage bed, the sleek black radio arcing through the air, and in this heightened moment, the truth crystalizes: He was not trying to smash Price's stained glass because Price had betrayed him. No, he was smashing the colored glass because it was the most elegant part of the bed, a small bright window of imperfect grace in his austere, square-cornered frame. Which was the same reason he went on through the house afterward, obliterating all his perfect work.

Jacob hears the whoosh of the roadway rushing past; then a savage ring of steel, as July hits the ledge. The bridge disappears. The wind gusts. He reels his arms the other way.

Out in the middle of the river he can see the salt bulker going away, pulled along by three small tugs. On the Portsmouth riverbank he sees a crowd of people—not watching the ship depart— they're watching him fall. He sees police cars, emergency vehicles, fire trucks, searchlights. He looks down, directly below, and sees seaweed floating, a cigarette butt, someone's discarded Dunkin' Donuts coffee cup.

His own reflection rises beside the cup, the beautiful stained cardboard cup.

Yes, indeed. A beautiful time to figure things out.

74

THE PISCATAQUA RIVER IS DEEP, ITS CURRENT IS STRONG, AND IN summer the river is filled with striped bass and bluefish and mackerel. But the water is much too salty to drink. When Jacob had drunk enough, somebody pulled him up.

He choked, then he vomited the water, and someone said, "Boredom."

Jacob felt more hands on him, then something slid forcefully under his back.

"Is he boarded? Strap him. Watch his arm. One, two—"

Jacob felt the river wash over him as he rose into the air. Someone was putting a blanket over him and tucking it under his shoulders. He coughed up more water, turned his head sideways to spit it out. A motor was chugging behind his head.

"My son," he gasped, "Max."

"Max is fine," someone said, holding his shoulder. "They're flying him down."

Jacob looked up at the bridge, all its structural steel; a helicopter hovered above the arch. A man wearing crooked bifocals looked into his face and asked, "Do you hurt anywhere?"

Jacob had to think about it, then the aching started. That's when he knew for sure that he was alive. His arm seemed to radiate pain all over his body.

"Are you sure?" he said. "Maxie's okay?"

"Perfectly fine," the man said. "He's coming down to see you."

Jacob watched the helicopter fly slowly overhead. Then he saw the concrete bridge pier rocking beside them, covered with barnacles to the high water mark, and it occurred to him that he had probably never appreciated anything as much as the sight of those barnacles.

"Can you wiggle your toes?" the man said.

Jacob did.

"Easy," the man said, holding his knee. "We'll be there in a minute."

The motor revved. They started to move. A woman knelt beside him and gently folded the blanket down from his shoulder. "I'm going to splint your arm," she said. "Try not to move."

She had a thin face and frizzy hair, and a wonderful smile. He felt her warm fingers on the back of his wrist.

"What about the girl?" Jacob said. "There was a girl up there."

The woman spoke sympathetically as she strapped his arm to a stiff plastic board. "I don't think she made it."

Jacob coughed some more, then looked back toward the bridge, where divers were dragging a body into a police boat. He saw the black hair hanging. July.

The woman patted his hand. "All set?" she said, and pulled the blanket to his shoulders again.

"How about inside?" said the bifocaled man, probing him gently, running his fingers along the back of Jacob's neck. "Ribs, belly, chest?"

His arm sent another throbbing message to his brain. "Starting to feel this."

"You will," the woman told him.

Jacob looked downriver again, where the tugs were hauling the salt bulker out to sea. Then his own rescue boat made a wide turn, heading for the Portsmouth dock, and Jacob heard cheering over the sound of the motor. He could see an ambulance parked on the pier, its red lights flashing, and a small crowd of onlookers kept back by yellow tape. Then he noticed Squeaky's red Impala parked on the other side of the salt pile. He tried to sit up, to see if Squeaky and Laura were there. Strange place to have parked the car.

"Take it easy," said the guy with bifocals, keeping his hand on Jacob.

Behind the firetrucks, he watched the helicopter land, its rotor slicing the morning air. That's when he saw Laura, with her father, pushing through the crowd on the pier—and Max running out of the chopper. Laura dropped to her knees and took him in her arms. Squeaky held them both.

Tears blurred Jacob's vision. He wiped his eyes. Then all other sounds disappeared.

"Dad! Hey, Dad!"

Max ran to the edge of the gangplank, looking like he wanted to dive into the river. He probably would have if two paramedics weren't holding him back.

"Dad!"

Max broke away from them and ran down the gangplank to the lower dock. Jacob pulled his good arm out of the strap, found the catch, and freed his chest.

"Mr. Winter, you need to wait for the stretcher."

"That's my son," Jacob said, and reached down for the middle strap. The boat bumped the dock, and Max was there waiting.

"Mr. Winter—"

"I can walk."

"He'll be okay," the woman said, freeing Jacob's feet. "Just be careful of your arm."

As a man tied the boat to the dock, Jacob climbed out and immediately hoisted his son in his good arm. Max hugged him back with his arms and legs. It almost made Jacob stop shivering.

"Mr. Winter, you need to come to the hospital," said a paramedic. There were two of them wearing blue jumpsuits. Close by, Laura stood with her father's arm around her.

Jacob held his son to his chest, savoring the warmth.

"Then I'd like a word," said a familiar voice.

Jacob looked up to see Susan Evangeline coming down the gangplank, flanked by two Portsmouth policemen.

Laura headed them off, saying, "Can I have a minute first?"

"Ma'am, he needs to be treated," said a cop.

Evangeline studied Jacob for a moment, then turned back to the cops. "Give them some privacy," she said. "Emergency's over."

Besides, the way Max was holding on to Jacob . . . He had never known the young daredevil to be frightened, until now, with his face buried in the crook of his father's jaw.

"It's okay, champ," Jacob said. "Everything's gonna be okay."

"Everything?" Max replied in a small voice.

Jacob felt a blanket drape over him. Laura tucked one corner around his chest and the other gently over his injured arm.

"I've been trying to come up with an apology," she whispered to Jacob, keeping her hands on him.

He took a breath, deep enough that it hurt his ribs, trying to swallow his injury. "What you said yesterday . . ." He gave her a questioning look.

She nodded. "Jake, I've never loved anyone but you."

He met her eyes, so full and beautiful, yet so tentative.

"If you can ever forgive me," she whispered, and then got her arms around him, so solid and warm that he almost forgot they were ever apart.

Jacob looked away, at the crowd of watchers, all the faces, until his gaze came to rest on Squeaky, standing off by himself behind the barrier, watching intently.

"I'm going to need someone to make furniture for the Seaview Inn," Laura said softly. "A desk man too. Part time, it wouldn't pay much, but you'd have free room and board. And all the time in the world to write."

Jacob looked back to the bridge. Could it work? After what they had been through, and put each other through, could they ever go back to the way they had been, Jacob, Laura, and Max? He breathed in the salt air off the river, then put his mouth close to Laura's ear.

"I don't think I'm ready," he answered, quiet enough so Max wouldn't hear.

She slipped her arm out from under his and stared up at him with regretful, liquid eyes.

"I'm sorry," he mouthed.

"We need you to lie on the stretcher, Mr. Winter," one of the paramedics said, reaching to take Max away, but the boy hung tightly to his father.

"Can he ride with me?" Jacob asked.

"I don't see why not," said the man. "There's a jump seat back there."

"Mr. Winter, when you're up to it," Susan Evangeline said, moving in, "I'll need to ask you some questions."

"Can it wait till he gets to the hospital?" said the paramedic.

"Also, this," Evangeline said, showing Jacob a yellow diskette. "One of the officers found this on the bridge. Someone said it might be yours."

"Throw it in the river," Jacob said. "I never knew what to write about, anyway."

"Don't."

Jacob looked over, saw Alix Callahan pushing to the front of the crowd.

"It's a good book," she told him. "Keep it."

Max reached for the diskette. Evangeline gave it to him, then said to Alix, "I need to talk to you too."

"Folks, we've got to move," the paramedic said, lifting Max out of Jacob's arm, the diskette tight in the boy's fist. While his partner helped Jacob lie back on the stretcher, then strapped him down and covered him with the blanket, Jacob gave Alix a questioning look. He was thinking of Sereno.

Alix must have sensed it. "He got what he came for," she said. "He won't be back."

Evangeline said, "You're talking about the man in your green-house—the dead man?"

"That's right," Alix said, but Jacob knew different.

As the medical team jacked the stretcher in the air, he said to her, "So, now that you're resurrected, I guess you're going to start taking in wayward kids."

Alix smirked.

"Can you two finish this up at the hospital?" one of the paramedics said while they wheeled Jacob into the ambulance and started closing the door.

"Would you like one now?"

"Wait." Alix stopped the door from shutting. "Would I like what?"

"A wayward kid," Jacob said. "I'm going to need a place to stay till I get my feet on the ground."

She gave him a look as though he were joking. Then, realizing he was not, her face changed quickly. She straightened herself. And in the glisten of her eyes, Jacob glimpsed a certain spark—and remembered the college girl, the elegant rebel, once so confident, mysterious, and cool . . . suddenly betrayed by a teary smile.

She said to him, "Guess I've got to start sometime."

From far downriver came another departing blast from the salt bulker. It was a 16,000-ton ship, once American, now Panamanian, with a crew that included Panamanians, Croats, Filipinos, and a Norwegian captain and chief engineer. Belowdecks were hundreds of places, cargo holds and cubbyholes, where a stowaway could hide during the day—that is, if a stowaway somehow managed to steal aboard—and lots of room to roam at night, when most of the crew were asleep, in search of food or water, or even medicines, if a man were in need.

In a few days the bulker would reach Great Inagua Island in the Bahamas, where it would pick up another load of salt from the distillery there. First, however, there was a load of Maine gravel destined for Peru. Who would ever know, in the dark of night as the ship made its way through the Panama Canal, if someone were to climb down? A man used to mountains and night travel might have no problem traversing the Cordillera de San Blas and making his way to the archipelago just offshore, a chain of islands inhabited by the Kuna Indians, a small-statured but proud and primitive tribe, among whom another small-statured man, knowledgeable in the ancient ways of healing and spirit flight and magic in the world, might find a home.

EPILOGUE

Thanksgiving, three months later

D AD, WE'RE SUPPOSED TO BE THERE. NOW."

With a frosty wind gusting out of the north, Max carried the last chair out to the road, the seat balanced on his head. There were eight in all, Windsor chairs made of ash, with ornate cockleshells carved in the top rails. Although Windsor chairs did not traditionally have top rails, these did, and they were curved to conform to the human back, with rounded seats and a single length of ash bent completely around, to form the back.

Jacob, standing on the rear bumper of his car, wearing his wool hat and winter coat, took the chair from Max and set it, with the others, atop the butterfly table he had also made, its own ornamental legs pointing up at the sky. The table had rounded drop-leaves, and cockleshells carved in the drawers. He had bought the wood for the dining room set with some of his thousand-dollar advance on *Bridge,* which a small Boston publisher was going to bring out in the spring.

"Here comes," he called, throwing the rope over the top of the load.

Alix caught it and pulled it tight. The furniture creaked. The remainder of Jacob's advance, he'd given to her for room and board.

"Mom's all worried," Max said. "She's afraid Gramp Frenetti and Professor Nielsen are gonna be the first ones there." Laura had dropped Max off after school the day before, so she could get everything ready for the dinner.

"What's she worried about?" Jacob asked.

"They don't know each other," Max said, steam pouring from his mouth. "What are they supposed to talk about?"

Alix tossed the rope back to Jacob. In the three months he had lived at Green Girls, he'd polished his novel and built the new dining room set, while Alix had begun rejuvenating her nursery and flower business.

"Mom's also worried about the food," Max said. "Like she hasn't been planning it for weeks. Besides the turkey, we're having shrimp *panzanella,* Thanksgiving *serpentone*—"

"Sounds good, what is it?" Alix said.

"Italian pastry," Jacob told her, "stuffed with cranberries, apples, and butternut squash. That reminds me, Maxie, did you put your pies in the car?"

"Only about an hour ago," Max said. He took the rope from his father, carried it around the car, and gave it to Alix. He had baked two pies the night before, with Alix's help: chocolate-cranberry and pumpkin. "Let's see, what else?" Max went on. "She's making *diavolillo* stuffing for the turkey. And your favorite, oyster-minestrone soup."

Jacob caught the rope from Alix, pulled it tight over the furniture, and tied a knot. He could feel his heart beating.

"She's been kind of nutty, you know," Max said, coming to take the rope from him.

"How so?"

"She only had her hair done twice yesterday. I thought she was gonna bust a gasket. Then she went out and bought three white shirts, and she kept trying on jeans, like ten different stores. So don't forget to tell her how beautiful she looks." He rolled his eyes and brought the rope around to Alix.

"Sounds like your day yesterday," she said to Jacob. "Hey, Maxie, ever seen your dad in a necktie?"

"Are you kidding? I never saw his hair combed, either."

Alix laughed, and carried the rope back to Jacob. "You look like a kid going to your first prom. How nervous are you?"

"Not very."

"Not much."

"Just remember what you always tell me," Max said to his father. "Head, not heart."

Jacob pulled down on the rope and knotted it twice. "I'm not so sure about that, Maxie. I don't think it works anymore."

"What do you mean?"

"He means don't think so much," Alix said. "Word for the day: bend."

"Bend?" Max looked up at his father. "So, Dad," he said, "what does work?"

Jacob tugged at the load to make sure it was secure. "Maybe you should tell me," he answered, then slapped the car roof. "Let's go, everyone, over the river and through the woods."

"Are you sure that's enough rope?" Max said. "It's pretty windy."

"It'll do," Jacob said.

Max gave him a quizzical look. And a minute later he gave his father the same look when Jacob steered the overloaded car onto the I-95 ramp, heading up over the high-level bridge.

"What's the matter?" Jacob asked him.

Max shrugged his shoulders. As soon as they merged with the traffic and were up in the open air, the wind buffeted the car, and the load shifted to the left. Jacob let the gust carry them into the passing lane.

"Don't worry," he said to his son, even though he knew that with the strength of the wind, the whole thing might let go and come crashing down around them.

But it didn't.

And as late as they were, Laura's turkey might have been cold by the time they got there, or overcooked.

But it wasn't.

With all the dining room furniture stacked on top of the car, everyone might be standing in the empty room, Squeaky Frenetti and Professor Nielsen not speaking.

But that wasn't the case, either. In fact, they were all in the kitchen, Squeaky carving the turkey, the professor mashing potatoes, and Laura putting the finishing touches on her shrimp *panzanella*, while Squeaky told them all about the Pennzoil 400, which Jeff Dakota had won.

"Dad," Max said, as they crossed over the bridge into Maine.

"Uh-huh?"

"I think I know what works."

"I'm listening."

Jacob gave Max a look, which Max wouldn't return.

"Tell me," Jacob said again.

Max kept his eyes focused on his knees. "You and Mom," he said. "And me."

Jacob touched Max's knee. "You know what?"

Max still refused to look up.

"Hey, Maxie."

He took hold of the boy's sticky hand.

"What?"

Jacob gave him a look, until Maxie met his eyes. Then he said, "I think that works for me, too."